Praise for the novels of Sherryl Woods

"Skillfully introducing readers to The Devaneys,
Sherryl Woods scores another winner."
—*RT Book Reviews* on *Sean's Reckoning*

"Sherryl Woods writes emotionally satisfying novels about
family, friendship and home. Truly feel-great reads!"
—#1 *New York Times* bestselling author Debbie Macomber

"Woods is a master heartstring puller."
—*Publishers Weekly* on *Seaview Inn*

"Woods's readers will eagerly anticipate her trademark
small-town setting, loyal friendships, and honorable mentors
as they meet new characters and reconnect with familiar ones
in this heartwarming tale."
—*Booklist* on *Home in Carolina*

"Once again, Woods, with such authenticity,
weaves a tale of true love and the challenges
that can knock up against that love."
—*RT Book Reviews* on *Beach Lane*

"In this sweet, sometimes funny and often touching story,
the characters are beautifully depicted, and readers…
will…want to wish themselves away to Seaview Key."
—*RT Book Reviews* on *Seaview Inn*

"Woods…is noted for appealing character-driven stories
that are often infused with the
flavor and fragrance of the South."
—*Library Journal*

"A whimsical, sweet scenario…
the digressions have their own charm, and Woods
never fails to come back to the romantic point."
—*Publishers Weekly* on *Sweet Tea at Sunrise*

#1 *New York Times* Bestselling Author

SHERRYL WOODS

The Devaney Brothers

MICHAEL & PATRICK

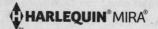

ISBN-13: 978-0-7783-1630-5

THE DEVANEY BROTHERS: MICHAEL AND PATRICK

Copyright © 2014 by Harlequin Books S.A.

The publisher acknowledges the copyright holder of the individual works as follows:

MICHAEL'S DISCOVERY
Copyright © 2003 by Sherryl Woods

PATRICK'S DESTINY
Copyright © 2003 by Sherryl Woods

Recycling programs
for this product may
not exist in your area.

For questions and comments about the quality of this book, please contact us at CustomerService@Harlequin.com.

Printed in U.S.A.

www.Harlequin.com

Dear Friends,

Years ago, I heard a question on *Jeopardy* about the most successful Disney movies of all time. It stated that they all had something to do with orphans. Well, who am I to argue with the Disney magic? Thus the Devaneys were born—five brothers, separated for years, thanks to a decision by desperate parents.

As each story unfolds and the brothers are reunited, more and more questions arise about why their parents allowed them to be separated. Readers have debated ever since about whether their reasons were valid or impossible to understand. As you come to know the brothers, I hope you'll share your thoughts with me, as well. Put yourselves in the parents' shoes and think about what you might have done under the same circumstances.

In the meantime, I'm delighted that the emotional stories of Ryan, Sean, Michael, Patrick and Daniel are coming back into print. I'll look forward to hearing from you.

All best,

Sherryl

CONTENTS

MICHAEL'S DISCOVERY

Prologue

Even through the haze of pain, Michael was aware of the charged atmosphere in his San Diego hospital room. The doctors had just delivered their dire predictions for his future with the Navy SEALS. Nurse Judy, normally a fountain of inconsequential, cheery small talk, was fluffing his pillow with total concentration, carefully avoiding his gaze. Clearly everyone was waiting for his explosion of outrage, his cries of despair. Michael refused to give them the satisfaction—not just yet anyway.

"Okay," he said, gritting his teeth against the hot, burning pain radiating through his leg. "That's the worst-case scenario. What's the best I can hope for?"

His doctors—the best orthopedic doctors anywhere, according to his boss—exchanged the kind of look that Michael recognized. He'd seen it most often when an entire op was about to go up in flames. He'd been seeing it a lot since a sniper had blasted one bullet through his knee, then shattered his thigh bone with another. The head injury that had left him in a coma had been minor by comparison. The patchwork repairs to his bones had apparently just begun.

He still wasn't sure how long he'd been out of touch, left for dead by the terrorist cell he'd penetrated. He did know that had it not been for a desperate, last-ditch effort by his team members, he would have died in that hellhole. He should be grateful to be alive, but if his career was over, how could he be? Though he was determined not to show it, despair was already clawing at him.

"Just tell me, dammit!" he commanded the expressionless doctors.

"That *was* the best-case scenario," the older of the two men told him. "Worst case? You could still lose your leg."

Michael felt a roar of protest building in his chest, but years of containing his emotions kept him silent. Only a muscle working in his jaw gave away the anguish he was feeling.

His entire identity was tied up with being a Navy SEAL. The danger, the adrenaline rush, the skill, the teamwork—all of it gave him a sense of purpose. With it, he was a hero. Without it, he was just an ordinary guy.

And years ago, abandoned by his parents, separated from his brothers, Michael had made a vow that he would never settle for being ordinary. Ordinary kids got left behind. Ordinary men were a dime a dozen. He'd driven himself to excel from his first day of kindergarten right on through SEAL training. Now these doctors were telling him he'd never excel again, at least not physically. He might not even walk…at least not for a long, long time. As for losing his leg, that was not an option.

With that in mind, he leveled a look first at one man, then the other. "Let's see to it that doesn't happen, okay? I'm a mean son of a gun when I'm pissed, and that would really piss me off."

Nurse Judy chuckled, then bit off the reaction. "Sorry."

Michael shifted slightly, winced at the pain, then winked at her. "It always pays to keep a man who's itchy to use a knife aware of the consequences."

She touched a cool hand to his cheek and studied him with concern. Since she was at least fifty, he had a hunch the gesture was nothing more than a subtle check of his temperature. The woman hadn't kept her hands to herself since he'd been brought in two days ago with a raging fever from the infection that had spread from his leg wounds throughout his body. She'd been with him when he was rushed straight into surgery to try to repair the damage that had occurred halfway across the world. The doctors in the field hospital had done their best, but there had been little doubt that his injuries would require a higher level of medical skill.

He gave the nurse a pale imitation of his usually devastating smile. She was beginning to show signs of exhaustion, but she hadn't left his side, unless she'd stolen a catnap while he'd been out of it in the operating room. Obviously she'd been hired by his bosses because she took her private-duty nursing assignments seriously. And given his own level of security clearance, hers was probably just as high in case he started muttering classified information in his sleep.

"How about some pain meds?" she asked. "You've been turning me down all morning. This stoic act of yours is beginning to get old. You'll heal faster in the long run if you're not in agony."

"I wanted to be alert for the prognosis," he reminded her.

"And now?"

"I think I'd better stay alert to make sure those two stay the hell away from my leg."

Just then there was a flurry of activity at the doorway, a hushed conversation, and then two tall, dark-haired men were pushing their way inside, ignoring the doctors' protests that no visitors were allowed.

"Why not take that medication, bro? We're here now. Nothing's going to happen to your leg on our watch," the older of the two said, pulling a chair up beside the bed and shooting a warning look at the doctors that would have intimidated an entire fleet of the Navy's finest.

An image floated through Michael's hazy memory. He looked again and suddenly a name came to him, a name he hadn't thought of in years. "Ryan?"

"It's me, kid," his oldest brother responded, squeezing Michael's hand. "Sean's here, too."

To his total chagrin, Michael blinked back tears. So many years, but there had been a time when he'd shadowed his two older brothers everywhere they went. They had been his heroes, at least until they had deserted him. To a shaken four-year-old that's how it had seemed on the day he'd been taken away to live with a different foster family—as if the cornerstones of his world had abandoned him. Coming on the heels of his parents' vanishing with the twins, it had been too much. He'd pushed all thoughts of the other Devaneys from his mind, kept them locked away in a dark place where the memories couldn't hurt him.

And now, all these years later, his older brothers at least were back, the timely arrival just as mysterious as the untimely disappearance.

"How did you find me?" he asked, his voice thick with emotion. "Where did you come from?"

"We'll get into all that later. Right now, you need some sleep," Ryan soothed.

Michael studied him, then sought out Sean. He would have recognized them anywhere, he thought. It was like looking in the mirror: the same black hair—even if his was military crewcut short—the same blue eyes. They'd all inherited Connor Devaney's roguish good looks, for better or for worse.

Their father had been a handsome devil, one generation removed from Ireland and with a gift for blarney. An image of him crept into Michael's head from time to time, always accompanied by deeply entrenched bitterness. If there was a God in heaven, Connor Devaney would rot in hell for taking his wife and their youngest sons and walking away from Michael, Sean and Ryan.

"Lieutenant, how about that pain medication now?" Nurse Judy asked gently.

Michael wanted to protest. He had so many questions he wanted to ask his brothers. But one glance at the way Ryan and Sean had settled in reassured him that they weren't going anywhere. Nor was any surgeon going to get anywhere near his damaged leg as long as *they* were around.

"Sure," he said, finally giving in.

Michael felt the prick of a needle in his arm, the slow retreat of pain and then his eyes drifted shut and for the first time since he'd been flown home to California, he felt safe enough to fall into a deep, untroubled sleep.

1

Six months later, Boston

Michael maneuvered his wheelchair across the floor and set the lock. He eyed the sofa and debated whether its comfort was worth the effort it would take to heave himself out of the chair. Every damn day was filled with such inconsequential challenges. After years of trying to sort through the life-and-death logistics of SEAL missions, it grated on him that the simple decision of where to sit to watch another boring afternoon of television took on such importance.

"You want some help?" Ryan asked, his expression neutral.

Over the past few weeks, when his brother had been popping in and out of California on a regular basis, Michael had learned to recognize that look. It meant that Ryan was feeling sorry for him and was trying not to show it.

The attempt was pretty lame, but Ryan was actually better at it than Sean. Sean's obvious pity was almost more than Michael could take, which was one reason Ryan had been designated to pick him up at the airport and to help him settle into his new apartment.

Michael had discovered that the grown-up Ryan was a low-key kind of guy. He ran his own Irish pub and had settled into family life with a woman named Maggie who seldom took no for an answer. Michael had already had a few encounters with her on the phone and discovered she masked an iron will with sweet talk.

Sean, however, was a recently married firefighter, an active man who would have chafed at the restrictions on his life, just as Michael did. Maybe that was the reason that Sean couldn't seem to hide his sympathy each time he saw Michael in this damnable wheelchair. They probably needed to talk about it, but neither one of them had gotten up the nerve. Besides, what was there to say?

"I still don't know how I let you all talk me into moving back to Boston," Michael grumbled as he waved off Ryan's offer of help and struggled to move from the wheelchair to the sofa on his own. "There must be a foot of snow out there. In San Diego, I could be basking in the sunshine beside a pool."

"But you wouldn't be," Ryan said wryly. "The way I hear it, you hadn't set foot outside since you left the hospital."

Michael scowled. His brother clearly had too much information about his habits. There were only a handful of people who could have given it to him, most of them men Michael could have sworn were totally loyal to him.

"Who ratted me out?" he inquired testily.

Ryan held up his hands. "I've been sworn to secrecy. Your men seem to think you have a particularly nasty temper when crossed."

At least he could still intimidate *somebody,* Michael thought with satisfaction. It was a consolation. He certainly hadn't been able to intimidate Ryan's wife, Maggie, though.

Maggie was the one who'd called every single, blessed day pestering him to come East. She'd ignored his cranky responses, talked right over his blistering tirades and pretty much won him over with her silky sweet threats. He wondered if Ryan knew what a weapon he had living with him. Michael was convinced that Maggie Devaney could take over a small country if she was of a mind to. Michael could hardly wait to meet her in person, though he'd prefer to be in top-notch form when he did.

"Why didn't your wife come to the airport with you?" he asked his brother.

"She thought you might like a little time to yourself to get used to things," Ryan said. "She did send along a list of therapists for you to consider. She said you'd been discussing it, but hadn't agreed to hire one yet."

Michael frowned at the understatement. "Actually, what I told her was that I wasn't interested. I could have sworn I'd made that clear."

"You're content to spend the rest of your life in that wheelchair?" Ryan asked mildly.

"The doctors are the ones who consigned me to a wheelchair," Michael responded bitterly. The shattered bone in his thigh had taken two additional surgeries, and the doctors still weren't convinced it would ever heal properly. His knee was artificial. He felt like the Bionic Man, only one who'd gotten faulty parts.

Even if everything healed and worked, he'd never have the agility to return to the kind of work he loved. His navy career was definitely over. He'd declined the offer to push papers behind some desk at the Pentagon. Michael shuddered at the very thought—he'd rather eat raw squid. So he was twenty-seven and out of work and out of hope. He'd learn to live with it…eventually.

Ryan leveled an uncompromising look straight at him. "Is that so? You're blaming this on the doctors? The way I hear it—"

"You apparently hear too damned much," Michael retorted. "Has it occurred to you that I was doing just fine before you and Sean—and your wives—came busting back into my life? I don't need you meddling now. If I decide to stay in Boston, I won't have all of you making me some sort of project." He leveled a daunting look of his own. "Are we clear on that?"

"No project," Ryan echoed dutifully.

Michael studied his brother with a narrowed gaze. That had gone a little too easily, he thought just as the doorbell rang. He scowled at Ryan. "You invite somebody else over?"

Ryan looked just the teensiest bit guilty. "It could be Maggie."

"I thought you said she was giving me some space."

Ryan shrugged. "Well, that's the thing with Maggie. She has her own ideas about how much space a man should have."

"Great. That's just great." Michael eyed his wheelchair with frustration. No way in hell could he haul himself back into the thing and get out of the room before Ryan opened the door. As curious as he was to see the woman who'd married his oldest brother, he wasn't ready for the meeting to take place today. Unfortunately, there was nothing he could do about it. He resigned himself to an early introduction to his sister-in-law.

Before he could catch his breath, Maggie burst into the room, her cheeks red, her eyes flashing and her hair like something from a painting of an auburn-haired goddess. No wonder his brother had fallen for her. Michael was half in love himself, but that was before he caught sight of the curly-haired toddler clutching her hand.

"This is Maggie," Ryan said unnecessarily. "And the pint-size replica is Caitlyn. She's just learned to walk, and she has only one speed—full throttle."

The warning came too late. Caitlyn took one look at Michael, broke free of her mother's grasp and hurtled straight toward him on her chubby, wobbly legs. She was about to grab his injured leg in her powerful little grasp when Michael instinctively bent forward and scooped her up.

Wide green eyes stared at him in shock. He expected immediate tears, but instead a slow smile blossomed on her little face, and he was an instant goner. He'd never realized a kid could steal a person's heart in less than ten seconds flat.

He sat her on his good leg. "Hiya, Caitlyn. I'm your Uncle Mike."

She studied him intently, then lifted a hand and patted his cheek.

"She's not saying too much yet," Maggie said, "but trust me, she knows how to make herself understood."

"Yeah, I can see that," Michael said, already thoroughly under little Caitlyn's spell.

"Think you can handle her for five minutes?" Maggie asked. "I have groceries in the car. I'm afraid I overdid it. I could use Ryan's help bringing them in."

"Sure. Miss Caitlyn and I will be fine." He wasn't sure how he knew that. It was just that it was the first time in months that someone wasn't looking at him with pity. His niece's expression was merely curious. He could deal with friendly curiosity, especially from someone who hadn't yet learned how to ask complete and probing questions.

But the instant Ryan and Maggie left, Michael had a sudden attack of nerves. He didn't know a whole lot about kids. He had dim memories of his twin brothers, but he'd been little more than a toddler himself when the family had split up. He'd been the youngest in his foster family. Now both of his foster sisters were married, but so far were childless. A couple of the guys on his SEAL team had children, but Michael had tended to steer clear of the gatherings when they'd been present. He didn't like the feelings of envy that washed through him when he was surrounded by tight-knit families.

"So, kid, what do you like to do?" he asked the toddler who seemed perfectly content to sit cuddled in his arms. "I'll bet you have a doll or two at home. Maybe a stuffed bear."

Caitlyn listened intently, but said nothing.

"Then, again, maybe you're one of those liberated little girls who has cars and trucks," Michael continued. "Your mom strikes me as the kind of woman who'd want you to grow up knowing that you have options."

Apparently he'd said the wrong thing, because Caitlyn suddenly looked around the room and huge tears promptly welled up in her eyes.

"Mama," she wailed loudly. "Mama!"

She sounded as if her little heart was breaking. Feeling desperate, Michael awkwardly patted her back. "Hey, it's okay. Your mama is just outside. She and your daddy will be right back."

That brought on a fresh round of tears. "Da-da-da!"

Michael was at a loss. He was about to panic, when the door swung open and Maggie and Ryan came breezing in. Maggie grinned, set the groceries beside the door and swooped in to pick up the squalling child.

"Hey, baby girl, what's all that noise?" Maggie chided.

Just like that, the wails trailed off and the tears stopped. "Mama," Caitlyn said contentedly, patting Maggie's cheek. Then she turned back to Michael and held out her arms.

Michael couldn't help chuckling. "Fickle little thing, aren't you?" he said as he reached for her. "You're going to grow up and break some man's heart."

"She won't be dating until she's at least thirty," Ryan said emphatically.

"Good plan. I can hardly wait to see how well you

stick to it," Michael said. "Especially since this one obviously has a mind of her own already."

"Don't laugh. You might be called on to help me chase off the boys," his brother informed him.

Michael looked at the little angel who was now snuggled against him, half-asleep. "Just say the word," he said solemnly.

"That reminds me," Ryan said, taking a slip of paper from his pocket and handing it to Michael.

"What's this?"

"Maggie's list of therapists. She reminded me just now to be sure and give it to you."

Michael's gaze narrowed. "And the connection to your daughter's social life would be?"

"If you're going to help me protect Caitlyn from hormone-driven teenaged boys, you're going to have to be in top form," Ryan said. "You might as well pick one and call. If you don't, Maggie will."

Michael glanced toward the kitchen where his sister-in-law was busily arranging his groceries and dishes so things would be within reach. He took the list and stuffed it in his pocket without comment.

It was only later, after Ryan, Maggie and Caitlyn had gone, that he took out the paper and glanced at the names. One jumped out at him: Kelly Andrews.

Years ago his best friend, Bryan Andrews, had had a sister named Kelly. Was it possible that this was the same girl? He remembered her as being a cute, shy kid, but by now she would have to be, what? Twenty-four most likely.

Michael had lost touch with Bryan years ago. Maybe

he'd track him down and ask if his sister was a physical therapist. Purely as a matter of curiosity. He had no intention of asking some therapist to waste her time on him, not when every doctor he'd seen had said that a full recovery was impossible.

And, he thought with self-derision, anything less meant he might as well be dead.

Kelly Andrews was as nervous as if she'd never worked with a patient before. She stood outside the small cluster of apartments in the freezing cold and tried to gather her courage. No matter how many times she told herself that Michael Devaney was a potential client, nothing more, she couldn't help the rush of emotions that filled her.

Michael had been her first teenage crush. Three years older than she was, he and her brother had been friends throughout high school. Michael had never given her so much as a second glance, not as anything more than Bryan's kid sister, anyway. That hadn't stopped her from weaving her share of fantasies about the quiet, dark-haired boy with the intense, brooding gaze and a body that even at seventeen had been impressively well muscled.

It was Bryan who'd told her about Michael being shot and the doctors' very real conviction that he would never walk, much less work as a SEAL, again. Bryan had come back from his visit with Michael sounding worried that his old friend was going to give up. That concern had communicated itself to Kelly.

"His brothers went out to San Diego and convinced

him to come back here to recuperate," Bryan had explained two nights before. "I spoke to Ryan after I saw Michael. He says his brother is going to be needing a lot of physical therapy, but so far Michael has flatly refused to ask anyone for help. He did ask about you, though."

Kelly's heart had taken an unsteady leap. "He did?"

"Apparently your name was on a list Ryan's wife made of prospective therapists." Bryan had regarded her with a knowing look. "You interested? I know how you love a challenge. I also know you always had a thing for Michael."

"I did not," she said, though the flush in her cheeks was probably a dead giveaway that she was lying.

As desperately as she wanted to be the one to be there for Michael now, she had hesitated. "From what you say, it's going to be a long, difficult process. He's going to need someone he trusts. Do you think he'll pay any attention to me? In his mind, I'm probably still your kid sister."

Bryan had grinned. "Sis, you forget, I've seen you in action at the clinic when I've come by to pick you up. You're hard to ignore. So, should I tell his brother you'll take the job, and that you won't let Michael's lousy, uncooperative mood scare you off?"

"Hold it. Back up a minute. You said that before—something about brothers. I thought there were only girls in his family."

"The Havilceks only had girls, but Michael was a foster kid."

"Of course. I knew that," Kelly said, suddenly remembering. "At least, I knew he had a different last name. I guess I never really gave much thought to it, because he didn't seem to. So, these brothers are his biological brothers?"

Bryan had nodded. "He hadn't seen them in years till they turned up in San Diego."

"That must have been a shock."

"It was. They were separated when his parents bailed on all of them. Michael was only four. He barely remembered them."

She'd stared at her brother with surprise. "Is this something you just found out, or did you know it when we were kids?"

He shook his head. "I knew he was a foster kid. But back then, Michael never talked about how he'd wound up with the Havilceks. Every time I started to ask about his real family, he told me the Havilceks were his real family, the only one that counted."

The story explained a lot…and added to her fascination with Michael Devaney, a fascination she was going to have to ignore if she was going to do her job the way it needed to be done.

"I'm scheduled at the clinic tomorrow, but tell Ryan I'll go by to see Michael the day after tomorrow," she had told her brother. "Whether I stay, though, is going to have to be up to Michael. I can't force him to do therapy if he's not willing."

Bryan had grinned at her. "Since when? I thought you specialized in difficult, uncooperative patients."

She did, but none of them were Michael Devaney, who'd always left her tongue-tied.

Since that conversation with her brother, she'd had

more than twenty-four hours to prepare herself for this meeting, but she was as jittery as if it were the first case she'd ever handled. Today she was only doing an evaluation, working up a therapy schedule and making sure that Michael was going to be comfortable having Bryan's kid sister as his therapist. She was counting on a brisk, polite half-hour visit.

She was not counting on the crash of something against the door when she rang the bell. Nor on the bellow telling her to go the hell away.

Oddly enough, the tantrum steadied her nerves and stiffened her resolve. She had a key in her pocket, passed along to her by Bryan, but when she tested the door, she found it was unlocked. Michael might be furious at the universe, he might be testing her courage, but he wasn't really trying to keep her out, or that door would have been locked tight with the security chain in place.

She plastered a smile on her face, squared her shoulders and called out a cheery greeting as she stepped across the threshold. From his wheelchair across the room, Michael glared at her, but he lowered the vase of flowers he had apparently been intent on heaving in her direction.

"Having a bad morning?" she inquired politely, ignoring the shock that seeing him had on her system. Incapacitated or not, he was still the most gorgeous man she'd ever seen.

"Having a bad life," he snapped back. "If you're smart, you'll turn tail and run."

She grinned, which only seemed to infuriate him more.

"I'm serious, dammit."

"I'm sure you are, but you don't scare me," she said with pure bravado. In truth, what really terrified her was the possibility that he'd force her to leave when he so clearly needed someone with her skills to get him out of that chair and back on his feet.

His scowl deepened. "Why not? I've scared off everybody else."

"How? Have you been waving a gun around?"

"Not likely. I believe they've all been removed from the premises," he said bitterly.

"Good. Then that's one less thing I need to worry about," she said. "Mind if I sit down?"

He shrugged. "Suit yourself."

She crossed the room, paused in front of his wheelchair and held out her hand. "It's good to see you again, Michael. You look great." And he did. Despite the exhaustion evident in his eyes, despite his unshaven cheeks, he looked exactly the way she'd remembered him—strong and invincible and sexy as sin. Not even his being in a wheelchair could change that.

For a minute he seemed totally taken aback by her comment, but eventually he clasped her hand in his. To her very deep regret, the contact sent a shock straight through her. She'd been hoping she was past being affected by him, that a girl's crush wouldn't inevitably mean that there would be a woman's attraction. It would make the next few weeks or months a lot easier on both of them if she wasn't fighting unreciprocated feelings of attraction.

"You look good, too," he muttered, as if he wasn't all that comfortable with polite chitchat. That much at least hadn't changed. Michael never had been much for small talk. He'd always been direct to the point of bluntness.

"I'm sorry you were hurt," she said.

"Not half as sorry as I am."

"Probably not. So let's see what we can do about getting you back on your feet."

His already grim expression turned to a glower. "Look, the doctors have already told me that I'll never work as a SEAL again, so let's not waste your time or mine."

"And that's the only profession out there for a man with a sharp mind?" she asked.

"It's the only one I care about."

She decided not to waste her breath trying to bully him out of such a ridiculously hardheaded, self-defeating stance. "Okay, then, if you're not motivated to walk again so you can get back to work, what about so you can do a few simple things like going for a walk in the park or maybe going out to get your own groceries? The way I remember it, you're an independent guy. Are you going to be content letting other people manage your life for you?"

He patted the wheelchair. "With a little more practice, I'll be able to get around well enough in this."

Now it was her turn to frown. "And you're ready to accept that?"

"It's not as if I have a real choice. The doctors said—"

She cut him off. "Oh, what do they know?" she asked impatiently. "The Michael I remember would take that as a challenge. Why not prove them wrong?" She looked him straight in the eye. "Or do you have something better you'd like to be doing?"

"I keep busy."

Kelly eyed the computer across the room. A bingo game was on the screen. "I imagine you can earn pocket change playing bingo, but I also imagine you'll be bored to tears in a couple of weeks." She shrugged. "Still, it's your choice. I certainly can't force you to do anything you don't want to do."

"Damn straight," he muttered.

She bit back a smile at the display of defiance. "So, Michael, what's it going to be? Do I go or stay?"

Once again, she'd obviously taken him by surprise by leaving the decision entirely up to him. He blinked hard, then sighed. "Stay if you want to," he said grudgingly.

She grinned at him. "Okay, then, let's do this my way," she said. "Here's what I'm thinking." She laid out the exercises and the rigorous schedule she'd already devised based on the medical information his brother had shared with her. "What do you think?"

"Do you have a masochistic streak I missed when you were a kid?" he grumbled.

Kelly grinned. "No, but I have what it takes to get you out of that chair."

For the first time since she'd arrived, he actually looked her directly in the eye, then slowly nodded. "You may have, at that."

"Then that's all that really matters, isn't it? I'll see

you first thing tomorrow. Be ready to work your butt off, Devaney."

He chuckled. "You're tougher than you used to be, Kelly."

"You'd better believe it," she said. "And I don't have a lot of use for self-pity, so get over it."

"Yes, ma'am," he said with a salute.

. She gave a nod of satisfaction. "It's always helpful when the client realizes right off who's in charge. Therapy goes much more smoothly."

"I'll try to keep that in mind."

"Not to worry. I'll make sure of it," she said, winking at him as she closed the door behind her.

She paused outside and leaned against the wall, unsuccessfully fighting the tears she hadn't allowed herself to shed in front of him. She'd put on a damn good show for him, but she'd been shaken. What if she couldn't do what she'd promised? What if she couldn't get him out of that wheelchair and back on his feet?

"Stop it," she muttered. Failure was not an option, not with Michael.

As for getting personally involved with a client, that wasn't an option, either, but she had a horrible feeling it was already too late to stop it.

2

"So, how did you and Kelly get along?" Bryan Andrews asked Michael when he stopped by for a beer at the end of the day.

Michael studied his one-time best friend with a narrowed gaze. He still wasn't sure how much he appreciated Bryan's unequivocal recommendation of Kelly for the job as his therapist. "Did she do a tour in the marines I don't know about?"

"Nope."

"I remember her as a sweet kid. She's changed." And that was a massive understatement that didn't even take into account the pale gold hair swept up in a knot that revealed the long, delicate line of her neck, the silky complexion and the woman's body with all the appropriate curves.

"She deals with a lot of cantankerous patients at the rehab clinic. She's had to change," Bryan said. He gave Michael a warning look. "Give her any grief and you'll have me to contend with, too."

"Trust me, I don't think she needs her protective big

brother butting in," Michael told him. "She could take me out in ten seconds flat."

"Are you telling me there's finally a woman who can get the upper hand with you?" Bryan taunted, clearly delighted. "And that it's my baby sister?"

"Only because of my weakened condition," Michael assured him.

"Good to know. Back in high school I used to envy the way you could take 'em or leave 'em. The rest of us were slaves to our hormones, but not you. There wasn't a girl in school who could twist you in knots."

That seemed like a lifetime ago to Michael. He'd had a purpose then, and he'd known that a teenage romance would only get in the way. "I was focused on what I wanted to do with my future. I didn't have time to get serious about any girl."

"That doesn't mean you couldn't have had any one you wanted," Bryan said. "It was great hanging out with you. The girls swarmed around *you,* and *I* ended up dating them."

Michael gave him a wry look. "I hope you're not counting on that happening now. I doubt any woman will give me a second look while I'm in this chair."

"If you ask me, that alone is a great reason to get out of it," Bryan said. "Stick with Kelly. She'll have you whipped into shape in no time." His expression sobered. "Seriously, pal, she's good. Cooperate with her. Let her do her thing. If anyone can help you, she can."

"Stop trying to sell her. She has the job. And it's not as if she's going to give me much choice about cooperating," Michael retorted, able to laugh for the first time in weeks as he thought of the way Kelly had held her own in the face of his display of temper.

Even as the unfamiliar sound of his laughter filled his cramped apartment, he realized that Kelly Andrews had brought two things into his life during her one brief visit—a breath of fresh air and, far more important, the first faint ray of hope he'd felt since his SEAL team had dragged him out of harm's way.

He immediately brought himself up short. He had been in some tricky, dangerous situations over the years, but nothing had ever scared him quite so badly as the sudden realization, that well-intentioned or not, Kelly might be holding out false hope.

Fear crawled up the back of his throat until he could almost taste it. If he tried to walk and failed, it might be far more devastating than never having tried at all. In the real world, how many miracles was one man entitled to? He'd gotten out of his last mission alive. Maybe that was his quota of good luck for one lifetime.

He looked up and saw that Bryan was regarding him with concern.

"You okay?" Bryan asked.

"Just reminding myself of something," he said grimly.

"Judging from that expression on your face, it wasn't anything good."

Michael shrugged. He wasn't about to tell Kelly's brother that he'd been reminding himself that she was a mere woman, not a miracle worker. It was a distinction he couldn't allow himself to forget, not for one single second.

* * *

"Are you sure you ought to be taking on this particular client?" Moira Brady asked Kelly, her expression filled with concern.

"I'm a professional. I can keep my feelings under control," Kelly insisted. "Besides, it's been years since I had my crush on Michael Devaney. I was a kid."

Moira regarded her skeptically. "Then you had absolutely no reaction to seeing him again? He was just a patient, someone you happened to know from years ago?"

"Absolutely."

"Liar."

Kelly frowned at her best friend, who also ran the rehabilitation clinic where Kelly worked part-time on days when she didn't have private patients scheduled. "I don't understand why you're making such a big deal about this, Moira."

"Because I don't want to see you get hurt," Moira said bluntly. "You always give your patients a hundred and ten percent, Kelly. You care about their progress. You feel guilty if they don't achieve the results you've been anticipating."

"Well, of course I do. Are you saying I shouldn't?"

"No, but add in your personal history with Michael Devaney, and I see a disaster waiting to happen."

"Oh, please," Kelly said derisively. "Michael and I don't have a personal history."

"But you fantasized about one," Moira countered. "I know that because you told me about him in glowing detail way back when we first met in college. He'd been gone for three years by then, but you hadn't forgotten the least little thing about him. Can you honestly tell me that there wasn't one teeny-tiny spark when you walked into his apartment yesterday?"

A spark? More like a bonfire, Kelly thought wryly. Not that she intended to admit it. "No spark," she said flatly.

Moira's gaze narrowed suspiciously. "Okay, is this one of those semantics things? What if I asked about fireworks? Would you admit to that?"

Kelly sighed. "It doesn't matter. Michael Devaney doesn't think of me in that way. I'm his friend's kid sister."

"Think he'll remember that when you're massaging his muscles?"

Kelly felt the heat climbing into her cheeks. She'd been wondering about that very thing herself. Anticipating it. She'd been itching to get her hands on those taut muscles of Michael's for years. Now she had the perfect excuse. She swallowed hard and banished the totally unprofessional thought.

Scowling, she reminded both of them, "I'm a professional, dammit!"

"Yeah, sure," Moira said. "You keep telling yourself that. And just in case you forget it, I'll mention it to you every chance I get."

Michael couldn't seem to get his pants on. Lately he'd taken to wearing sweatpants because they were easy and comfortable and warm, but he'd gotten it into his head to put on a pair of jeans for this first session with Kelly. His bum leg wasn't cooperating.

He had the pants half on and half off when the doorbell rang. Scowling, he gave one more forceful yank

on the jeans and barely managed to stifle a howl of
agony. Or at least he thought he had, until he looked
straight up into Kelly's worried gray eyes. Her cheeks
were flushed and she was still wearing a bright pink
ski jacket over a sweater that looked so soft he immediately wanted to stroke his hand over the material...
and the woman under it.

"Are you okay?" she asked.

"Aside from having an uninvited guest appear in my
bedroom, I'm just peachy," he growled.

Her chin shot up and fire blazed in her eyes. "Not
uninvited. I'm here for our appointment, and I'm not
even a minute early. I only came in because you didn't
answer the door and I thought I heard you cry out."

"I didn't answer the door because I wasn't dressed,"
he retorted. "How the hell did you get in, anyway?"

"Your brother gave me a key," she said. "And since
you're obviously okay, I'll head on into the living room
and get set up. You might as well strip out of those pants
before you join me."

The suggestion probably couldn't have been more
innocent, but something that felt a whole lot like desire
slammed straight through him. "I beg your pardon?"

Kelly gestured toward his jeans. "The pants. Lose
them. I'm going to start with a massage to loosen up
those tight muscles."

Michael swallowed hard. She intended to put her
hands all over him? He frowned at her. "Did we talk
about that when you were here yesterday?"

"I'm sure it came up," she said briskly. "Five minutes, okay? I have another client in an hour, so there's
no time to waste."

Michael stared after her as she left his room. They most definitely had not talked about this. He would never have agreed to letting her put her soft as silk hands on his body. He might be injured, but he wasn't dead. One touch and he suspected this could go from a therapy session to something else entirely. It had been too blasted long since he'd felt a woman's hands on his bare skin. His best friend's baby sister was not the woman who should be testing his willpower.

Still wearing his jeans—zipped up and securely in place now—he wheeled himself into the living room. "We need to rethink this," he said tightly. "It's not going to work out."

She leveled a look straight at him. "Oh? Why is that?"

"I don't think you ought to be touching me."

He could almost swear that her lips twitched at that, but she managed to cling to a perfectly serious expression.

Hands shoved into the pockets of her own snug-fitting jeans, she inquired curiously, "I don't make you nervous, do I?"

"Of course you make me nervous," he retorted. "What man wouldn't be nervous when an attractive woman he barely knows suddenly announces that she's going to be massaging him?"

"You've known me since I was fourteen," she reminded him. "And it's therapy, not seduction."

"Tell that to my body," he mumbled under his breath, very aware that the conversation alone was having an extremely interesting effect on certain parts of his anatomy. This was Kelly, dammit. What was wrong with him? Bryan would mop the floor with him—and rightly so—if he heard about Michael's reaction to his sister.

"What was that?" she inquired, her expression all innocence.

"Nothing."

"Come on, Michael. You were a SEAL. The way I hear it, they're the bravest of the brave. Are you actually going to fire me before we even get started, just because I'm going to massage you? What would your buddies think of that?"

The challenge hung in the air. The woman was good. Really good. She knew exactly how to play him. He scowled at her. "If I had half a brain, I would."

She did grin then. "Is that a yes or a no?"

Michael considered his options. He could fire her right now and hire somebody else—preferably some ox of a man—or he could try getting through at least one treatment before calling it quits. He owed Kelly for one session anyway, and something told him she wouldn't take a cent if he didn't let her do her job. He weighed fairness against self-preservation, and opted for fairness.

"We'll see how it goes today," he said finally.

She gave the slightest little nod of satisfaction. "Okay, then, let me help you out of those pants."

One fierce look from him stopped her in her tracks. "Or you can get them yourself," she said.

Wincing at the shooting pain that accompanied every movement, Michael finally managed to shed the pants and heave himself onto her portable massage table. At least he was on his stomach, so he wouldn't have to see her face when she saw the jagged scars from the surgery. He didn't miss her sharp intake of breath, though.

He felt a soft splash of warm oil on his injured leg, then the skimming touch of her hands as she smoothed it down the back of his thigh and over his calf. Her touch was gentle rather than provocative, but that didn't stop the sudden shock of awareness that flowed through him. Michael forced his mind to detach itself from her actions and concentrate on counting backward from a thousand. It was a tactic that had served him well in other situations involving slow torture.

"Am I hurting you?" she asked.

The simple question dragged her from the periphery of his consciousness right back into his head. "No," he said tersely, trying to mentally haul himself back to that nice, safe place.

For a few moments, blessed silence fell. Michael made it all the way down to nine hundred and two before she spoke again.

"What happened?" she asked.

He resigned himself to staying in the disconcerting moment. "When?"

"When you were hurt."

"I walked into a trap," he said, still filled with self-loathing at the stupidity of it. He should have known what was going on. He should never have trusted the intelligence report that the caves had been cleared of terrorists. He'd always relied on his own surveillance, his own instincts, but this one time he'd gotten anxious, a little careless. It was a bitter lesson that would have served him well in the future...if only he had one.

"Where were you?"

Too many years of keeping silent about his work kept him cautious even now. "I can't say."

"But you were a Navy SEAL, right? So I can assume that this had something to do with the war on terrorism?"

"You can assume anything you want to assume."

Her fingers began to massage a little deeper, working muscles too long unused. Knots of tension in his legs seemed to ease, at least as long as she didn't venture too close to the scars. That area was still amazingly tender. He yelped the first time she touched the bullet's exit wound on the back of his thigh.

"Sorry."

"I'll survive."

"I'm sure of that," she agreed. "But I'll be more careful around the scars. I can't ignore them, though, because that skin's going to need to be stretched."

"Whatever you say."

She patted his leg. "That's it for today, then."

He glanced up and regarded her with surprise. "You're finished?"

"It's been nearly an hour, and I have another appointment across town."

"At this rate, we're not going to make much progress," he said, suddenly disgruntled by the too-quick end of the session and the complete lack of anything remotely like measurable improvement. "I thought you were going to work my butt off, or am I misquoting you?"

"Nope, that's what I said, and that day will come. I've got you scheduled for two hours, day after tomorrow. We'll start the exercises then." She met his gaze. "That is, if I passed today's probation."

He ought to tell her to get the hell out and stay away, but he couldn't seem to make himself do it. He was too afraid of the disappointment or disdain he'd see in her eyes. Either one would make him feel like a jerk. Besides, a part of him couldn't help clinging to the possibility that she was his best hope for getting back on his feet again.

He met her gaze. Now that he was willing to give therapy a try, he wanted to see progress. He wasn't scared of a little pain or hard work. In fact, he looked forward to it. "Make it three hours, day after tomorrow."

"You're not ready for three hours," she said flatly.

He scowled at her reaction. "Let me be the judge of what I can handle. I've gone through training so rigorous, it would make your therapy seem like child's play."

"Have you done it since having several bones shattered, to say nothing of going through—what was it— three surgeries?" she inquired tartly.

The woman was tough as nails. It was a trait he couldn't help admiring. "Okay, you made your point. Two hours, but if I'm up to it, we'll go to three the next time," he bargained. "Is it a deal?"

Kelly looked for a moment as if she might argue. Finally she held out her hand. "Deal."

Michael took her hand in his and instantly regretted it. It had taken every ounce of willpower he possessed to ignore the way her hands had moved over his body earlier. Now, with something as simple as a handshake, he was once more thoroughly aware of her as a desirable woman.

Her skin was amazingly soft, her grip strong. A faint hint of the aromatic oil she'd used for the massage lingered in the air. It wasn't the least bit feminine-quite the opposite, in fact—but it suddenly turned erotic. If he'd been another kind of man in a different situation, he would have brought her hand to his lips and brushed a kiss across her knuckles. Instead, he released her hand as if he'd been burned.

A faint flicker of surprise flashed across her face, followed almost instantly by understanding. To his disgust she'd apparently guessed that for one brief second he'd let himself cross some sort of line.

"Is there anything I can do for you before I go?" she asked.

A thousand and one wicked possibilities slammed through him. "Not a thing," he said tightly.

"Are you sure?"

"I thought you were in a hurry."

"I can spare five minutes," she said, regarding him with amusement. "I could fix you some breakfast if you haven't had any."

Forget breakfast, and five minutes wouldn't be nearly long enough to act on a single one of those wicked possibilities, Michael thought wryly. He wondered what she would do, though, if he suggested, say, a kiss.

It wasn't propriety or the thought of Bryan pounding him to a pulp that stopped him. It was the very distinct likelihood that it would backfire on him. If he was already having totally inappropriate thoughts about Kelly after one very brief therapy session, a kiss could very well send him over the edge. He might start obsessing about the way she'd feel in his arms. He might forget all about the reason she was there…to help him get back on his feet, not to help him prove he was still first and foremost a man.

Michael sighed heavily, determined to ignore the tantalizing sparks sizzling in the air. "I'll see you day after tomorrow."

She almost looked disappointed. "Whatever you say."

To keep himself from doing anything foolish, he deliberately turned his wheelchair in the direction of the kitchen, putting his back to her. "Lock the door on your way out," he said.

He expected to hear the door open and close, the lock click into place. Instead, there was nothing, not even a whisper of movement.

"What are you going to do with the rest of your day?" she asked finally.

"Planning my activities is not part of your job," he retorted more sharply than necessary.

"I was asking, not planning," she responded, evidently undaunted by his tone. "I hate to think of you being shut away in here all alone."

"You might not think my company has much to recommend it," he said. "But I'm content with it."

"Have you called the Havilceks and told them you're back? Have you even told them what happened to you?"

Back still to Kelly, Michael frowned at the question. He'd made one call to them from San Diego to let them know he'd been injured, but that he was recuperating. To his astonishment, Mrs. Havilcek had wanted to fly out right away, but he'd explained about Ryan and Sean being there.

"Oh, Michael, that's wonderful," she'd said with what

sounded like total sincerity. "I won't come now, then, but you call me if you need me. I can be there the next day."

The memory of that promise had been enough to warm him whenever loneliness had crept in after Ryan and Sean had headed back East. It was enough to know that Mrs. Havilcek would come if called, and amazing to think that after all the years she'd cared for and loved him, that he'd even doubted for a minute that she would.

"Have you gotten in touch with them?" Kelly prodded.

"Not since I got to Boston," he admitted.

She regarded him incredulously. "Why on earth not?"

He wasn't sure he could explain it. He loved his foster family. The Havilceks had been great parents to him. And he couldn't have been any closer to the girls if they had been his real big sisters. But when Ryan and Sean had turned up, he'd felt almost disloyal to the Havilceks, as if having feelings for his biological brothers was some sort of betrayal of all his foster family had done for him. He was still wrestling with how to handle keeping all of them in their rightful place in his life, a life that had changed dramatically since he'd last seen them.

"I'll call them," he told Kelly, "once things are a little more settled."

"You mean after you're back on your feet? Don't you want them to see you when you're not a hundred percent? Do you think they'd care about that?" she demanded indignantly.

He found the suggestion that he was acting out of

misplaced pride vaguely insulting. "No, of course not. It's not about that at all."

"What then?"

He regarded her with a wry expression. "You know, Kelly, maybe there's something we ought to get straight. You're here to help me walk again. Leave the rest of my life to me."

"I would, if you weren't so obviously dead set on wasting it," she shot back. "But that's okay. I'll drop it for now."

"For good," he countered.

She flashed him a brilliant smile. "Sorry. I can't promise that."

Before he could threaten to fire her if she insisted on meddling in things that were none of her concern, she was out the door. The lock clicked softly into place, just as he'd requested.

Michael should have felt relieved to have her gone, relieved to be alone with hours stretching out ahead of him to do whatever struck his fancy, at least given the limits of his mobility.

Instead, all he felt was regret.

3

If Michael had been anticipating a lonely, boring day to himself after Kelly's departure, he should have known better. Despite his admonition to Ryan that he was to be no one's project, his brothers and sisters-in-law were apparently determined that he not have a single minute to himself to sit and brood. In fact, by the end of the day he wouldn't have been surprised to discover a schedule of their assigned comings and goings posted outside his door.

Maggie was first on the scene, with Caitlyn in tow. His niece came in dragging a purple suitcase on wheels, which he discovered was filled with her favorite picture books and a doll that was apparently capable of saying all the words Caitlyn had yet to master. She shoved the doll in his arms, then climbed up beside him on the sofa, put a book in his lap and regarded him expectantly.

"She wants you to read to her," Maggie said, as if that hadn't been perfectly obvious, even to a novice uncle like him.

Michael studied the thick board book with its

brightly colored pictures, started to flip it open to the first page, only to have Caitlyn very firmly turn it back to the cover and point emphatically. He gathered he was supposed to begin with the title.

"The Runaway Bunny," he began.

Caitlyn nodded happily, then snuggled closer.

Michael glanced in Maggie's direction, caught her satisfied smile and gave in to the inevitable. He discovered that reading to a one-year-old might not involve complex plots, but it had its own rewards. Caitlyn was a very appreciative audience, clapping her little hands together with enthusiasm and giggling merrily.

Even so, after five books, he was more than ready for a break. He uttered a sigh of relief when Maggie announced that lunch was ready. He prayed it would be accompanied by a good stiff drink, but since he hadn't found a drop of liquor in his cabinets after Maggie had stocked them, he wasn't holding out much hope.

"Shall I bring lunch in there?" she asked.

"Nope. I'll come to the kitchen," he responded. He glanced at Caitlyn. "How about it? Want to hitch a ride with Uncle Mike?"

She nodded happily and held out her arms.

"Whoa, sweet pea. Let me get settled first." He struggled into the wheelchair, then lifted her to his lap and wheeled into the kitchen, where Maggie was pointedly ignoring the fact that it had taken a much longer time for them to get there than it would have taken for her to bring the lunch into the living room to him and Caitlyn.

"How did your first therapy session go?" she asked

as she served the thick sandwiches and potato salad she'd prepared.

"Why am I not surprised that you knew it was this morning?" he inquired dryly. "And why am I stunned that it took you this long to get around to asking about it?"

Maggie gave him an irrepressible smile. "I'm learning restraint."

Michael laughed. "How's it going?"

"Pretty well today, apparently." Her expression sobered. "So, how *did* it go? You didn't scare Kelly off, did you? She seemed like a nice young woman when she came by the pub to pick up a key to this place from Ryan."

"About that," he began, intending to explain that his key wasn't to be handed out at random to anyone who asked or professed a need for a copy.

Maggie held up a silencing hand. "I know. I told Ryan he should have consulted with you first, but he was afraid she'd show up for the consultation and you wouldn't let her in. He figured the key would assure that you'd see her at least once." She met his gaze. "You can always ask her to give it back. Did you?"

"No," he admitted, not entirely sure why he hadn't. Maybe it was best not to examine his reasons.

Maggie seemed to be struggling with a grin. "I see. Then things have gone okay with Kelly?"

He was not about to admit that Kelly had actually left today before he was ready for her to go. Maggie would clearly make way too much of that, though whether she'd deduce it was enthusiasm for therapy or for the therapist was a toss-up.

"She'll be back day after tomorrow," he conceded grudgingly, and let it go at that.

"Terrific."

He studied his sister-in-law intently. "So, Maggie, who has the afternoon shift?"

She regarded him blankly. "Excuse me?"

"Is Sean coming by to take over when you take the peanut here home for her nap? Or maybe his wife? Then, again, Deanna has already called in today, so maybe it's Ryan's turn."

Color bloomed in Maggie's cheeks.

Michael sighed. "I thought so. You all divvied up the assignment so I wouldn't be alone for more than an hour or so at a time, didn't you? I'm amazed nobody took the night shift, or is somebody that I don't know about sitting in the hallway from midnight to seven in the morning?"

Maggie's chin rose, eyes flashing. "Your brothers are concerned about you. It's perfectly natural."

"Where was that concern twenty years ago? Or even five years ago?" he demanded heatedly. "Hovering now won't make up for all those years they didn't do a damn thing to find me."

Maggie regarded him in silence.

"No answer for that?" he pushed, even though he knew he was being totally unreasonable by taking years of pent-up anger out on her. "I didn't think so."

Before he could wheel himself away from the table,

Maggie rested her hand on his. "They were hurt, too, you know."

"Not by me, dammit!"

"No, of course not. But you were all kids," she reminded him with gentle censure. "None of you could have been expected to fight the system to find your way back to the others."

"We've all been adults for a long time now," he retorted.

She regarded him with an unflinching stare. "Then I'll ask you this—did you look for Ryan or Sean?"

Michael's heart throbbed dully as he thought of how hard he'd worked to block out all memories of his big brothers. He'd substituted the loving Havilceks for his family. They would never have turned their backs on one of their kids, not even him, though he'd spent a lot of years with his heart in his throat expecting the worst.

"No," he admitted, "but—"

"Can't you let it be enough that your brothers are back in your life now? We're family, Michael. It may be late, but let's not waste any more time by tossing around a lot of useless recriminations."

Gazing into his sister-in-law's troubled green eyes, Michael fought off the desire to prolong the argument. Maggie was right. There was nothing to be gained by holding grudges, and maybe quite a lot to be gained by forgiveness.

"Okay, then," he said at last. "I'll work on putting aside the past, if you'll do something for me in return."

"Anything," she agreed readily.

"Can the hovering," he said bluntly. "I have to learn

to do things for myself. And if there's something I can't manage, I'll call and ask for help."

She studied him skeptically. "You promise that you won't shut us out completely?"

He grinned at that. "As if you'd let me. No, Maggie, I won't shut any of you out. You're welcome here any-time…just not *all* the time."

She laughed. "Okay, I get it. I'll speak to Ryan, Sean and Deanna."

"Thank you."

"You're welcome. Of course, that puts you in my debt, at least a little, docsn't it?"

He eyed her warily. "A little, I suppose. Why?"

"Will you come to the pub on Friday night? There will be Irish music, and the special's fish and chips. Ryan can come by to pick you up."

Michael was surprised to find that the prospect held some appeal. "You're a tough negotiator, Maggie De-vaney."

"I know," she said with unmistakable pride. "I had to be to win your brother's heart. You may find this hard to believe, but he was even less trusting than you are."

"You're right. I do find that hard to believe."

"Well, it's true." She smiled at him. "Will you come?"

"I'll come," he agreed. "But I'll get there on my own."

She opened her mouth, but he cut her off before she could protest. "If I can't manage it, I'll call."

"Fair enough, then. I'll do these dishes and get out of your hair."

Michael glanced at his niece and saw that she was nodding off in her booster seat at the table. "I think maybe you ought to get Caitlyn home for her nap, instead. I can clear things away in here."

"But—"

He deliberately scowled at her. "Go, Maggie, before you undo all the warm and fuzzy feelings I'm developing toward you."

She laughed at that, picked up her daughter, then bent and kissed his cheek. "I'm glad to have you as part of our family. You'll get to meet the rest of the O'Briens on Friday night. You might want to brace yourself. My family can be a little overwhelming. Ryan and I have been married for nearly two years now, and they still make *him* nervous."

"Now there's a fine recommendation," Michael responded dryly. "I'm really looking forward to Friday night, after that."

"The music will compensate for the chaos. I promise."

Michael believed her, which was a bit of a miracle in and of itself. Other than the men on his SEAL team, he'd long ago lost his faith in promises.

Kelly wasn't sure what to expect when she arrived for her second therapy session with Michael. Even though during her last visit he'd agreed to continue with his rehabilitation, he wouldn't be the first patient to have a change of heart between sessions, especially if he'd spent the intervening hours brooding.

She rang the bell at his apartment promptly at

10:00 a.m., then waited to see what sort of greeting she got. She counted it a positive sign when nothing crashed against the door. Nor were there any cries of pain from inside. So far, it was going better than either of her earlier visits.

When another full minute had passed, she rang the bell again. "Michael, it's me. Is everything okay? Should I come on in?"

More silence. She frowned at the door. Had he bailed on her, after all? Or was he inside, simply ignoring her, hoping she would go away? She was about to put her key in the lock, when the front door of the building crashed open. Kelly whirled around and found herself staring straight into Michael's very blue eyes.

"Sorry," he said as he awkwardly tried to manipulate the chair into the foyer. "I had to go out. I thought I'd be back before you got here, but everything took longer than I expected."

Kelly stared at him. "You went out?" she said blankly. Where? How? She resisted the urge to ask questions he would no doubt find intrusive, if not downright insulting.

"To the store," he said, holding up two small plastic bags crammed with groceries. He looked astonishingly pleased with himself.

"How did you manage?" she asked. "Did you call a taxi?"

"Of course not. The store's only a few blocks away."

Her incredulity grew. "You went in your wheelchair?"

"I sure as hell didn't walk," he retorted, his good mood evaporating.

Kelly immediately felt guilty for spoiling his moment of triumph. "Sorry. I just wasn't expecting it. It's terrific that you were able to manage on your own."

His scowl stayed firmly in place. "You're not out of a job just yet, if that's what's worrying you."

"No, of course not. You caught me off guard, that's all." She gestured toward the apartment. "And I was worried when you didn't answer the door."

"Well, I'm here now, and that clock of yours is no doubt ticking, so let's get started."

Filled with regret about the tension she'd managed to cause, she merely nodded and stepped aside. "Go on in. I'll be right behind you."

He wheeled past without comment. Kelly leaned against the wall for a second and drew in a deep breath. Why was it that she couldn't manage to have one single encounter with this man without some sort of misunderstanding? She'd never had problems making herself clear before, but Michael managed to keep her off-kilter and tongue-tied. When she finally did speak, everything kept coming out wrong. Sure, he was understandably prickly, but she seemed to have a special knack for setting him off.

Determined not to let it happen again, she squared her shoulders and carried her equipment inside. While Michael was putting his groceries away, she got set up.

A few minutes later he came into the living room wearing a pair of boxers, a T-shirt and a frown. He gestured toward the massage table.

"Are we starting with that again?"

Kelly nodded.

He struggled awkwardly from the chair to the table, then stretched out facedown. Kelly put some of her aromatic oil on his injured leg and began to massage, trying to ignore the body heat the man put out. If she were ever stranded outdoors in a blizzard, Michael was definitely the man she'd want with her. He emitted heat like a blast furnace.

His muscles were also knotted with tension, probably due in part to her. She smoothed her hands over his powerful thigh and down the length of his calf until she finally felt the tension begin to ease.

The massage probably went on longer than necessary because she enjoyed touching him so much, enjoyed the fact that for once they weren't at odds, enjoyed even more the soft sigh of pleasure that eased through him.

It was the sigh, though, that snapped her back to reality and reminded her that the massage was not about her enjoyment, or even his. It was therapy, a prelude to some of the stretching exercises she'd scheduled for today. Kelly had a feeling that one reason she'd put off getting to those was the knowledge that Michael was going to be indignant that she wasn't assigning him anything more strenuous.

"Okay, that's it," she forced herself to say finally.

Michael sat up slowly and regarded her with confusion. "For the day? We're finished?"

She smiled at his obvious dismay. "Not just yet. I have some stretching exercises for you to try. It'll help with getting those torn muscles and ligaments back into shape."

As she'd expected, he frowned.

"Stretching?" he asked disdainfully. "Come on, Kelly, can't we move beyond that?"

She regarded him evenly. "You straighten that injured leg out and do ten leg lifts and we'll reevaluate my plan."

"Piece of cake," he boasted.

"Okay, then, let's see it," she said, her arms folded across her chest as she stood back and waited.

She wasn't the least bit surprised when he couldn't get his leg to straighten completely. Nor when his first attempt to lift it in the air had sweat beading on his brow. He was wincing in obvious pain as he finally managed to raise the leg a scant three or four inches.

"Okay, you win," he grumbled, scowling fiercely. "But nobody likes a know-it-all woman, you know."

"I don't need you to like me," she said cheerfully. "I just need you to trust me."

"Sweetheart, there are very few people on earth I trust," he said bitterly. "I don't know you well enough for you to make the cut."

The comment tore straight through her, but she forced herself not to let it show. "Then maybe we need to do something to change that."

His gaze narrowed. "Such as?"

"Spend some time together."

Her response clearly startled him.

"You're asking me out?" he inquired warily.

Kelly's pulse skittered crazily at the idea, but she

kept her tone even. "As if I'd date an ill-tempered old man like you," she taunted.

He frowned at that. "I'm only three years older than you."

She grinned. "I notice you didn't try to argue with the ill-tempered part."

He shrugged. "Didn't see much point in it. When you're right, you're right. I'll try to stop taking my bad moods out on you."

"Thank you."

"So, if you weren't suggesting a date, what were you suggesting?"

"Just getting out in the world. It'll give me a chance to evaluate your motor skills in a more realistic setting, and you can ask me whatever questions are on your mind."

He regarded her doubtfully. "And you think that will build trust?"

"Couldn't hurt," she said.

"What do you think your brother will have to say about you and me going out?"

"Bryan doesn't interfere in my work. For that matter, though, he's welcome to come along." Maybe her brother could smooth things over between them, keep her from saying the wrong thing, or at the very least, keep Michael from misinterpreting what she said and taking offense. "Is it a deal?"

He seemed to be struggling with the offer, weighing it from every angle to see if he could find a catch. Kelly could almost see the wheels in his head turning. She realized then that this whole trust business was a far larger issue than she'd first assumed. Obviously it had to do with his family background. How on earth could she be expected to overcome that kind of distrust in a few short therapy sessions?

She looked him in the eye. "Or would you prefer to start over with another therapist."

"No," he said at once.

She might have found the quick response flattering if she didn't suspect it had more to do with his dread of wasting time searching for someone new than it did with her.

"Okay, then," she said. "Pick a day and we'll get together."

"Friday," he suggested finally. "I promised my sister-in-law today that I'd go to the pub Friday evening. Why don't you and Bryan come along?"

Kelly nodded. "Sounds good. Want us to pick you up? You're on our way."

"Sure," he said eventually, as if he'd wrestled with that decision, too.

She grinned at him. "You're not sacrificing your independence, you know. You really are on our way."

He gave her a self-deprecating grin that made Kelly's heart flip over.

"I know," he admitted. "That's why I finally gave in. I'm stubborn. I'm not an idiot."

She laughed then. "A distinction I'll try to remember."

His expression sobered. "So will I. I really am sorry for giving you such a rough time. It's just that all this is so blasted frustrating."

She patted his hand. "Compared to some people I've worked with, you're downright sweet-natured."

Michael winced at the description, just as she'd expected him to.

"Don't worry," she reassured him. "I won't let it get around. I imagine you big, tough SEALs pride yourselves on being as cantankerous as they come."

"You'd better believe it," he agreed, his fierce expression belied by the twinkle in his eyes. After an instant, the sparkle dimmed. "Of course, *ex*-SEALs are another breed entirely."

There was no mistaking the return of bitterness and despair in his tone. Kelly desperately wanted to make things better, but she wasn't sure if she could find the right words. She made herself try, though.

"You know, Michael, it seems to me that in some ways it takes as much bravery to face a future all alone without the SEALs as it does to take on some dangerous, covert mission surrounded by an entire team of highly trained experts," she told him.

"In other words, if I don't get over myself and face this whole therapy thing head-on, I'm a coward?" he asked.

"Your words, not mine," she said.

He sighed heavily. "Then maybe that's exactly what I am," he conceded, his expression bleak. "Because if I'm no longer a SEAL, then I don't know who the hell I am."

Kelly could have offered a whole string of platitudes that would have meant nothing at all to him, but she didn't. Instead, she merely touched his shoulder. "But you'll figure it out," she said quietly.

"I wish I were as sure of that as you seem to be."

"You're a smart man, you'll find your way," she insisted. "Trust me."

His gaze captured hers and held. "Which brings us full circle."

She gathered up her things and headed for the door. "I'll see you Friday night and we'll work on it," she said, because suddenly there was nothing on earth more important to her than gaining Michael Devaney's trust... unless it was giving him back his faith in himself.

4

Bryan was staring at Kelly as if she'd suddenly grown two heads. "Tell me again how this came about?" he demanded, when she invited him to join her and Michael at Ryan's Place on Friday night. "You asked Michael—your patient—out on a date? How many rules does that break?"

"None precisely," Kelly retorted defensively. "And it's not a date. Michael admits he has issues with trust. I find it's impossible to do my job if my client doesn't trust my judgment. I thought it might help if he got to know me better as someone other than your baby sister. Apparently he agrees, because he suggested going to Ryan's Place on Friday night. Now do you want to come along or not?"

"Oh, I'm coming," Bryan said, his expression grim. "If only to make sure you don't do anything stupid. You seem to forget that I can read you like a book. It may be an issue of trust for Michael, but it's a whole lot more for you."

Kelly found her brother's attitude extremely annoying, to say nothing of patronizing. "I am not going to try to seduce him, if that's what you're worried about," she said heatedly.

"What if *he* tries to seduce *you?* Will you take him up on it?" Bryan asked with the sort of bluntness he normally reserved for the patients he counseled in his psychology practice.

Much as she wanted to believe that Michael attempting to seduce her was a possibility, Kelly was a realist where Michael Devaney was concerned. He was not going to try to get her into bed, not Friday night, most likely not ever. More's the pity.

She regarded her brother with a sour look. "I'll let you know if the issue arises. Then, again, maybe I won't. It's not really any of your business."

"How can you say that? Of course it is. I'm your brother, and I'm the one who talked you into taking this job."

"Oh, for heaven's sake, Bryan, you didn't talk me into anything. You mentioned it. I spoke with Ryan and then consulted with Michael. He and I were the ones who agreed to give it a try. At best, you gave me a lead on a job. You've done it a hundred times before without working yourself into a frenzy over the outcome."

"But this was different."

"Why?"

"Because we're talking about Michael," he replied with evident impatience. "I knew you'd jump at the chance to help him because you always had a thing for him."

She kissed her brother's cheek. "Too late for regrets now, worrywart. I'm a big girl. I can handle this."

"You can handle Michael's therapy," he corrected. "I don't have a doubt in the world about that. But this? This is social. Michael's not thinking straight these days, and neither, apparently, are you. You'll end up getting your heart broken."

She frowned at him. "Thanks for the vote of confidence."

"You know what I mean. I thought for sure you'd be over your crush by now, but you aren't, are you?"

"I was barely a teenager when you first brought Michael home. He was gorgeous. Naturally I was intrigued by him," she said, ignoring the fact that none of those feelings had gone away. She was still very much attracted to Michael, something her big brother definitely didn't need to have confirmed. Maybe it was time to turn the tables, put him on the hot seat. "Now let's talk about your love life—or should I say your lack of one."

His scowl deepened. "Nothing to discuss," he said tightly.

"Oh, really? Then that fling with what's-her-name is really over?" she pressed, in part because she knew of someone else who was ready and willing to take on Bryan, if he'd finally wised up.

"It wasn't a fling," he said defensively. "And you know her name. It's Debra."

"Short for dim-witted," Kelly muttered. "You know, for an intelligent man who has a degree in psychology, you have exceptionally lousy taste in women."

"Thank you for sharing your opinion," her brother

retorted. "Next time you feel so inclined, bite your tongue."

She grinned at him. "Advice you should consider following when it comes to Friday night."

Bryan sighed heavily, picked up his jacket and headed out without saying another word.

Now it was Kelly's turn to sigh. She should have kept her mouth shut about Friday, because if she knew her brother at all—and she did—he was on his way straight to Michael's, probably to warn him to behave or get his teeth knocked down his throat.

Kelly considered calling Michael to warn him, but why bother? Bryan was a great guy, but he definitely leaned more toward intellectual pursuits than physical prowess. Michael could probably use a good laugh. He might be in a wheelchair, but she had a feeling he could still take her brother in a fight. Maybe it would do both of them good for Michael to remember that.

Michael was watching the Celtics game on TV and cursing the fact that there wasn't a beer in the place, when the doorbell rang. Since he'd all but banished his brothers from stopping by uninvited, he figured he shouldn't just tell his visitor that the door was unlocked. He wheeled across the room and found Bryan on his doorstep, a scowl firmly in place and a six-pack in his hand.

"Talk about your mixed messages," Michael said, moving aside to let his friend in.

Bryan stared at him blankly. "What?"

"Hey, you're the psychologist," Michael reminded

him. "Shouldn't you understand that arriving with a frown on your face and a peace offering in your hand could be a bit confusing?"

"Was I frowning? Sorry," Bryan said, though the apology sounded halfhearted.

Michael studied him curiously. The Bryan he'd once known had always been upbeat, always able to put a positive spin on things. He could spot the silver linings on the cloudiest days. It was a trait that probably contributed to his skill as a psychologist. Clearly, something had to be weighing mighty heavily on him to put this scowl on his face.

"Something on your mind?" Michael probed cautiously.

"You could say that."

"Why don't you pour a couple of those beers and tell me all about it?" Michael suggested. Listening to somebody else's problems for a change would be good for him, he decided. It might make him forget his own.

While Bryan headed for the kitchen, Michael went back in the living room and muted the sound on the TV. He didn't have to listen to the game, but he wasn't going to skip it. Basketball was the one thing he'd missed when he was off in various godforsaken locations. Of course, he'd also missed playing it, but for now he'd have to settle for the vicarious thrills of watching a good game on TV.

Bryan returned, handed Michael his beer, then sank down on the sofa, still looking worried.

"Woman problems?" Michael asked.

"Not the way you mean. It's Kelly."

Now it was Michael's turn to frown. "Has something happened to your sister? She was here this afternoon, and she seemed perfectly fine."

"Yeah, well, since then, she's apparently lost her mind."

Michael stared at him. "What the hell are you talking about?"

"This whole cockamamy scheme that the two of you should spend time together," Bryan explained. "Whose idea was it?"

"Hers," Michael said at once, still not seeing why Bryan was making such a big deal out of it. "What's wrong? It's not as if we're dating—though, frankly, it would be none of your business if we were."

Bryan snorted. "Yeah, that's what she said, too."

"Well, then, what's the problem?"

"I don't like it, that's the problem," Bryan said, regarding him defiantly. "Therapy's one thing. This— whatever *this* is—is something else entirely. Kelly's no match for you. She's been in Boston her whole life. She's dated some, but the men were nothing like you."

"Which makes her what? Naive? Stupid?"

Bryan's scowl deepened. "Of course not."

"Glad to know you're smart enough to see that. But if Kelly's not the problem, then I must be," Michael concluded. "Do you figure I'm some sort of macho, sex-starved male who can't keep his hormones in check?"

His friend flushed a dull red. "No, but you are experienced."

Michael couldn't deny that. "Maybe so, but I would never take advantage of your sister," he said flatly.

"After all the time we spent together, you ought to know me better than that."

"I suppose, but it's been a lot of years since you and I hung out, Michael. You could have changed," Bryan said defensively.

"I haven't," Michael said, meeting his gaze evenly.

Bryan nodded slowly. "I'll take your word, then, that you won't take advantage of her."

"Thank you." He slanted a look at Bryan. "So, does she have any idea you're over here warning me off?"

"Probably," Bryan said.

Michael regarded him with amusement. "And you got out of the house in one piece? Amazing. You must be quicker than I remembered."

"Very funny."

"Look, I admire the fact that you care about what happens to your sister, but I swear to you that I'm not a threat. I'll say it one more time—this whole pub visit is strictly professional. She thinks it will help the therapy if I can put my trust in her."

Bryan rolled his eyes. "And you bought that hogwash?"

Something in his reaction sent a little chill of apprehension down Michael's back. He regarded Bryan with a narrowed gaze. "You think she has another agenda?"

"She might not even be aware of it herself, but, yes, I think she has another agenda." He leveled a warning look at Michael. "And so help me, if you take her up on it and break her heart, I'll make you regret it."

"Whoa!" Michael protested, reeling from the possibility that Bryan viewed his own sister as the one who couldn't be entirely trusted to exercise good judgment. "It's a long way from spending one evening in a pub with family to breaking your sister's heart. Trust me, that is not a road I intend to go down."

"As long as you're clear on the consequences," Bryan said flatly.

"Very clear. Are you clear on the fact that I'm not the least bit interested in getting involved with *anyone* these days? Fixing my own life is pretty much an all-consuming task."

"Okay, then," Bryan said, clearly relieved. "Now turn the sound up on the game, while I get us another beer."

Michael stared after him as he left the room. Bryan's little wake-up call hadn't exactly scared him. He could handle an irate Bryan. But the memory of the way he'd felt when Kelly had her hands all over him gave him pause. He was suddenly far less confident about whether he could handle Kelly, if she really did have something other than therapy on her mind.

Michael was still feeling a little leery about Kelly's intentions when they got to Ryan's Place on Friday night. Fortunately, with nearly a dozen members of his own family and the O'Briens around, it was easy enough to put some distance between himself and Kelly.

When the boisterous crowd got to be too much for him, he made his way to the bar where Ryan was trying to keep up with the orders. Michael couldn't hide his grin at how natural his big brother looked pouring ales and Irish whisky and joking with the customers.

"This place suits you," he told Ryan, when his brother finally turned his attention to him.

"You like it, then?" Ryan asked.

"There's a warm, comfortable feel to it I haven't run across since a vacation in Ireland a few years back."

"Then I've done it right," Ryan said, obviously pleased. "And having you and Sean in here couldn't make me happier. For a long time, I thought I could be content just to have this place with its crowd of regulars. Then Maggie came along and made me see what I was missing." He nodded toward the crowd across the room. "The O'Briens are special. I didn't trust all that love they shower on everyone at first, but it's the real thing."

Michael nodded. "I can see that. Not five seconds after we met, Nell O'Brien fussed over me as if I were one of her own brood."

"You are now," Ryan said simply. His expression turned thoughtful. "You know, if you wanted to invite your foster family here sometime, it would be fine with me. I'd like to get to know them. I never stayed with any of mine long enough to get attached. Sean had better luck, but he doesn't see them much anymore. Of all of us, I think you're the one who came closest to finding a real home."

Michael tried to imagine the Havilceks here and, surprisingly, found that he could. "Maybe I will," he said. "One of these days. I haven't told them I'm back in Boston."

Ryan regarded him with shock. "Why not?"

Michael tried out the same explanation he'd used on Kelly to see if it sounded any better now. "I wanted to sort things out for myself. My foster mom is great, but she'd take over and try to fix things." He grinned. "The girls are no better. I had measles when I was maybe eight or nine and they just about nursed me into a mental institution with all their hovering. I couldn't think straight. Even a cold was enough to bring out all their Florence Nightingale tendencies." He tapped his still-useless leg. "Just imagine the frenzy they'd go into over this."

"Would that be so awful?" Ryan asked, an unmistakable trace of envy in his voice.

Michael sighed. He'd learned only a little of what his big brother had gone through in foster care, but he knew their experiences were vastly different. He could understand why Ryan might not get how Michael would chafe under all that attention. "Trust me, it's better this way. They'd be hurt if I refused to move in with one of them."

"Will they be any less hurt when they find out you've been hiding out from them for months?"

"Not months," Michael insisted. "Another week or two, just till I see if my prognosis improves at all."

Ryan nodded. "Okay, then, I'll back off for now." He glanced across the room. "I was a little surprised to see Kelly and her brother with you tonight."

Michael shook his head, thinking about how complicated this simple outing had turned out to be. "Kelly's here because she thinks therapy will go more smoothly if I start to trust her."

"And Bryan?"

"He's here because he's afraid I'm going to make a move on Kelly," Michael admitted dryly.

Ryan barely contained a chuckle. "And do you intend to make a move on her? You could do a lot worse, you know."

Michael turned and studied Kelly. She was a beautiful woman, no question about it. And there were definitely some sparks between them. Even so, he shook his head. "Too complicated."

"Because you and Bryan are friends?"

"No, because she's my best shot at getting out of this wheelchair. I don't intend to do anything that might distract from that."

Ryan's gaze narrowed. "There are a lot of therapists in Boston, you know. Maggie's still got her copy of that list she made. A new therapist could uncomplicate things."

"I've made my peace with having Kelly underfoot. I don't want to start over," Michael said flatly.

"That might be a shortsighted view, especially if you're attracted to her," Ryan said, refusing to let the subject drop.

"I'm not," Michael insisted.

A grin spread across Ryan's face. "I hope you were more convincing when you tried that line out on her brother."

Michael sighed. "Probably not."

"Just make me a promise, then," Ryan pleaded. "When you two decide to have it out, don't do it in here, okay? The bar glass is expensive."

"I'll keep that in mind." Michael glanced toward Kelly and saw that she was watching him. "Guess I'd better bite the bullet and get back over there. I've managed to stay out of Kelly's path most of the evening, which pretty much defeats the avowed purpose of bringing her here."

Ryan stepped out from behind the bar and blocked his path. "Look, I know you didn't ask for any advice from your big brother, but I'm going to offer some just the same. Therapy might get you back on your feet, but it's going to take more than that to heal your soul. If Kelly's offering more, don't be so quick to turn your back on it."

"I suppose you gave in the very first second that Maggie came into your life," Michael speculated.

Ryan laughed. "Hardly. I'm just trying to save you a little time. You can learn from my mistakes and give in to the inevitable."

"There's nothing inevitable about Kelly and me."

"If you say so," Ryan said doubtfully.

"I do," Michael said very firmly.

Unfortunately, Ryan didn't look as if he believed the denial any more than Michael did himself.

In terms of building a bridge between herself and Michael, the evening had been a bust so far, Kelly concluded as he rejoined the group who'd clustered around several tables in the middle of the pub. She noted he was careful to stay on the opposite side of the table from her.

Unfortunately for him, Bryan had just asked Katie O'Brien to dance, so the chair right next to Michael had just opened up. She made her way around the table.

"You've been avoiding me," she accused lightly as she took the vacant seat.

"Bryan's orders," he said just as lightly.

She laughed. "I probably ought to kill him."

"You probably should."

"Then, again, I'm surprised you scared off so easily."

"A smart man knows to pick his battles and his enemies."

Kelly regarded him with dismay. "Is that what I am, the enemy?"

He winced. "No, of course not. Neither is your brother. We're just caught up in a complicated situation."

"It docsn't have to be all that complicated. I'm trying to get to know you. I'm not asking you to marry me or even to sleep with me."

"Thank heavens for that," he said fervently. "Your brother really would kill me, then."

She decided to play it cool. "Only if you took me up on it," she teased. "Would you?"

"Kelly." Her name came out part warning, part plea.

"Yes?"

"You're playing a dangerous game."

"Only if you're the least bit tempted," she said.

"I'm a man," he said, as if that said it all.

"So, of course, you're not capable of resisting temptation?" she scoffed. "Please, Michael. Don't try to make me believe you'd take advantage of the situation, if I happened to throw myself at you."

A dull flush crept into his cheeks. "We'rc never going to know, because you are not going to do that. Are we clear?"

The direct order made her see red. Something dark

and dangerous came to life inside her. Before he could make his demand again, she leaned forward, clamped a hand around the back of his neck and kissed him.

Somewhere in the back of her mind, she'd only intended the gesture to be a belligerent response to his unreasonable order. Big mistake. No, *huge* mistake. Because the instant her lips met the hard line of his mouth, she felt as if the entire world was spinning out of control.

And when his mouth opened and his tongue thrust between her lips, she was completely lost to sensation... greedy, urgent sensation that made her pulse hum and her heart thump wildly. Liquid heat pooled low in her belly and desire made her want to cling and savor and taste. Only a low growl in Michael's throat had her tearing herself away, her cheeks flushed, her breath coming in quick, unsteady gasps.

She rocked back in her chair and raked her fingers through her hair. "I'm sorry," she whispered, embarrassment flooding through her. Only the dazed look in Michael's eyes kept her from feeling like a complete fool.

"Don't," he said, his voice harsh. "Don't apologize. I shouldn't have—"

She cut him off. "Shouldn't have what?" she asked with self-derision. "Responded when I all but attacked you?"

He smiled faintly at that. "I dared you," he pointed out.

"You did not," she said, then thought about it. Maybe he hadn't dared her in so many words, but the challenge in his voice was exactly what she'd responded to. She studied him in confusion. "Okay, maybe you did. Did you do it on purpose?"

He looked almost as bewildered as she felt. "I wish to hell I knew."

Before they could explore it any further, her brother arrived, a glowering expression on his face. "I see that my warning was taken to heart by both of you."

"Oh, stuff a sock in it," Kelly retorted.

Bryan ignored her and looked at Michael. "What about you?" he demanded indignantly. "What do you have to say for yourself?"

"I think 'stuff a sock in it' pretty well sums up my view, as well."

Bryan scowled from Michael to Kelly and back again. "Okay, then, I wash my hands of this. You two are on your own."

"Fine by me," Kelly retorted.

"I always have been," Michael said, his expression already distant and withdrawn.

Bryan hesitated. He seemed as if he were about to relent, but then he whirled around and headed for the bar.

Kelly instinctively reached for Michael's hands and held them tightly. "You are not on your own anymore. Look around you. You never have to be alone again."

Michael surveyed the assembled Devaneys and O'Briens warily, as if he still didn't quite trust what they were offering. In that instant, Kelly felt something deep inside herself shift. Years ago what she had felt for Michael Devaney had been a teenage crush on a handsome, mysterious boy. What she felt right now was so much more. She wasn't quite ready to put a label on it, especially not one he would reject out of hand.

But if it took her a lifetime, she would find some way to wipe that bleak expression from his eyes and prove to him that he was a man worthy of being loved.

5

The memory of that soul-searing kiss kept Michael awake most of the night. It had taken him totally by surprise on so many levels, his mind was still reeling.

Even after Bryan's warning, he hadn't actually expected Kelly to make a move on him. A part of him still thought of her as Bryan's kid sister. That she had impulsively and thoroughly out-of-the-blue locked lips with him had shocked him right down to his toes. That wasn't some kid's move. It was the act of a woman willing to take what she wanted.

That he had responded, that he had all but devoured her right there in the middle of his brother's pub in front of a whole slew of witnesses—including her disapproving brother—had been almost as shocking. Maybe that head injury he'd dismissed had left his brain more addled than he'd realized.

He'd admitted to Kelly that part of the blame was his. He had—albeit unintentionally—pretty much challenged her to kiss him. What red-blooded, healthy, spirited woman wouldn't have reacted exactly as Kelly had?

That didn't make it right. It certainly didn't make it smart. And it most definitely didn't make it something that could be allowed to happen again.

Unfortunately, short of firing her, he wasn't entirely clear on how he was going to guarantee that there wouldn't be a repeat, especially now that they both knew exactly the kind of fireworks they'd be avoiding. Most men—and even a few women—would not willingly turn their backs on that kind of instantaneous combustion, no matter how dangerous.

Michael muttered a sharp oath under his breath. Why hadn't he seen that kiss coming? He could have deflected it, laughed off the incident and gotten a decent night's sleep. Instead, he'd tossed and turned, his body half-aroused by lingering memories of the way Kelly's mouth had felt on his. Here it was nearly eight in the morning and he was as stirred up as he had been within seconds after she'd dragged her lips away from his. Worst of all, there wasn't even enough time for him to haul himself into an ice-cold shower before Kelly arrived for their Saturday morning session.

Well, there was only one thing to do, he finally concluded. He had to face the whole situation squarely and give Kelly the option of quitting or sticking around under a stringent set of hands-off guidelines.

There was just one tiny little flaw in that plan. Massages were part of the therapy. He'd discovered already that there were a dozen different reasons why it was necessary for her to touch him. Trying to ban all contact between them was pretty much self-defeating in terms of his recovery. Not banning it was dangerous for entirely different reasons.

Michael thought of the thousand and one dangerous situations in which he'd found himself during his years as a SEAL. How could he possibly let one sexy little therapist scare him out of doing what needed to be done? He couldn't, not if he ever expected to look at himself in the mirror again.

Bring her on, he thought with renewed determination. Let her tempt him. He would be strong. He would resist. He would concentrate on the reason she was in his life…to make him whole again, to get him back on his feet. He would pretend she looked like a frog and had the skin of an alligator.

He choked on the image. Maybe he should forget about trying to deceive himself into thinking she wasn't attractive and concentrate on developing the willpower of a saint.

"You did what?" Kelly's boss at the rehab clinic asked incredulously when Kelly stopped by with coffee and blueberry muffins on her way to Michael's on Saturday morning.

The coffee and treats were a Saturday ritual. The stunned expression on Moira's face was a rarity. So was the hard look that followed. Kelly found herself wincing under that intense, disapproving scrutiny.

"Tell me again," Moira commanded. "I can't believe I heard you right the first time."

"I kissed Michael," Kelly repeated. "I flat out, on

the lips, kissed him." Her chin shot up in a display of defiance. "And I would do it again, if I got the chance."

That said, her belligerence wilted. "Not that I'm ever likely to have another chance," she said. "He'll probably fire me when I walk in there this morning."

"He should," Moira said without the slightest trace of sympathy. "Of all the unprofessional, self-defeating things you could have done—"

Kelly cut her off. The lecture wasn't really unexpected, but it was unnecessary. "You're not telling me anything I haven't already told myself a thousand times since last night. What do I do now?"

"Go over there and face the music," Moira said. "And don't be surprised if it's a funeral dirge."

"That's what I love about you, Moira. You always paint such a rosy picture of things," Kelly said wryly.

"What did you expect?"

"I suppose I was hoping you'd mix a tiny bit of compassion in with the lecture," she admitted. "Imagine that this was a guy you'd had the hots for during most of your adult life. Wouldn't you have done exactly what I did, given the chance?"

"You weren't exactly given the chance," Moira reminded her. "You stole it."

"A technicality," Kelly insisted. "Remember, he did kiss me back."

"Which only proves he's a red-blooded male."

"You don't intend to give an inch on this, do you?" Kelly asked wearily.

"And let you off the hook? No way." Moira's disapproving frown did lift ever so slightly, though. She leaned forward and subjected Kelly to a thorough survey. "Judging from the pink in your cheeks and the sparkle in your eyes, the kiss must have been worth putting your professional reputation on the line."

Kelly sighed. "Oh, yes," she confided dreamily. "That kiss was everything I ever dreamed of, and then some. I can only imagine what kissing him would be like if his heart was really in it."

"Probably best not to go there," Moira said. "You might be tempted to try it again."

"Oh, I suspect I will be," Kelly admitted. Before her friend could react to that, she squared her shoulders with renewed resolve. "But the next time, I'm going to resist. I'm going to remind myself that I am not in Michael's life as a woman, but as a therapist. That I have a job to do, and I won't be able to do it if there's all that kissing going on."

"Great logic," Moira said, laughing. "Tell me again why you were at the pub."

"So we could get to know each other better."

"Well, kissing would definitely accomplish that," Moira noted.

"Actually, it was all about gaining his trust," Kelly corrected. "I don't think the kissing accomplished that. If anything, it probably did the exact opposite. He's probably terrified to be alone in a room with me for fear I'll find some new way to test his code of honor."

"Could be," Moira confirmed. "I guess you'll find that out when you get over there."

Kelly sighed. "And there's no point in putting that off, is there? Wish me luck."

"Always," her friend said, her expression sobering. "I just wish I knew if you wanted luck on the professional front or the personal."

"That is the heart of the dilemma, isn't it?" Kelly said as she left Moira's office to make the drive to Michael's.

Until she heard him call out in response to her ringing of the bell, she wasn't sure she would even find him at home. Apparently he was less cowardly about this meeting than she was. She wanted to turn and run.

She didn't, though. She walked into the apartment with her head held high and a plan forming in the back of her mind for keeping Michael as a client despite her behavior the night before. One look at him had all of that flying right out of her mind.

"What happened? Are you sick?" she demanded, taking in his ashen complexion, unshaved cheeks and still-mussed hair.

"No sleep," he said tersely. "I finally gave up about twenty minutes ago. I haven't even had my first cup of coffee."

Her heart skipped a heat. "Why were you having trouble sleeping?"

"Do you even need to ask?" he asked, his expression daunting.

Kelly winced at his harsh tone. "The unfortunate kiss," she said.

"The unfortunate, never-to-be-repeated kiss," he confirmed, then almost immediately scowled at her. "There you go again."

She stared at him in confusion. "What?"

"What I said before, it was not a challenge."

"Of course not," Kelly agreed at once, though she had to admit a tiny part of her had reared up in defiance of that *never-to-be-repeated* edict.

"Then why did you get that same glint in your eyes that you got last night right before you kissed the daylights out of me?" he asked.

Kelly stared at him. "A glint? Really?"

"Don't give me that innocent look. If I'm going to have to watch every word out of my mouth around you, this is never going to work. I can't have you thinking that everything I say is some sort of challenge or invitation or something."

Kelly seized on the fact that he apparently hadn't decided to fire her outright. "I'll behave myself. I promise. What happened last night was a fluke. I swear to you that I am not in the habit of throwing myself at my clients."

"Good to know," he said, his mood lightening ever so slightly. "How did you happen to make an exception in my case?"

"Like I said, it was a fluke. I must have had too much to drink."

"One ale that you nursed all night?" he asked skeptically.

Kelly shrugged. "I'm not a big drinker."

A grin tugged at his lips. "Also very good to know. I guess it wouldn't be wise to invite you over for beers and basketball."

"I don't think the basketball would be a problem," she said thoughtfully, then winced as his grin spread. "Sorry. You were teasing."

"Just a little," he conceded.

"Michael, I really am sorry. What I did was inappropriate and unprofessional, and I assure you that it won't happen again. I hope you'll give me another chance." She drew in a deep breath, then dove into her planned speech. "In fact, I was thinking that we could move the sessions to the rehab center where I work part-time, if that would make you feel more comfortable. There would be other patients, other therapists around. We'd never be alone." She'd figured that alone would sell him on the idea, but just in case it wasn't enough, she added, "And there is equipment there that would be helpful."

His frown deepened as she spoke. "Forget the center. I don't want to work with a lot of people staring at me. We can go on working right here."

"But the equipment there really would be helpful. At some point you'll need to go there, anyway."

"When that time comes, we'll discuss it," he said flatly, clearly refusing to give the idea any more consideration. "Not until then. As for avoiding a repeat of what happened last night, I told you then that part of the blame is mine. I take full responsibility for my part in it, and you've apologized for yours. That's sufficient. We'll just forget about this and make sure it never happens again. There's no point in denying that there's some sort of attraction going on here, but we're both adults. We can deal with it and keep ourselves from acting on it." He met her gaze. "Deal?"

"Deal," she agreed eagerly, so overcome with relief that she wanted to hug him, but wisely managed to resist. Instead, she injected a brisk note in her voice and said, "Now, why don't I make some coffee and we can get started?"

"The coffee can wait," Michael said. "We've already wasted too much of this session. I want you to give me a real workout today, and in case there's any doubt in your mind, that *is* a challenge, and I expect you to take me up on it."

Kelly nodded. She didn't even try to hide her relief that he was giving her a second chance. And if the only thing he wanted from her was a grueling schedule of therapy, she would bury the memory of just how good that kiss had been and accommodate him.

At least for now.

The increasingly demanding exercises were excruciatingly painful. Sweat was beading on Michael's brow, but Kelly had asked for ten more repetitions and, by God, he was going to give her ten. A SEAL never quit. Sometimes, in the weeks and months following his injury, he'd had a hard time remembering that. For a few weeks in San Diego, the news had been relentlessly discouraging. Eventually he'd taken it to heart and resigned himself to his sedentary fate.

But ever since the morning after that unforgettable kiss, Kelly had flatly refused to let him sink for one single second into a morass of self-pity. Whenever he muttered about all this effort being a waste of time, she sent him a chiding look and demanded even more from him. In the last couple of weeks, he'd learned to keep his mouth shut and do whatever she asked without protest.

The two hours she spent with him three days a week

flew by. And after she left, it took him hours to recover from pushing himself to the limit, but he would not allow himself to quit.

She thought he was making excellent progress. He disagreed, but kept his opinion to himself. If he so much as hinted that he was discouraged, he was afraid that one of these days she would stop responding with extra work and simply walk out the door. If she did that, she would take his only hope with her.

Besides, aside from the rigors of her therapy, he enjoyed spending time with her. He liked the way she got in his face, refusing to back down. He liked even more the faint feminine scent she wore. He was beginning to remember just how much he liked having a woman in his life. Not one special woman, just someone to flirt with, maybe dance with, make love to.

He sighed, then realized that Kelly was staring at him with a puzzled expression.

"Where did you go just then?" she asked. "You stopped right in the middle of the eighth leg lift."

"Sorry. I guess my mind wandered."

"Really?"

"It happens," he said gruffly.

"Of course it does, but you're usually so focused."

He reached for a towel and wiped his face. "Well, today I'm not. Sue me."

There was no mistaking the hurt in Kelly's eyes. It wrenched Michael's heart. He honestly couldn't blame her for being on the brink of tears. His mind had wandered down a forbidden path and now he was unreasonably taking it out on her. Why was it that he could look into the eyes of soulless terrorists and remain completely unmoved, but one glance into Kelly's soft gray eyes and he was lost?

"Sorry," he said, apologizing yet again for his thoughtless behavior.

"Why don't we quit for the day?" she suggested, her tone neutral. "You've been working too hard for the past couple of weeks. You could use a break."

Michael was smart enough to acknowledge that she was right. He had been overexerting himself and his muscles were complaining. The last thing he needed was a tear or some other injury that would put his rehabilitation on hold. Nor did he need to risk offending Kelly any more than he had already.

"I'll tell you what," he said, trying to make amends. "I need to go see someone today. If you have time to give me a lift over there, I'll buy you lunch on the way."

Kelly seemed so taken aback by the suggestion, he couldn't help chuckling. "I'm not scared to be alone in a car with you," he teased. "Or in a restaurant. You've been on very good behavior lately. I think I can let down my guard for a couple of hours."

She gave him a rueful smile. "You have no idea how stressful it's been," she responded.

Michael had the distinct impression that she wasn't actually joking. He could understand exactly where she was coming from. Despite his overwhelming relief that they'd been adhering to the ground rules about no intimate contact, the strain of it was telling on him, too. Maybe that was one more reason why he'd suggested lunch. He figured they both deserved a reward for their incredible restraint.

"Probably best not to go down that road," he told her. "Not when we've been doing so well."

An expression of what might have been disappointment flashed in her eyes, but then she regained her composure.

"So where are you going that you're willing to risk spending time alone in a car with me? It must be important."

He nodded slowly. "It is. I'm going to stop by to see the Havilceks."

"Your family," she said at once, her expression brightening. "I met your mother a few times when we were kids. I guess she was actually your foster mother, though, right?"

He nodded. "I didn't think of her that way, not for long, anyway. She wouldn't allow it. She said that even if she couldn't adopt me, she intended to be my mother. No boy could have had a better one."

"Then why have you waited so long to get in touch with her since you got back to Boston?" she asked. "I still don't understand that."

"Self-protection," he admitted candidly. "She's the kind of woman who assesses a situation, then takes over. It doesn't matter to her that I've been a grown man for a long time and that I've handled extraordinary responsibilities with the Navy, I'm still her baby."

"Hard to picture anyone thinking of you that way," Kelly said, surveying him with blatant appreciation. "Then again, that's exactly how my folks treat Bryan and me. It would probably help if Bryan and I moved into our own places, but it's been so comfortable living at home, neither of us have bothered. Hovering and worrying is probably just a universal parental trait."

"That doesn't make it any less annoying, especially in a situation like this," Michael said.

"No, it certainly doesn't." Kelly regarded him with undisguised curiosity. "Do you remember your real..." She immediately stopped and corrected herself, "I mean, your biological mother at all?"

Michael had thought about that very question a lot over the years, even more so since Ryan and Sean had found him in San Diego. They both had such vivid memories of their mother, but Michael's were all hazy. When Mother's Day rolled around, it was Doris Havilcek—with her sweet smile, graying hair, sharp intelligence and steely resolve—whose image filled his head. Kathleen Devaney was a name on his birth certificate, nothing more. She stirred no sentimental feelings in him at all.

"Not really," he told Kelly. "I don't have the same kind of anger about her and my dad that Ryan and Sean feel, either. Maybe if I'd been a little older or if I'd wound up in a different situation the way they did, I'd hate them, too, but basically when it comes to my biological parents, I feel nothing at all."

Sorrow spread across Kelly's expressive face. "Aren't you even the least bit curious about them? I know I would be. I'd want to know what they're like, why they did what they did, where they are now."

"Why bother?" he said cynically. "There are no good

explanations for any of it. If it were up to me, Ryan would give up searching for them, but he's determined to finish what he started. Sean has some reservations, but in general, I think he's backing him up. I think one reason they're so determined to find our parents is to find out what happened to the twins. For all we know, they were abandoned along the way, too, when it got to be too inconvenient to keep them around."

"Twins?" Kelly repeated incredulously. "There were more of you?"

He nodded. "Twin brothers, Patrick and Daniel. They were only two when we were all split up. Ryan seems convinced our parents took them when they left." He tried to dismiss the little twinge of dismay that stirred in him, but he wasn't entirely successful. If it was true, it made the whole mess even more despicable.

He met Kelly's gaze. "If you ask me, Ryan's going to be opening up a whole lot of emotional garbage by tracking them down. If they did have all those years with our parents, how the hell are they supposed to react when three older brothers come charging back into their lives? And I doubt if either Ryan or Sean can claim to be entirely indifferent to the fact that our parents chose to keep Patrick and Daniel while dumping the rest of us into foster care."

"But it could be wonderful to be reunited," Kelly insisted.

"Maybe in an ideal world," Michael said. "But something tells me it's not going to be a picture-perfect moment, not for anyone."

He shrugged off his dread of that day and forced a smile. "Have you actually agreed to my invitation yet?"

She laughed. "Probably not, but if you think I'd miss the chance to see you reunited with your mom, you're crazy. Of course I'll take you, and lunch will be great."

"You won't mind pushing me around in this chair?" he asked, even though the real question was how he was going to feel letting her do it. He had a hunch she'd be more comfortable in the situation than he was likely to be.

"Don't be ridiculous," she said, confirming his guess. "But you might want to change first. Otherwise the restaurant's likely to make us eat outside, even though the temperature's in the teens today."

Michael glanced at his sweaty workout clothes and feigned indignation. "You think I need to improve on this?"

"Oh, yeah," she said fervently. "Not that I haven't always been rather fond of a truly male scent, but everyone's not like me."

"Maybe you should come back in a half hour," he suggested.

She frowned at him. "Make it an hour. I could use a little sprucing up myself. Will that still give us enough time for lunch before you're due at the Havilceks'?"

"Sure," he said, unwilling to admit that he hadn't exactly warned them that he was coming by. He hadn't wanted to give his mother time to work up a good head of steam about his failure to get in touch the second he hit town. He was hoping the surprise of finding him on her doorstep would take the edge off of her annoyance.

Kelly grinned at him. "You haven't told them you're coming, have you?"

"Nope," he said unrepentantly.

She laughed. "This is going to be fun. I'm not sure which I'm looking forward to more—the joyful reunion or listening to your mother deliver a blistering lecture about the way you've been hiding out in Boston the last few months."

Michael regarded her with chagrin. "Something tells me you'll get a chance to evaluate both options and decide which has the most entertainment value. The only person I've ever met who's tougher on me than you is my mother. None of my commanding officers in the navy even came close."

"Then I can definitely hardly wait to meet her," Kelly said. "Maybe she'll give me some tips on how to handle you."

He leveled a look straight into eyes suddenly churning with emotion. "Trust me, that is not a lesson you need to learn."

Kelly looked incredibly pleased by the backhanded compliment. "Even an expert can use an occasional pointer from someone with more experience."

Michael groaned. What had he been thinking? The prospect of having Kelly and his mother ganging up on him was almost more daunting than trying to get out of this damned wheelchair.

6

Kelly deliberately chose the most wheelchair accessible restaurant she knew for their lunch. Though she wasn't absolutely certain, she was fairly sure that this was the first time Michael had ventured out to eat anyplace other than his brother's pub. She didn't want the experience to be so stressful that he refused to try it again. He was a proud man and he was already chafing enough at letting her assist him with getting in and out of her car.

"Is this okay?" she asked as she walked along beside him as he rolled himself toward the street-level entrance.

"Looks fine," he said, his expression grim as he contemplated the door. When Kelly started toward it, he grabbed her wrist. "I'll get the damn door."

Arguing seemed pointless. She waited until he'd maneuvered himself around and could hold it while she stepped inside. Then he faced the dilemma of how to get in himself without having the door crash into him. His face was a study in concentration as he shouldered the door open, then eased his chair through the entry. She didn't release her pent-up breath until he was safely inside the restaurant.

There were more obstacles to come. The only vacant table in the busy restaurant was all the way across the room. When the room was empty, Kelly imagined the aisles were wide enough, but now with chairs jutting erratically out, they were all but impassable. Michael's expression was filled with tension as he tried to make his way between tables without knocking into the backs of other customers, most of whom were completely oblivious to his difficulties. The hostess had long since placed their menus on the table and gone back to her post by the time Michael finally crossed the room.

"You did great," Kelly said, taking her seat.

"I don't need a pat on the head for getting across a damned restaurant," he snapped.

She bit back a sharp retort of her own and turned her attention to the menu. She was still fighting the sting of tears when she felt his hand cover hers.

"Kelly?"

"What?" she responded, still holding her menu up to mask the fact that she was about to cry over something so ridiculous, especially when she could totally understand his level of exasperation. For a man whose work had required a peak level of physical fitness and agility, to adjust to being anything less had to be difficult.

"I seem to spend my life apologizing to you, but I am sorry. It's just so damned frustrating to be tied to this chair," Michael said, his tone full of contrition.

She lifted her gaze then and met his. "It won't be

forever. And even if it were, it wouldn't be the end of the world."

"It's already the end of my world," he said quietly. "No matter what, I won't be going back to work as a SEAL. For months, in the back of my mind, I was convinced I could if I just worked hard enough." He sighed. "But for weeks now I've been struggling to face the fact that that's not going to happen."

"I know I can't begin to understand what it's like to lose something that's been so important to you, but you will find something else just as challenging," she told him earnestly. "There are plenty of things a man with your intelligence can do. And a career's not everything. You can marry, have a family. Your life isn't over."

"The only one I ever wanted is over," he said flatly.

"If that's going to be your attitude, then I feel sorry for you," she told him, refusing to back down when a dull, red flush climbed into his cheeks. "There are plenty of people who will never walk again. You *will* get out of that wheelchair. So it's taking a little longer than you'd like. And you won't be able to do some of the rigorous things you once did, so what? You're alive, dammit! Stop feeling so sorry for yourself and concentrate on what you still have, instead of what you've lost."

For what seemed like an eternity she wasn't sure if he was going to explode with anger or simply turn around and wheel himself right back out of the restaurant. She was still wondering when their waiter appeared and, completely oblivious to the tension, announced that he was Henry and he'd be taking care of them today.

"Just what I need," Michael muttered. "Somebody

else who thinks it's his mission in life to take care of me."

Henry stared at him in confusion. "What? Did I say something wrong?"

Michael's smile wasn't exactly wholehearted, but it was a smile. "No, I'm just having a bad day. How's your day going, Henry?"

Henry still looked uncertain, but he said gamely, "Fine, sir. Have you two decided on what you'd like to drink?"

Michael glanced questioningly toward Kelly.

"I'll have a cup of tea," she said.

Michael nodded. "The lady will have tea, and I'll have your strongest poison."

Henry blinked furiously. "Sir?"

Kelly bit back a chuckle. "Don't mind him, Henry. He thinks he's being amusing. Bring him a cup of very strong coffee. I want him wide-awake while I finish telling him what I think of him."

"Yes, ma'am," the waiter said, backing away from the table with undisguised relief.

"Think he'll ever come back?" Michael asked.

"He shouldn't," Kelly said. "You were awful to him."

"And to you," Michael said. "I thought I'd save you the trouble of having to put something lethal in my coffee by asking him to do it."

"Don't think I wouldn't, if I had any murderous tendencies," Kelly told him. "Unfortunately, I still think you're worth salvaging."

He studied her intently. "Why?"

"Why what?"

"Why do you think I'm worth saving?"

She got the impression that he sincerely wanted to know, maybe even needed to know. "Because underneath all that exasperating self-pity, you're a good guy. You've spent your life being a hero for your country. You're smart, occasionally funny and breathtakingly handsome, though I wouldn't let that go to your head. Good looks rarely make up for a lousy disposition."

A smile tugged at his lips. "I'll try to remember that from now on."

Kelly regarded him seriously. "Michael, there really are a lot of blessings in your life. You should try counting them, instead of focusing on what you've lost."

"I will," he promised, his own expression suddenly serious. "I hope you won't mind if I put you at the top of the list."

Kelly's breath caught in her throat and the tears she'd fought off returned with a vengeance. "Dammit, why did you have to go and say something so blasted sweet?" she asked, swiping impatiently at her cheeks. "I was just getting comfortable being furious with you."

He reached over and caught a tear streaking down her face, then brushed it gently away. "Well, now, I couldn't have that, could I?"

She sniffed and tried not to notice the way his fingers felt against her skin. "Why not?"

"You were liable to go off and leave me stranded in here," he told her with a perfectly straight face.

Kelly choked back the laughter that bubbled up. "I should have known your reason would be totally self-serving."

He grinned. "That's the kind of guy I am," he said unrepentantly.

"No," she said emphatically. "That's the kind of guy you want me to *think* you are." She leveled a look deep into his eyes. "Which makes me wonder why you feel it's necessary. Are you deliberately trying to scare me off, Michael? Is this part of your tactic to keep some distance between us?"

He seemed to consider the question for an eternity before finally shrugging. "I honestly don't know."

"Then you should know that it takes a lot more than a bad temper to scare me away."

He sighed heavily. "Yeah, I think I'd already figured that out."

The entire scene at the restaurant had been totally draining. Given a choice, Michael would have gone back to his own apartment and hidden out for the rest of the day, but he wasn't about to admit to Kelly just how shaken he was, both by the struggles he'd had adjusting to a world in which he wasn't agile as a cat and to the discovery that her opinion of him mattered. It mattered far more than it should.

Which was also why he wasn't going to back out on this visit to see his folks. He wasn't going to give Kelly one more reason to think of him as a coward.

Given his state of emotional turmoil, he shouldn't have been surprised by his reaction to seeing the home in which he'd grown up, but he was. It was as if a hard knot he hadn't even known was there, deep inside, finally eased.

The house, an unimpressive, two-story brick Colonial on a quiet street, looked exactly the way it had since the first day he'd walked through the door. There was ivy climbing up one side, despite his father's frequent attempts to destroy it. The shutters, despite his mother's avowed intention to paint them red, were still the glossy black his father preferred, as was the front door with its gleaming brass knocker. His gaze drifted along the front walk, then froze at the sight of the steps. There were so blasted many of them. How had he forgotten?

Apparently Kelly saw his dilemma at the same instant, but she was quicker to adjust. "You can go in through the garage," she said swiftly. "It opens directly into the kitchen, doesn't it?"

Michael didn't bother asking how she knew that. She had been in the house from time to time. If the visits hadn't been especially memorable to him, apparently they had been to her. He was grateful for that at the moment.

"That'll work," he said at once. "The garage door's not locked and it's not automatic. Think you can lift it?"

She grinned and feigned flexing a muscle. "I may be little, but I'm mighty."

She went on ahead as Michael tried to navigate the driveway. It seemed to take forever. He was surprised that no one glanced outside and caught a glimpse of him struggling up the slight incline. What if no one was home? Granted it was Saturday afternoon and his mother had always baked on Saturdays, but maybe things had changed.

As he considered that, he realized that Kelly had the

garage door open. His mother's car, the same dull gray sedan she'd driven for far too many years now, was right where it had always been. He bit back a sigh as he thought of how many times he'd offered her money to buy herself something newer, and how many times she'd told him to save his money for a rainy day.

Just then the door from the kitchen was flung open and there she was, her cheeks rosy from the heat of the oven, wisps of graying curls framing her face and an expression of pure delight on her face.

"Oh, my," his mother whispered. "I heard the garage door, but I never imagined… Oh, my." She was down the driveway, her arms around him before Michael could even blink away the tears that threatened.

"Mom, you have to stop crying," he said as he held her tightly. "I'm okay, and any second now you're going to have me blubbering. How will that look?"

"I don't care how it looks," she said, still not releasing him. She shook him just a little. "There's nothing wrong with a man showing emotion. I thought I'd taught you that."

Michael laughed. "You certainly tried."

His mother stood up at last, then surveyed him thoroughly. "Oh, Michael, you look wonderful. Why didn't you let us know you were coming?"

"I didn't want you to make a fuss," he said, knowing now how futile that had been. Surprise or no surprise, there would eventually be a fuss. He took her hand and gestured toward the garage. "There's someone here you've been ignoring. Do you remember Kelly Andrews?"

His mother spun around, and her eyes lit up. "Bryan's little sister," she said at once, then grinned. "The one who always had a crush on you."

Michael winced. "Mom, don't embarrass her."

But Kelly was laughing. "And I thought I'd hidden it so well."

"A mother always knows," his mother told her. "It's wonderful to see you again. But how…?" Understanding obviously dawned, and she whirled on him. "Michael Devaney, how long have you been back in Boston?"

"Not long," he said evasively.

She turned to Kelly. "How long?"

Kelly looked straight at him and didn't even hesitate. "I believe it's been about six weeks now, hasn't it, Michael?"

"Traitor," he said.

"Honesty should be prized," his mother scolded. "What on earth am I thinking keeping the two of you out here when it's bitter cold? Come inside where it's warm, so I won't feel guilty making you listen to me tell you just how annoyed I am with you, Michael Devaney."

He felt a little like saying, "Aw, Ma, do I have to?" Unfortunately he knew exactly the sort of reaction that would get. He might as well go in and get the deserved lecture over with.

Looking up, he gave his mother his most appealing smile. "I don't suppose you've been baking today, have you?"

She frowned at him, though there was a twinkle in her eyes. "I've just finished baking for the social hour after church tomorrow, as you perfectly well know, since I've been doing it every Saturday for the past thirty or more years. I don't imagine anyone there will object if I cut one of the apple pies for you and Kelly." She gave him a knowing look. "And I imagine you'll be wanting ice cream on top."

"Is there any other way?" he asked as his mother stepped behind the chair and briskly wheeled it inside as if she'd been doing exactly that forever.

The kitchen smelled of cinnamon and sugar and apples. While he and Kelly took off their coats, his mother bustled around cutting the pie, putting ice cream on top and setting it on the table. Only after he'd taken the first bite and made all the appropriate comments about her incredible baking did she pull out a chair and glower at him.

"Now, then," she said in a tone with which he was all too familiar, "we'll talk about why in heaven's name you thought you had to keep your presence here in Boston a secret from me."

Kelly grinned and settled back more comfortably in her chair. "I think I'm going to enjoy seeing you try to wriggle off the hook."

His mother frowned at her. "You're not off the hook, either, young lady. You know the phone number here. You could have tipped me off."

Kelly instantly looked so incredibly guilty that Michael took pity on her. "Don't blame her. I swore her to secrecy."

It was a slight overstatement of the truth, but Kelly didn't deserve to get one of his mother's blistering lectures on his account. Hiding out had been his choice, though for the life of him, he couldn't think now why he had thought it was necessary.

"Then you explain it," his mother challenged.

He met her gaze and said simply, "I needed to get my bearings."

"And you couldn't do that under this roof?" she demanded incredulously.

"No," he said quietly. "I'm not the same man I was when I left here."

"Don't be ridiculous," his mother said with obvious impatience. "Of course, you are, certainly in every way that counts. You're going to have to do much better than that, Michael."

Both women seemed to be watching him expectantly, but Michael didn't have any answers for them. None his mother was likely to accept, certainly.

"I'm glad I'm here now, Mom. Isn't that enough?"

Her eyes misted again. "Yes, I suppose it is," she said softly, then reached for his hand. "Your father is going to be so pleased. He'll be home soon. You can wait, can't you? And I can call your sisters. I'm sure they'd want to be here to welcome you."

Michael noticed that even without him having to say it, she'd apparently gotten the message that he wouldn't be staying here with them. "Of course I can wait, as long as Kelly's not in a rush."

She immediately shook her head. "I'm in no rush. In fact, that will give me time to try to pry this pie recipe out of your mother."

Nothing Kelly could have said would have done more to ingratiate her with his mother, Michael thought as he saw the pleasure bloom on Doris Havilcek's face. Before he knew it the two of them were sharing recipes as if they'd been at it for years. He sat back, closed his eyes for an instant and let the sound of their excited talk flow over him.

It didn't take long for the rest of his family to assemble. His foster sisters Jan and Patty, were the first to arrive, welcoming him with hugs and more stern admonishments about his failure to get in touch the instant he hit town. He was trying to fend them off with good-natured teasing when the man he'd always considered his father walked in.

Kenneth Havilcek was a big, burly man who'd spent his life in construction. He'd loved athletics and privately bemoaned the fact that his daughters weren't the least bit interested in any of the sports he loved. When Michael had come into his life, he'd said Michael was the gift of a son he'd been dreaming about. Sports had been their bond. No father could have been prouder when Michael excelled at both football and basketball in high school. He'd never missed a single game.

He was halfway across the room, a welcoming smile on his face, when he spotted the wheelchair and faltered. When he finally met Michael's gaze, there was a shared misery in his expression. Clearly, he understood better than most of the others in the room the full implications of Michael being unable to walk, however temporarily.

The moment lasted only a heartbeat, then he was bending over, giving Michael a hearty bear hug and a slap on the back. "Welcome home, son. I imagine your mother has already given you an earful about keeping us in the dark about being in Boston, so I won't add to it." He waved a finger under Michael's nose. "But don't think for a second I'm not as irritated by it as she is."

"Sorry, sir."

His father nodded. "I should think you would be. Now, then, what's this I've been hearing about your biological brothers finding you?"

His sisters reacted with shock. "You've heard from them?" Jan demanded. "Why didn't anybody tell me?"

"Or me?" Patty asked. "This is huge news. Where are they? Have you actually seen them? What are they like?"

Michael held up his hands. "Whoa! One question at a time. They came to San Diego when I was in the hospital, so, yes, I have seen them."

"*They* were in San Diego and you wouldn't let us come?" Jan said, her indignation plain.

"I didn't invite them," he protested. "They showed up."

"I guess there's a lesson there for us," Patty said to her sister. "When it comes to our baby brother, we shouldn't wait for an invitation. So where do they live? What are they like?"

"They're right here in Boston," he admitted. "We have a lot of old baggage to work out, but I do like them. And they're dying to meet all of you. Ryan would like you to join us at his pub one evening."

Patty stared at him with sudden comprehension. "Not Ryan's Place?"

Michael nodded. "You know it?"

"I've been there half a dozen times for the Irish

music. Ryan is your brother? I can't believe it." She tilted her head and studied him. "Now that you say it, though, I can see the resemblance. This is so amazing. When can we go?"

Everything was moving a little too fast for Michael. He wasn't sure what sort of reaction he'd expected from his family, but it hadn't been this. Then, again, he should have known that people who could welcome a little boy into their home with such open hearts would be just as eager to welcome those who mattered to him.

"How about next Friday night?" he said eventually. He turned his gaze to Kelly, who'd been sitting quietly throughout his reunion with his father and sisters. "Can you make it then?"

Michael caught the pleased look that his mother exchanged with his father and knew exactly what it meant. She already had him romantically linked with Kelly, though they'd never given her so much as a hint that Kelly was anything more than his therapist.

Kelly must have seen the same look, because she hesitated.

"I'd like you to come," he told her, not sure why he felt it was so important to include her. He just knew that this whole day had been easier because she was by his side. He wanted her there when his two families met for the first time. "Please."

She smiled then. "Of course, I'll come," she said, studying him intently. "But if you don't mind, I think we should be going now."

His sisters protested, but his mother took Kelly's side

and within minutes Michael was outside in Kelly's car. He glanced over at her as they pulled away.

"How did you know I was ready to leave?" he asked.

She shrugged off the intuition. "Something in your eyes, I suppose."

Michael sighed. It should be terrifying that she could read him so easily, but for some reason, it wasn't. Tomorrow, when he was less exhausted, he'd have to try to figure out why.

7

Kelly had known she was in serious emotional trouble the minute she'd started sharing recipes with Doris Havilcek. There had been something so wonderfully comfortable about it, as if she were already a member of the family that had taken Michael in when he was a boy. Even as warmth had stolen through her, she had realized that she was heading down a very dangerous road. Being accepted by the obviously warmhearted Mrs. Havilcek was a far cry from having Michael indicate that he wanted her in his life in any meaningful way.

She had tried to remain on the fringes of the family's reunion, staying silent and unobtrusive so that no one else would get the idea that she and Michael were a couple. Clearly his foster mother had jumped to that conclusion, and that was likely to be awkward enough.

Kelly had spent the rest of the weekend trying to think of some way to extricate herself from the visit to Ryan's Place, but nothing came to mind—probably because the truth was that she wanted to be there to see how the Havilceks and Devaneys blended together, and whether Michael was at ease among them.

Even so, on Tuesday she attempted to make an excuse as she and Michael were finishing his therapy session. The two hours hadn't gone especially well, and he was in a particularly foul temper because of it. She probably should have waited to broach the subject of Friday night until his mood improved, but she wanted to get it over with.

"One more thing," she said as she gathered up her equipment. "I've been thinking about Friday, and I don't think that's going to work for me."

Michael's gaze shot up, a surprising display of alarm in his eyes. "Why not?"

"It's just not. I…" The lie faltered on her lips, but she sucked in a breath and managed to get it out. "I have a date."

He regarded her curiously. Suddenly his anger seemed to fade. "Is that so?" he said mildly. "Can't be much of a date, if you didn't even remember it when the subject of Friday night came up on Saturday." His gaze narrowed. "Or did you make it after that?"

Kelly hated the faint hint of contempt in his eyes at the possibility that she was breaking her plans with him to go out with someone who'd issued a later invitation. "No, of course not," she insisted, unwilling to carry the lie to that extreme. She didn't want him to dislike her. Nor did she want to destroy the fragile trust they were building. She merely wanted to protect her heart. "It was on my calendar. I'd just forgotten about it."

"Is this date with a man?" he asked.

Kelly studied him curiously. He'd almost sounded jealous, but that couldn't possibly be. Or could it? She decided to play out the charade a little longer to try to gauge his reaction. "Don't women usually go out with men?" she asked. "Besides, my private life is none of your concern. We set up the ground rules weeks ago."

He sighed at that. "Technically, no," he agreed. "But this family thing is important to me. I thought you understood that I want you to be there."

"Of course I understand that it's important, but you don't need me there," she said, instantly feeling guilty for trying to wriggle off the hook. "Look at this another way. If I stay away, we'll avoid all sorts of potentially embarrassing questions."

"Such as?"

"What I'm doing at what should be a very private meeting between the Havilceks and the Devaneys," she explained. "That's likely to stir up all sorts of speculation."

Michael suddenly grinned. "So that's it," he said as if he'd just discovered some huge secret. "You're scared my mother's about to start making wedding plans. You should have thought of that before you started asking her for the recipe for all my favorite dishes."

She frowned at his obvious amusement. Maybe it was a big joke to him, but it wasn't to her. "Aren't you worried about that?"

"Not particularly."

"Why?" she asked, bewildered by the fact that he wasn't the least bit concerned.

"Because my mother is basically harmless. And

if she does start getting any crazy ideas, I'll set her straight. It's not a big deal, Kelly. I can handle my mother."

"Yeah, I could see that on Saturday," she said dryly.

He laughed. "Okay, I can *usually* handle my mother." His expression sobered. "Come on, Kelly, tell the truth. You don't really have a date, do you?"

Continuing to lie was obviously pointless. Apparently she wasn't all that good at it. "No," she finally admitted with a sigh.

"Then come."

"Why is my being there so important to you?"

Now it was his turn to look vaguely bewildered. "It just is," he said finally. "I feel more…" He paused, searching for a word. "I feel more normal when you're around."

The explanation left her more confused than ever. "Normal how?"

He looked away as if he were almost embarrassed to make the admission. "You don't get that expression in your eyes when you look at me that everyone else gets," he said.

Kelly was beginning to get the picture. "No pity?"

"Exactly. And you don't let me off the hook when I'm behaving badly. Everyone else does, as if I deserve a pass because I'm in this damned chair. That's the last thing I need. I need to be held accountable for my actions. I need *you* right now."

Kelly swallowed hard against the tide of emotion rising in her throat. Michael's admission that he needed her—that he needed anyone—took her breath away.

It was a huge breakthrough for a man who'd probably gone through his whole life trying to convince himself that he didn't need anyone. How could she possibly turn him down after that?

"What time?" she asked, resigned.

As he realized what she was saying, a smile spread slowly across his face. "Pick me up at seven?"

Kelly almost agreed, then recalled that he'd told his family to meet at the pub at six-thirty. "Isn't that a little late?"

He gave her a rueful look at having been caught. "I was hoping they'd get all the introductions out of the way before I got there."

She shook her head. "I don't think so. I'll pick you up at six-fifteen, and no dillydallying. Be outside and ready to go. I'll remind you of that when I'm here on Thursday."

Michael laughed, clearly in a much better frame of mind now that she'd caved in to his request. "Yes, ma'am."

Impulsively she went back and touched his cheek. The faint stubble was rough against her palm. His heat and masculinity drew her as no other man's ever had. It was getting harder and harder to go on with the charade that she was immune to him. "It's going to be okay, you know."

He placed his hand over hers and held it in place. "With you there, something tells me it will be."

Michael still wasn't used to Kelly having her hands all over him. It didn't seem to faze her, so he knew he shouldn't let it bother him, but it did. In fact, it was driving him crazy. As if worrying about Friday night weren't bad enough, today he couldn't seem to keep his thoughts from straying to what it would be like if Kelly's touches were a little—okay, *a lot*—less impersonal.

"How do you do it?" he asked finally when it felt as if he might explode if she stroked her hands over his thigh one more time. He'd spent the past few weeks trying to hide the fact that he was in a perpetual state of arousal when she was around and it was beginning to get to him.

"Do what?" she asked, sounding oddly distant.

"The massage thing."

"I took classes."

He glanced back over his shoulder and frowned. "Not what I meant, and you know it."

She met his gaze, then looked hastily away, her cheeks suddenly rosy.

"Doesn't it bother you?" he persisted.

"It's my job," she said, her tone as prim as someone's elderly maiden aunt. "You're a client."

"I'm also a man," he reminded her. Some wicked instinct had him rolling over to prove the point. He was thoroughly aroused...and that was despite a concerted attempt to remain completely disconnected from the massage.

Kelly's attention was immediately drawn to the evidence. She swallowed hard, then deliberately looked away. Michael tried to gauge her reaction. It had almost seemed as if she was more fascinated—maybe even secretly pleased—than embarrassed. Maybe she wasn't as immune as he'd thought.

"Look, I..." Her words dwindled off.

He reached out and clasped her hand in his. "I don't mean to make you uncomfortable. I really don't. Actually, I was curious about how you remain detached from what you're doing."

She met his gaze. "The truth?"

"Of course."

"The issue has never really come up before."

"Before?" he repeated, a certain measure of gloating creeping into his voice. "Meaning it has with me? You aren't unaffected by touching me?"

She pulled away. "Don't sound so blasted pleased with yourself. We really shouldn't be having this conversation. It's inappropriate and totally unprofessional on my part. Besides, we had an agreement."

She was so clearly dismayed that he instantly backed off. Besides, he had the answer he wanted. The attraction wasn't as one-sided as he'd imagined. Satisfied with that knowledge, he rolled back on his stomach and rested his head on his arms. "I'll drop it, then," he murmured.

"Thank you."

"But don't be surprised if it comes up again tomorrow night when you're not on the clock."

Her hands on his leg stilled. "Michael!" she protested weakly.

"Kelly!" he responded, teasing.

She sighed heavily. "What am I going to do about you?"

"An intriguing question," he told her. "Let's put that on the agenda for tomorrow night, too."

"You realize if these topics come up tomorrow night, we might never actually make it to the pub?"

He hid his grin. "Definitely an added bonus," he conceded.

She smacked his uninjured leg. "Forget it, Devaney. I'm not providing you with an excuse to get out of introducing your families to each other."

"Oh, well, it was worth a try," he said with an air of resignation.

And getting Kelly to admit that she was not oblivious to the effects of these massages had definitely been a side benefit. Of course, it was also likely to fuel his own fantasies so that he wouldn't get a minute's rest between tonight and tomorrow. He figured the sacrifice of a little sleep was worth it.

Kelly was a nervous wreck on Friday night. She told herself she was worried for Michael's sake, that she merely wanted everything to go well, but it was more than that. The entire conversation they'd had about the impact of her massages on him had been disconcerting at best. His assurance that he intended to get into the subject again tonight the instant they were alone had her feeling edgy with anticipation of an entirely different sort.

She had been stunned when he'd revealed that he was thoroughly aroused. Stunned and, she was willing to admit, thrilled that she could have that kind of impact on a man she'd been convinced didn't think of her as a woman at all. There was little question now that Michael saw her as a desirable grown-up, not a kid. But what would he do about it? Would he do the noble thing and ignore it because of his friendship with her brother and her role as his therapist? She hoped not. She'd been waiting far too long for him to notice her.

Of course, that wistful thought lasted only the length of time it took to say "lost license." She could just imagine what Moira would have to say if Kelly revealed that there was anything the least bit provocative about her contact with a client.

She should get a grip, she told herself sternly, and tell Michael he had to do the same. Or she should quit. One or the other. She certainly couldn't let things continue as they had been, not if she valued her professional reputation.

But the prospect of not seeing Michael on a regular basis was inconceivable. He'd come to mean too much to her. Her childish infatuation was developing into something far more important. Something she had to ignore, though, if she wanted to see him through his rehabilitation. And she did want that. She wanted to be there when his leg was strong and he was finally able to walk again. Which meant she was going to have to push her personal feelings for him aside and pretend they didn't exist, no matter how badly he tormented her.

When she arrived Friday night to pick him up, he was dutifully waiting for her outside, despite the fact that the temperature had dropped and there was a threat of snow in the damp air.

"Are you crazy?" she demanded as she got out to

open the door and help him into the car. "Why didn't you wait inside?"

"You told me six-fifteen and that I wasn't to dilly-dally," he reminded her.

"And you always do what I say?"

He gave her his most winning smile, the one that made her heart flip over. "I try."

Kelly noticed that he was able to transfer himself to the car a bit more easily than he could the previous weekend. He was actually able to put a little weight on his bad leg. When he was settled, she put the wheelchair in the back, then got back behind the wheel and glanced over at him.

"You ready?"

"No."

She grinned at his sour expression. "Too bad."

"We could run away to the Caribbean. Spend a month or two in the sun getting a tan," he suggested, regarding her seriously. "My treat."

"As much as the possibility of spending a few days on a beach where the temperature is at least fifty degrees warmer than it is here appeals to me, I'm afraid I'll have to say no to that, too."

"You're no fun," he accused.

His words, clearly spoken in jest, hit a raw nerve. "So I've been told," she said, unable to keep the old hurt out of her voice.

Her response clearly startled him. His gaze narrowed. "What idiot said a thing like that?"

"The last man I dated."

Something in his expression turned dark and dangerous. "He hurt you, didn't he?"

"Well, it's never pleasant being told that one is a bore," she said, trying to make light of it.

It wasn't that Phil Cavanaugh had devastated her. She hadn't cared enough about him for his opinion to matter that much, but she had been shaken. It had made her question if that was why no relationship she'd been in had lasted more than a few months. Had Phil been speaking the truth? Was that the conclusion her other dates had eventually reached?

"Why would he say such a thing?" Michael prodded.

"Look, just forget about it," she said. "It's not important. I shouldn't have mentioned it."

"You mentioned it because even though I was joking, I apparently struck a nerve. Now, tell me," he ordered, "what gave this jerk the idea that you weren't much fun? Was there some specific incident, or was he just insulting you on general principle?"

Kelly had never examined that awful exchange from that exact perspective before. She considered Michael's question thoughtfully. It hadn't been an out-of-the-blue comment on her personality at all. Phil had made the accusation when she'd refused to join him at a nightclub for swinging singles, who enjoyed sharing their partners. She'd been stunned that he'd asked in the first place. He'd professed to be shocked by her refusal. Obviously they hadn't known each other at all. For months afterward she'd struggled to figure out why he'd ever thought she would go along with such an idea. She'd refused every invitation, terrified that the man who asked had the same low impression of her morals that Phil had had.

Suddenly she felt Michael's hand cover hers.

"Kelly, what happened?" he asked, regarding her with concern. "I really want to know."

And oddly enough, she found that she wanted to tell him, but how to explain it so that she didn't feel even dirtier than she had that night? "He made a rather insulting suggestion about how we could spend an evening and I turned him down," she said finally, skirting the specifics.

"Some men don't take rejection well," he noted.

Her lips twitched slightly. If only it were that simple. "As I recall, not five minutes ago you made the same comment when I turned your invitation down."

"Yes, but I was joking and you knew it." He studied her intently. "You did know it, didn't you?"

"Honestly, yes, but that didn't stop me from having an instant of déjà vu."

"I'm sorry. Not that I don't think running away to the Caribbean with you to be an excellent idea, but I was only trying to buy myself some time." He lifted his wrist, looked at his watch, and a triumphant grin spread across his face. "Which I have successfully done."

Kelly glanced at the clock on the dashboard and realized it was indeed after six-thirty. All thoughts of the slimy Phil Cavanaugh fled. She scowled at Michael. "You rat!"

"At least acknowledge that I'm a clever rat," he teased.

"Not a chance. I intend to tell everyone who'll listen that we're late because you're not only sneaky, but you're also a total chicken."

He regarded her with mock ferocity. "You wouldn't dare," he said direly.

"Watch me."

He didn't say another word as she started the car and drove the short distance to Ryan's Place, but as soon as she'd parked and come around the car to help him into his wheelchair, he snagged her hand and pulled her closer.

"I know one way to stop you," he said, amusement threading through his voice.

"Oh? How?"

"Like this." He gave a firm tug that had her tumbling into his lap. His mouth covered hers in a kiss that robbed her of breath and definitely cut off both thoughts and speech. Her pulse was scrambling by the time he released her.

She stood up shakily, cleared her throat and regarded him through dazed eyes. "You won't do that, though," she said, her voice unsteady.

"I won't?"

"No," she said with confidence. "It would stir up too many questions."

He laughed. "Do you honestly think I'm afraid of a few questions? Especially when the trade-off is a chance to kiss you thoroughly? Sweetheart, remember that I've been trained to withstand the worst kind of torture without breaking."

Kelly didn't like the gleam in his eye. She realized suddenly that he meant exactly what he was saying.

He would kiss her into silence and enjoy every outrageous minute of it.

So would she, but that was another issue entirely, and she was not about to share that little tidbit of information with him.

For once, kissing Kelly had served a purpose other than completely and fruitlessly turning him on. He was feeling downright cheerful and relaxed when they finally went into his brother's pub. Unfortunately, his sister-in-law was the first to spot them. Maggie was on the two of them like a hummingbird after nectar.

"My, my, my," she said, subjecting both of them to a thorough survey. "Rosy cheeks, avoiding looking at each other. Hmm, what could it mean?"

"Nothing," Kelly insisted, her cheeks burning an even deeper shade of pink.

Maggie's gaze settled on Michael. "You going to lie to me, too?"

He grinned. "Not a chance. I know better."

Maggie patted his back. "Good man," she said approvingly. She winked at Kelly. "Fibbing is a waste of time, anyway. I saw you two through the front window. It was quite a show, at least until that kiss pretty much fogged up the window. Then I had to rely on my imagination to guess what was going on."

"Oh, God," Kelly whispered, obviously embarrassed. "Did everyone see?"

Maggie wrapped a consoling arm around her shoulders. "Only me and Ryan," she said, then added, "and the people at the table by the door."

Kelly whirled in that direction, then groaned when she saw it was Michael's folks. His mother seemed especially pleased by what she'd observed. His father was merely studying the two of them with a speculative look.

Maggie laughed. "Definitely a fascinated audience, am I right?"

Michael shook his head at Maggie's obvious pleasure in their discomfort. Ryan definitely had his hands full with her. Michael couldn't decide if he pitied him or envied him. Add in Caitlyn, and the balance definitely tilted toward envy.

"I gather you've met the Havilceks," he said to Maggie.

"Yes," she responded cheerfully. "Why don't you two go on and join them? Ryan's going to move some more tables together in a minute. Sean and Deanna will be here soon."

"And your folks?" Michael asked.

"They decided to wait until another time. They didn't want to intrude."

"Which I shouldn't be doing, either," Kelly said, suddenly backing away as if she were about to make a break for the door. "Michael, I'm sure someone here will give you a lift home. I'll see you tomorrow for your therapy session."

She moved quickly, but even confined to his damnable chair, Michael was faster. He blocked her way and waited until her nervous gaze finally met his.

"I thought we'd settled this earlier in the week," he chided. "I want you here."

"But what must they think of me?" she whispered. "Kissing you right out there in public. What was I thinking?"

"Frankly, I don't think either one of us were doing much thinking," he retorted. "And for the record, this time I kissed you, not the other way around."

"In the grand scheme of things, I think that qualifies as a pretty puny technicality," she retorted.

Suddenly his mother's voice cut through their debate. "When are you two going to stop bickering and get over here?" she asked.

"My master calls," Michael said. "Are you going to dare to defy her?"

For an instant, he thought Kelly might do just that, but then she sighed and visibly squared her shoulders. "Let's go," she said. "But just so you know, you are going to pay for this. I have an exercise that will bring you to your knees."

Michael grinned at her. "An intriguing concept. I can hardly wait," he said, his tone deliberately wicked.

He noticed Kelly was still sputtering in indignation as she swept past him and went to join his parents. All things considered, the evening was off to a much better start than he'd anticipated.

8

It took less than an hour for Kelly to forget about how thoroughly flustered she'd been by Michael's kiss and Maggie's teasing. The heat she'd expected to keep her cheeks a permanent shade of embarrassed pink finally cooled, and she began to relax. After all, this evening wasn't really about her at all. It was about the Havilceks and the Devaneys getting to know each other.

Although Michael had clearly dreaded the entire occasion and she'd been expecting it to be awkward, they'd both evidently forgotten about the warmth exuded by his foster mother and his sister-in-law. Doris Havilcek and Maggie Devaney were like a couple of cruise ship social directors determined to see that everyone had a good time. Introductions were accompanied by anecdotes designed to provide insight and provoke good-natured laughter. Kelly was in awe of them, and more than a little envious.

So, apparently, was Michael. She turned to find him watching his foster mother with a dazed expression.

Leaning close, she noted, "She's an amazing woman, isn't she?"

"Even more so than I realized," he admitted. "I thought she'd feel threatened by having my brothers suddenly thrust into the middle of our lives, but she's not. She's simply opening that generous heart of hers and adding them to her family as if they'd just been rediscovered after a long absence. And my dad and sisters are following her lead."

"I'm glad for you," Kelly told him sincerely. "It would have been hard if they hadn't gotten along. I'm sure you would have felt torn."

Before Michael could respond, Scan moved into the vacant seat on his other side. "You really lucked out in the foster family department," Sean told him. "The Havilceks are terrific people."

Michael nodded. "No question about it."

"I've tried to get my last foster family in here to spend some time with Ryan and Maggie, but they're not much interested. Deanna and I go by to see them once in a while, but I always have the feeling if we stopped going they'd hardly notice. They're good people, but they've moved on. I always had the feeling that they knew there would always be another foster kid waiting just around the corner, so they tried not to get too attached to any of us."

Sean shrugged as if it didn't matter to him, but Kelly could see that it did. And it must be even harder on Ryan, who'd never stayed with the same foster family for more than a few months at a time. There was no one from his past to whom he felt the slightest sentimental attachment.

"Well, it looks to me as if you can all count on being part of the Havilcek clan from now on," Kelly told Sean. "Mrs. Havilcek will see to that."

Sean grinned. "Fine by me. I've heard about her apple pie."

Ryan joined them. "Did I hear somebody mention apple pie? Who's baking?"

Michael shook his head and regarded his big brother with amusement. "You'd think that a man who owns his own pub wouldn't have any trouble getting all the food he wants."

"Rory is a genius when it comes to cooking up an Irish stew or anything else he learned in Dublin, but he's yet to master an American apple pie," Ryan said with apparent regret. "Maggie's offered to teach him, but he's vowed to leave the day she starts trying to take over his kitchen the way she's taken over the rest of this place. Now, when my Caitlyn gets a little older, it'll be another story. That daughter of mine has our Rory wound around her little finger. She could sit in the kitchen all day long, banging on his favorite pots and pans with a spoon, and he'd never complain about the noise or the scratches."

"Speaking of Caitlyn, where is my niece tonight?" Michael asked.

"Upstairs with the baby-sitter and, with any luck, sound asleep," Ryan said.

"As is my son," Sean said. "Though I imagine he's playing video games rather than sleeping. He told us he wasn't a baby like Caitlyn, so Deanna bribed him to stay out of our hair for a few hours. I think Kevin's destined for a top-level management career in business. He's already a tough negotiator. Deanna and I come out on the losing end more than I'd like to admit."

Kelly listened with fascination as the talk centering on the kids went on for several minutes. Apparently both Ryan and Sean had been able to put their own bad experiences with abandonment behind them and had taken to parenting like the proverbial ducks to water. She wondered if Michael would eventually do the same. Because he'd been younger and because he'd landed with the Havilceks right at the beginning, he seemed to have fewer issues than his older brothers had had growing up.

And yet, she sensed that Michael still had moments when he felt like an outsider. His failure to call the Havilceks the minute he returned to Boston was evidence of it. Though he'd made perfectly rational excuses for that, Kelly wondered if he hadn't been just a little bit afraid of how they would perceive him now that he was no longer going to be a strong, able-bodied hero. He should have known better, but there had to be lingering insecurities from being abandoned by his own parents. How could there not be?

She snapped back to the present when she heard Ryan mention the search for the rest of the Devaneys.

"The investigator says he has a lead. It's not a sure thing, but he's found a Patrick Devaney up in Maine," Ryan told them. "He thinks it could be one of the twins.

The age is about right. They'd be nearly twenty-six by now."

Sean's expression darkened. "Is he going up there to check it out?"

"Actually, I thought maybe we should be the ones to go," Ryan said slowly.

"Forget it!" Sean said with surprising heat. "Finding the two of you has been great, but I've been giving it a lot of thought. I think that's going to be it for me."

Ryan turned to Michael, who looked as if he might object, as well. "Do you feel the same way?" Ryan asked him.

Kelly wasn't sure what she expected Michael to say or even what was right. This was an incredibly delicate situation, and clearly each of the brothers was coming at it from an entirely different perspective. And the twins might very well bring about a reunion between the three brothers and their biological parents.

"I need to think about it," Michael said, his earlier good mood suddenly vanishing. He glanced worriedly toward the Havilceks, as if he feared they might overhear the conversation. When he turned back to Ryan, he said, "This is a big step. We're getting closer to our parents. This guy's not going anywhere, right?"

"It doesn't sound like it," Ryan said.

"Then let me and Sean give it some more thought and we'll talk later, okay?"

"Sure. No problem," Ryan said. "Trust me, I've got mixed feelings about this myself. Not so much about finding Patrick and Daniel. I think that would be great.

But like you said, if they're going to lead us to our folks, I'm not sure how I feel about that."

"I know exactly how I feel," Sean said bitterly. "If they haven't bothered to look for us in all these years, it's their loss."

"We don't know they haven't looked," Michael suggested quietly.

Sean scowled at him. "Of course we do. If they had, they would have found us. It didn't take Ryan all that long to track me down, and the two of us were able to find you. It's not as if any of us had changed our names and moved to the far ends of the earth."

"Sean, believe me, you're not saying anything I haven't thought myself," Ryan responded. "But maybe none of us will really be at peace with the past until we know the truth about what happened. Maggie's forced me to see that." He patted Sean on the back. "But it's up to you. You two get back to me once you've thought it over. I'd better get back to the bar for a bit."

Ryan started away, then turned back to Michael. "By the way," he began casually, "there's a guy who comes in here once in a while who runs a fleet of charter boats. I'd like you to meet him sometime."

Kelly watched Michael's already stormy expression turn even darker.

"Oh? What does that have to do with me?" Michael asked.

"A guy with your background has to have an interest in boats, right? You must have been trained on every kind imaginable," Ryan responded. "I just thought you'd have a lot in common. And he's told me he has a hard time finding captains who know the equipment."

"The day won't come when I'll steer a bunch of damned tourists around Boston Harbor," Michael said heatedly.

Ryan shrugged as if his response were of no consequence. "It was just an idea. What would it hurt to talk to him? Add that to your list of things to think about, okay?"

He walked away without waiting for Michael's response.

Sean gave Michael a searching look, then sighed. "I think I'll go upstairs and check on the kids," he said.

After his brothers had gone, Michael faced Kelly with a troubled expression. "So, what do you think about this search of Ryan's?"

She noticed he didn't mention the job prospect Ryan had dangled in front of him. Apparently he really had dismissed it out of hand.

"It's really none of my business," she said finally.

"And that's stopped you from forming an opinion?" Michael asked skeptically.

"Hardly," she admitted with a rueful grin.

"Tell me."

"I understand why all of you would hesitate, but I think Maggie's right. I'm sure every one of you has wondered all these years why your parents disappeared and left you behind. I can't even begin to imagine what kind of impact that's had on your lives." She searched his face, trying to gauge how he was responding, but his expression was neutral. "Come on, Michael, isn't it better to find out the truth and put it behind you, once and for all?"

"Then the answer's pretty much black-and-white to you," he concluded. "You think we should go and see if this Patrick is one of the twins?"

"Yes, I do."

Michael's expression turned thoughtful. "Think about this, though. He was barely two when everything happened. He might not even remember that he had brothers. He and Daniel and our parents might have had this tight-knit, perfectly happy family all these years. How's he going to feel if three of us show up out of the blue and announce it was all a fraud?"

"It wasn't a fraud," Kelly replied. "It was simply *his* experience as a Devaney versus the ones each of you had."

"But it could forever alter his trust in our parents. Do we have the right to do that?" He seemed genuinely tormented by the question.

"You know what I think? I think it's amazing that you're thinking of his feelings at all. That's something a big brother would do. How can he not want to know that he has three older brothers who care deeply about him despite years and years of separation?"

Michael shook his head. "I think you're being overly optimistic. I think he's going to resent the hell out of us for coming in and destroying his world."

"Then you'll apologize and let him go on just as he has been."

"You're being naive, Kelly," Michael accused her.

"It doesn't work that way. The damage will have been done."

Kelly could see his point, but that was only one scenario. She pointed out another. "What if all these years, he has remembered having older brothers?" she asked. "What if he's always felt as if a part of his life was missing? Are you ready to deny him the answers he needs to feel complete?"

Michael frowned at her questions. "If only we could predict which way it was going to go," he said plaintively.

She put her hand over his and squeezed. "We can't. We can only calculate the risks and make the best choice possible. No one should understand that better than you do. You've made a career out of taking calculated risks."

"Yeah, but those are the kind of risks I understand," he said.

"They're life-and-death risks," she countered.

"And this isn't?" he asked wryly.

"Certainly not in the same way," she insisted.

"Remind me to have this conversation with you again when your entire world's been turned upside down," he said.

Little did he know that it already had been…on the day he'd come back into her life.

Despite Kelly's opinion that things would turn out all right, Michael was still feeling uneasy about this search for the rest of his biological family. On the one hand, it had turned out okay when Ryan and Sean had found him, but on the other, he sensed it was going to be very different with the twins.

As for finding his parents, he wasn't even ready to go there yet. He was not as bitter toward them as Ryan and Sean obviously were. He simply didn't care much one way or the other. That was a hornet's nest he didn't particularly want to disturb, but more and more it was growing inevitable that he would have to unless they called a halt to the search now. Whatever they did, they needed to be united, because all their lives were going to be affected. He honestly didn't know which decision was the right one.

There was one person, though, whose opinion he trusted more than anyone else's when it came to matters of family—his foster mother. Impulsively, the minute his therapy session ended and Kelly had gone, he called a cab and went over to the Havilceks. The fact that his mother would be in the midst of her Saturday baking wasn't entirely coincidental.

It grated on him that he had to ask the cabdriver to go up to the house and let his mother know to let him in through the garage, but the beaming smile on her face negated that momentary humiliation. She shivered as she waited for him just inside the garage.

"Come on in here, Michael," she said briskly. "It's freezing out there this morning. What brings you by? It's too early for the pies to be out of the oven, you know."

He regarded her slyly. "But not the cinnamon rolls, I'll bet."

She grinned. "With milk or coffee?"

"Milk, of course."

She waited until he was settled at the kitchen table before sitting opposite him, her expression suddenly serious. "What's on your mind, Michael? Did you and Kelly have a fight last night?"

Startled by the question, Michael paused with a fork-ful of gooey cinnamon roll halfway to his mouth. "No. Why would you think that?"

"Something changed during the evening. You were so clearly happy when you came in, but when you left, you both looked…" She hesitated, then said, "Serious, I guess. I thought something might have happened."

He let the cinnamon roll practically dissolve on his tongue as he studied his mother. "You like her, don't you? It would really bother you if we'd fought."

"Well, of course I like her. The two of you seem good together, but it's your feelings that count."

He ought to be pleased by the assessment, but instead it made him uneasy. "We're not dating, you know. She's my therapist."

His mother grinned. "If you say so, dear."

Michael frowned. "I do."

"Then you might consider not kissing her quite so enthusiastically," she teased. "It could give people, including Kelly, the wrong impression."

"I'll try to keep that in mind," he said wryly.

His mother studied him intently. "Okay, then, if you didn't come to talk about Kelly, why are you here?"

"You and the cinnamon rolls aren't excuse enough?"

"We certainly could be, and I'd be flattered if we were, but I have my doubts."

"Do you realize how disconcerting it is to have a mother who can virtually read your mind?"

"I can be vague if you'd prefer it," she offered.

"Hardly. Okay, here it is. Ryan thinks he may have found one of our younger brothers in Maine. He wants all of us to go up and check it out."

She nodded slowly. "I see. And you don't want to go?"

"It's not that. I just keep trying to put myself in Patrick's place. He was little more than a baby when the family split up. For all we know, he's lived happily ever after, and now here we come barging in to tell him that his idyllic situation cost the rest of us a family."

She regarded him knowingly. "Are you so sure it's Patrick you're worried about?"

"Of course."

"Michael," she chided in the tone she used when she thought one of her children wasn't being entirely forthright.

He frowned at the unspoken accusation. "Okay, maybe I'm the one with the problem. I lucked out. I wound up with the best family a boy could ask for, but a tiny part of me resents the fact that the twins got to keep our biological parents and the rest of us were sent away. I don't think I even realized how much I resented it until last night when Ryan said his investigator had a lead on Patrick."

"You know that none of this was Patrick's fault," his mother said. "Any more than it was yours or Ryan's or Sean's."

"Yes, but..." He sighed. "You know what I really

don't get is why Ryan's suddenly so anxious to find the twins and our parents. He should be the angriest of all, and, deep down, I think he is. It's Maggie who's convinced him to do this."

"Maybe he's simply wise enough to realize he'll never let go of that anger until he has the whole story."

"Then you think we should go," he concluded, knowing that was exactly what he'd expected her to say when he'd come here. Maybe he'd wanted her blessing even more than he'd wanted her advice.

She rested her hand against his cheek. "Michael, I love you as much as if you were one of my own," she said quietly. "But this is not my decision. You need to listen to your heart."

That was going to be hard to do for a man who'd grown used to ignoring anything his heart had to say, especially if it happened to be the least bit inconvenient. He'd always thought of himself as a man of cool actions, not emotion.

"And while you're at it," she added slyly, "you might see what your heart has to say about Kelly. You could be surprised."

"Careful," he teased. "Some men might find your meddling annoying."

"Not the smart ones," she retorted. "Now, shall I turn off the oven and give you a lift home? Or can you stay for dinner?"

"Not tonight. I have some thinking to do. And don't worry about the lift. I'll call a cab."

"Let me do it," she said, already moving toward the phone.

Michael shrugged into his jacket and jockeyed the wheelchair into the garage.

"I'm not opening that door yet," his mother warned. "The cab company said it would be at least ten minutes. I wish you'd just let me take you."

"This is fine, Mom."

"One of these days you'll be driving yourself places again," she said with confidence. It was the first time she'd ventured any sort of comment about his future.

"I hope so."

"I know so," she said emphatically. "Now give me a kiss." She bent down and accepted his kiss. "I love you."

"I love you, too."

She regarded him intently. "Finding your biological parents won't diminish that."

He smiled. "I know that."

"Just thought I'd mention it, in case it was on your mind."

"Have I told you lately how incredible you are and how lucky I am to have you in my life?"

"You never had to say it," she said, though there were tears in her eyes. "Mothers can usually see straight into their children's hearts."

"You can," he told her. "I'm not so sure Kathleen Devaney could."

"You won't know that until you see her again."

Michael sighed. "Will you be disappointed in me if I decide against it?"

"I could never be disappointed in you as long as you make your choice for the right reasons," she said with conviction.

The arrival of the taxi saved him from having to think about what his mother would consider valid reasons for leaving things just as they were.

But finding Kelly waiting on his doorstep pretty much guaranteed that he wasn't off the hook for the day, after all.

Michael didn't look especially overjoyed to see her, Kelly concluded as he exited a taxi and made his way up the walk to where she waited. She wasn't sure what had drawn her back to his place after she'd finished with her last client. Maybe it had been his distraction during their morning session. More likely, it was the uneasy conversation they'd had the night before. She'd avoided asking about the search that morning, but it had clearly been on his mind. He'd hardly said two words to her during the entire session.

"What brings you back?" he asked as he maneuvered the wheelchair past her and into the foyer. "Did you forget something?"

"No." She'd been waiting for a half hour and in all that time she hadn't managed to come up with a halfway plausible excuse for returning aside from wanting to see him. "If you're busy, I can leave."

"I'm not busy," he said. "Are you hungry? We could order a pizza or something."

She was surprised by the invitation. "Are you sure you don't mind me being here?"

"To be perfectly honest, I'm glad you're here."

His response startled her, but she didn't want to make too much of it. "Oh?"

"I was over at my mom's. She gave me a lot to think about, but to be frank, I'm not looking forward to all the soul-searching required."

"If you're looking for a distraction, maybe I should go rent us a couple of videos, too."

He grinned. "Perfect."

"Action, romance or comedy?"

"What do you think?"

"One action movie for you, one chick flick for me," she concluded. "That's only fair."

He nodded. "What do you want on your pizza? I'll order while you're gone."

"Nothing slimy."

Michael laughed. "Besides anchovies, what exactly does that exclude?"

"Onions and mushrooms."

"Fine by me. I'll get half pepperoni and half sausage."

"You have beers or sodas?"

"Plenty of both," he confirmed.

"Then I'll be right back." She started down the walk, then turned back. "When was the last time you went to the movies, just so I don't get something you've already seen."

"The last movie I saw was *Lethal Weapon*."

"Which one?"

He stared at her blankly. "There was more than one? Movies weren't something I paid any attention to once I hit my teens. I was too wrapped up in sports."

Kelly laughed. "I can see you have a lot of catching up to do."

It took her less than twenty minutes to pick up *Lethal Weapon II*, along with *Die Hard* and *Pearl Harbor*, and for her, the romantic comedy *Return to Me*, which she'd already seen twice before. She grabbed a package of microwave popcorn at the checkout counter while she was at it.

Back at Michael's, she arrived at the same time as the pizza. She paid the delivery man, then juggled everything and almost dumped it on the floor twice before finally getting the door open.

She noted that Michael had already poured a beer for himself and a soft drink for her and was seated on the sofa with a basketball game on TV. He instinctively started to get up, then fell back with a muttered oath.

"Sorry," he mumbled.

Kelly merely nodded, took the pizza over to the coffee table, then held up the movie selections. "You pick first."

He pointed to the Bruce Willis film. "Somehow testosterone goes better with pizza and beer."

"A matter of opinion," she noted, but she slipped it into the tape player and sat down beside him.

As requested, the movie was noisy and filled with action, so no conversation was required, but Kelly still felt as if Michael was holding something back. As soon as it was over, rather than slipping a second tape into the machine, she turned to him.

"Are you sure you don't want to talk about whatever's on your mind?"

He leveled a look at her and slowly shook his head. "I'd rather do this," he said, reaching for her.

Kelly sighed and murmured, "Me, too," just as his mouth covered hers.

9

The kiss did what nothing else had been able to do. It drove all thoughts of the search for the rest of the Devaneys from Michael's head. All that mattered was the silky brush of Kelly's lips across his, the intoxicating heat that curled through him like a slug of fine Scotch, and the thundering of his heart. For a few minutes, he forgot that he couldn't walk, forgot that his future was filled with uncertainty. All that mattered was here, now and the woman in his arms.

Then, somewhere in the back of his head where his values and conscience resided, he heard the first faint whisper that lust was a poor substitute for deeper feelings. And sex was no way to block out problems that needed to be dealt with.

There was little question that he could spend the next few hours, perhaps even the whole night with Kelly in his bed and his problems on hold. But he'd never used a woman like that before, and he wasn't about to start with one he genuinely liked. He sighed against her delectable lips and slowly released her.

Forehead pressed against hers, he murmured an apology.

"For?" she asked cautiously.

"I keep swearing that I won't do this again."

"Have I complained?"

His lips curved. "No, but you should. There are a million and one reasons why it's a bad idea."

"Name two," she challenged.

"Your professional reputation," he said, tossing her own frequently stated argument back at her. "And the fact that I'm at a crossroads. I have nothing to offer you. Until I figure out who and what I'm going to be now that I'm no longer a SEAL, I have nothing to offer to anyone."

Eyes sparkling with indignation, she frowned at that. "Michael Devaney, if that's not the most ridiculous thing I've ever heard. You don't have to put yourself in harm's way for your country to be a worthwhile human being. The reality is that very few men do what you've been doing the last few years, and most of the rest live perfectly respectable, fulfilling lives with women and children who love them. Are you suggesting that any one of them is less of a man because of what they do or because they don't do what you did?"

"Of course not," he said fiercely. "I would never say anything like that. It's about being able to do what you love, what you're good at. I was good at being a SEAL. I loved it, the same way Ryan loves running his pub or Sean loves being a firefighter. It's about being passionate about something, and then losing it. We were talking about your professional reputation the other day.

That wouldn't matter if your career weren't important to you, right? So, what if you lost it? What if they took your license away? How would you feel?"

Her expression faltered at that. "I'd hate it," she said at once, then added with absolute certainty, "but I'd get over it and find something else."

"Just like that?" Michael asked skeptically. "You think it's that easy?"

"No, of course it's not easy, and maybe it wouldn't happen overnight, but I wouldn't give up or think my life was over," she insisted.

Though he didn't share her belief that she could move on so easily, Michael accepted the fact that she believed it. "Fair enough," he said. "All I'm saying is that I've only reached the point where I can accept that my life isn't over. That's a long way from knowing what I can do with it."

"Ryan offered one option the other night," she said cautiously. "You didn't even consider it, did you?"

"No, because it's ridiculous."

"Why?" she persisted. "Because being a charter boat captain is somehow demeaning?"

Michael hesitated. That was part of it, but there was more, something obviously Ryan and Kelly hadn't even considered. "It's not something I can very well do unless I'm back on my feet."

"But you will be," Kelly said fiercely. "I believe that with all my heart."

"I wish I were as confident."

"Make me a deal, then. *When* you're back on your feet, you'll at least meet your brother's friend."

As reluctant as he was to do it, he nodded slowly. "Okay, that's fair enough."

"I'll remind you, you know."

He grinned. "I'm sure of it."

She regarded him with a suddenly wistful expression. "Are you saying you can't sleep with me until then, either?"

"I shouldn't," he said emphatically, fighting a whole slew of regrets as he said it. "And I won't."

Kelly tilted her head and gave him a considering look. "Then I hope you won't mind if I bring you a few books on changing careers next time I come by, just in case the charter boat thing doesn't work out."

For the first time in days, Michael laughed. "In other words, you intend to do your best to speed up the process?"

"Yes." She locked gazes with him and ran her thumb across his lower lip. "And be warned, in the meantime, I also intend to make it all but impossible for you to resist me."

Michael's pulse scrambled at the challenge. "Kelly," he protested.

"Save your breath," she said. "That's just the way it's going to be. Until tonight I wasn't absolutely certain you wanted me this way, but now I am."

"And what about all the professional considerations you've mentioned?"

"Easy," she said with a shrug. Her gaze locked with his. "As of tonight, I quit."

He pulled away, shocked by the feeling of desperation that cut through him at her words. "Hey, you can't do that," he protested.

"Sure I can."

"But I need you," he said.

A faint spark of something that might have been satisfaction lit her eyes at his words. "You need a good therapist. It doesn't have to be me. But actually, I have no intention of letting you find one. I'll go on helping you. I just won't let you pay me for it."

"And that makes it okay for you and me to…?" He hesitated over the precise description.

"Have sex," she supplied bluntly, her eyes twinkling at his discomfort.

"Yes, that," he agreed.

She grinned. "It can't hurt. Besides, who's going to turn me in?"

Michael could think of one possibility in particular. Her brother might at least threaten to turn her in to save her from making a huge mistake that would cost her everything. "Bryan," he suggested.

"I'll deal with my brother, not that he's likely to know if you and I are sleeping together."

"Trust me, he'll know," Michael said dryly.

"How?"

"Men always know when their friends are getting lucky."

"Because you all like to brag?"

"No, because we're a whole lot less cranky."

Kelly laughed. "I don't think we need to worry about that in your case. You have lots of excuses to be cranky that have nothing to do with sex. I doubt that will change."

"Thanks," he said, unable to keep a hint of irritation out of his voice.

"Just calling it like I see it."

"I think it's time for you to go," Michael said stiffly.

"It's not that late," she argued.

"Oh, yes, it is."

She regarded him curiously. "Are you afraid you're going to grab me and haul me off to bed right now?"

Michael groaned.

Kelly's expression turned gloating. "That's it, isn't it?"

"A smart woman would stop tempting fate and get out of here before we both regret it."

For what seemed like an eternity, Michael was terrified she was going to refuse. He wasn't sure his willpower was strong enough to withstand even five more minutes of her deliberate teasing.

Finally, her expression thoughtful, she nodded. "You win. For now."

She grabbed her coat and purse, started for the door, then came back and kissed him so thoroughly, he had to wonder if he'd lost his mind when he'd all but kicked her out.

"I'll see you Tuesday bright and early," she called out when she reached the door.

She sounded so blasted cheerful, Michael was tempted to pick up the nearest heavy object and hurl it after her.

But he didn't. He murmured a polite farewell, hit the

remote and started another movie. For a long time after she'd gone, he was oblivious to what was playing on the TV screen. Then he noticed that it was a romantic comedy and muttered an oath that could probably be heard down the block.

He shut off the VCR and flipped through the channels until he found a basketball game. Just what he needed, he thought happily, reaching for what was left of his beer. He understood basketball. He understood sweat and competition. He apparently didn't know a thing about women or he would have seen this whole thing with Kelly coming a mile away and he could have gotten out of the damned way.

Kelly sat across the table from her best friend and flinched under Moira's knowing stare. There was no question that this unusual Sunday breakfast was a command performance. The message on her answering machine the night before had made that clear. Now that they were here, she wished Moira would just get it over with. Kelly pushed her eggs around on her plate and waited for the lecture to start. When the minutes dragged on and Moira said nothing, Kelly's nerves finally snapped.

"Just say it," she commanded.

Moira regarded her innocently. "Say what?"

"Whatever you're thinking."

"You don't want to know what I'm thinking."

"Probably not," Kelly murmured morosely, staring at her plate because she couldn't bear to see the censure in the other woman's eyes. "Say it anyway."

"I'm not sure whether to start by asking if you've lost your mind or if you're happy."

"Both," Kelly said.

"Then you are involved with your *client,*" she said, making sure that Kelly understood exactly what was at stake. "I was afraid of that."

"We're not involved," Kelly said. "Not yet, anyway. And I quit last night."

"And that's supposed to make it all right?"

"Look, I know I'm skating on thin ice, professionally speaking, but Michael matters to me. I thought I could keep my personal feelings out of it, but I can't." She shrugged. "So I quit."

"Is he planning to hire another therapist?"

"I don't think so."

"And you intend to go on with his therapy in the meantime?"

Kelly nodded.

Moira met her gaze. "He's that important to you?"

"Yes, he is."

Moira sighed. "How does he feel about you?"

"He wants me," she said. "He doesn't want to, but he does. I figure that's got to be a good start."

"Or a disaster waiting to happen," Moira predicted.

"Come on," Kelly coaxed. "Stop being so gloomy. This could be the best thing that ever happened to me. I've been half in love with Michael Devaney for most of my life. I'm finally getting a chance to see if that's real." She gave Moira a penetrating look. "Are you telling me that if you had the same chance to test things with my brother, you wouldn't grab the opportunity with both hands?"

Moira's pale, lightly freckled complexion flushed a bright red. "Let's leave my feelings for your brother out of this."

It had been an unspoken topic between them for years now. Kelly decided it was past time to put an end to the silence. "Why?" she demanded. "You've been carrying a torch for him forever. Why should both of us continue to deny it?"

"Because it's pointless. Bryan has never given me a second glance. Besides, you're just trying to change the subject to take the heat off of you."

"Yes, I am," Kelly admitted cheerfully. "As for Bryan not giving you a second look, maybe that's because you try to fade into the woodwork whenever he's around. I'll bet he'd take notice if you gave him half a chance. You're a wonderful woman, and you'd be terrific for Bryan. He's a dreamer with his head in the clouds most of the time. You're real. You're grounded. You'd balance each other perfectly."

"In your opinion," Moira pointed out. "If Bryan thought that, he would have asked me out before now. He's had plenty of opportunities."

"If that isn't the pot calling the kettle black," Kelly chided. "You think it, and you haven't done anything about it. It's pitiful actually. You're shy and he's dense. I could fix that."

Hope stirred in Moira's eyes. "Fix it how?" she asked warily.

Kelly wondered why she hadn't thought to push

the two of them together before. Maybe she'd wanted to believe fate would take care of it, but she was discovering lately that fate sometimes needed a helping hand.

"Leave it to me," she told Moira. "What are you doing Friday night? Are you free?"

"I usually do laundry on Friday night."

"Oh, please," Kelly said, dismissing the feeble excuse. "You're free. Meet me at Ryan's Place at seven. It's an Irish pub."

"I know what it is, but why there?"

"Because it's owned by Michael's brother and it's become the Friday night place to be for his family." She gave her friend a wicked grin. "And for my brother."

Moira, who was as confident about most things as any woman Kelly knew, regarded her uncertainly. "I don't know. Won't it be obvious that it's a setup?"

"To my myopic brother?" Kelly scoffed. "Hardly. Don't even think of arguing with me about this. I'm not taking no for an answer. Seven o'clock, and wear something blue. It's Bryan's favorite color, and you happen to look great in it."

"Okay, fine. You win," Moira finally agreed. "But I'm only saying yes so I can meet this man who has you taking crazy chances."

"Of course you are," Kelly teased.

"Just because you're trying to fix me up with your brother does not mean you're off the hook," Moira insisted. "I'm still worried about you."

"There's nothing to worry about," Kelly said. "I

know exactly what I'm doing where Michael's concerned."

In fact, she was growing more and more certain of it with each passing day.

"So, you'll do it?" Kelly was asking, as she massaged the taut muscles in Michael's calf.

"Do what exactly?" he asked, trying to drag his attention away from the heat that was spreading through him with each strictly professional caress.

"Ask Bryan to join us at the pub Friday night," she explained with obvious impatience. "Weren't you listening to anything I said?"

"Every word," he assured her. Most of them just hadn't registered. It was impossible to concentrate when she was rubbing warm oil into his skin. He'd never thought eucalyptus to be an especially provocative scent, but he was rapidly beginning to change his mind. He forced himself to pay attention to the conversation. "This has something to do with your friend. What was her name again?"

"Moira Brady."

"And Bryan knows her?"

"Yes, but he doesn't pay any attention to her, at least not the way he should."

"So, basically what you're doing is matchmaking, and you want my help?"

"Exactly."

"No way," he said emphatically.

Her hands stilled, and Michael almost regretted

being so adamant. Clearly she wasn't pleased with his response.

"Why not?" she asked, her tone suddenly chilly.

"Because men don't meddle in their friends' love lives."

"You don't have to meddle. You just have to ask him to meet us at the pub. It's not as if you've never asked him to join you there before."

"Why can't you ask him? Moira is your friend."

"Because that's too obvious," she said impatiently. "Don't you know anything?"

"Apparently not when it comes to matchmaking, thank God."

This time when her hands stroked his leg, there was something far more sensual than therapeutic about it. Michael responded accordingly. He had to will himself to stop paying attention to those long, lingering strokes and concentrate on counting backward from a thousand. He was getting to be quite good at it.

"Michael, please," she coaxed softly. "It's not such a big deal. There will be a whole crowd of us there, right? It's not as if we're asking him to spend a deadly dull evening all alone with a total toad."

Michael groaned. He was going to say yes eventually and hate himself for it. A few months ago he'd barely remembered Kelly's existence and now he was considering conspiring with her against a man he'd always thought of as his best friend. He suspected traitors could fry in hell for less.

Kelly leaned closer, her breath whispering against his cheek. "Are you thinking about it?"

"How can I think when you're all over me?" he muttered irritably.

She laughed. "I'll take that as a compliment."

"It wasn't meant that way," he groused.

"No, I'm sure it wasn't. But you are going to do this one tiny thing for me, aren't you?"

He rolled over, dragging the sheet with him to cover his unmistakable reaction to her sneaky massage technique. "I'll do it on one condition."

"Great!" she said, obviously pleased.

"Hold on. You haven't heard the condition. I want you to look me in the eye and tell me exactly what put this little scheme into your head. Have you ever fixed your brother up with one of your friends before?"

"No," she admitted, looking decidedly uneasy.

"Then why now? Why Moira?"

"I think they'd be perfect for each other," she said, sticking to her story.

Michael wasn't buying it, not entirely anyway. "And you just reached that conclusion this week? Out of the blue? After knowing this Moira for how long?"

"A while," she conceded.

"And the inspiration to matchmake never struck you before?"

"Not exactly."

"Then I have to ask again, why now?"

She frowned at him. "I sort of owe her."

"For?"

"Keeping her mouth shut about something," she told him grudgingly.

Suddenly it all became perfectly clear to him. "Moira's the woman who runs the rehab clinic where you work part-time, isn't she? And she found out about the two of us."

He didn't have to see the telltale flush in Kelly's cheeks to know he'd hit the nail on the head. He would have known it by the way she suddenly found a million little things to do to avoid meeting his gaze. When she started lining up her selection of free weights according to size, he shook his head.

"You can't avoid answering me forever," he said.

"Sure I can," she said with obvious bravado.

"So, the price of Moira's silence is a date with your brother," he said, drawing his own conclusions. "And this is a woman you want me to trick him into spending an evening with?"

She scowled at that. "You make it sound so sleazy. It's not that way at all. Moira is a terrific woman. She's just a little shy. She gets all tongue-tied when Bryan is around. And just so we're very clear, this was my idea, not hers."

"But she went along with it," he reminded her.

"Reluctantly. Come on, Michael, what's the harm?"

"There are so many possibilities, I can hardly list them all," he responded.

"Name one."

"Your brother could be furious."

Kelly shrugged. "It won't be the first time or the last. Brothers and sisters are always at each other's throats."

"He could be furious at me," Michael corrected. "And that would be a first. I'm at a disadvantage, you know. Under normal conditions, I'd be a more than even match for him, but right now I'd prefer to pick fights I can win with words."

"So you'll smooth things over, if it comes to that," she said, clearly not taking his fears seriously. "It won't. I'm telling you, he's going to thank you. And I will certainly find some inventive way to demonstrate my gratitude."

Michael choked at the immediate image that slammed through him. "Inventive, huh?"

She grinned, clearly sensing victory. "Absolutely."

"Care to give me a small sample, just a little incentive offered in good faith?"

"Roll over," she ordered.

Michael cast one last, lingering look into her suddenly smoldering eyes and did as she'd asked. The sheet fell away. He wasn't entirely sure what he expected, maybe some new, exotically scented oil that would drive him wild. Maybe the light skim of her fingers just a little too high on the back of his thigh.

What he absolutely, positively had not expected was the light brush of her lips against the back of his calf, the back of his knee, the back of his thigh. If it hadn't been for one small, but very strong hand placed squarely in the small of his back, he would have jolted off the massage table and dragged Kelly straight into his arms and then onto his bed without giving propriety a second thought.

When she finally finished her little demonstration, his breathing was ragged and his resolve in tatters. He sighed heavily and tilted his head to meet her gaze.

"Bring me the phone."

She grinned, a cat content with its expected reward of cream.

"And don't look so damned smug," he added.

"Aye, aye, sir," she said cheerfully as she handed him the phone.

"I know I'm going to regret this," Michael muttered as he dialed Bryan's number.

Then he thought of the way Kelly's clever mouth had felt against his skin and concluded that even if her scheme blew up in their faces, he still might die a happy man.

10

Her brother truly was the biggest dolt on the planet, Kelly concluded as she watched him all but ignore Moira, who was seated next to him. And if sparks didn't start to fly soon, Michael was never going to let her forget it.

In fact, he chose that precise moment to lean in close and whisper, "It's going well, don't you think?" The edge of sarcasm in his voice was unmistakable.

"Well, do something," she snapped back.

His eyes widened. "Me? This was your idea."

"I'll make it worth your while," she offered.

He had the audacity to laugh at that. "Promises, promises."

One advantage of being with a man in a wheelchair was that his attention could be refocused in a heartbeat. Kelly snagged the handles on his chair and aimed him toward her brother and Moira. "Now, talk," she muttered.

The look Michael shot at her would have wilted the resolve of a lesser woman, but Kelly was feeling desperate. She wanted this evening to work out, not to guarantee Moira's silence—truthfully, that was a given anyway—but to try to ensure her happiness. If her friend was foolish enough to be interested in Bryan, then he was the man Kelly wanted for her. Not that she would ever have promoted such a scheme if she hadn't also believed that Moira was exactly right for her brother, she added piously.

"Great music," Michael ventured to Moira. "Are you enjoying it?"

Kelly had to fight a smile at his charming awkwardness. Clearly social graces had never been high on his list of achievements. She actually found that reassuring. She'd always assumed he'd been a rogue who flirted with anything in skirts, especially once he'd joined the navy. Handsome as he was, though, she doubted he'd needed much in the way of charm to have women circling around him.

When Moira remained absolutely silent, Kelly firmly poked an elbow in her ribs. "Michael asked you about the music."

Moira gave them both a weak smile. "Sorry. I guess I was thinking about something else. The music's very nice," she agreed politely.

"Are you very familiar with Irish music?" Michael asked, still doing his best to get the conversation rolling.

Kelly nearly groaned when her friend merely nodded. She knew for a fact that Moira loved Irish music and had been to a dozen or more pubs on a trip to Ireland. She would have sworn this was the perfect topic to get her friend to be a little more animated and to catch

Bryan's attention. He considered himself something of an expert on Irish folk tunes.

"You have been to Ireland, though," Kelly prodded. "How does this compare?"

Finally, Moira seemed to forget Bryan's apparently intimidating presence. Her expression brightened. "The lead singer's the best I've heard this side of Dublin," she said with her more familiar enthusiasm.

Bryan's attention was finally snagged. He regarded Moira intently. "You've been to Ireland?"

Moira blinked at him, clearly startled that he'd finally taken notice of her. "Well, of course," she said. "With a name like Brady, how could I not have gone at least once? Have you been?"

"Twice. Once on a tour by horseback. Another time hiking."

Moira's eyes lit up. "You actually went hiking? Where? Which tour company did you use?" The questions poured out of her. "I've been thinking of doing that next summer, but I can't decide which tour to take. Just when I think I've decided, I see another brochure that looks even better."

Kelly secretly congratulated herself on a job well done as the two of them put their heads together, shutting Michael completely out of the conversation. He turned back to Kelly slowly, his expression vaguely bewildered.

"What just happened there?"

"You asked the right question. I provided an extra push. And they took over from there." She patted his hand. "Nice work. You obviously have a knack for this sort of thing after all."

He frowned at that. "Don't go getting any ideas. This was a one-time thing, just to get you out of a bind." His gaze locked on hers. "Though I have the strangest feeling that your friend Moira was never any threat to your career in the first place. She doesn't seem the type to resort to blackmail to get a guy."

Kelly feigned surprise. "Really?" She shrugged. "Well, you never know. Better safe than sorry."

His gaze darkened as he subjected her to a thorough survey that had her skin heating.

"So, what do you think? Can we get out of here now?" he asked, his voice low and husky.

Something in his tone, in his eyes made her suddenly nervous. "And miss seeing the fruits of our labor? Why would we want to do that?"

He snagged her jacket off the back of her chair and tossed it to her. "Because we have better things to do," he said, already heading for the door.

Heat spiraled through her along with a little thrill of anticipation. "We do?" she asked, automatically trailing after him just as he'd obviously assumed she would.

"Remember all those inventive ideas of yours?" he said cheerfully. "It's time to pay up."

Her step faltered. "Now? Tonight?"

"Can you think of any reason to wait? A deal is a deal, right?"

"Well, sure, but tonight?" She glanced back to see that her brother and Moira still had their heads together. "What if they need us?"

"Their problem," Michael said succinctly. "We've done our good deed for the day, maybe for the year."

He leveled a look straight into Kelly's eyes that made her stomach flip over.

"Unless there's some reason you want to back out on our deal?" he suggested lightly.

Honestly, she had been sure that Michael would be the one backing out. After all, he was the one who'd listed all those reasons why they should keep their emotions in check and their hands to themselves. Her promise had been made half in jest, though with at least a modicum of wistful hope. Now that it appeared he was taking her up on it, she had to wonder if she'd made a mistake. As desperately as she wanted it, were they really ready to take this next step? Maybe they should think it over a little longer, weigh the pros and cons.

Was she crazy? This was exactly what she'd been wanting from the day she'd set eyes on him years ago. If they were finally on the same wavelength, why wait?

She held his gaze, her expression serious. "Lead on," she said quietly, accepting his challenge.

For an instant, Michael seemed startled by her ac-quiescence. Then he latched on to her hand and pulled her down until her face was even with his.

"Once we get in your car and head for my place, there's no turning back," he said tightly.

"We're not playing some silly game of chicken, Mi-chael. I know that," she told him.

"Just so we're clear."

"Never more clear," she replied evenly. She was amazed at how cool she sounded, when her heart was hammering at least a hundred beats a minute. This was it, then, the night she'd been waiting for forever. And she was going to blow it by asking the one question guaranteed to bring on an attack of conscience in Michael.

"Why tonight?" she asked, studying his face intently.

His expression faltered ever so slightly. Most people wouldn't even have noticed, but Kelly did. She sighed heavily as regrets came crashing down around her.

"I thought so. No real reason, except that I offered you a deal, right?"

Now it was his turn to sigh. "That, and the fact that I'm an idiot. Scratch that. I'm a randy idiot. I want you, and you gave me the perfect excuse to take what I wanted."

"You still can," she said and meant it, even if the warm and fuzzy glow was fading rapidly.

He pressed her knuckles to his lips and kissed them. "Another time. Go back in there and keep an eye on your brother and your friend."

She knew it was the smart thing to do, the only thing, really. "How will you get home?"

He gestured toward the street where a taxi sat waiting, its motor running. "I already had Ryan call a cab for me. For a minute there, I was going to send it away, but saner minds prevailed."

Kelly stared at him incredulously. "You were testing me?"

"And myself," he said. "It was a stupid thing to do, and I apologize. At least we both learned a valuable lesson."

She wasn't much in the mood to view things in a particularly generous light. "Oh? What's that?"

"That it's increasingly likely that we're going to tempt fate once too often."

She frowned at him. "Don't be too sure of that," she said heatedly. "I think the lesson I learned is entirely different."

"Oh?"

"When it comes to playing games, you're a master, and that is definitely *not* a compliment."

That said, she whirled around and went back inside, leaving Michael to stare after her, his mouth open. Whatever words he'd been intending to say to try to pacify her this time, she hoped he choked on them.

Michael was getting exactly what he deserved, no question about it. Kelly's frosty attitude when she'd walked away on Friday night had lingered all through Saturday's therapy session and on into the couple of calls he'd made to try to apologize again for his inexcusable behavior. He'd taken something important and turned it into a contest to see which of them was stronger. He'd expected to be the winner by a mile, but he had to admit it had turned out to be a draw. Kelly was no slouch when it came to good sense and willpower.

Which left them exactly where? Truthfully, he was surprised she'd even shown up on Saturday, but clearly that powerful work ethic of hers had kicked in, along with a healthy dose of pride. It was evident, though, that the attraction between them could no longer be ignored.

The first time Michael had linked Kelly and hot,

steamy sex in the same thought, he had cursed himself for an idiot. A few stolen kisses were one thing. They'd both been driven to distraction by circumstances, he had assured himself.

The second time his mind invented an image of the two of them naked in his bed, tangled together, he pictured just how many ways Bryan could devise to make him pay for taking advantage of his kid sister. That had temporarily put a damper on his desire to steal anything more than an occasional kiss.

Friday night he'd come too damned close to making those images a reality. He feared that the next time, his brain wouldn't kick in at all.

The only way to avoid temptation would be to fire her. Of course, that ignored the fact that she'd already quit...specifically so they could become more intimate, if they so chose. How was he supposed to fire someone who didn't technically work for him in the first place? And how could he explain it to her without making himself out to be even more of a jerk than she already thought him to be?

When Kelly's knock came promptly at 10:00 a.m. on Tuesday, he sucked in a deep breath and resolved to clear the air between them. He was halfway to the door when she used her key and came breezing in, a phony smile firmly in place. A desire to kiss her until that smile turned real slammed through him. That was not a particularly good sign.

"Good morning," he said, regarding her warily as he tried to gauge her real mood.

"Is it? I hadn't noticed." She flipped open her massage table and locked the legs into place. "Are you ready to get to work?"

Michael noted that the frost from Saturday had now turned to icicles. He had to hold back a sigh of regret.

"Sure," he said, climbing onto the table.

The first touch of her cold hands on his back was a shock. He noted that she hadn't bothered to warm the oil she was using today, or else it was simply no match for her body temperature or her mood.

"Starting Thursday, I think we should have our sessions at the rehab clinic," she informed him. "I've already spoken to Ryan and Maggie, and they'll be happy to drive you over there."

Something deep inside Michael turned hot and angry at her presumption. "What right did you have to go to my brother before coming to me?"

She didn't react to his tone. "I wanted to be sure transportation wouldn't be a problem. Since it isn't, I assume you have no objections to the change."

Michael moved away from her. "Are you scared, Kelly? Is that what this is about?"

"Don't be ridiculous," she snapped, her eyes flashing furiously. "You don't scare me. You're ready for equipment I can't haul around. You'll make faster progress if you have it. It's as simple as that."

"Then it's just a bonus for you that we won't be alone anymore?"

"Exactly," she said tightly.

Michael wanted to force her to admit that it wasn't his recovery, but her anger at him that was behind this sudden announcement. Instead, he put his head down without further comment, and let her continue with the massage.

He felt the brush of her breasts as she leaned closer to massage the tight, cramped muscle in his thigh. Instinctively, he glanced to his left and his gaze landed on her cleavage. Not that she was wearing anything the least bit revealing, just her usual V-neck T-shirt. It just so happened that it had dipped provocatively lower than normal. The sight of that smooth, pale skin snapped the last tiny hold he had on his restraint.

This time when he reached for her and closed his mouth over hers, he knew things were going to be different. Unless she slapped him silly—which she probably should—he was going to do more than taste her lips. He was going to close his mouth over the pebbled tip of her breast. He was going to skim his tongue over that swell of satiny skin.

He was going to burn in hell.

He uttered a curse and pushed her away. She drew in a deep, raspy breath and stared at him.

"Why?" she began in a choked voice.

"Why did I kiss you again? I think we both know the answer to that," he said wryly. He raked a hand through his hair. "I swore I wasn't going to touch you, but you could tempt a saint. It's even worse when you get that chilly don't-touch-me note in your voice."

A smile played at the corners of her mouth. "Apparently you like a challenge."

"What man doesn't?" he said wryly. "Can you imagine what would happen if you got it into your head to try to seduce me?"

"I…I couldn't," she stammered, looking shocked. "I wouldn't."

"But not because you don't want to," he said. "Or because I don't want you to."

"Because it's wrong," she said flatly. "That was the conclusion you reached all on your own. On top of that, we've discussed this, Michael. We've gone over it every which way. I totally agree with you now that it's a bad idea."

"I know," he soothed gently, even as he reached for her again and brushed his lips over hers. "Are you absolutely sure that we ruled this out? I can't seem to remember anything except how much I want you."

"When you do that, I can't remember anything, either," she admitted, then moaned as he claimed her mouth again.

Michael swore he was going to take only a quick taste of her minty sweetness, but it only made him crave more. "I'm sorry," he murmured against her lips. "Do you want me to stop?"

"Yes," she whispered, clearly dazed, then, "no."

His lips curved. "Which is it?"

"Oh, God, I wish I knew," she said, closing her mouth over his again.

Her kiss was hot and needy and sent desire ricocheting through him in a way he'd never expected to experience again. Her hands slid over his chest, the touch nothing like the professional strokes of her massages. This left a trail of wicked fire and yearning in its wake.

Michael found himself wanting to experience her pale, smooth skin in the same way. He tugged her T-shirt free from the waistband of her jeans and caressed the bare, hot flesh beneath. He stroked the curve of her breasts with his thumbs, then skimmed a finger across the already taut nipples. She jolted at the touch, then arched into it, a murmur of pleasure low in her throat. He flipped open the snap on her jeans and reached lower, dipping toward her moist, hot core.

"Come up here with me," he urged, wanting her on top of him, rubbing against the throbbing heat of his own arousal. Right? Wrong? He didn't care anymore. It was all about the sensation, the need that she stirred in him and the promise of pleasure that was just out of reach.

He had his hands around her waist and was about to lift her when she seemed to snap out of the sensual daze she'd been in.

"No," she said shakily. "I need more than this from you. I deserve more than this."

Shaken by her words and by the suddenness with which she pulled away, he simply stared, breathing hard and trying to make sense of what had just happened. Given how many times he'd ended things before they got carried away, he supposed he had no right to complain, but he wasn't feeling especially rational at the moment, just needy.

"Was this some new therapy technique?" he inquired, hoping to lighten the charged atmosphere.

Something that looked an awful lot like hurt flashed in her eyes.

"Sure, that's exactly what it was," she said, the ice

back in her voice. "Be sure to recommend me to your friends."

Before he knew it, she'd grabbed her purse and left without so much as a word of goodbye.

Michael stared after her, his heart thudding dully. "Well, you certainly blew that," he muttered. Driving her away was getting to be a habit, a truly lousy habit.

He spent a miserable two days worrying and wondering if she'd come back or if she'd send another therapist in her place. He should have realized that Kelly was made of sterner stuff. He'd certainly seen all the evidence of that.

Thursday morning at precisely 9:30, Maggie turned up. "Ready to go to the clinic?" she inquired cheerfully.

He had forgotten all about the damned clinic and Kelly's edict that further sessions would be conducted there with lots of witnesses around to prevent a repeat of their last couple of encounters. However, he was not about to let Maggie see his dismay. Heaven knew what she would make out of it.

"Let's go," he said grimly, reaching for his coat.

After they were in the car, his sister-in-law slanted a knowing look at him. "Anything wrong?"

"What could possibly be wrong?" he asked sourly.

"I thought maybe you were unhappy about no longer having Kelly to yourself for these sessions."

"Why would that bother me?"

She struggled with a grin. "No reason. You just seem a little off this morning."

"I've been a little off ever since I got shot," he retorted. "Or hadn't you noticed?"

"Well, of course, I have no way of knowing what your disposition was like prior to your getting shot, but you seem a little crankier than usual today, if you don't mind me saying so."

Michael sighed. "Would it stop you if I *did* mind?"

She laughed. "Not likely." Her gaze suddenly turned serious. "Why don't you just admit you're crazy about her? It would be a lot easier on everyone, you included."

"I can't be crazy about her," he said flatly.

"Why on earth not?"

He scowled at the question. "Do you even have to ask? She doesn't need an out-of-work man who can't even stand on his own two feet in her life."

Maggie shook her head. "There are so many things wrong with that statement, I hardly know where to begin."

"I don't suppose you could be persuaded to keep all of them to yourself?"

"Oh, please," she said, regarding him with disdain. "First, if not having a job is an issue, get one. Ryan's friend is still anxious to talk to you. Second, you'll be back on your feet eventually, so that's a ridiculous excuse. And third, you need to stop feeling so blasted sorry for yourself and think about Kelly's feelings for a change. You're selling her short. You're assuming that she's some superficial twit who cares only about whether you have a good job or can run a marathon."

"I never said any such thing," he retorted indignantly.

"Maybe not in so many words, but the message is clear, just the same."

"It's not about her, it's about me," he said with frustration.

"Well, it's time to get over yourself, Devaney, and get on with the business of living."

"Have you ever considered a military career?" he inquired, more shaken by the scolding than he'd ever been by a dressing down from a superior officer in the navy.

"Nope. Couldn't take the discipline," she said at once.

"Then find some small country that needs a dictator. You'd be good at it."

She laughed. "If I get tired of running a pub with your brother, I'll keep that in mind. I'm not the one who's averse to considering other options," she said as she pulled to a stop in front of the clinic. "I'll get your wheelchair out of the back. Do you need help getting inside?"

He considered the doors and the challenge in Maggie's eyes. "I'll manage," he said tightly.

"Good answer," she said and gave his shoulder a reassuring squeeze.

Oddly enough, her approval made him feel marginally better as he went inside to face Kelly.

He spotted her at once, working with a young girl whose gait was awkward as she clung to two metal rails on either side of her. The girl couldn't have been more than sixteen and her brow was furrowed in concentration as she struggled to put one foot in front of the other and inch along between the bars. She hadn't gone more than a couple of feet, when Kelly beamed at her and patted her hand.

"Good work, Jennifer," she praised as she helped her

into a wheelchair and took her over to a woman who'd been watching the scene with a shattered expression on her face.

Kelly smiled at the older woman. "Great progress today, don't you think?"

"Wonderful," the woman said, forcing a smile for the girl.

Jennifer searched the older woman's face as if she were looking for signs that she wasn't telling the truth, but the smile never wavered, and eventually Jennifer's lips curved into a half smile.

"I'm going to walk again, Mom. I really am," she said with gritty determination.

"Of course, you are," Kelly agreed. "I'll see you again on Saturday."

Shaken by the entire scene, Michael waited until they'd gone before joining Kelly.

"What happened to her?" he asked.

"Automobile accident," she said succinctly.

"How long ago?"

"About the same time as your injuries."

He caught the underlying message without her having to spell it out for him. Young Jennifer was braver and more determined than he was. In that instant, he knew what real shame felt like.

"Okay, then," he told her. "Let's get to work and get me up to speed." His gaze locked with hers. "After that we need to talk."

"No, we don't," she said emphatically.

Michael's leg might be all but useless, but his arms

were as strong as ever. He latched on to her hand and tugged until she was standing right in front of him.

"Okay, then, we'll talk first. I'm sorry," he apologized.

She finally met his gaze. "For?"

"Making light of what happened between us the other day."

She shrugged. "It was a kiss. No big deal."

"It was more than a kiss and it was a big deal," he insisted. "I guess that's why I did it. I felt guilty for taking advantage of you."

"You?" she said incredulously. "I'm the one who took advantage. I'm the one who broke the rules."

He struggled with a grin. "You have rules about that kind of thing?"

"The two of us made rules about it."

"Then who better to break them?" he asked.

"We can't keep doing this," she said plaintively.

"It was a kiss," he said, echoing her words before adding, "A great kiss."

The beginnings of a smile tugged at her lips and she slanted a look at him. "Great, huh?"

He laughed at the hint of satisfaction in her voice. "Phenomenal."

"Okay, don't overdo it," she said. "I can live with great. Now, let's get to work."

"In a sec. There's one last thing I wanted to say."

"Oh?"

"I'm glad you haven't given up on me. It's more than I deserve."

She sighed. "There was never a question about that,

Michael. I'm here for as long as you need me. There's nothing you could do that would chase me away."

The heartfelt commitment took him aback. Few people in his life had made that kind of commitment to him. His own parents certainly hadn't. The Havilceks had, but because adoption had been out of the question, there had never been that final leap to becoming a real family that he believed he could count on forever. The reservation had been his alone. He'd been scared to allow himself to feel too much for the Havilceks.

Beyond that, though he and Bryan had been as close as brothers, or at least as close as he'd remembered brothers being, they hadn't stayed in touch once he'd joined the navy.

Now here was a beautiful, compassionate, loving woman telling him she was in his life for as long as he needed her. An unfamiliar feeling filled his chest. He tried to pin a label on it, but couldn't.

Only later that night, when he was all alone in his cold bed, his leg throbbing, did it dawn on him what that feeling had been: contentment. If he could feel such a thing at the worst time of his life, then he owed the woman responsible. He owed her more than respect and fair play. He owed her his heart, and it was past time he proved he was capable of giving it.

11

When there was a knock on Michael's door about six o'clock on Friday evening, he opened it, anticipating that he'd find Kelly on the other side. Instead, it was Sean, his usual jovial expression far more grim than Michael had ever seen it.

"Come on in. Is there a problem?" Michael asked his older brother.

"We need to talk," Sean said, looking around the apartment with a cursory glance.

Since it was the first time Sean had been to visit since Michael had returned to Boston, Michael assumed it had to be important, especially when they were supposed to see each other at the pub in less than an hour.

"Okay," Michael said cautiously, gesturing for him to come in. "I take it this is something we couldn't get into later at Ryan's Place."

"Too many people around," Sean said. "I figure you and I need to work this out and present a united front."

Michael sighed. "Then it's about the search for the rest of the family," he guessed.

Sean nodded. "You know where I stand on that. Where do you stand?"

Despite the conversation he'd had with his mother, since then Michael had tried to avoid giving the matter any serious thought at all. He'd been secretly hoping that Ryan would simply take the matter out of their hands and do whatever it was he felt the need to do.

"Have a seat," he said to Sean, just to buy himself some time to put his thoughts into words.

"I'll stand."

"And make me get a stiff neck trying to look you in the eye?" Michael inquired.

Sean immediately looked chagrined. "Sorry, man. I wasn't thinking." He sat down on the edge of the sofa. "Are you doing okay?"

Michael shrugged. "Kelly thinks I'm making progress."

"Well, she's the expert."

He thought of the young girl he'd seen at the clinic the day before and how guilty he'd felt when he'd seen how hard she was struggling to overcome her injuries. "Kelly's idea of progress and mine differ slightly, but that's going to change," he said with determination. He'd wallowed in self-pity and given lip service to his therapy long enough. Maybe he'd never be a SEAL again, but everyone had been right—there were plenty of things he could do. He just had to find the right one, something that challenged him mentally and physically. Captaining a charter boat might not be it, but there was something out there.

Sean regarded him with obvious discomfort. "I'm

sorry I haven't been around much to help out. It's not that I didn't want to, it's just…"

Sean's voice trailed off, and Michael knew that his assessment of his brother's careful distance had been right on target. "It's just that my situation made you uncomfortable," he said. "I understand. I think when people like you and me, who work in a profession that requires top-notch fitness, run into a situation where someone's physically impaired, we see ourselves. The guys on my SEAL team were the same way when I was in the hospital in San Diego. They came around because they felt duty-bound to come, but they couldn't look me in the eye. It made all of us uncomfortable, me most of all."

Relief spread across Sean's face. "That's it exactly. It's sort of the there-but-for-the-grace-of-God-go-I thing. I got trapped in a fire last year trying to get my partner out. It turned out okay, but I think that brush with a potential tragedy put the fear of God in me. And now that I have Deanna and Kevin to consider…" He shrugged. "Maybe it's time to think about a new line of work."

"Would you be happy doing anything else?" Michael asked.

"Nothing I can think of," Sean admitted.

Michael sighed. "Same with me." He felt as if he and his brother were sharing a rare moment of being totally in sync, the way brothers ought to be. It was a strange—and oddly comforting—sensation.

"It doesn't do a damn bit of good to tell you it will all work out, does it?" Sean asked.

"Not much."

With nothing left to be said, Michael pushed the topic out of his mind. It wasn't a situation they could resolve today. Maybe they could figure out the pros and cons of this hunt for their parents and twin brothers, though.

"Sean, just how vehemently against this search are you?" he asked. "You've had longer to make peace with the idea than I have, yet you haven't done it."

"It's a funny thing about that," Sean said, looking pensive. "For years I waited for our folks to turn up to claim me. When I grew up and that hadn't happened, I told myself it didn't matter. In fact, I deliberately took pains to make it difficult for them to locate me—an unlisted phone number, no credit cards, the whole nine yards." He gave Michael a rueful look. "Ryan found mc anyway."

"Which led you to believe that our parents never even tried," Michael concluded. That's the way he would have interpreted things, as well. And it would have hurt, if he'd allowed himself to dwell on it, just as it so clearly hurt his brother.

"They certainly didn't look hard enough, anyway." Sean's eyes were filled with bitterness and belligerence as he met Michael's gaze. "So, why should I care about finding them?"

"I can't argue with that," Michael said. "The way I see it, we don't owe them a damned thing, but maybe finding them is like finding a missing piece of a puzzle. You don't really care about it and it may not mean much in the grand scheme of things, but clicking that last piece into place can still complete things you'd never even realized you were wondering about. It can bring about a sense of closure where the past's concerned."

Sean sighed heavily, clearly unhappy with Michael's assessment. "Then you're saying we should go to meet this Patrick."

Michael nodded slowly as he reached his own decision. "Yeah, I think I am. I thought I had a lot to lose by looking for the rest of the family. I thought it would hurt the people who'd given me a home and raised me as if I were one of their own kids. But my mom made me see that I can never lose them, not really. I can only gain some answers, maybe even get my old family back."

"You sure you want them?" Sean asked wryly.

Michael grinned. "Hey, if it goes badly, you, Ryan and I still have each other, which is more than we had before Ryan started looking. And it could go well. If that happens, well, a man can never have too many decent brothers watching his back, can he?" He regarded Sean intently. "But that's the way I see it. It doesn't mean you have to reach the same conclusion."

"Yeah, right," Sean said. "But if I don't, the two of you will see me as holding out just out of pure stubbornness."

"I won't," Michael reassured him. "It's your call, Sean. Seems to me like this is one of those times when the majority shouldn't necessarily rule. I don't know how Ryan will feel, but I say we need a unanimous vote to move on."

Sean didn't look entirely convinced, but he finally sighed. "I'll go along with it," he said, not even trying to hide his reluctance. "I know Deanna thinks I should.

And you and Ryan have given it a lot of thought. So what happens next?"

"If you're absolutely sure, then we'll tell Ryan tonight that the trip is on."

"When do you want to go?"

Michael regarded his brother with an innocent expression. "Just as soon as I'm out of this chair and can go on my own two feet."

Sean reacted with surprise. "After everything you just said, you want to wait?"

Michael chuckled. "I said I wanted answers. I didn't say I was in a hurry to get them."

Friday nights at Ryan's Place had turned into a regular thing, not only for the Devaneys, the O'Briens and the Havilceks, but for Kelly, Bryan and Moira. It had been two weeks since Kelly and Michael had set up her brother with her best friend, and the two had been pretty much inseparable since that awkward beginning.

Kelly glanced toward the tiny dance floor where Moira was attempting to teach Bryan an Irish jig. It wasn't going well. Kelly's brother had two left feet, which he kept tripping over. Moira was trying to hide her laughter, even as she patiently demonstrated the steps yet again.

Watching them instilled a feeling of melancholy in Kelly. Bryan and Moira hardly knew each other, but you could tell just looking at them that there was something special happening. She thought of her own situation with Michael and wondered if they would ever share that kind of closeness. They were totally in sync in so many ways and the chemistry was certainly powerful, but when it came to the important stuff, they kept bumping into roadblocks.

Even as the thought began to nag at her, she realized how contradictory it was, given the steamy kisses they'd shared. Yet something was missing in their relationship, something she could no longer deny. Sizzling attraction wasn't commitment, and that was what she wanted from Michael. She wanted forever, maybe not right now when he was still doing so much soul-searching about his own future, but at least the promise of forever once those questions were resolved.

"Hey, why the frown?" Michael asked, regarding her worriedly.

"Just thinking," she said evasively. This wasn't the time or the place to get into a discussion about their relationship. Maybe there was no appropriate time to get into it. Maybe she needed to accept that there would never be a relationship—at least not the kind she'd been hoping for—and move on with her life just the way she'd been encouraging Michael to do when it came to his career.

"It must be some pretty heavy thinking," he said, tracing his finger lightly over the furrow in her brow. "Anything I can help with?"

"No. It's under control." She forced a smile. "You said earlier that Sean came by. How was that?"

"Pretty great, actually. We really connected."

"I'm glad," she said with total sincerity. "It's wonderful that this whole reunion thing is working out so well for you."

He frowned. "Okay, that's it."

"What?" she said, startled by his reaction.

"You're suddenly being too blasted polite and—I don't know—distant, I guess. What's going on?"

"Nothing."

His scowl deepened. "So much for honesty and trust."

The jab hit home. Kelly sighed. "Okay, the truth is I was thinking about us, about how there really isn't an us, might never be an us, and I was trying to decide what to do about that."

"I see," he said slowly.

Since he looked more troubled than angered, she decided to press on. She regarded him earnestly. "I love being here with you, with your family," she told him honestly, "but it's an unhealthy situation for me."

He stared at her as if she'd suddenly started spouting Greek. "What the hell does that mean?"

"It means that I'm starting to care too much, not just about you, but about all of this," she said, gesturing around the table at the gathering of Devaneys, Havilceks and Maggie's relatives. "Right now, I'm your therapist. That's the only relationship that's real between us, the only one you're allowing to be real."

Michael looked genuinely bewildered by her claim. "Those kisses felt damn real to me."

She closed her eyes and tried to ignore the sensation of pure longing that suddenly swamped her. "I know," she said softly. "But they're not enough. Not anymore."

"What are you saying?"

She drew in a deep breath and faced him evenly.

"I'm going to start seeing other people, and I won't be hanging out here anymore."

His expression turned hard. "Your choice."

A tide of hurt washed over her. If only he'd objected, fought even a little to change her mind, but he didn't. And that said everything. It said that whatever they had, he didn't think it was worth fighting for.

Kelly stood up, grabbed her coat and spun away from the table before anyone could see the tears that were starting to slide down her cheeks. As she raced for the door, she heard several people call her name, but she pretended she hadn't. She needed to be alone, needed to tell herself—probably a million and one times before she believed it—that she had done the right thing.

She was also going to need every single second between now and tomorrow morning to brace herself for having to face Michael at the rehab clinic, because even though it would be the smart, safe thing to do, she had no intention of abandoning him in the middle of his therapy.

Michael still wasn't entirely sure what the devil had happened the night before. One minute Kelly had been looking a little thoughtful, the next she'd been announcing that she was through with him. Maybe he was only a clueless male, but it didn't make any sense. He honestly had no idea what had triggered her announcement or her abrupt departure, not even after every single person in all of the combined families had tried to pry it out of him.

That had irritated him most of all, that Kelly had

walked out, and he'd been left to answer an endless barrage of questions about what *he'd* done to make her go. Clearly everyone assumed that she couldn't possibly be the one at fault. He intended to have quite a lot to say about that when he saw her this morning at the clinic—*if* he saw her at the clinic.

He arrived with his heart admittedly in his throat as he scanned the mirrored therapy room for some sign of her. He spotted Jennifer, the teenaged patient who had inspired his own renewed dedication to his therapy, but she was working with someone else. His heart sank.

"Looking for Kelly?" Moira inquired, her tone every bit as cool as it had been the night before when she'd assumed that he had somehow driven Kelly from the pub.

He nodded.

"She's in a meeting with Dr. Burroughs. She should be free soon."

Michael couldn't describe the feeling of relief that spread through him. "Thanks." When Moira would have turned away, he caught her hand. "I didn't do anything to upset her last night. I swear it."

"If you say so."

"I do. I'm as confused as you are."

"If Bryan or I find out differently, there will be hell to pay," she said fiercely. "You know that, don't you?"

He had to admire that kind of loyalty, even if it did make him feel as if he'd been unwittingly targeted. "Everyone should have friends as protective as you are," he said. "I'll wait over there."

He felt Moira's gaze on his back as he wheeled himself across the room. He turned his back to the mirrored wall. He hated those mirrors. When he looked into them, he couldn't ignore his condition.

A few minutes later, he heard Kelly's laughter before he actually saw her. She emerged from an office with a man dressed in carefully creased slacks, a designer dress shirt and a lab coat. He was the epitome of everything Michael wasn't at the moment—suave, sure of himself and physically fit. Michael hated him on sight. Watching the way the man looked at Kelly set Michael's teeth on edge. If he'd been in any shape to do it, Michael would have slugged the man on the spot just as a matter of principle.

Even as the desire to punch the guy's lights out rocketed through him, he brought himself up short. He was jealous. He—a man who'd never had a jealous bone in his body—was feeling totally and thoroughly possessive about a woman he'd never even had a right to claim as his own. Well, hell. He was going to have to take a good long look at the reason for that, just not right now. Right now, he had to get across the room and protect his interests, even if he wasn't entirely sure why it mattered so much.

Kelly noticed him before her companion did. She frowned when she realized that he was heading straight for her, even though she was in the midst of a private conversation.

"Bill, I've got a client scheduled, and he's here now," she said. "I'll see you tonight at seven."

The doctor glanced in Michael's direction, gave him a distracted greeting, then turned his disgustingly toothy, white smile on Kelly. "I'll look forward to it."

"You didn't waste much time, did you?" Michael said sourly when Kelly finally turned to him.

"I beg your pardon?"

"Big date with the doc tonight, or did I misunderstand?"

"Whether I have a date with Dr. Burroughs tonight or not is none of your business," she told him coldly. "Are you ready to get to work today?"

He scowled at the dismissal of his question, but decided not to make an issue of it right now. First things first. He needed to get back on his feet, so he could show the doctor a thing or two about which of them was the better man.

By the time she got through the tense therapy session with Michael, Kelly's nerves were strained to the limit. It took everything in her not to go whining to Moira and ask that she recommend another therapist for him. The truth was, she didn't want to give up the time with him. And she wanted to be the one there with Michael when he walked on his own again.

She prayed that a hot shower and fifteen minutes of rest would improve her mood before her date. She had known Bill Burroughs for a couple of years now. He frequently referred his orthopedic patients to her when they needed rehab. He was attractive, intelligent and on his way to being filthy rich, even in today's fiscally tightfisted medical environment. He actually treated her as if she were a precious commodity. Most women would have been flattered, perhaps even charmed by his attentiveness and respect.

All Kelly could think about was the cantankerous man who'd kissed her till her toes curled, then apologized for making a joke out of it. Her teenage crush was turning into a full-blown case of grown-up lust, one she was determined to ignore if she and Michael were to go on working together. This date was supposed to help her accomplish that.

And it should have. It really should have. Bill pulled out all the stops. He took her to an elegant, romantic restaurant, ordered the finest champagne, told her how beautiful she looked.

When the orchestra played, he held her in his arms as if she were more fragile than spun glass and more valuable than diamonds. She gazed up into his dark brown eyes and wished they were other eyes, crystal-blue eyes.

"You seem distracted," Bill said. "Worried about one of your patients?"

"In a way," she said, hoping he'd let the subject drop.

He gave her one of his brilliant smiles, but suddenly it seemed practiced and artificial, not like the blinding sunlight of one of Michael's rare smiles.

"Do you want to talk about it? Maybe I can help."

And he would, too. Bill was always generous with his time, always willing to offer treatment suggestions whenever she had doubts about the appropriate course for a particular patient. Now, though, she shook her head. "Thanks, that's okay."

He led the way back to their table, then studied her for a long time. "You need a break, Kelly. You've been working too hard."

"No time," she said.

"Make time," he said firmly. "If there's one thing I've had to learn, it's that too much work winds up being counterproductive. You end up making bad decisions when you're under stress."

She heard what he was saying and knew he was right. Maybe she could use a break, even a week away might bring some perspective to the whole situation. And a week off from his therapy wouldn't set Michael back that much, or if he insisted, Moira or someone else could fill in.

"I'll think about it," she promised Bill.

His gaze warmed. "Don't think. Go with the flow. I could take a few days off and we could go someplace with warm beaches and tropical drinks. How does that sound?"

It was twenty degrees outside and snow was threatening. How did he think it sounded? If Michael had asked, she'd have been packing. As it was, she simply stared at Bill in shock. "You want me to go away with you?"

"Why not? It doesn't have to be a big deal."

Memories of Phil's sleazy proposition rang in her head. Was she the kind of woman men expected to be easy? Why the heck was Michael the only one who ever showed any restraint around her?

She met Bill's expectant gaze. "Call me old-fashioned, but to me it does sound like a big deal. We hardly know each other."

"Then what better way to get to know each other than a few uninterrupted days together in some romantic setting?" he asked, clearly confident that he could overcome her objections.

"Sorry, I can't," she said flatly.

Unlike Phil, Bill took her refusal with a smile. "No problem," he said, as easygoing as ever. "Let me know if you change your mind."

She didn't say it, but if tonight had proved nothing else, it was that she wasn't even the tiniest bit interested in Bill Burroughs, despite all the superficial things they had in common. In fact, she had pretty much spent the entire evening feeling like a fraud.

Minutes later, she told him she thought it was time to be going. He accepted that, as well.

When he walked her to her door, she let him kiss her, hoping that it would banish the memory of another kiss. Instead, it was a tepid reminder that real passion required more than simply locking lips.

"Thanks, Bill. I had a lovely time," she said politely.

"So did I. We'll do it again soon," Bill said.

Kelly shook her head. "I'm sorry, Bill. You're a great guy, but…" Her words faltered.

Bill regarded her knowingly. "But your heart belongs to somebody else. I spent this whole evening hoping I was wrong about that. But it's the man I met at the clinic this morning, isn't it? I could sense that there was more going on there. He looked as if he'd like to beat me to a pulp for talking to you."

She regarded him with surprise. She hadn't expected him to see her feelings so clearly when she was still grappling with the truth herself. As for his assessment of Michael's feelings, she'd missed that completely.

"You're an intuitive man. My heart does belong to someone else." She saw no need to confirm that it was Michael. "I think it always has. I'm sorry for wasting your time. You planned such a lovely evening. I didn't deserve it."

Bill leaned down and pressed a chaste kiss to her cheek. "Nonsense. Don't be sorry. Spending an evening with you could never be a waste of time. Whoever he is, he's a lucky guy. And if things don't work out, give me a call. I'd like another chance. That tropical beach will still be there."

After she'd gone inside and settled into a warm bath filled with fragrant bubbles, Kelly allowed herself to think about Bill's words. She wondered if Michael would consider himself lucky if he knew how she felt.

As hard as she was trying—as hard as they both were working—she could never give him the one thing he clearly wanted. Oh, she would get him walking again. No question about that, given the progress they were already making.

But, even though they mostly avoided the subject, they both knew his career with the SEALs was over and he was a long way from making peace with that. She couldn't help thinking that he'd consider her love to be little more than second prize.

12

Saturday had been the longest damn night of Michael's life. He'd refused several offers of company and spent the entire evening brooding over what Kelly and her date might be up to. The mere fact that she even *had* a date was annoying. Granted, things between the two of them were a little uncertain, but all that heat had to mean something. How could he have misread the signals between them so badly? Why the hell had she felt the need to take off with that pretty-boy doctor? What did he have to offer that Michael didn't, besides a body on which all the parts presumably worked?

Just thinking about what the two of them could be up to soured his mood. His bad temper didn't improve on Sunday or Monday. In fact, by the time he got to the rehab center on Tuesday morning, he was half out of his mind with imagining the worst—that she'd gone and fallen head over heels in love with that annoying, expensively dressed jerk of a doctor. He wasn't prepared to examine why that seemed to matter so blasted much to him.

As Kelly approached him, Michael studied her face, looking for evidence that something had changed. She looked a little wary, a little pensive, but other than that, he couldn't read anything into her expression. When she finally met his gaze, she managed to muster an unenthusiastic smile, then went into what he'd come to recognize as her crisp, no-nonsense professional mode.

"I thought we'd try getting you out of that chair today," she chirped cheerfully. "Are you game?"

Michael debated calling her on the phony attitude, but her plan for the day caught his attention. "I've been getting out of the chair," he pointed out.

She gestured toward the parallel bars where he'd first seen Jennifer struggling to walk. Hope—along with something that felt a whole lot like panic—swept through him.

"You want me to walk?" he asked incredulously.

She did smile at that. "Hasn't that been the idea all along? I thought you were chomping at the bit to get back on your feet. I think you're strong enough now. Your arm and shoulder muscles were already in great shape. The weight work has strengthened your leg muscles the last couple of weeks. It's time to start standing on your own two feet again, Michael. I'm not expecting you to run a marathon. Standing up for a few minutes to put some real weight on that leg will be good enough."

"But…" The protest died on his lips. This was what he wanted, maybe too much. What if he stood up and fell flat on his face?

"You're not going to fall," Kelly reassured him, as

if he'd voiced the fear aloud. "You'll have the bars to hold on to and I'll be there."

Falling into her arms was not an option. He'd never survive the humiliation of it. He weighed that against the cowardice implied by not trying at all. It was no contest. He had to do this, and maybe it was better that she'd taken him totally by surprise. He hadn't had to spend the whole weekend worrying about it.

Totally focused now, he met her gaze evenly and gave her a curt nod. "Let's do it."

She guided his chair to the bars, then placed herself between them and in front of him. "Want some help getting out of the chair?"

"No," he said tersely. If he was going to do this, he was going to do it on his own. He needed to learn to rely on himself again, the way he once had without giving it a second thought.

Kelly shrugged off his tone and gestured for him to get up on his own.

Michael set the brake on the chair, then reached for the bars and pulled himself up, grateful for the years of SEAL training that had, indeed, kept his shoulders and arms powerful. But once he was upright between the bars, his legs felt as wobbly as a newborn's, despite all the work they'd been doing to strengthen the muscles.

"Just take a minute and steady yourself," Kelly said quietly. "Remember this isn't some sort of test on which you're going to be graded. A step or two will be enough. Let's see how that injured leg takes to having some weight put on it."

Michael held himself upright by sheer will, terrified

to put any weight at all on his bum leg. What if the surgeries and the pins weren't going to be enough, after all? What if the bones hadn't healed sufficiently? What if he crumpled to the floor right here? He could tolerate whatever pain there might be, but not the disappointment of failing, especially in front of Kelly.

But what if he didn't fail at all? He clung to that thought as he sucked in a deep breath and put his foot down gingerly. Slowly he began to put a little weight on it. To his relief, nothing immediately snapped in two. His bones and the various pieces of hardware the doctors had installed were apparently strong enough to keep him upright, at least. He added a little more weight until he was evenly balanced on both feet. It was an odd sensation, scary and exhilarating at the same time. Who would have thought that just standing up would give him such a sense of accomplishment, after the thousands of far more strenuous exertions to which he'd subjected his body?

Standing there, clinging to the bars with a white-knuckled grip, he ventured a glance at Kelly. Seeing her from this perspective—the way a man ought to be able to look a woman straight in the eye—made him want to drag her straight into his arms, but he forced the wistful thought aside.

"Looking good," Kelly said, giving him an encouraging smile. She backed up a step. "Now come here."

He met her gaze. "What's the incentive?" he asked, a deliberate dare in his voice.

One brow arched. "Walking again's not enough?" she asked.

"I was thinking such a momentous stride forward in our therapy ought to at least net me a kiss."

She frowned at that. "Take the step, then we'll talk about it."

"A peck on the cheek, then," he coaxed, enjoying the patches of color blooming on her face. He studied her with a considering look. "What's the harm, unless you and the good doctor are now an item?"

Her cheeks paled. "Leave Dr. Burroughs out of this."

Michael promptly took heart. "Bad date?" he inquired sympathetically. "I could have told you that. The guy is obviously too self-absorbed to be good company."

Kelly scowled at him. "I don't know how you came up with that," she snapped. "He was very good company. And why are we talking about him at all? You're supposed to be concentrating on taking that first step."

"Frankly, right this second, I'm finding this conversation a whole lot more fascinating," he said. "Something tells me you didn't have a good time."

"And you find that something to gloat about?"

"No, I merely find it interesting. Tell me, how did it go?"

Her scowl deepened. "Why are you pushing this? My date is none of your business."

"That's not the way I see it," Michael told her.

She gave him an impatient look. "I do."

"Come on, Kelly. I think I have a right to know if the woman who's been willing to risk her professional reputation to kiss me has found some other man she'd prefer to spend her free time with." He gave her a considering look. "Well, have you? Are you planning on spending more evenings with the preppy doctor?"

"If you must know, the answer is no. I won't be seeing Dr. Burroughs again."

He grinned, not even trying to hide his relief. "Glad to hear it. Does that mean I get my kiss?"

Suddenly the ice in her eyes seemed to melt. She gave him one of her more irrepressible grins. "If you can catch me," she said, backing up another step, then one more for good measure.

Michael's grin spread. "Sweetheart, don't you know you should never dare a SEAL?" If it took every last ounce of strength he possessed, he was going to meet her challenge. He'd been obsessing about kissing her all night long. He wasn't about to lose his chance now.

The first step was awkward and painful. It was impossible to imagine that walking, running and mountain-climbing had once been second nature to him. Sweat beaded on his brow and the muscles in his arms quivered with the tension of holding himself upright.

Thank God, he had long legs. He could reach her in one more stride. He took that step thanks to sheer grit and determination. As he steadied himself, he closed one hand over hers where it rested on the bar and gazed deep into her eyes.

"Pay up," he said softly.

There was no mistaking the heat that flared in her eyes as she lifted herself on tiptoe and brushed a quick, disappointing kiss across his lips.

"Oh, no, you don't," he whispered against her mouth, leaning heavily against one bar, while he slipped an arm around her waist and held her tight. "I caught you fair and square. Now, pay up with a kiss that means something."

He heard her breath hitch, felt the heat radiating from her as she sighed and leaned into him, her breasts soft against his chest, her lips parted under his.

"Better," he murmured, as he plunged his tongue deep inside to taste her…to claim her.

When they were both breathing hard, he released her, then realized that the kiss had drained him of every last ounce of strength. Cursing his weakness, he struggled to turn himself around and make his way back to his wheelchair, angrily brushing off Kelly's offers of assistance.

Only after he was safely seated again did he allow himself to meet her gaze. To his amazement, she was grinning broadly.

"What?" he growled, feeling like a toddler who'd taken his first brave step, only to land solidly on his backside.

She regarded him as if he were crazy to have to ask. "You walked, Michael! You did it!"

As the enormity of that sank in, his irritation faded and a grin began to spread across his face. "By God, I did, didn't I?" He'd felt less triumphant after surviving a dangerous mission. He met Kelly's gaze. "If I could dance you around the room, I would."

"I'll hold you to that," she said. "Something tells me it won't be long."

Meeting her gaze, wanting her, Michael knew that no matter when it happened, it wouldn't be nearly soon enough.

* * *

Those first couple of faltering steps could be either the beginning of something or the end, Michael concluded when he had time to himself later that night. In a few weeks, Kelly would start cutting back on his therapy, leaving him to his own devices while she moved on to use her considerable skill with another patient who needed her more. As badly as he wanted to feel whole and able-bodied again, the prospect of losing Kelly forever was out of the question. He didn't know why he was so sure of that, but he was.

Whatever the pace of his recovery from here on out, he was going to have to make damn sure that Kelly stayed in his life, at least until he could figure out the hold she seemed to have over him. There would be no more little adventures for her with the Dr. Burroughses of the world. He wanted to be the one who occupied her thoughts and her time.

For a man who'd spent much of his life being totally driven and goal-oriented, this was just one more challenge to be met. Like any SEAL mission he'd ever planned and executed, it was a matter of logistics and precision. He intended to start with his Thursday therapy session, since that was the one time he could be guaranteed that she wouldn't bail on him. He was going to dazzle her with his progress, then set out to capture her heart.

For the forty-eight hours between sessions, he practiced standing until he could remain upright and steady without grabbing on to the nearest stable object to break an impending fall. By the time night came, his muscles ached from the strain and his leg was giving him fits, but it was a small price to pay.

On Thursday he wheeled himself into the rehab center with a renewed sense of confidence and purpose. Kelly seemed to sense the change in attitude, because she studied him with a quizzical expression as he hefted himself out of the chair and onto the parallel bars without being asked.

"I gather you're ready to start," she said, a spark of amusement in her eyes.

"I am," he said firmly. "Back up."

She hesitated. "I think it's better if I stay here."

He scowled until she finally shrugged and backed away, leaving nothing to impede him should he actually be able to manage to walk the entire length of the parallel bars. Gritting his teeth, Michael took the first step. It was actually easier than it had been at his apartment without any solid support to cling to. His confidence grew with the second step and then the third.

"Michael, don't push too hard," Kelly warned as he kept coming. "You don't want another injury now."

"I'm not going to fall," he insisted, his voice tight as he tried to gauge the remaining steps. Four, maybe. Three, if he could lengthen his stride to something better than these shuffling half steps. He sighed. Maybe he'd better settle for baby steps, as exasperating as that was. It was better than falling flat on his butt at her feet.

He noted that despite her warning, she hadn't rushed forward to cut him off, but she was holding her breath.

"You know, if you don't let out that breath you're

holding, you're going to turn blue," he admonished lightly.

She sighed. "Sorry. I'm just afraid you're moving too fast."

He snorted at that. "I've seen snails move faster."

"You know what I mean, Michael."

All the while they bickered over whether or not he was overexerting himself, he kept moving forward with his awkward, shuffling gait. And then he was there, toe-to-toe with her, close enough to see the spark of admiration in her eyes, despite the admonitions tripping from her lips.

His legs were protesting the strain he'd put on them. His powerful arms were the only things keeping him upright, which meant he had to get through this next part in a hurry. Still standing, he met her gaze.

"Have dinner with me tomorrow night," he suggested.

She blinked rapidly. "What?"

"It's not a difficult concept. I asked you to have dinner with me."

"Why?"

He grinned at her reaction. "The usual reasons. Man meets woman. Man is attracted to woman. He asks her on a date. That is how it goes, isn't it? I'm not that much out of touch." He shrugged, trying not to make too much out of it. "Besides, I think we're past due for a celebration. You certainly deserve one for putting up with me all this time."

"Tomorrow's Friday," she pointed out.

Michael grinned. "I know that."

"You usually go to the pub on Fridays, and I told you how I feel about going there."

"You don't want to give my family any ideas about the two of us," he recited. "I know that, too. This is a date, Kelly. I'm asking you out on an honest-to-goodness date. No pub. No family. Just the two of us. You'll have to drive, but other than that I'm in charge for a change. We'll go wherever you want. Someplace fancy with candlelight and good wine. I'm afraid dancing's out, but who knows, maybe I'll buy you a corsage."

She laughed then. "Nobody buys corsages except for proms."

"Too much?"

"Definitely."

"Champagne, then. What do you say?"

She took so long answering that he thought she might actually turn him down, but finally she nodded. "I would love to go to dinner with you, Michael. What time should I pick you up?"

"Seven sound okay?"

"Perfect," she agreed more eagerly. "I'll pick the place and make a reservation."

He shook his head. "Tell me. I'll call. I need to remember how it's done."

"I think it will all come back to you fairly quickly," she said wryly.

Her belief that he'd been a bit of a scoundrel was very flattering, but the truth had been something else entirely. Before joining the navy, he hadn't wanted to get distracted by a woman. During his years as a SEAL, the unpredictability of his life had kept him from getting too close. His relationships had been hot and steamy for a time, but there wasn't one he could look back on as being remotely meaningful.

"This is different," he told her with total sincerity.

"How? Because it's been so long?"

"No." He met her gaze and felt the familiar thunder of his pounding heart. "Because it's you."

Because it's you. Because it's you.

Kelly couldn't seem to stop Michael's words from echoing through her head. What had he meant? It had almost sounded as if he was genuinely worried about getting it right because she mattered to him in some way all the other women had not.

"Don't be ridiculous," she muttered as she tossed aside what had to be the tenth outfit she'd tried on. She had deliberately picked an informal restaurant, despite Michael's offer of champagne. He was still taking occasional pain medications and had no business drinking more than the occasional beer he indulged in with his pizza at home. Besides, her wardrobe was far more suited to casual than fancy.

Even so, she couldn't seem to find a blasted thing in her closet that satisfied her. She finally settled for a sage-green cotton sweater that somehow made her gray eyes seem more the soft green of jade. She added a pair of camel-colored wool slacks and a gold locket that her mother had given her for her thirteenth birthday. Inside, still, was a tiny picture of Michael she'd clipped from a snapshot that had been taken of him and Bryan on a trip to Cape Cod that summer. She'd kept that locket in her jewelry box for years, but something told her tonight was a perfect night to bring it out again. Of course, if he happened to ask what was inside, she'd probably die of embarrassment.

Michael's exuberant mood from Thursday afternoon had faded by the time she arrived to pick him up. His face was tight with pain. She took one look at him, assessed that he was paying for having overdone it the day before, and firmly closed the door behind her.

"Did you take your pain medication?" she asked as she moved briskly past him and headed for the kitchen where he kept the pills.

He shook his head.

She whirled on him. "Dammit, Michael, that's what the medication's for."

"Who said I was in pain?" he snapped.

The man's determination to be a stoic no matter the cost exasperated her beyond belief. She regarded him with amusement. "Are you saying you're not?"

"No more than usual," he insisted.

"Okay, then, get on your feet and let's get out of here."

The withering look he shot her would have terrified most people. Kelly simply stood there and waited.

"Okay, dammit, get the pill," he said, his voice tight with fury. "Just one."

She brought back the pill and a glass of water. "Why don't I fix dinner right here?"

He shook his head. "Absolutely not. I promised you a celebration."

"Michael, we can celebrate right here. It's private.

The refrigerator's well stocked. I can whip something up in no time."

"It doesn't seem like much of a date."

"It works for me."

His gaze searched hers. "You really wouldn't mind?"

"Being alone with you? Hardly," she said lightly, then fled to the kitchen before he could react.

She heard the whispered glide of his wheelchair as she was pulling dishes from the cabinet, then the locking sound of the brake. When she finally turned around, Michael was struggling to his feet.

"What are you doing?" she demanded, starting forward.

"Stay where you are," he commanded.

"But—"

"Just this once, do what I ask," he said, slowly walking toward her. "And set those dishes down."

She regarded him with confusion. "Why?"

"Because if I do this right, you'll just wind up dropping them," he said, his expression solemn.

Filled with a sudden rush of anticipation, Kelly set the dishes down with a thump just before Michael drew her into his arms. He tucked a finger under her chin, searched her face intently, then lowered his mouth to cover hers.

Tenderness exploded into urgent need. Years of pent-up longing gave way to the thrill of satisfaction as Michael's kiss turned dark and dangerous. This was the way a man kissed a woman he wanted, Kelly thought as her senses went spinning.

"I want you," he murmured against her lips. "I'd intended to do this right. A little wining and dining the way you deserve, then trying to coax you back here and into my bed. If it's a lousy idea, tell me now."

Kelly could barely breathe, barely think, her heart was pounding so hard. "It's the best idea you've had in years," she said with conviction.

"Dinner?"

"I'll turn off the oven." She met his gaze. "Condoms?"

He grinned at that. "In the nightstand."

"Which means we have to get to your bedroom," she said.

For an instant, he looked uneasy. "The gallant thing would be to carry you," he said.

She glanced toward the wheelchair. "I could always ride in your lap."

For an instant, she thought he might refuse her out of stubborn pride, but then apparently the possibilities began to intrigue him. He sat and she settled into place, wriggling a bit in the process.

"Watch it," he warned.

She regarded him with deliberate innocence. "Am I bothering you?"

"Sweetheart, you've been bothering me since the first day you walked through my front door all full of sass and determination."

"Is that so?" she asked, pleased. "Then your patience is amazing."

"I thought so."

The trip to the bedroom took a whole lot longer than

it needed to, simply because Kelly did her best to bother him along the way.

"Game's over," he said when they were beside the bed.

Kelly met his gaze, let the heat between them build to a slow simmer, then shook her head. "No, Michael. It's just beginning."

13

Over recent months, Kelly thought she'd learned just about everything there was to know about Michael's body. After all, she'd massaged him, she'd seen his undeniable reaction to her touches. She knew the power of his shoulders and arms, the slowly fading scars on his legs, the less visible scars from old injuries he'd refused to discuss. But all of that had been different. She'd forced herself to hold back, to try not to react to him as a woman. She'd been at least moderately successful.

Now, however, she was able to give free rein to her curiosity, to caress his hard muscles and explore his body far more intimately than prior prudence had allowed.

In the bedroom, he shifted from the wheelchair to the edge of the bed. Kelly knelt beside him and tugged his dress shirt free from his slacks. For the first time, she realized how much care he'd taken with his appearance tonight.

"It's almost a shame to get you out of this," she said,

even as she began undoing the buttons. "You look incredibly handsome. The blue matches your eyes."

"Is that so?" he said, as if it were a surprise and of little consequence. Instead, his intense gaze seemed to find the quick work she was making of his buttons fascinating. "You're awfully good at that."

"What, this?" she asked innocently, as she slowly spread the flaps of his shirt apart, then helped him shrug out of it. Then she slipped her fingers under the edge of his white T-shirt, her knuckles grazing warm, supple skin. She took her time lifting the soft cotton shirt higher and higher, allowing herself the titillating pleasure of a slow, deliberate revelation of his bare chest with its swirls of dark, crisp hair.

Tossing aside the T-shirt with its fresh laundry scent, she bent to press a kiss to his skin. The heat seemed to come off of him in waves. She was half-surprised it didn't sear her lips. As if it might, she kept her mouth moving, tasting him, peppering little kisses across his shoulders and the base of his throat. She could hear the hitch in his breath, feel the pounding of his heart under her palm. Knowing that she could make Michael respond to her was amazing. She had never felt more desirable in her entire life.

Still contemplating the wonder of his reaction, she gasped when his arm suddenly circled her waist and he lifted her around to stand between his legs.

"My turn," he announced, his gaze hot as he lifted the soft green sweater over her head. The action tousled her hair, but he reached up with total concentration and gently smoothed it back into place, his touch lingering on her cheeks.

"You're so soft," he whispered, his voice husky and filled with something that might have been awe.

What could have been an agony of indecision raced across his face, before he met her gaze. "This could be a bad idea."

Kelly immediately guessed his concern. Touched that he had let his need for her supercede his vulnerability, she reached for him, feeling the hard press of his arousal through his slacks.

"It doesn't seem like such a bad idea to me," she reassured him.

"I'm not exactly agile," he said, sounding suddenly angry and defensive, reactions more in keeping with a man who was putting his masculinity to the ultimate test, rather than an injured leg that had affected only his mobility.

She grinned and smoothed away the furrow in his brow. "But I am," she said. "Lay back and enjoy it, Devaney. Everything works that needs to work."

Heat and yearning glinted in his eyes. "You surprise me."

"Glad to hear it," she said, already fumbling for the buckle of his belt.

Michael covered her hands and stilled them. "Slow down. There are a few things I know I can still do," he said, regarding her with renewed eagerness. "Then you can take over."

Swift, sure hands swept over her breasts, releasing the front hook on her bra in the blink of an eye. Michael smoothed away the scraps of lace, his smoldering gaze steady as he surveyed her.

"You are so gorgeous," he whispered, his voice satisfyingly husky. A wry grin tugged at his lips. "And I keep waiting for your brother to come charging in here to smash my face in."

Kelly chuckled. "Not an image to dwell on. Besides," she reassured him, "I have it on very good authority that his time is otherwise occupied tonight."

"Moira?"

"Moira. They're a hot item, thanks to us."

Michael grinned. "Well, good for us," he said, then closed his mouth over the tip of her breast.

The action sent a jolt of fire straight through her. Conversation died, lost to a rising tide of sensation that threatened to pull Kelly under, gasping for breath and clinging to Michael like a lifeline.

He might claim not to be agile, but he had more than enough moves to sweep her off her feet and onto a roller-coaster ride that left her feeling exhilarated and needy as they raced for the precipice and then, finally, at long last plunged over the edge in a giddy, amazing descent that had her screaming out with the wonder of it.

This was what she'd waited for her whole life, Kelly thought as the satisfying shudders slowly faded and contentment settled in. This was what sex was meant to be when two people really, truly connected on every conceivable level. This was what people meant when they talked about sex being transformed into making love.

And now that she'd discovered it, there was no way in hell she would ever let it go.

* * *

Michael woke up sometime later feeling astonishingly rested and satisfied in the way a man only felt after rambunctious, steamy sex. Okay, it hadn't been all that rambunctious, but it had been a helluva ride. And Kelly had ridden him over the brink, astonishing him with her abandon.

Discovering that he was still able to please a woman in bed did more for Michael's recovery than all the other therapy Kelly had provided. He'd needed not just the physical release, but the reassurance that his diminished agility hadn't really reduced him to a shell of the man he'd once been, at least not in one important facet of his life. He'd known all along that his assumptions about himself were exaggerated and based on fear, not common sense, but until now he hadn't been able to let go of them. Now, he thought, he was finally ready to move on, put his weaknesses into perspective and work to overcome them.

So what if he couldn't scramble up the side of an enemy ship with the quickness of a cat? So what if he'd never again run at a sprinter's pace? In time he would eventually be able to do most physical activities at a level equal to that of many civilians. And even now, when his first steps were still awkward and tortured, he'd been able to do the horizontal mambo in a more than satisfactory manner. If he could bring pleasure to Kelly—and himself—then complaining about the rest seemed pointless.

He had pleased her, too. There was no mistaking the flare of heat in her eyes, the soft moans of pleasure, the quick, urgent thrusts of her hips as they'd climbed higher and higher before tumbling together into a stormy sea of sensations.

He'd also read something else in her eyes, something he wasn't entirely sure how to interpret, something that terrified him. While he'd been selfishly grabbing at the one act guaranteed to reassure him that he was still a man, he suspected Kelly had been turning her long-ago crush into a full-fledged love affair. Though what had just happened between them had been incredible—inevitable, even—he wasn't quite ready to pin a label on it. He certainly wasn't ready to build a future around it.

Okay, maybe he was jumping the gun. Maybe Kelly was no more anxious for marriage and commitment than he was. Maybe she was perfectly capable of handling a torrid affair that stemmed from all the restless heat simmering between them for weeks now.

He glanced over at her tousled hair, her rosy cheeks and innocent expression and muttered a curse under his breath. No way was this woman ready for a torrid, meaningless affair. No way did she deserve anything less than happily-ever-after. And deep down, in a place he'd been trying to avoid examining too closely, he wanted to give her that. He just wasn't sure he could, not until he had answers to all the questions still burning in his gut.

Beyond passion and the promise of a pension from the navy, what did he really have to offer her? He was still only a shadow of his former self. Oh, he would be back on his feet, capable of walking more than a few feet, in a matter of weeks now, but what the devil was he going to do with himself then? More than most, he knew the value of having a profession that mattered, not for the money, but for the self-respect, something that despite the Havilceks' best efforts had eluded him until he'd become a SEAL. How was he going to find that self-respect again in his altered world?

Up until now he'd been consumed with proving the doctors wrong and walking again. Now he was going to have to face the fact that the fight ahead to find a new role for himself was going to be just as challenging. And, unfortunately, this was one challenge Kelly couldn't help him meet. He was going to have to face it squarely on his own.

He glanced down at her as she sighed and snuggled more tightly against him. At least now, though, he had a reason outside of his own ego to make something of his life. He'd desperately needed that motivating factor, probably in a way that wasn't entirely smart or healthy. Bottom line, though, Kelly had given him a reason to move on.

As if she sensed his turmoil, Kelly turned restless, then slowly stretched and blinked before finally focusing on his face.

"Hi," she murmured, reaching for the sheet as if she'd suddenly turned shy.

Michael kept the sheet just out of reach. "Don't," he chided. "I like looking at you."

She seemed startled by that. "You do?"

He grinned. "Come on now. You're a gorgeous woman. I'm a red-blooded male. Who knows what looking might lead to."

Her eyes sparkled with sudden fascination. "Really? Tell me."

"Why don't I show you?" he said, reaching for her. It took him over an hour to make his point to his thorough and complete satisfaction. Kelly gave herself up completely to him, holding nothing back. She was remarkable.

For Michael, the effort proved one thing beyond a shadow of a doubt. He had to be able to come to her as the kind of man she deserved...or he had to let her go.

Kelly knew she was probably behaving like a giddy schoolgirl when she arrived at the rehab clinic early Saturday morning for her weekly coffee and sugar-laden treats date with Moira, but she couldn't help it. Last night had been the most magical night of her life. If it showed on her face, if she couldn't seem to stop smiling, well, too bad. Moira was the one person she could count on to understand completely. She'd been grinning a lot lately, too.

Kelly walked into her boss's office and plunked the bag of doughnuts on Moira's desk, then handed her the paper cup of latte from the trendy coffee shop down the street. Moira glanced up from her pile of paperwork, tossed down her pen and studied Kelly's face with searing intensity.

"Uh-oh," she said eventually. "Something happened between you and Michael, didn't it?"

"Did I ask you to tell all when you and Bryan got together?" Kelly inquired airily.

"You didn't have to ask," Moira pointed out. "I babbled like an infatuated idiot. You owe me the same courtesy."

"You'll just tell me what a mistake I'm making by mixing business and pleasure."

Moira sketched an *X* across her heart. "No, I won't. I promise. I'm taking a break from making judgments. Today I'm just your friend."

It was true. Moira really was the best friend she'd ever had. If it weren't for their professional relationship, Kelly would have spilled everything the second she'd walked into the room.

Finally she sighed. "I didn't believe it was possible, but I am more in love with him than ever."

"In other words, you slept with him," Moira interpreted. "And it was fabulous."

"Beyond fabulous."

"What about Michael? Is he in love with you?"

Kelly wished she could say an unequivocal yes, but the truth was, she'd detected shadows in Michael's eyes this morning. She hadn't pressed for answers, because she honestly hadn't wanted anything to spoil what had been so incredibly magical for her.

"He cares about me," she said slowly. "I know he does."

"And that's enough for you?" her friend asked skeptically.

"It is for now. He still has a lot to sort out. His whole world has changed. He can't go back to doing the work that he loves. He's known that all along, but I think he's just now starting to face the full ramifications. I'm pretty sure he's finally willing to start looking for an alternative line of work, rather than bemoaning what he's lost."

"Facing it could leave him bitter and resentful. He could even blame you—irrationally, I know—for not finding some way to make things turn out differently."

Kelly hadn't even considered that scenario. A man in Michael's position might well look for someone to blame. She frowned at Moira. "Why not blame the sniper who shot him? Why would he ever turn on me?"

"Because the sniper was a faceless enemy. You're right here and you're the person who's supposed to be helping to make him whole again."

"I can only do that within limits," Kelly said defensively.

"I know that, but does he?"

"Of course," Kelly said, but she wasn't entirely certain of it. She set down her half-eaten doughnut and now-cold coffee. Frowning, she added accusingly, "You've certainly managed to put a damper on my good mood."

"I'm sorry. I just want to be sure you're facing facts."

"Possibilities, not facts," Kelly argued.

"You know I only want you to be happy, don't you?" Moira asked, her expression plaintive. "I would never deliberately try to hurt you."

Kelly gave her hand a reassuring squeeze. "I know that, especially since you know I could tell my brother all your secrets," she teased.

"I don't have any secrets," Moira retorted, then grinned. "Darn it all."

Kelly laughed. "I could always make some up."

"I'll think about it. Bryan might respond well to a few hints that my life hasn't been deadly dull up until now. I'd hate for him to get the idea he's saving me from total boredom."

"Sweetie, you travel. You have a successful business. You have friends. I'd hardly call that boring," Kelly chided.

"But your brother has done all sorts of fascinating things," Moira protested.

Kelly shrugged off Bryan's activities. "He's only told you the highlights. Believe me, he spends most of his time with his head buried in these stuffy tomes about dead psychoanalysts or locked away in his office with people who think their lives are a mess."

Moira grinned. "I'm sure he'd love to know how deeply you respect his work."

"I do. He's very good at what he does. It's just not very exciting. He's hardly in a position to cast stones at your life. That's why you're going to be so good for each other. You can spur each other to take some chances, have a few adventures." She winked at her. "Or you can cuddle up together and read all those boring medical and psychology journals side by side in bed, then toss them aside and do far more interesting things."

"Trust me, we have not been sharing the bed with any journals," Moira said, then blushed furiously.

"Told you that you didn't need to worry about being boring," Kelly taunted. "I've got to go. Jennifer's due any second for her therapy and I want a few minutes with her mom first."

Suddenly all business, Moira asked, "How's Jennifer's progress?"

"She's doing great, but her insurance is about to run out. I want to work something out so we can continue with her treatment."

"Let me know if I can help," Moira said. "I'm good at yelling at insurance bureaucrats."

"I may do that." Kelly glanced out the window in the office door and felt her heart skip a beat. Michael was here an hour early and already at work on the parallel bars with no one to spot him. "Gotta run. Michael's out there."

Moira came to stand beside her. "Looks to me as if he's developed a renewed determination to get back on his feet." She gave Kelly a knowing look. "Wonder what—or who—inspired that?"

"I'll let you know if I find out," Kelly said as she walked out and closed the door behind her.

She forced herself to take slow, measured steps across the therapy room, even though she wanted to race over and plant herself in front of Michael to prevent a fall. When she reached him, he'd made his way to the midpoint of the bars. There were white lines of tension around his mouth and furrows of concentration on his brow. She had to resist the urge to yell at him. Instead, she stepped between the bars blocking his path.

"You're ambitious this morning."

A fleeting grin tugged at his lips. "I'm motivated."

"You're overdoing it," she countered.

He regarded her with surprise and a hint of anger. "Don't you think it's about time? I've wasted weeks."

His words cut through her as if they'd been an accusation. "Are you suggesting I haven't worked you hard enough?"

Dismay spread across his face. "No, of course not. I'm the one who's been balking. I haven't gotten with the program, not really. Believe me, I know what tough, rigorous training is like. I can take it and from now on out, I intend to do just that."

Kelly bit back a protest that he might reinjure his leg. She didn't totally understand this sudden need to push himself, but it was obviously important to him. And what were the chances that he might really harm himself?

"I'll make you a deal," she said.

He frowned at that. "Who gave you bargaining rights in this?"

"You did."

"When? When I slept with you?"

She hadn't realized that he had the power to hurt her so badly. Tears stung her eyes, but she blinked them away. "No," she said quietly, "when you hired me as your therapist."

Forgetting about the deal she'd been about to make with him, she whirled around and walked blindly away.

"Kelly!"

She ignored his urgent call, for once glad that he couldn't move quickly enough to stop her. Spotting Jennifer and her mother in the waiting area, she paused long enough to compose herself, plastered a smile on her face and headed their way, certain that Michael wouldn't interrupt. She would have to deal with him again eventually, but by then she could steel herself to do it unemotionally.

And if she couldn't, well, telling him to go to hell would feel really good about now.

Michael knew he'd made a total jackass of himself with Kelly. He wasn't sure why he'd suddenly made the kind of cutting remarks he knew would hurt her. He wished he could blame the entire incident on her thin skin, rather than his own boneheaded behavior, but he couldn't.

Maybe it was the fact that she'd implied he couldn't do the hard work just when his ego was finally convinced it was past time to start pushing his limits. Maybe it was the whole sex thing and the uncomfortable issues it had stirred about the future.

The future. He sighed just thinking about it. He'd put off a visit to the navy doctors for weeks now, despite repeated reminders from the West Coast physicians that he was overdue to check in with the specialists they'd recommended. He couldn't put an examination off forever, even if he didn't want to hear the final, if inevitable, verdict that he'd never go back on active duty.

It was time now. Past time. Sucking it up like the supposedly brave man he was, he made an appointment with the navy doctors he'd been avoiding. He might be dreading it, but he needed an honest assessment of what the future might hold. He wasn't expecting them to tell him anything the doctors in San Diego hadn't said months ago, but he was still holding out hope for a miracle.

The examination was painstakingly thorough, the grim expressions pretty much what he'd expected. He could hang on to his job, as long as he was willing to settle for desk duty.

"I'm sorry," the orthopedic surgeon told him. "I don't see any way around it."

"Not even with intensive physical therapy?" Michael asked, trying to keep a pleading note out of his voice. He'd come here knowing it was time to accept things. He needed to do it and stop fighting for something that could never be.

"Not even then," the man said, removing all hope.

That night, Michael received a call from his commanding officer. "I heard the news," Joe Voinovich told him. "I'm sorry as hell about this."

"Me, too."

"Are you going to take the job they're offering in Washington?"

"No," Michael said flatly. Whatever happened, he was staying in Boston. He'd find something to do eventually. And Kelly was here. Sooner or later he'd coax her to forgive him. Or find the courage to let her go and make some sort of future with a man who had his act together.

The incident at the rehab clinic hadn't been mentioned since it had happened. In the days since, when the time had come for his therapy session, she'd been right on time, a phony smile firmly in place, her voice discernibly chillier than usual. He knew she deserved an apology, but so far he hadn't been able to bring himself to utter one. He was still debating whether it was better to let the relationship die before it really got started.

Then he thought of the way it was between them, the heat and passion, the tenderness and thoughtfulness, and he wasn't sure he could bear it if he lost her. Until he knew what was best, though, the distance between them was safe. In fact, he probably ought to assure that there would be even more distance. He'd let other women go. In fact, he'd made a habit of it. So why was it so difficult to get the words out now?

Maybe because he knew that as soon as he uttered them, he couldn't take them back. He knew they would change everything, that Kelly had enough pride to make her walk away for good, certain that he'd used her and was tossing her aside now that she'd served her purpose.

And wasn't that exactly what he was doing?

"No, dammit." He uttered the words aloud without realizing it.

Kelly's gaze shot toward him. It was one of the rare times lately when she'd looked him in the eye. "What?"

"Nothing," he said. "Talking to myself."

She regarded him with a penetrating look. "What's wrong?"

Now was the time. He owed her honesty. Hell, he owed her his life.

"There's something we need to talk about," he said.

Alarm flashed in her eyes, but she quickly glanced away. When she looked back, there was only mild curiosity in her expression. "Sure. What?"

He gestured toward a nearby workout bench. "Let's sit a minute." She followed him, her steps dragging ever so slightly. When they were seated, he forced himself to look directly into her eyes. "I think you know what a lifeline you've been for me," he began. "You've been amazing."

"But I've outlasted my usefulness," she said quietly.

"Don't say it like that," he said, hating how the words he'd been struggling to form sounded when she said them with such an air of resignation. She looked as if she might be fighting tears, but she kept her gaze steady.

"But that's the bottom line, isn't it? You want to go on from here on your own."

"Kelly, you're an incredible woman. You deserve the best and I don't have anything to offer you. I'm getting out of the navy. I have no idea yet what I'll do next. It would be wrong of me to ask you to sit around and wait while I figure things out."

For a moment, it looked as if she might argue. Michael braced himself to try to counter whatever she said. Instead, though, she sighed, her expression unbearably sad.

"As long as you believe that, then you're right, you don't have anything to offer me."

She stood up, fiddling nervously with the pen she'd been using to make notes on his therapy, not quite looking him in the eye. "Michael, the only thing I ever wanted or needed was your heart."

14

Kelly hadn't known it was possible to feel so empty inside. Just when she'd thought she'd finally found something real and permanent and remarkable, Michael had deliberately yanked it away. And why? Because he was so convinced that he was nothing without his stupid uniform, without a job that put his life at risk.

She blamed the Devaneys for having done that to him and she hated them for it. She prayed when Ryan, Sean and Michael eventually found their parents that she would be granted five minutes alone with them to given them a piece of her mind for abandoning those three young boys and destroying their sense of self-worth in the process. It was little wonder that Michael thought he wasn't worthy of being loved by her, when his own parents had drilled that lesson into him at such an early age.

She sighed and turned to find her brother studying her with a worried expression. "What?" she demanded. "Why are you even home tonight? Shouldn't you be with Moira? You've been spending all your free time at her place lately."

Bryan held up his hands. "Hey, don't jump down my throat. I just came over here to ask you if you'd like to come to the pub tonight with Moira and me. Word is you've been holed up here for days now, refusing to go anywhere, including work. Moira's worried sick. Your clients are about to rebel. They don't like any of the substitute therapists she's assigned to them."

Kelly felt a momentary pang of guilt. She knew her clients shouldn't have to suffer because her life was falling apart. "Then I'll go back to work," she said eventually. She could avoid Michael if she only scheduled patients on Mondays, Wednesdays and Fridays at the clinic.

"When?" her brother pressed.

"Soon."

"Whatever that means," he said. "In the meantime, what about tonight? Come with us. You have to start getting out sometime."

She frowned at him. Either he was being deliberately insensitive or he was an awfully lousy psychologist who couldn't even read his own sister.

"Are you crazy?" she asked sourly. "The pub is the very last place I'd ever show my face."

It was his turn to sigh. "I thought so," he said, sinking down in a chair across from her. "Your crummy mood obviously has something to do with Michael. You might as well tell me, Kelly. What did he do to you? I'll kill him."

"Stay out of it," she ordered. "I don't need my big brother fighting my battles for me."

"Then fight them for yourself," he said mildly. "Come with us tonight. Show him that you're not about to let him ruin your life."

"My life is not ruined just because Michael Devaney broke up with me," she said fiercely.

"Then prove it."

"I don't have to prove anything to anybody. I don't want to come to the pub. That's a little too in-your-face for my peace of mind."

"You like it there."

"I liked it there when I was with Michael," she corrected. "If you'd been paying the slightest bit of attention, you'd know that I opted out of spending time there a couple of weeks ago. I didn't want to have to answer a lot of questions when I eventually wound up in exactly the position I'm in now, cast aside by a man who's too self-absorbed or too scared to make a commitment to another living soul. Who needs it?"

"You apparently," Bryan said wryly.

"I don't need Michael," she said emphatically.

"Okay, then, you could meet someone else. There's a guy who's been coming in lately with Maggie's folks. Seems like a good guy." He grinned. "He's almost as handsome as I am."

She frowned at her brother. "That's not saying much."

"Kelly, don't shut yourself away. Michael's my best friend and I love him like a brother, but he's not worth a broken heart."

"Who said anything about my heart being broken?"

He regarded her evenly. "Am I wrong? Tell me I'm wrong and I'll back off. Tell me you have another date tonight, maybe with that doctor you went out with awhile back."

There was no date and she wouldn't lie to him. "Can't you just let me be miserable in peace?"

"Sorry, kid. No can do. Moira and I will pick you up. Be ready at six o'clock."

Her gaze narrowed. "Why so early?"

"It'll be easier if you get there first and stake out your turf. Let Michael be the one who's on the defensive when he finds you there."

What her brother said made a lot of sense, but Kelly wasn't sure she was masochistic enough to take his advice. She'd spend the entire evening being miserable. Why go under those conditions? Why risk having her already aching heart suffer another blow if Michael flat-out ignored her? Staying away would be the smart-safe—thing to do. But she'd never played it safe in her life.

And the pitiful truth was that she desperately wanted to catch a glimpse of Michael, to see if maybe, just maybe, he was as miserable as she was. Maybe by now he'd come to his senses, she thought hopefully, then chastised herself for being an idiot. If Michael had had second thoughts, he knew her phone number and he certainly knew where she lived. He'd started coming there as a teenager.

"I'll go," she told her brother finally, because she found it all but impossible to resist. "But you bring me home the second I ask you to, okay? No questions and no arguments."

"Deal," he said at once. "And if you change your mind and want me to punch him out, just say the word."

Kelly sighed. "Don't even tempt me."

Michael fully expected a visit from Bryan. In fact, he was looking forward to it. He figured a good thrashing was the least he deserved for hurting Kelly, even if he hadn't meant to, even if he'd thought with some misguided sense of honor that he was protecting her. Instead, though, he heard nothing from his best friend. That left him to sit and stew with his own regrets.

When he finally tired of that, he called his brother. It was time—past time—to act. For a man who'd thrived on action, he'd been way too passive for months now.

"Hey, Ryan, you remember that guy you were telling me about, the one with the charter boats?"

"Sure. You interested after all?" Ryan asked cautiously.

"Maybe."

"Want me to set up a meeting?"

Michael drew in a deep breath. It was now or never. Maybe this prospect would turn out to be nothing, but he had to start someplace.

"No," he said eventually. "Is he there tonight?"

"Sure is. You coming by? Everyone's here. We've been missing you. Caitlyn's been asking for you every day."

Michael felt his mouth curve into the first genuine smile since he'd broken things off with Kelly. "I can't disappoint my niece, can I? I'll be there in an hour. Have your friend stick around if he can."

"Will do. See you soon."

Now that he was committed, he managed to shower and dress in record time. For some reason, his heart felt lighter than it had in months. He should have done something like this long ago, instead of wallowing in self-pity and fear. He was feeling almost upbeat by the time he reached Ryan's Place.

Then he spotted Kelly, sitting at a table separate from the Devaneys and the Havilceks. Bryan and Moira were with her, one on each side as if they felt the need to protect her.

Michael's heart climbed into his throat. She looked fabulous, and sad. Knowing that he was responsible for her sorrow cut right through him. The guilt was almost enough to make him turn tail and run, but he didn't. Tonight was all about getting his act together at long last and Kelly was the reason he couldn't put it off a moment longer.

He forced himself to go right past her table, to stop and utter an impersonal greeting to all three of them, though his gaze never left Kelly's face. Her chin jutted up and she met his gaze without flinching.

"Everything going okay?" he asked her.

"Fine," she said in a terse tone that said everything was far from fine. "I see you're walking with a cane now. That's great progress."

Michael nodded, not sure what to say to that. "I'm here to talk to that friend of Ryan's about a job."

For an instant there was a spark of genuine excitement in her eyes. "The charter boats?"

He nodded.

"I thought you weren't interested in that."

"I've had second thoughts," he told her, his gaze unwavering. "About a lot of things."

"I see," she said, returning to her mask of cool indifference. "Well, good luck, then." She glanced at Bryan. "I'd like to leave now, if you don't mind."

Bryan cast a hard look at Michael, then stood up. "Sure thing, Kelly. Moira, you want to wait here? I'll be back in ten or fifteen minutes."

Moira nodded. "I'll wait." She gave Michael a pointed look. "Why don't you have a seat?"

"Moira!" Kelly protested sharply, hesitating with her coat halfway on.

"I'm not going to kill him," Moira said. "I can be as civilized as the next person."

Michael grinned at that. "I don't doubt it, but I have a couple of prior engagements, first with my niece and then about a job. You'll have to give me a rain check on the inquisition."

Moira sighed. "Too bad." She stood up and grabbed her coat. "I guess I'll go along with you guys, then."

Michael stood where he was and watched them leave. Kelly never once looked back.

"Woman problems?" Ryan asked sympathetically, coming up beside him.

Michael nodded. "I'm still not sure how I let things get so out of hand. I never meant to hurt her."

"Then fix it," Ryan said simply.

"I'm not sure I know how. I do know that finding a job is the first step, one I have to take for me before I can give any thought at all to the future."

"Does Kelly agree that work should come before her?"

"Probably not," Michael admitted. "But that's the one thing I am sure of."

"Okay, then, let me introduce you to Greg Keith." Ryan led the way across the restaurant to a man seated at a table in the corner. Not until Michael was next to the table did he realize that Greg Keith was in a wheelchair. He had to fight not to show any visible sign of his shock.

Greg grinned at him. "You can ask," he said, when Ryan was gone and Michael had taken a seat opposite him.

"Ask what?"

"About old ironsides here. We've been together a long time now."

"It's none of my business," Michael said.

"It is if you're going to come to work for me. I don't see much point in ignoring my limitations. If I do, then they're controlling me, and believe me, that's not a situation I can tolerate."

Michael nodded. He was just beginning to relate to the sentiment. "What happened?"

"A bullet in the spine during an operation in the Persian Gulf War. I came out of the SEALs with a nice pension and some money in the bank. As soon as I got out of the hospital, I started looking around for a boat to buy. I couldn't imagine my life anywhere except around water. I have a fleet of ten charter boats now, everything from a tall ship to a couple of fishing trawlers." He regarded Michael with a penetrating look. "I assume you're here because Ryan told you I'm always looking for good captains."

Michael nodded slowly, trying to digest what Greg Keith had done with his life once he'd been dealt a devastating blow. It was one more reminder that he had nothing to complain about.

"I'll be honest," he told Greg. "I'm not sure if this is for me, but I'd like to take a look around, see if it feels right."

"Fair enough. Does tomorrow morning suit you?" Greg grinned at Michael. "I guarantee you that once you set foot on deck and get back out to sea, it'll give you a whole new lease on life."

Michael thought of the woman who'd just left the pub and the future that could await them, if he ever found the courage to try. "I truly hope so."

To his shock and ultimately to his relief, Michael discovered that he liked being back on the water, even if he couldn't be heading out to face some sort of incredible danger. The serenity he'd always found at sea hadn't changed just because the type of vessel had.

He also discovered that Greg was a remarkable man, whose accomplishments and whose positive outlook on the hand he'd been dealt quickly became an inspiration to Michael. In no time at all, he felt as if he'd found a new life that was worth living. There was just one thing missing—Kelly.

He finally worked up the nerve to call her, only to be told that she was away on an extended vacation. An hour later, Bryan called him back.

"What the hell were you thinking calling here?" he demanded. "You're the one who made the decision to end things with my sister. Leave her in peace."

"Is she at peace?" Michael dared to ask. If she was, maybe he didn't have any right to try to stir things up again. Maybe the love he felt for her, but hadn't acknowledged in time would never be enough to make things right.

"She's getting there," Bryan said.

"Look, I know I made a lot of mistakes," Michael told him. "I just want a chance to fix things."

"Fix them how?" Bryan asked skeptically.

The truth was that Michael wanted what they'd once had back. He wanted to marry her, but he was not saying that to Bryan before he had a chance to say it to Kelly. Her reaction was the only one that mattered.

"That's between Kelly and me."

"No," Bryan said flatly. "You've done enough to mess up her life. I'm telling you to stay away from her. If our friendship ever meant anything to you, you'll listen to me and do as I ask."

"Sorry, man. You know I respect you, but I don't think I can do that."

"Dammit, Michael, having you walk out on her devastated her. Isn't that enough?"

"I want to make it right," he said again.

"I don't think that's possible," his friend said bluntly. "This vacation she's on, she went with someone."

Michael's heart began to thud dully. "The preppy doctor?"

"I don't think that's any of your business. Just stay away from Kelly, or I'll make you regret it."

Michael might have laughed, if Bryan hadn't sounded so deadly serious. The fact that he was willing to resort to violence to protect his sister told Michael volumes about how badly Kelly had been hurt. Heartsick, he sighed heavily.

"I'll stay away," he promised at last.

Michael kept his promise to Bryan for weeks, going to work seven days a week, hiding out in his apartment during his little bit of free time. He was getting exactly what he deserved for being such a first-class jerk. Kelly had offered him the sun and the moon, to say nothing of her heart, and he'd thrown it all back in her face.

It was a visit from Ryan and Sean that finally pulled him out of his latest bout with self-pity.

"Okay, bro, we've had it," Sean said. "We're tired of waiting for you to come to us, so here we are."

To forestall the pep talk they so clearly intended, Michael offered them beers and some of the large pepperoni pizza that had arrived just ahead of them.

"You're not getting off the hook that easily," Ryan said, as he polished off the last piece of pizza. "We came here, in part at least, because we think it's time to go to Maine and meet Patrick."

The announcement took him by surprise. "Why now?"

"Because of you," Sean said.

"Me? What the hell do I have to do with it?" He looked at Sean. "I thought you wanted to put this meeting off till doomsday, if at all possible."

Sean nodded. "I did till I started seeing how the past is affecting you."

"Nothing in my life has anything whatsoever to do with the past," Michael said emphatically.

"I think you're wrong about that," Ryan said, just as fiercely. "Unless I'm very much mistaken, you've just abandoned a woman you love the same way our parents left us. Maybe it's not even the first time. Don't you think, for your own sake, you need answers so you can break the pattern before you spend the rest of your life alone? I certainly needed a wake-up call to get my life on track. So did Sean. Otherwise, we both might have turned our backs on Maggie and Deanna."

Michael wasn't interested in their version of pop psychology. "Are you crazy?" he demanded. "Breaking up with Kelly had absolutely nothing to do with the past. If anything, it had to do with the future. It took me a while but I finally got over that. Unfortunately, it was too late."

"Says who?"

"Her brother."

Ryan stared at him. "You took Bryan's word on something that important? What the hell were you thinking?"

"Why would he lie to me?" Michael asked defensively.

"To protect his sister," Sean suggested. "Geez, bro,

that one's so obvious, even I could see it. For an ex-SEAL, you're awfully gullible."

"He said she went away with someone," Michael retorted. "That sounds as if it's too late to me."

Sean groaned. "She did. She and Moira went to Ireland for a week."

Michael stared. "Ireland? With Moira?" He'd given up on her because she'd gone away for a few days with her best friend? Maybe he had been a little too quick to accept the possibility that she didn't care about him because of his past. Maybe he'd bought into the idea that he wasn't worth loving. He could see it so clearly now, how he'd been influenced by his parents' abandonment. After all, if they had found him so unlovable, then sooner or later wouldn't Kelly likely reach the same conclusion? Why fight for someone he was destined to lose anyway? If that had been his thinking when he took Bryan's words at face value, then he really was pitiful.

As for Bryan's role in all this by deliberately misleading him, Michael resolved to deal with that later.

He stood up suddenly and headed for the door. "You guys stick around and finish your beers," he told his brothers. "I've got someplace I need to be."

"Think he's going out for more pizza?" Sean joked.

"Not if he's half as smart as I think he is," Ryan retorted.

Michael grinned at them. "I'm smart enough to go after the best thing that ever happened to me."

"Of course you are," Ryan confirmed. "Whatever the

past, at least the three of us have started a new Devaney family tradition."

"What's that?" Michael asked.

"We hang on to the people we love."

15

The trip to Ireland had been everything Kelly had always imagined it would be, but she hadn't enjoyed herself. An image of a dark-haired, moody Irishman back home kept intruding. If it hadn't been for Moira, she would have cut the trip short and gone home early.

But to what? she wondered despondently. She had her work, of course, but there would be no social life, not as long as the memory of one man refused to let her alone. She'd never been the type who could counter a broken heart with a whirlwind of dating, especially when none of the men ever measured up. Maybe she needed to accept the fact that she was a one-man woman and always had been.

She looked across the table in the pub where she and Moira were having dinner and saw that her best friend was regarding her with a worried frown, the same frown she'd been wearing for most of the trip.

"We might as well go home," Moira said with resignation. "You're obviously having a terrible time."

"Don't be silly," Kelly said, instantly consumed with

guilt. "I'm not going to spoil your vacation by cutting it short."

"Believe me, that would probably be better than traveling from village to village with a woman who's not really seeing the scenery."

"I'm sorry."

"Don't be sorry. Suggesting this trip was probably a bad idea in the first place. I just wanted to get you away from all the bad memories in Boston for a while. Bryan agreed it was a good idea."

"Bryan was just scared I'd cave in and go looking for Michael," Kelly said.

"Would you have done that?"

Kelly sighed heavily. "More than likely. I love him. I can't help it. I think I've loved him since I was a kid. These past few months have only deepened what I feel for him."

"The man hurt you," Moira reminded her, sounding as fiercely protective as Bryan would.

"I know," Kelly acknowledged. "But he didn't do it intentionally. I all but threw myself at him before he was ready to think about anything but getting back on his feet again. I was ready for a relationship. He wasn't."

"And you think that's changed by now?"

"I honestly don't know, but there's only one way to find out."

This time it was Moira who sighed deeply. "By going home," she concluded. "We can make the arrangements to leave in the morning."

Kelly knew her friend would do that, too, but she couldn't let her. "I have a better idea. Let's call Bryan and see if he can't come over here and join you. I know the two of you were planning a trip together before you decided to rescue me. When he gets here, then I'll leave. Until then, I'll try to throw myself into the spirit of things." She glanced toward the small dance floor. "I might even try an Irish jig."

There was no mistaking the faint spark of excitement that stirred in Moira's eyes. "I can live without watching you trip over your own feet," she said wryly. "As for calling Bryan, are you sure you wouldn't mind going back alone?"

"I'm a big girl. I can fly by myself," Kelly responded with a chuckle. "Stop worrying. I'm not going to throw open the door and dive into the Atlantic."

Moira regarded her indignantly. "Well, I should certainly hope not."

"A couple of weeks ago, I wouldn't have been so quick to say that," Kelly said. "But now I'm going to go home and fight for the man I love. He's not going to know what hit him."

Moira finally grinned. "Good for you."

"It might be best, though, if we don't tell Bryan that," Kelly warned her. "It might give him second thoughts about coming over here to join you."

A blush tinted Moira's cheeks. "Oh, I think I can keep your brother's mind otherwise occupied."

Kelly studied her friend and noted the new sense of confidence. It made her more attractive than ever. "Yes, I imagine you can. Any hint of wedding bells?"

"Not yet," Moira conceded. "But then I haven't taken

him on my tour of quaint Irish chapels yet. That ought to get him thinking along the right lines."

"Maybe you'd be better off just asking him outright to marry you," Kelly suggested. "Bryan's head is usually in the clouds. The direct approach has its advantages with a man like that."

"Is that what you intend to do with Michael, ask him to marry you?"

"Absolutely not," Kelly said as if she were utterly horrified by the idea. Then she grinned. "Actually I intend to plant the idea in his head and then let him think he was the one who came up with it. Michael has definite control issues, but now's not the time to work on them."

Moira lifted her glass of ale. "To us, then, and the men we love."

"To love," Kelly said, then added silently, *and to getting Michael to believe in it.*

Well, this was turning out to be damned frustrating, Michael decided as he spent days trying to catch up with Kelly.

He'd finally heard she was back from Ireland...from his mother. Apparently Kelly had paid her a visit on her return. She'd brought Doris Havilcek a lovely book of Irish recipes.

And Kelly had been spotted at the pub. Maggie reported that Kelly had dropped by with a list of Irish musicians who had upcoming tours to the United States and would be happy to play at Ryan's Place.

There had been sightings at the clinic, as well. Jennifer told him shyly that Kelly had been there for her last session, which had been rescheduled from Tuesday to Wednesday, a day when he wasn't likely to be around.

His plan for getting to Kelly and making things right was being foiled at every turn. He was mentally threatening to stake out her parents' place, when he concluded that maybe he needed to put a little more thought into his approach. It certainly wouldn't hurt to have a specific plan in mind.

Years of SEAL training had taught him that every last detail of an operation had to be ironed out in advance to assure success, even if the best-laid plans occasionally went wildly awry and he wound up scrambling. Looking at the alternatives from every angle might mean delaying the start of the mission, but it could guarantee achieving the results he wanted.

While he was at home pondering the best way to handle things, he got a call from an admiral at the Pentagon requesting a meeting.

"Sir, I've already resigned," he pointed out.

"I've got the paperwork right here on my desk," Admiral Stokes agreed. "Haven't signed it yet."

Michael bit back a curse at the delay. He'd wanted the ties severed once and for all. "Why is that, sir?"

"It occurs to me that you might not be thinking too clearly after what you've been through."

"Believe me, I've been over this a thousand times," Michael countered. "I'm not suited to a desk job. Whatever contribution I was able to make to the navy came because I was a highly skilled operative. That's over."

"Hell, man, your brain still functions, doesn't it?"

The harsh tone cut right through Michael and made him sweat. "Yes, of course, but—"

"Oh, stop trying to make excuses and get down to D.C.," Stokes commanded. "We've spent too much damned time and money training you to think like a SEAL to have you wasting it by running a bunch of tourists around so they can catch some fish."

Michael didn't waste time asking how the admiral knew what he'd been up to.

"We need to talk," Stokes continued. "Be here at oh-eight-hundred hours. And that's an order, Lieutenant. You're not out of the navy yet."

"Yes, sir," Michael said and slowly hung up the phone. To his astonishment, rather than fury over the presumptive arrogance of the admiral, what he felt was a faint stirring of excitement.

Kelly was feeling really pleased with herself. She'd made very sure that Michael knew she was back in town, while managing to avoid him catching so much as a glimpse of her. If she knew him half as well as she thought she did, he was probably going a little crazy by now. The fact that he'd been trying to catch up with her added to her conviction.

She had one last stop she wanted to make, possibly the riskiest one of all, because she wasn't entirely sure she could avoid getting caught this time. She headed to Greg Keith's charter boat headquarters, ostensibly to make an inquiry about chartering a boat that was captained by Michael. She wanted him to hear about the

request, wanted him to wonder why she'd suddenly decided to take up fishing.

"To be honest," Greg told her, "I'm not so sure Mr.
Devaney's going to be taking out any more fishing char-
ters."

Kelly stared at him in shock. The announcement
was the last thing she'd expected when she'd come here.
"He's not? Why? Did something happen? He's not injured again, is he? His recovery is still on track?"

The ex-SEAL, whom Ryan had willingly sent her to,
grinned at the barrage of questions. The smile transformed his face from a rugged ruin to something in-
triguingly handsome.

"Whoa," he ordered. "Don't panic. Michael's fine.
It's just that he's gone out of town for a few days, and
I'm not sure what's going to come of the trip."

"He went away on business? What kind of business?"
The only kind of business Michael had, as far as she
knew, was SEAL business.

"I'm not at liberty to discuss it. Why not ask him
yourself when he gets back?"

"When will that be?"

"Hard to say," he said with a shrug. He seemed to
be enjoying her growing agitation. "Should I tell him
you've been by asking a lot of questions? Men usually
like to know when a beautiful woman's been poking
around in their life."

Kelly slapped a business card on his desk. "Yes, indeed, you be sure to tell Michael that I came by. And
tell him that I am interested in chartering a boat, but
only if he's at the helm."

"Got it," Greg said, his grin spreading.

She was at the door, when he called after her. She turned around and saw him studying her card.

"If things don't work out between you and Michael," he said, "you give me a call. Something tells me you're the kind of woman who only comes around once in a man's lifetime."

She laughed. "Tell that to Michael. See what he says."

His dark, serious gaze never wavered. "I just might do that."

Oh, my, Kelly thought. Greg Keith might be confined to a wheelchair, but he could definitely give a woman a run for her money. If he reported their encounter to Michael the way she intended, she'd have to reciprocate by finding him a woman who'd be up to the challenge.

Michael was still in a daze when he got back from Washington. The admiral had been extraordinarily persuasive. Michael had left his office with a promotion to lieutenant commander and a job in the counterterrorism intelligence unit, working out of Boston. Being able to stay close to his family had sealed the deal. His days of fishing were pretty much over. He'd enjoyed the work, but he couldn't honestly say he regretted the dramatic turn things had taken during his Pentagon visit.

Now he just had to get Kelly on board. En route to her place, he took three detours: one to a jeweler's, one to a florist's and one to Greg's office to resign.

Greg took one look at the bouquet and grinned. "For me? You shouldn't have."

"Very funny."

"I don't suppose those are for Kelly Andrews, are they?"

Michael froze in place. "What do you know about Kelly?"

"She stopped by while you were gone. She wanted to charter a fishing boat for the day, with you as captain."

"Are you serious?" he asked incredulously.

"I am. She seemed to be, too. Attractive woman. You going after her?"

Michael nodded. He was definitely going after her, though before he proposed, he might ask what the hell she thought she'd been up to the past couple of weeks. If he didn't know for a fact that she believed in the direct approach, he might have concluded she'd been deliberately taunting him.

Greg gave him a penetrating look. "I assume I can cross you off my list of available captains, then?"

"In more ways than one," Michael said. "I really appreciate you giving me a job, Greg. It helped to get my confidence back in ways I can't even begin to explain."

"You staying in the navy?"

Michael nodded. "I'm just discovering that there's more than one way to skin an enemy. You ought to think about that."

"Not me. I like my laid-back lifestyle. You go on and get the bad guys." He winked. "And while you're at it, good luck with getting the girl."

"Thanks, pal. I'll be by from time to time and I'm sure I'll see you at the pub."

"Count on it."

From the office, Michael headed for home to change,

then went straight to Kelly's. When he finally showed up at her door, he was in his dress uniform and carrying a bouquet of spring flowers that had cost an arm and a leg in midwinter.

When she opened the door, there was a brief moment when he thought she might turn right around and slam it in his face. Instead, she squared her shoulders and stood fast. That little display of courage made him want to scoop her up and kiss her, but he resisted the urge.

"Can I help you?" she asked.

She spoke in a cool tone that didn't quite go along with her recent forays into all the corners of his life. Still, it was disconcerting. Suddenly hesitant, he thrust the flowers toward her and said, "I brought you these."

She accepted them with apparent reluctance, breathed in the sweet scent, then looked at him over the extravagant bouquet. "Why?"

He shifted uneasily at her lack of enthusiasm. "Could we go inside?" He didn't want a lot of witnesses if she turned him down flat.

She shook her head. "I don't think so. I see you're wearing your uniform. Does that mean you're going back to work for the navy?"

He nodded. "I'll tell you about that in a minute. The important thing is, I'm gainfully employed again."

"I thought you were gainfully employed by Greg Keith."

His lips twitched. "Yeah, I heard you'd paid him a visit. What's with the sudden desire to go fishing?"

"I'm exploring new interests. I thought it might be fun."

"And spending the day at sea with me had nothing to do with it?"

"Not really."

"Then why didn't you go through with the charter?"

She shrugged. "Changed my mind."

"That's not the way I hear it, Kelly."

"Men have a tendency to imagine things and then exaggerate," she told him.

"I see. Okay, then, let's get back to the reason I'm here."

"I figured you wanted me to know you'd gone back to work for the navy," she said. "Now I know. Did you really think that mattered to me?"

"No, but settling into a career mattered to me," he said.

"And fishing's not good enough?"

"No, dammit. Stop twisting everything I say. It wasn't about money, Kelly. Or about prestige. It was about self-respect. I need to do something that matters."

A flicker of understanding warmed her eyes, but then that shuttered expression fell back into place. "I'm happy for you, truly I am, but if that's all you came to tell me, I need to get going."

She was about to close the door, when Michael jammed his foot in it. "Wait."

She looked into his eyes.

"I love you," he said, blurting it out before he messed up again. "*That's* what I came to tell you. That and to ask you to marry me." He fumbled in his pocket and drew out a ring, a diamond solitaire that could never in a million years match the sparkle in her eyes when she was happy. "I know I'm the worst sort of fool and I don't deserve you, but no one will ever love you more or work harder to make you happy."

Her eyes unexpectedly filled with tears and made his heart wrench.

"Are you sure, Michael?" she asked, her voice shaky. "Really, really sure? Because this is it. If you take it back this time, I will never forgive you."

"I won't take it back," he promised, hardly daring to believe that he'd finally gotten it right. "I love you and I want to marry you." He searched her face, looking for a clue about what she was feeling. "If you'll have me. Will you, Kelly?"

She stepped toward him then and lifted her hand to his cheek. "Oh, Michael," she whispered, "all you ever had to do was ask."

Epilogue

"I still don't understand why you're in such a hurry," Bryan said to Michael as he ran a finger around the collar of his tuxedo. "I know my sister. If she hasn't changed her mind about you after all these years, she's not going to. There's no rush."

Michael frowned at him. He'd had enough trouble waiting the month Kelly had insisted it would take her to plan the perfect wedding. "I take it you're in no big hurry to get Moira to the altar."

Bryan stared at him blankly. "Married? Me and Moira?"

"You haven't even considered it? I thought you were in love with her."

"I am, at least I think I am. I'm not even sure I know what love is."

"And you're a psychologist," Michael said, shaking his head. "I pity your clients."

"Wait a minute, how did we go from discussing this rush into marriage you and Kelly are taking to picking apart my relationship with Moira?"

"Just a diversionary tactic," Michael admitted cheerfully. "Plus, if you were in love, you'd understand why we don't want to wait. Too bad, because I really thought you and Moira had something special. Mind if I introduce her to someone at the reception?"

Bryan's expression turned dark. "Forget about it."

Michael gave his best man a triumphant look. "*That,* my friend, is love."

Bryan looked vaguely bemused by his analysis. "Do you suppose that's why she kept dragging me into all those little churches all over Ireland? Was she trying to tell me something?"

"I'd say that's a safe bet," Michael said, regarding him with a pitying look. "Have a couple of glasses of champagne at the reception and ask her."

"Ask her what?"

"Ask her to marry you, idiot."

"Oh." A slow smile spread across Bryan's face. "Maybe I will at that."

Kelly stood at the back of the church and studied the man waiting for her in front of the altar, his back ramrod straight, his cane nowhere in sight. He was stunning in his uniform, but he was darned good-looking out of it, too. In fact, she preferred him that way, naked and eager. A blush climbed into her cheeks at the wicked thought. On her wedding day and in church, no less. She was surprised a bolt of lightning didn't strike her dead on the spot. Then, again, she was about to marry the man. Why do that, if he didn't get to her?

"You ready, pumpkin?" her father asked.

"Absolutely," she said without hesitation.

"Have been for a long time, haven't you? Michael's always been the one."

"Always," she agreed. "This just proves teenage fantasies can come true."

"Not without a little nudge from your brother," he reminded her. "You given him the credit he's due?"

She feigned a frown. "I gave him my best friend and he's too dense to make the most of it. Do you know Moira came back from Ireland without a ring on her finger?"

"Stop fretting about that," Moira said when she overheard Kelly's complaint. "It's your wedding day. Enjoy it. I know I intend to. I've already spotted three gorgeous men who came without dates."

Kelly grinned. "You go, girl."

Her father shook his head. "If I'm not mistaken, it's time for all of us to go. Isn't that the wedding march starting up now?" He leaned down and pressed a kiss to Kelly's cheek. "Be happy, pumpkin."

"I will be," she said with absolute confidence. She looked at Michael and caught his eye. His gaze was filled with so much love, it made her knees weak.

The Havilceks must have spotted it, too, because Doris Havilcek smiled, tears in her eyes, and even her husband looked as if he might shed a tear or two when Michael took several steady steps to meet her partway down the aisle and take her arm.

Behind them were the Devaneys—Ryan, Maggie and Caitlyn next to Sean, Deanna and Kevin. There was a third dark-haired man there, as well, a man who was unmistakably from the same gene pool. Kelly shot a curious glance toward Michael.

"Patrick?" she mouthed.

Michael nodded. "I didn't want to say anything, because I wasn't sure he would come. We went up to Maine and all but dragged him down here. We told him this was a family occasion, and that the Devaneys stick together now."

"Are you happy he's here?"

"I'm reserving judgment. Patrick has some issues. I don't want them affecting the rest of us. And before you ask, I am not getting into that right here when the priest is about to marry us."

Kelly grinned. "Oh, right. I almost forgot."

"As if," he said dryly. "You've been planning this day since the day you ignored my temper tantrum and walked into my apartment."

"Longer, actually," she confessed unrepentantly. "I love you, Michael Devaney."

Kelly repeated those words during the ceremony, then added, "And I will make your family mine—the Havilceks, and each and every one of your brothers and their families." She cast a look toward Patrick, who managed to appear removed from all the others even though only inches separated him on the pew from Ryan. "We're stronger together than we are apart."

"Amen," Michael said softly.

The priest beamed at them. "Then I now pronounce you man and wife. May you live in love all the days of your lives."

"No question about it," Michael whispered just before he kissed her until her toes curled.

"No question at all," Kelly agreed.

There were discoveries to be made and challenges to be met. The future stretched out before them with all its bumps and twists and turns, but their love would remain constant. She was sure of that. Gazing deep into Michael's blue eyes, she saw that he finally believed it, too.

* * * * *

PATRICK'S DESTINY

1

Spring came late to Widow's Cove, Maine, which suited Alice Newberry just fine. Winter, with its dormant plants, icy winds off the Atlantic and stark, frozen landscape, had been more appropriate for her brooding sense of guilt. The setting had been just as cold and unforgiving as her heart.

But she was working on that. In fact, that was the whole reason she'd come home to the quaint Victorian fishing village where many of her female ancestors had lost husbands to the sea. Eight years ago she'd had a bitter disagreement with her parents and left, determined to prove to them that she could make it on her own without any help from them.

She'd done it, too. She'd worked her way through college, gotten her degree in early childhood education and spent several years now teaching kindergarten, happily nurturing other women's children. She'd assumed there would be ample time ahead to make peace with her parents, many more years in which to have a family of her own.

Then, less than a year ago, on a stormy summer night, John and Diana Newberry had died when their car had skidded off a slick road and crashed into the sea. The call from the police had shaken Alice as nothing else in her life ever had, not even that long-ago rift when she'd been little more than a girl. Not only were her parents dead, the chance for reconciliation had been lost forever. So many things between them had been left unspoken.

From that instant, a thousand *if onlys* had plagued her. It tormented her that they'd died with only the memory of her hateful words echoing in their minds…if they'd thought of her at all.

Alice had wondered about that. She'd been haunted by the possibility that they'd pushed all thoughts of her completely out of their heads on the day she'd climbed onto the bus leaving Widow's Cove for Boston. While she had lived with a million and one regrets and too much pride to ask for forgiveness, had they simply moved on, pretended that they'd never had a daughter? The possibility had made her heart ache.

When their will had been read, she'd had her answer. John and Diana Newberry had left everything to her— "their beloved daughter"—and that had only deepened the wound. For eighteen years she'd been their pride and joy, a dutiful daughter who never gave them a moment's trouble. And then she'd gone and they'd had no one left, at least no one important enough to bequeath their home and belongings to. She'd had to face the likelihood that they'd been not just alone, but lonely, in her absence.

Coming home after the school year to settle their affairs, Alice had spent a lot of time in the cozy little house on the cliff overlooking the rolling waves of the Atlantic and tried to make peace with her memories...of the good times and the bitter parting. She'd realized by July it was something that couldn't be accomplished in a few weeks or even a few months. So she'd applied for a teaching position in Widow's Cove and come home for good in August.

This first school year in Widow's Cove was passing in a blur, the seasons marked only by the falling of the leaves in autumn, winter's frozen landscape and her own unrelenting dark thoughts.

Now, finally, in mid-April, spring was creeping in. There were buds on the trees, lawns were turning green and daffodils were swaying in a balmy breeze. She hated the fact that the world was having its annual rebirth, while she was as lonely and as tormented by guilt as ever.

Worse, as if to emphasize how out-of-step she was with the prevailing spring fever, her kindergarten students were as restless as she'd ever seen them. She'd broken up two fights, read them a story, tried vainly to get them settled down before lunch, then given up in defeat. The noise level in the classroom was deafening, an amazing accomplishment for barely a dozen kids. Her head was pounding.

Desperate for relief, she clapped her hands, then shouted for attention. When that didn't work, she walked over to the usual ringleader—Ricky Foster— and pointedly scowled until he finally turned to her with a suitably guilty expression.

"Sorry, Ms. Newberry," he said, eyes downcast as

the other students promptly followed his lead and settled down.

That was the wonder of Ricky. He could stir up mischief in the blink of an eye and just as quickly dispel it. He could charm with a smile, apologize with utter sincerity or assume the innocent face of an angel. A child with that kind of talent for leadership and spin control at five was destined for great things, assuming some adult didn't strangle him in the meantime.

"Thank you, Ricky," she said. "Since it's such a lovely day outside, it occurred to me that perhaps we should take our lunches and go for a walk." Maybe the fresh air and exercise would work off some of this pre-spring-break restlessness and she could actually teach something this afternoon. Maybe it would cut through her own malaise as well.

"All right!" Ricky enthused, pumping his fist in the air.

A chorus of cheers echoed his enthusiasm, which only made Alice's head throb even more. Even so, she couldn't help smiling at the children's eagerness. This unchecked excitement and wonder at the world around them was exactly what had drawn her to teaching kindergarten in the first place.

"Okay, then, here are the rules," she said, ticking them off on her fingers. "We form a nice, straight line. We stay together at all times. When we get to the park, we'll eat our lunches, then come back here. No running. No roughhousing. If anyone breaks the rules, we come back immediately. Is that understood?"

They listened to every word, expressions dutifully

serious as they nodded their understanding. "Yes, ma'am," they said in a reassuring chorus.

Alice figured they would forget everything she'd said the minute they got outdoors, but she refused to let the prospect daunt her. She'd been teaching for several years now. No five-year-old had gotten the better of her yet, not for long, anyway.

"Do all of you have your lunches?" she asked.

Brown bags and lunch boxes were held in the air.

"Then line up, two-by-two. Ricky, I want you in front with Francesca."

Ricky immediately made a face. Francesca was a shy girl who never broke the rules. Maybe she'd be a good influence, Alice thought optimistically.

With Ricky right where Alice could keep a watchful eye on him, they made their way without incident to the nearby park, which the school used as a playground. As the kids sat at picnic tables and ate their lunches, Alice turned her face up to the sun and let the warmth ease her pounding headache.

She'd barely closed her eyes when she felt a frantic tug on her arm and heard Francesca's panicked whisper.

"Ms. Newberry, Ricky's gone."

Alice's eyes snapped open and she scanned the park. She caught a glimpse of the errant boy heading straight for the waterfront, which every child knew was off-limits.

"Ricky Foster, get back here right this second!" she shouted at the top of her lungs. She saw his steps falter and shouted again. "This second!"

His shoulders visibly heaved with a sigh and he reluctantly came trotting back. She was there to greet him, hands on hips. "Young man, you know the rules. What were you thinking?"

"The fishing boats just came in. I was going to see if they brought back any fish," he said reasonably. "I told Francesca not to tell, 'cause I was coming right back." He scowled at the tattler. "How come you had to go and blab?"

"Francesca is not the one who made a mistake," Alice informed him as predictable tears welled up in Francesca's eyes. "You know that."

"But it's really cool when the boats come in." He gave her a pleading look. "I think we should *all* go. We could have a lesson on fishing."

Alice considered the request. Five minutes each way and they would still be back in the classroom in time for one last lesson.

And truthfully, it was hard to resist Ricky. If she had trouble ignoring that sweet face and coaxing tone, it was little wonder that the other kids were putty in his hands. Besides, she could remember what it was like when the air finally warmed and spring fever set in. There were too many tempting possibilities around the sea to sit still for long. At their age, she'd been just as bad, always eager to run off to the beach, to feel the sand between her toes and the splash of waves, no matter how cold.

"Why should I reward you for misbehaving?" she asked Ricky, trying to hold out as a matter of principle.

"It's not a reward for me," he said piously. "It would be punishing everybody else if you didn't let us go." He regarded her earnestly. "They don't deserve to be punished."

Alice sighed. "No, they don't. Okay, then, I suppose

we can go for a walk to see the boats," she agreed at last. "The key word is *walk*. No running. Is that understood?"

"Yes, ma'am," Ricky said, his head bobbing.

"Class?"

"No running," they echoed dutifully.

Satisfied that she at least had a shot at keeping them under control, she had the children throw away their trash, then line up. They looked like obedient little angels as they waited for permission to start. She knew in her gut what an illusion that was, but she wasn't quite prepared for chaos to erupt so quickly.

Ricky spotted something—Alice had no idea what—and took off with a shout, his promise to remain with the group forgotten. Three others followed. Francesca immediately burst into tears, while Alice shouted ineffectively at Ricky, then set off in hot pursuit. The remaining kids galloped in her wake, obviously thrilled to have the chance to run at full throttle without fear of disapproval.

As she tried to catch the errant children and their sneaky little leader, Alice wondered where in her life she'd gone so wrong. Was it when she'd decided on this outing? Was it when she'd come back to Widow's Cove? Or had it been years before, when she'd defied her parents just as rebelliously as Ricky had just defied her?

Whenever the beginning, her life was definitely on a downward spiral right this second, and something told her it was about to get a whole lot worse.

A dozen pint-sized kids thundered across the rickety, narrow dock straight toward certain disaster. Patrick Devaney heard their exuberant shouts and looked up just in time to see the leader trip over a loose board and nosedive straight into the freezing, churning water.

Muttering a heartfelt oath, Patrick instinctively dove into the Atlantic after the boy, scooped him up and had him sitting on the edge of the dock before the kid was fully aware of just how close he'd come to drowning. No matter how good a swimmer the kid was, the icy waters could have numbed him in no time, and his skill would have been useless.

Patrick automatically whirled on the woman accompanying the children. "What the *hell* were you thinking?" he demanded heatedly.

Clearly frozen with shock, cheeks flushed, she stared at him, her mouth working. Then, to his complete dismay, she burst into tears. Patrick barely contained a harsh expletive. A near drowning and a blubbering female. The day just got better and better.

Sighing, he jumped onto the deck of his fishing boat—which also happened to be his home at the moment—grabbed a blanket and wrapped it around the shivering boy. He shrugged out of his own soaked flannel shirt and into a dry wool jacket, keeping his gaze steady on the kid and ignoring the ditzy woman responsible for this near disaster.

"You okay, pal?" he asked after a while.

Eyes wide, the boy nodded. "Just cold," he said, his teeth chattering.

"Yeah, it's not exactly a perfect day for a swim," Patrick agreed. The temperature was mild for a mid-afternoon in April on the coast of Maine, but the ocean was cold enough to chill a beer in a couple of minutes.

He knew, because he'd done it more than once lately. The sea was more efficient than a refrigerator. And if the water was that effective on a beer, it wouldn't take much longer than that to disable a boy this kid's size and have him sinking like a rock straight to the bottom. He shuddered just thinking about the tragedy this accident could have become.

The kid watched him warily. "Don't blame Ms. Newberry," he pleaded. "I tripped. It wasn't her fault."

Patrick could have debated the point. Who in their right mind brought a bunch of rambunctious children onto a dock—a clearly marked *private* dock—without sufficient supervision? He scowled once more in the woman's direction, noting that she'd apparently recovered from her bout of tears and was carefully herding the rest of the children back onto dry land. Her soft voice carried out to him as she instructed them firmly to stay put. He could have told her it was a futile command. Children as young as these were inevitably more adventurous than either sensible or obedient. Besides, they outnumbered her, always a risky business when dealing with kids.

"Ms. Newberry's going to be real mad at me," the boy beside him confided gloomily. "She told us not to run. We were supposed to stay together."

Patrick bit back a smile at the futility of that order. "How come you didn't listen?"

"'Cause I was in a hurry," he replied impatiently.

Patrick understood the logic of that. He also thought he recognized the kid. It was Matt Foster's boy. Matt rushed through life the same way, always at full tilt and without a lick of common sense. "You're Ricky Foster, aren't you?"

"Uh-huh," he said, head bobbing. "How come you know that?"

"Your dad and I went to school together. I'd better call him and tell him what's happened," Patrick said. "You need to get home and into some dry clothes."

"I'll see that he gets home," the woman in charge of the group informed him stiffly.

"You sure you can handle that and keep an eye on the others, too?" Patrick inquired, nodding toward the brood that was already racing off in a dozen different directions.

Muttering a very unladylike oath under her breath, she charged back to shore and rounded up the children for a second time. She looked as if she'd like nothing better than to tie each and every one of them to a hitching post.

Patrick took pity on her and carried the still-shivering Ricky back to join the others. With two adults presenting a united front, maybe they'd have a shot at averting any more disasters.

"Let's take 'em all over to Jess's where they can warm up while you call Matt Foster and get him down here," Patrick suggested. He headed off in that direction without waiting for a reply. A firm grip on his arm jerked him to a stop.

"I don't think a bar is an appropriate place for a group of five-year-olds," she told him.

He frowned down at her. "You have a better suggestion?"

"We could take them back to the school. That's what

we *should* do," she said, though without much enthusiasm.

Patrick understood her reluctance. The school's principal, Loretta Dowd, had to be a hundred years old by now, and she wasn't known for her leniency. Patrick knew that from his own bitter experience. He'd been every bit as rambunctious as Ricky at his age. There would be hell to pay for this little incident.

"Miss Dowd knows about this outing, then?" he asked, guessing that it had been an impromptu and ill-advised decision. "Permission slips to leave the school grounds are all on file?"

She faltered at that, then sighed. "No," she admitted. "I suppose the bar is a better choice, at least for a few minutes."

"It won't be busy at this time of day," he consoled her. "Most of the fishermen came in hours ago. And you know how Molly likes to cluck over kids."

Jess's had been catering to Widow's Cove fishermen for three generations. Jess had long since passed on, but his granddaughter ran the place with the same disdain for frills. Molly served cold beer and steaming hot chowder, which was all that mattered to her regulars.

When Patrick and Ms. Newberry trooped inside with the children, Molly came out from behind the bar, took one look at the dripping wet Ricky and began clucking over him as predicted.

"What on earth?" Molly asked, then waved off the question. "Never mind. It doesn't matter. I'll have hot chocolate ready in no time." She looked at the teacher and frowned. "Alice, you look terrible. Sit down before you faint on me. Patrick, get the children settled, then for heaven's sakes go and put on some dry pants and a warm shirt under that jacket. I have some of grand-dad's I can lend you. They're hanging in the pantry on the way to the kitchen. Help yourself. I'll be back in a minute. While I'm in the kitchen, I'll give Matt a call and tell him to get over here to pick up Ricky."

Patrick knew better than to balk openly at one of Molly's orders. She might be his age, but she'd had Jess as an example. She could boss around a fleet of marines without anyone questioning her authority. Besides, one glance at Alice Newberry told him that she was in no condition to take charge. He'd never seen a grown woman look quite so defeated. He had a hunch that today's misadventure was the last straw in a long string of defeats.

He studied her with a bit more sympathy. Every last bit of color had drained out of her delicate, heart-shaped face, and her brown hair had been whipped into a tangle of curls by the wind. The fact that she was making no attempt at all to tame them spoke volumes. Her hands were visibly trembling, as well. If she wasn't in shock, she was darn close to it. He tried not to feel too sorry for her, since she'd brought this mess on herself, but a vulnerable woman could cut through his defenses in a heartbeat. Usually he knew enough to avoid them like the plague. This one had reached out and grabbed him when his defenses were down.

"Sit," he ordered her as he passed by on his way to the bar. Hot chocolate might be great for the kids, but she clearly needed something a lot stronger. He could use the heat from a glass of whiskey himself. He poured two shots and took them back to the table where she was sitting, then slid in opposite her. He wasn't the least bit surprised when she reacted with dismay.

"I can't drink that," she said. "It's the middle of the day and I'm working."

Patrick shrugged. "Suit yourself." He tossed back his own drink, grateful for the fire that shot through his veins. It was only a temporary flash of heat, but it was welcome and would do until he could get home and into his own dry pants.

When he glanced across the table, he found Alice Newberry's solemn gaze locked on him. He had a feeling a man could drown in those golden eyes if he let himself.

"I never thanked you," she said. "You saved Ricky's life. I don't know what I would have done if you hadn't been there."

"You would have jumped in after him," he said, giving her the benefit of the doubt.

She shook her head. "I couldn't," she said in a voice barely above a whisper. "I froze. It's like it happened in slow motion and I couldn't move."

"You only froze for a second," he said, surprised by his reluctance to add to her obvious self-derision. "It all happened very quickly."

"That's all it takes. In a second, everything can change. One minute someone's there and alive and healthy...the next, they're gone."

Something told him she was no longer talking about Ricky Foster's misadventure. Something also told him he didn't want to know what demons she was wrestling with. He had more than enough of his own.

Now that he knew who she was, he had a dim recollection of hearing the gossip that the new kindergarten teacher in Widow's Cove was returning home after some personal tragedy. Everyone spoke of it in whispers. Patrick hadn't listened to the details. They hadn't mattered to him. He made it a practice to keep everyone at a distance, to remain completely uninvolved in their lives. It was the one sure way to avoid being betrayed. He had no family in Widow's Cove and few friends. And he liked it that way.

"Yeah, bad stuff happens like that," he said neutrally, in response to Alice's lament. "But all's well that ends well. Ricky will be fine once he gets into some dry clothes. You'll be fine once the shock wears off."

She studied him with surprise. "You didn't sound so philosophical down on the dock. I believe you asked me what the hell I was thinking."

He shrugged. "It seemed like a valid question at the time." Now that the crisis was over, his temper had cooled and his own share in the guilt had crept in.

"It was a perfectly reasonable question," she agreed, surprising him.

"I don't suppose you have a perfectly reasonable answer, do you?"

She nodded. "Actually, I do. The children were getting restless at school. Spring break starts tomorrow. I thought a walk would do them good. The next thing I knew, Ricky spied the last of the fishing boats coming in. He begged to come and see what kind of catch everyone had. He swore to me that he'd stay with the group. Everyone agreed not to run. I took them at their word."

She shrugged and gave Patrick a wry look. "Obviously, I should have known better. Five seconds later,

Ricky spied something, who knows what, and forgot all about his promise. He took off, and the next thing I knew they were all off and running. I've been teaching five-year-olds long enough now to have anticipated something like that."

"Maybe so, but you couldn't anticipate Ricky tripping," Patrick replied, then conceded with reluctance, "Besides, the fault's as much mine as yours. I've known that board was loose since I bought the dock, but I keep forgetting to pick up some nails when I'm at the hardware store. I've gotten so used to it, I just walk around it. Nobody else comes down that way. That dock's supposed to be private."

She regarded him with surprise. "In Widow's Cove?"

Patrick chafed under the hint of disapproval he thought he heard. "I bought and paid for it. Why shouldn't I put up No Trespassing signs?"

"It's just unusual in a friendly town like this," she said. "Most people don't see the need."

"I don't like being bothered." No need to explain that the signs were meant as a deterrent for certain specific people, Patrick thought. If they kept everyone else away, too, so much the better.

He glanced up and caught sight of Matt Foster coming through the door. "Ricky's dad's here," he told Alice, making no attempt to hide his relief. "I'll speak to him and tell him what happened, then I'll be getting back to my boat."

"I'll explain," Alice insisted, her chin jutting up with determination as she slid from the booth. "It's my responsibility."

"Whatever," he said with a shrug. "One word of advice, though. Next time you think about taking your class for a stroll, think again. Either that or keep 'em away from the docks."

There was a surprising flash of temper in her eyes at the order he'd clumsily tried to disguise as advice. For an instant Patrick thought she was going to address him with another burst of unladylike profanity, but one glance at the children silenced her. Discretion didn't dim the sparks in her eyes, nor did it quiet her tongue. She looked him straight in the eye and said, "If the occasion ever arises again, I'll certainly consider your point of view, Mr. Devaney."

The fact that her meek tone was counterpointed by sparks of barely restrained annoyance pretty much ruined the polite effect he was sure she intended. Patrick shook his head.

"Just keep 'em away from my dock, then," he said, dropping all pretenses. "And that's not a simple request, Ms. Newberry. That's an order."

She was still sputtering indignantly when he spoke to Matt and then walked out the door.

Something about that little display of temper got to him, made his blood heat in a way it hadn't for a while. He savored the sensation for a moment, then deliberately dismissed it. All it proved was that he needed to keep his distance from Alice Newberry. If a woman could get under his skin with a flash of temper, then he'd been seriously deprived of female companionship for far too long. He suspected the kindergarten teacher with the tragic past and the vulnerable expression was the last woman on earth he should choose to change that.

2

The minute he'd taken a hot shower and changed into dry clothes, Patrick headed for the hardware store in downtown Widow's Cove. Today's near tragedy had been just the wake-up call he needed to repair the dock once and for all.

He'd let too many things slip the past few years, not caring about anything more than the hours at sea, the size of his catch and a cold beer at the end of a hard day. Ricky Foster's plunge into the ocean had shocked him back to reality. Unless he planned to move to some uninhabited island, Patrick couldn't keep the world at bay forever. And since he couldn't, he'd better be prepared for the intrusions, if only to make sure that no one could sue his butt off.

That cynical response aside, he had another pressing issue to consider—his disturbing reaction to Alice Newberry. He could fix the dock to keep some other kid from tripping, but he wasn't nearly as sure how to go about protecting himself from the likes of the teacher.

Maybe Molly would give him some pointers on that

score. The two women were obviously acquainted. He figured, knowing Molly, that asking questions would stir up a hornet's nest, but that was still better than risking another encounter when Alice Newberry could catch him off guard and get to him with those big golden eyes of hers.

At the old-fashioned hardware store, which was stacked from floor to ceiling with every size nut and bolt imaginable, along with tools for everything from fixing a leak to building a mansion, Patrick picked out the nails he needed to repair the dock, added some treated lumber to replace the boards that were warped beyond repair, then went up to the counter. Caleb Jenkins, who'd taken over the store from his father fifty years ago and modernized very little beyond the selection of merchandise, gave him a nod and what passed for a smile. "Figured you'd be in," he said.

"Oh?"

"Heard what happened on the dock," Caleb explained. "Board's been loose since Red Foley bought that dock thirty years ago. Told him a hundred times, the dang thing was a danger. Would've told you the same thing, if you'd come in here before now, but you've been making yourself scarce since you moved over here from your folks' place."

Patrick's grin faltered at the mention of his parents, but that was a discussion he didn't intend to have—not with Caleb Jenkins, not with anyone. He'd written his folks off, and the reasons were his business and his alone. The fact that they were less than thirty miles away meant he was bound to run into people who knew them from time to time. It didn't mean he had to discuss his personal business.

Instead he focused on the rest of Caleb's comment. "Doubt I'd have listened any better than Red," he told the old man.

"Probably not." Caleb shook his head. "You get old and finally know a thing or two and nobody wants to listen. Heard the boy's okay, though."

"Just wet and scared," Patrick confirmed. "I imagine Matt will have quite a bit to say to him."

"Doubtful. Matt never had a lick of sense. Always in a hurry, Matt was. Boy's the same way," he said, confirming Patrick's previous thought that like father, like son.

"You have a point," Patrick agreed.

"Matt lived to tell a tale or two about his narrow escapes. I imagine his son will, too."

"Hope so," Patrick said. He peeled off the money to pay for the nails and lumber, anxious to get home, finish the needed work and put this day behind him.

Caleb gave him a sly look as he handed back the receipt. "Hear Alice Newberry took what happened real hard."

"She was upset, but she'll get over it. After all, there was no real harm done."

"Doubt Loretta will see it that way," Caleb said, shaking his head. "How that woman ended up principal of a school is beyond me. She never did understand kids. You gotta let 'em explore and discover things for themselves. They're bound to make a few mistakes along the way, but that's just part of living, don't you think?"

Patrick hadn't given the topic much thought, since

he had no kids of his own and didn't intend to. "Makes sense to me," he said, mostly to end the conversation. He had a hunch Caleb was leading up to something Patrick didn't want to hear.

Unfortunately, Caleb wasn't the least bit daunted. "Maybe you ought to go by the school and have a word with Loretta."

Patrick gave him a hard look. "Me? Why should I get involved?"

"You are involved," Caleb pointed out. "The boy fell off your dock. Besides, a man ought to be willing to help out a woman when she needs looking after. That's the way of the world."

The old-fashioned world, maybe, Patrick thought. He wasn't sure he had any reason to get involved in Alice Newberry's salvation. As well, he had a hunch she could stand up for herself just fine. Aside from that brief display of tears, which he attributed to shock, she hadn't hesitated to speak her mind to him. She seemed to have some sort of fixation on personal accountability, too. He doubted she would appreciate him running to her rescue.

"I'll think about it," he told Caleb.

"Not much of a gentleman if you don't," the old man said, his tone chiding.

"If I hear Ms. Newberry needs any help, I'll talk to Loretta," he promised.

"That'll do, I suppose," Caleb said, looking disappointed.

"I imagine you'd go rushing over to the school right now," Patrick said, feeling the weight of the subtle pressure.

Caleb's expression brightened at once. "There you go. Best to nip this sort of thing in the bud. Be sure to give Loretta my regards."

"I never said I was going to the school," Patrick pointed out.

"Of course you are. It's ten minutes away. Won't take you but a couple of minutes to put things right with Loretta, and you can be back on that dock of yours in no time. You'll have done a good deed."

"I thought diving in the freezing ocean *was* my good deed," Patrick grumbled.

"One of 'em," Caleb agreed. "A smart man knows he needs a lot of 'em on the ledger before the day comes when he faces Saint Peter."

Patrick sighed heavily. "I'll keep that in mind."

He noticed that Caleb was looking mighty pleased with himself as he watched Patrick gather up his purchases. Just what he needed in his life…a nosy old man who thought he had a right to be Patrick's conscience.

Nevertheless, he drove to the school, then stalked through the halls that still smelled exactly as they had twenty years ago—of chalk, a strong pine-scented cleanser, peanut butter sandwiches and smelly sneakers. He followed the all-too-familiar path directly to the principal's office and hammered on the door, determined for once not to let Loretta Dowd intimidate him. He was all grown-up and beyond her authority now.

"Come in," a tart voice snapped.

Patrick entered and faced Loretta Dowd with her flashing black eyes and steel-gray bun. He promptly felt as if he were six years old again, and in trouble for the tenth time in one day.

"You!" she said. "I might have known. There's no need to break my door down, Patrick Devaney. My hearing's still perfectly fine."

He winced at her censure. "Yes, ma'am."

"I imagine you're here to tell me that it wasn't Alice's fault that Ricky Foster fell off your dock."

Patrick nodded.

"Did you take him from his classroom to the waterfront?"

Patrick barely resisted the desire to squirm as he had as a boy under that unflinching gaze. "No."

"Did you lose control of him?"

"No."

"Then I don't see how this is your fault," she said. "You may go now."

Patrick started to leave, then realized what she hadn't said. He turned back and peered at her. "You're not firing Ms. Newberry, are you?"

She frowned at the question. "Don't be ridiculous. She's a fine teacher. She just happened to make a bad decision today. Spring makes a lot of people do crazy things. We've addressed it. It won't happen again."

Thank the Lord for that, Patrick thought. "Okay, then," he said.

He turned to leave, but Mrs. Dowd spoke his name sharply.

"Yes, ma'am?" He noticed with some surprise that there was a twinkle in her eyes.

"It was very gallant of you to roar in here in an attempt to protect Ms. Newberry. You've turned into a fine young man."

Warmth flooded through him at the undeserved compliment. "I imagine there are quite a few who'd argue that point," he said, "but thanks for saying it, just the same."

"If you're referring to your parents, I think you know better."

Patrick stiffened. "I don't discuss my parents."

"Perhaps you should. Better yet, you should be talking to them. And to your brother."

"They're in my past," he told her, not the least bit surprised that she felt she had a right to meddle in his life but resentful of it just the same.

"Not as long as there's breath in any of you," she told him, her tone surprisingly gentle. "One phone call would put an end to their heartache." She leveled her gaze straight at him. "And to yours."

"My heart's just fine, thanks all the same, and I didn't come here to get a lecture from you," he said. "I left grade school a long time ago."

"But you haven't outgrown the need for a friendly nudge from someone older and wiser, have you?" she chided.

It was the second time in less than an hour that someone in town had seen fit to pull rank on Patrick. It was Caleb's push that had gotten him over here, and for what? He hadn't done a thing to help Alice Newberry, and he'd gotten another lecture on his own life in the bargain.

"Forgive me for saying this, Mrs. Dowd, but in this case you don't know what you're talking about."

"I know enough to recognize a miserable man when I see one standing in front of me," she said. "You won't be truly happy until you settle this."

"Maybe it can't be settled and maybe I don't care about being truly happy," Patrick retorted. "Maybe all I care about is being left alone."

That said, he whirled around and left the school, regretting that he'd ever let Caleb talk him into coming over here in the first place. Some days a man would be smart to listen to his own counsel and no one else's.

Alice had never been so humiliated and embarrassed in her life. Of all the boneheaded things she could have done...not only had she lost control of her students and let one of them nearly drown, she had done it in front of Patrick Devaney.

Everyone in Widow's Cove knew that Patrick had turned into a virtual recluse. He lived on that fishing boat of his, ate his meals at Jess's and, for all Alice knew, drank himself into oblivion there every night as well. What no one knew was why, not the details, anyway. There had been some sort of rift with his parents, that much was known. He'd left his home, about thirty miles away, and moved to Widow's Cove. That thirty miles might as well have been thirty thousand. From what she'd heard, none of them had bridged the distance.

Alice almost hadn't recognized Patrick when he'd emerged from the ocean dripping wet and mad as the dickens. His hair was too long and stubble shadowed his cheeks. He looked just a little disreputable and more than a little dangerous, especially with his intense blue eyes shooting angry sparks.

Alice remembered a very different Patrick from high school. Although she'd been two years older, everyone at the county high school located here in town knew each other at least by sight. Even as a sophomore, Patrick had been the flirtatious, wildly popular, star football player; his twin brother, Daniel, the captain of the team. The two of them had been inseparable. Now they barely spoke and tried to avoid crossing paths. No one understood that, either.

Alice hadn't been surprised that Patrick hadn't remembered her. Not only had she been older, but in high school she'd kept her head buried in her books. She'd been determined to go to college, to break the pattern of all the women in her family, going back generations, who'd married seafaring men, borne their children and lived in fear each time a violent storm approached the coast.

Too many of those men had been lost at sea. Too many of the wives had raised their children alone, living a hand-to-mouth existence because they'd had no skills of their own to fall back on. It had been such a bitter irony that her own father had been lost to that same sea—not in a boat, but in a car—and that he'd taken Alice's mother to her death with him.

Alice could still recall the heated exchange when she'd told her parents of her plans. They'd both thought she was casting aspersions on their choices, that by wanting more she was being ungrateful for the life they'd struggled to give her.

Maybe that was why, even when Patrick had been lambasting her for what had happened this afternoon, Alice had felt a strange sort of kinship with him. She knew all about family rifts and unhealed wounds. He, at least, still had time to heal his before it was too late.

Maybe they'd met so that she could pass along the message she'd learned, assuming they ever crossed paths again.

She was about to leave school for the day when the screechy public address system in her room came on with a burst of static. "Alice, my office now, please," Mrs. Dowd said in her usual tart manner.

Alice sighed. She thought they'd already been over today's transgression and moved on. Apparently she'd been wrong. Maybe Matt Foster had called and made an issue of what had happened to Ricky. Maybe he'd forced the principal's hand.

Gathering her things, she headed for the office, filled with a sense of dread. Even though living in Widow's Cove hadn't yet brought her the peace she'd hoped for, she didn't want to leave, and that was exactly what being fired would mean, since there was no other kindergarten class for miles and miles along this remote stretch of coast.

She tapped lightly on the principal's door, then walked in when the woman's sharp tone summoned her.

"There's something I thought you should know before you go off on break for the next week," Loretta Dowd said, a surprising hint of a smile on her usually stern lips.

"Yes?"

"Patrick Devaney was here."

Alice stared at her. Had he come to complain that she wasn't responsible, that she had no business being in charge of a classroom full of children?

"Why?" she asked, barely able to squeeze the word out past the sudden lump in her throat.

"I believe he wanted to save your job if it was in jeopardy. I told him it wasn't, but I think the attempt spoke very well of him, don't you?"

Alice nodded, too shocked for words. Patrick had come rushing to her rescue? He'd been furious with her. Obviously someone was behind it. Molly perhaps. Of course, as fast as news spread in Widow's Cove, it could have been anyone. Few people in town hesitated to share their opinions of right and wrong under the guise of being helpful. Someone had definitely given him a nudge, no question about it.

"Be sure to thank him when you see him," the principal said, a twinkle in her eyes.

"I hadn't planned—"

"The man dove into the icy water to save one of your students," Mrs. Dowd said, cutting her off. "And then he came charging into my office to save you. Don't you think the least you can do would be to take him some homemade soup as an expression of gratitude?"

Alice stared at her, trying to process this bit of advice. If she wasn't mistaken, Loretta Dowd was matchmaking. "What are you up to?" she asked, stunned that the woman even had an interest in Alice's love life.

The principal drew herself up and gave Alice one of her most daunting looks. "I am not up to anything," she declared fiercely, but the indignation came too late.

Alice could see quite clearly now that Loretta Dowd was a complete and total fraud. She was not the strict, unfeeling disciplinarian everyone feared. She had a heart.

"If you can't make soup, I made a fresh pot of chowder this morning," the principal added.

Alice grinned. "I can make soup. In fact, I made some last night and there's plenty left. I baked several loaves of bread, too."

"Well then, what are you standing around here for?" Mrs. Dowd said with her familiar exasperation. "Get on over to that boy's boat before he catches his death of cold."

"Yes, ma'am."

Relieved to have an excuse to force her to do what she'd been half wanting to do, anyway, Alice walked to her house, filled a container with some of her home-made beef vegetable soup, added a loaf of her home-baked bread to the basket, and headed right back to Patrick Devaney's private, No Trespassing dock.

Once there, she took a certain perverse pleasure in pushing open the flimsy gate and making a lot of noise as she approached his trawler. She wasn't the least bit surprised when he emerged from below deck with a scowl already firmly in place.

"Which part of 'stay away' didn't you understand?" he inquired, leaping gracefully onto the dock and blocking her way.

"I figured it didn't apply to me, since I come bearing gifts," she said cheerfully, holding out the soup and bread as she took note of the fact that there were several new boards in place underfoot. "You never mentioned the fact that you were in that freezing ocean because of me—"

"Because of Ricky," he corrected.

She shrugged at the distinction. "I thought some hot soup might ward off a chill. I don't want it on my conscience if you get sick because of what happened. Besides, I need to thank you for going to see Mrs. Dowd this afternoon. She was impressed."

His mouth curved into an arrogant grin that made her heart do an unexpected flip.

"I don't get sick," he informed her. "And I didn't go by the school to impress Loretta Dowd."

"Which makes it all the more fascinating that you did," she replied. "As for your general state of good health, having some nutritious soup won't hurt."

"You casting aspersions on Molly's chowder?"

"Hardly, but you must be tired of that by now."

The grin faded. "Meaning?"

She faltered. She hadn't meant to admit that she knew anything about his habits. "She says you're there a lot, that's all."

"You asked about me?" He didn't even attempt to hide his surprise.

The arrogant tilt to his mouth returned, and Alice saw a faint hint of the charming boy he'd once been. She wasn't here to inflate his already well-developed ego, though. "I most certainly did not," she said. "Molly tends to volunteer information she thinks will prove helpful."

He sighed at that. "Yeah. I keep talking to her about that. She seems to think she can save me from myself if she gets enough people pestering me."

"What do you think?" Alice asked curiously.

"That I don't need saving."

She laughed. "I keep telling her the same thing. It hasn't stopped her yet. Now we've both got Loretta Dowd meddling in our lives. She's the one who insisted on the soup. We're probably doomed."

"Don't remind me," he said. "I imagine Mrs. Dowd will want to know exactly how polite I was when you came over here. She and Caleb Jenkins will probably compare notes."

"How on earth did Caleb get involved in this?" Alice asked.

"He thought I should speak to Mrs. Dowd on your behalf."

"Ah, that explains the trip to the school. I guessed it wasn't your idea."

"Oh, I suppose I would have come around to it sooner or later on my own," he claimed. "The point is, there are any number of fascinated bystanders in this town. I'll hear about it if I act ungrateful and send you away." He pushed off from the railing and held out his hand. "You want to come aboard and share a bowl of that soup? Looks to me like there's plenty for two."

Alice hesitated. Wasn't this the real reason she'd come, to see if she and Patrick Devaney had as much in common as it seemed? Wasn't she here because of that feeling of kinship that had sparked to life in her earlier?

"Are you sure?" she asked. "You don't seem very receptive to company." She nodded toward the No Trespassing sign.

He gave her a steady, intense look. "It doesn't apply to invited guests, and where you're concerned, I'm not sure of anything," he said in a way that sent a surprising shiver of awareness racing over her.

"Want to wait till you are?" she asked, startled by the teasing note in her own voice. She almost sounded as if she were flirting with him. Of course, it had been a long time, so maybe she wasn't being as obvious as she thought.

"Hell, no," he said, grinning. "I've gotten used to living dangerously."

Alice laughed, then reached out to accept his outstretched hand as she stepped onboard. She noted that unlike the previously decrepit dock, the boat was spotless and in excellent repair. Every piece of chrome and wood had been polished to a soft sheen. Fishing nets were piled neatly. Apparently Patrick Devaney used the time he didn't spend socializing or shaving to pay close attention to his surroundings.

Below deck in the small cabin, it was the same. The table was clear except for the half-filled coffee cup from which he'd apparently been drinking. The bed a few feet away was neatly made, the sheets crisp and clean, a navy-blue blanket folded precisely at the foot of the bed.

Moving past her in the tight space, Patrick took a pot from a cupboard, poured the soup into it and set it on the small two-burner stove, then retrieved two bowls and spoons from the same cupboard. Alice was all too aware of the way he filled the cramped quarters, of the width of his shoulders, of the narrowness of his hips. He'd filled in since his football-playing days, but he was definitely still in shape. It was the first time in ages she'd recognized the powerful effect pure masculinity could have on her.

From the moment she'd lost her parents, nearly a year ago, she'd gone into an emotional limbo. She let no one or nothing touch her. She even kept a barrier up between herself and her students, or at least she had until Ricky Foster had scared the living daylights out of her this afternoon. Nothing had rattled her so badly since the night the police had called to tell her that her parents had driven off that road they'd traveled a thousand times in all kinds of weather.

Don't go there, she thought, forcing her attention back to the present. One appreciative, surreptitious glance at Patrick's backside as he bent to retrieve something from the tiny refrigerator did the trick. It was all she could do not to sigh audibly at the sight.

Don't go there, either, she told herself very firmly. She was here for penance and for soup. Nothing more. A peek at Patrick Devaney sent another little shock of awareness through her and proved otherwise.

Oh, well, there was certainly no harm in looking, she decided as she sat back and enjoyed the view. Even a woman living in a self-imposed state of celibacy had the right to her fantasies, and any fantasy involving Patrick Devaney should definitely not be dismissed too readily.

3

Patrick wasn't sure what had possessed him to invite Alice Newberry aboard the *Katie G.*, a boat he'd named for his mother as a constant reminder that people weren't to be trusted. For eighteen years he'd considered his mother to be the most admirable woman he'd ever known. Now, each time he caught a glimpse of the name painted on the bow of the boat, it served as a reminder that everyone had secrets and that everyone was capable of duplicity. It was a cynical attitude, but experience had taught him it was a valid one.

Maybe he'd invited Alice to join him because he was getting sick of his own lousy company. Or maybe it was because he had a gut instinct that she'd learned the same bitter lesson about humanity's lack of trustworthiness. Not that he planned to commiserate. He just figured she was probably no more anxious than he was to start something that was destined to end badly, the way all relationships inevitably did.

Oddly enough, for all that they'd had going against them, his own parents were still together. He supposed there was some sort of perverse love at work, if it could survive what they'd done to their own family. Funny how for so many years he'd thought how lucky he was to have had parents who'd stayed together, parents who preached about steadfastness and commitment and set an example for their sons.

He and Daniel had had a lot of friends whose parents were divorced, kids who'd envied them for their ideal home. Not that Patrick or Daniel had shared the illusion that everything was wonderful in the Devaney household. There were arguments—plenty of them, in fact—mostly conducted in whispers and behind closed doors. And there were undercurrents they'd never understood—an occasional expression of inexplicable sorrow on their mother's face, an occasional hint of resentment in their father's eyes—just enough to make him and Daniel wonder if things were as perfect as they wanted to believe.

In general, though, he and Daniel had had a good life. There had been a lot of love showered on them, love that in retrospect he could see was meant to make up for the love their parents could no longer give to their other sons. There had been tough times financially, but they'd never gone to bed hungry or doubting that they were loved. And in later years, his father had settled into a good-paying job as a commercial fisherman, working not for himself but for some conglomerate that guaranteed a paycheck, even when the catches weren't up to par. After that, things had been even better. There were no more arguments over rent and grocery money.

He and Daniel had been eighteen before they'd discovered the truth, and then all of those whispered fights and sad looks had finally made sense. Not that their parents had confessed to anything in a sudden flash of conscience. No, the truth had been left for Patrick and Daniel to find discover by accident.

Daniel had been digging around in an old trunk in the attic, hoping to use it to haul his belongings away to college, when he'd stumbled on an envelope of yellowing photos, buried beneath some old clothes. It was apparent in a heartbeat that the envelope was something they'd never been meant to see.

Patrick still remembered that day as if it were yesterday. If he let himself, he could feel the oppressive heat, smell the dust that swirled as Daniel disturbed memories too long untouched. To this day, if Patrick walked into a room that had been closed up too long, the musty scent of it disturbed him. It was why he'd chosen to live here, on his boat, where the salt air breezes held no memories.

He remembered Daniel shouting for him to come upstairs, remembered the confused expression on his twin's face as he'd sifted through the stack of photographs. When Patrick had climbed the ladder into the attic, Daniel looked stunned. Silently, he held out the pictures, his hand trembling.

"Look at them," he commanded, when Patrick's gaze stayed on him rather than the photos.

"Looks like some old pictures," Patrick had said, barely sparing them a glance, far more concerned about his brother's odd expression.

"*Look* at them," his brother had repeated impatiently.

The sense of urgency had finally gotten through to Patrick, and he'd studied the first picture. It was of a toddler with coal-black hair and a happy smile racing toward the camera at full throttle. He was a blur of motion. Patrick had blinked at the image, thoroughly confused about what Daniel had seen that had him so obviously upset. "What? Do you think it's Dad?"

Daniel shook his head. "Look again. That's Dad in the background."

"Okay," Patrick said slowly, still not sure what Daniel was getting at. "Then it has to be one of us."

"I don't think so. Look at the rest of the pictures."

Slowly, Patrick had worked his way through the photos, several dozen in all, apparently spanning a period of years. His mom was in some of them, his father in more. But there were happy, smiling boys in each one. That first toddler, then another who was his spitting image, then three, and finally five, two of them babies, evidently twins.

Patrick's hand shook as he studied the last set of pictures. Finally, almost as distressed and definitely as confused as Daniel, he dragged his gaze away and stared at his brother. "My God, what do you think it means? Those babies, do you think that's you and me?"

"Who else could it be?" Daniel had asked. "There are no other twins on either side of the family, at least none that we know of. Come to think of it, though, what do we really know about our family? Have you ever heard one word about our grandparents, about any aunts or uncles?"

"No."

"That should have told us something. It's as if we're some insular little group that sprang on the world with absolutely no connections to anyone else on earth."

"Don't you think you're being overly dramatic?" Patrick asked.

"Look at the damn pictures and tell me again that I'm being too dramatic," Daniel shouted back at him.

Patrick's gaze had automatically gone to the top photo, the one of five little dark-haired boys. "Who do you suppose they are?"

"I don't even want to think about it," Daniel said, clearly shaken to his core by the implications.

"We have to ask Mom and Dad. You know that," Patrick told him, feeling sick. "We can't leave it alone."

"Why not? Obviously, it's something they don't want to talk about," Daniel argued, far too eager to stick his head right back in the sand.

It had always been that way. Patrick liked to confront things, to lay all the cards on the table, no matter what the consequences. Daniel liked peace at any cost. He'd been the perfect team captain on their high school football squad, because he had no ego, because he could smooth over the competitive streaks and keep the team functioning as a unit.

"It doesn't matter what they want," Patrick had all but shouted, as angered now as Daniel had been a moment earlier. "If those boys are related to us, if they're our *brothers,* we have a right to know. We need to know what happened to them. Did they die? Why haven't we ever heard about them? Kids don't just vanish into thin air."

"Maybe they're cousins or something," Daniel said, seeking a less volatile explanation. It was as if he couldn't bear to even consider the hard questions, much less the answers.

"Then why haven't we seen them in years?" Patrick wasn't about to let their folks off the hook…or Daniel, for that matter. This was too huge to ignore. And it could explain so many things, little things and big ones, that had never made any sense. "You said it yourself, the folks have never once mentioned any other relatives."

Even as he spoke, he searched his memory, trying to find the faintest recollection of having big brothers, but nothing came to him. Shouldn't he have remembered on some subconscious level at least? He scanned the pictures again, hoping to trigger something. On his third try, he noticed the background.

"Daniel, where do you think these were taken?" he asked, puzzled by what he saw.

"Around here, I guess. It's where we've always lived."

"Is it?" Patrick asked, studying the buildings in the photos. "Have you ever noticed a skyscraper in Widow's Cove?"

Daniel reached for the photo. "Let me see that." He studied it intently. "Boston? Could it be Boston?"

Patrick shrugged. "I don't know, I've never been to Boston. You went there with some friends last Christmas. Does it look familiar to you?"

"I honestly don't know, but if it is Boston, why haven't Mom and Dad ever mentioned that we took a trip there?"

"Or lived there?" Patrick added. "We have to ask, Daniel. If you won't, then I will."

Patrick remembered the inevitable confrontation with their parents as if it had taken place only yesterday. He'd been the one to put the photos on the kitchen table in front of their mother. He'd tried to remain immune to her shocked gasp of recognition, but it had cut right through him. That gasp was as much of an admission as any words would have been, and it had stripped away every shred of respect he'd ever felt for her. In a heartbeat, she went from beloved mother to complete stranger.

"What the hell have you two been doing digging around in the attic?" his father had shouted, making a grab for the pictures. "There are things up there that are none of your business."

But all of Connor Devaney's blustery anger and Kathleen's silent tears hadn't cut through Patrick's determination to get at the truth. He'd finally gotten them to admit that those three boys were their sons, sons they had abandoned years before when they'd brought Patrick and Daniel to Maine.

"And you've never seen them again?" he'd asked, shocked at the confirmation of something he'd suspected but hadn't wanted to believe. "You have no idea what happened to them?"

"We made sure someone would look after them, then we made a clean break," his father said defensively. He looked at his wife as if daring her to contradict him. "It was for the best."

"What do you mean, you made sure someone would look after them? Did you arrange an adoption?"

"We made a call to Social Services," his father said.

"They said someone would go right out, that the boys would be taken care of," his mother said, as if that made everything all right.

Even as he'd heard the words, Patrick hadn't wanted

to believe them. How could these two people he'd loved, people who'd loved him, have been so cold, so irresponsible? What kind of person thought that making a phone call to the authorities made up for taking care of their own children? What parents walked away from their children without making any attempt to *assure beyond any doubt* that they were in good hands? What kind of people chose one child over another and then pretended for years that their family of four was complete? My God, his whole life had been one lie after another.

Patrick had been overwhelmed with guilt over having been chosen, while three little boys—his own brothers—had been abandoned.

"How old were they?" he asked, nearly choking on the question.

"What difference does it make?" his father asked.

"How old?" Patrick repeated.

"Nine, seven and four," his mother confessed in a voice barely above a whisper. Tears tracked down her cheeks, and she suddenly looked older.

"My God!" Patrick had shoved away from the kitchen table, barely resisting the desire to break things, to shatter dishes the way his illusions had been shattered.

"Let us explain," his mother had begged.

"We don't owe them an explanation," his father had shouted over her. "We did what we had to do. We've given the two of them a good life. That's what we owed them. They've no right to question our decision."

Patrick hadn't been able to silence all the questions still churning inside him. "What about what you owed your other sons?" he had asked, feeling dead inside.

"Did you ever once think about them? My God, what were you thinking?"

He hadn't waited for answers. He'd known none would be forthcoming, not with his mother in tears and his father stubbornly digging in his heels. Besides, the answers didn't really matter. There was no justification for what they'd done. He'd whirled around and left the house that night, taking nothing with him, wanting nothing from people capable of doing such a thing. It was the last time he'd seen or spoken to either one of his parents.

Daniel had found him a week later, drunk on the waterfront in Widow's Cove. He'd tried for hours to convince Patrick to come home.

"I don't have a home," Patrick had told him, meaning it. "Why should I have one, when our brothers never did?"

"You don't know that," Daniel had argued. "It's possible they've had good lives with wonderful families."

"Possible?" he'd scoffed. "Separated from us? Maybe even separated from each other? And that's good enough to satisfy you? You're as bad as they are. The Devaneys are a real piece of work. With genes like ours, the world is doomed."

"Stop it," Daniel ordered, looking miserable. "You don't know the whole story."

Patrick had looked his brother in the eye, momentarily wondering if he'd learned things that had been kept from Patrick. "Do you?"

"No, but—"

"I don't want to hear your phony excuses, then. Leave me alone, Daniel. Go on off to college. Live your life.

Pretend that none of this ever happened. I can't. I'll
never go back there."

He'd watched his brother walk away and suffered a
moment's regret for the years of closeness lost, but he'd
pushed it aside and made up his mind that he would
spend the rest of his life living down the Devaney name.
Maybe what that meant wasn't public knowledge, but
he would live with the shame just the same.

That was the last time he'd gotten drunk, the last
day he'd wandered idly. He'd gotten a job on a fishing
boat and started saving until he'd been able to afford his
own trawler. His needs were simple—peace and quiet,
an occasional beer, the infrequent companionship of a
woman who wasn't looking for a future. He tried with
everything in him to be a decent man, but he feared
that as Connor and Kathleen's son, he was a lost cause.

He spent a lot of lonely nights trying like the very
dickens not to think about the three older brothers who'd
been left behind years ago. He'd thought about hunting
for them, then dismissed the notion. Why the hell would
they care about a brother who'd been given everything,
while they'd gotten nothing?

He heard about his folks from time to time. Widow's
Cove wasn't that far from home, after all. And in the
past twenty-four hours, he'd heard far too many refer-
ences to his family, first from Caleb Jenkins, then from
Loretta Dowd. As for Daniel, Patrick knew his brother
was in Portland much of the time, working, ironically,
as a child advocate with the courts. Daniel had found
his own, less-rebellious way of coping with what their
parents had done.

Patrick sighed at the memories crashing over him

tonight. He concentrated harder on the soup he was heating, then ladling into bowls, on the crusty loaf of homemade bread he sliced and set on the table with a tub of margarine.

Over the past few years of self-imposed isolation, Patrick had lost his knack for polite chitchat, but he quickly discovered that tonight it didn't matter. Alice was a grand master. From the moment he sat down opposite her, his presence at the table seemed to loosen her tongue. Maybe it came from spending all day talking to a bunch of rowdy five-year-olds, trying desperately to hold their attention. She regaled Patrick with stories that kept him chuckling and filled the silence better than the TV he usually kept on as background noise. In his day, Ricky Foster would obviously have been labeled a teacher's pet, because his name popped up in the conversation time and again. Alice clearly had a soft spot for the boy.

"Then today wasn't Ricky's first act of rebellion?" he asked when she'd described another occasion on which the boy had gotten the better of her.

"Heavens, no. I'm telling you that boy will be president someday." She shrugged. "Or possibly a convicted felon. It depends on which way his talents for leadership and conning people take him."

"His daddy always lacked the ambition for either one," Patrick said. "I suppose in retrospect a case could be made that Matt had attention-deficit disorder. He couldn't sit still to save his soul. Maybe that's Ricky's problem, too."

Alice regarded him with surprise. "You know about ADHD?"

Patrick leaned closer, then lowered his voice to a whisper. "Why? Is it a secret?"

She blushed prettily. "No, it is not a secret. I just didn't expect..." Obvious embarrassment turned her cheeks a deeper shade of pink as her words trailed off in midsentence.

"Didn't expect a fisherman to know anything about it?" he asked, trying not to be offended.

"I'm sorry. That was stupid of me."

"Making assumptions about people is usually the first step toward getting it totally wrong," he replied. Then, because he couldn't resist teasing her, he added, "For instance, right now I am trying really, really hard not to assume that you're here because you want to seduce me."

The color staining her cheeks turned a fiery red. "I see your point. And in case there's any doubt, you would definitely be mistaken about my intentions."

Something about the hitch in her voice told him he wasn't nearly as far off the mark as she wanted him to believe. "Is that so?" he asked, tucking a finger under her chin and forcing her gaze to meet his.

"I came to thank you for saving Ricky," she insisted. She swallowed hard as he traced the outline of her jaw. "And for going to see Mrs. Dowd."

"I'm sure you believe that," he agreed, noting the jump in the pulse at the base of her throat when he ran his thumb lightly across her lower lip.

"Because it's true," she said.

Patrick deliberately lowered his hand and sat back, noting the sudden confusion in her eyes. He shrugged. "Sorry, then. My mistake."

Confusion gave way to another one of those quick flashes of anger that had stirred him earlier in the day.

"That sort of teasing is totally inappropriate, Mr. Devaney," she said in a tone she probably used when correcting a rambunctious five-year-old.

Patrick imagined it had the same effect on Ricky Foster that it had on him. It made him want to test her.

He stood up, picked up his empty soup bowl, then reached for hers. He clasped one hand on her shoulder as he leaned in close, let his breath fan against her cheek, then touched her delicate earlobe with the tip of his tongue. She jumped as if she'd been burned.

"Mr. Devaney!"

Patrick laughed at the breathless protest. "Sorry," he apologized, perfectly aware that he didn't sound particularly repentant. Probably because he wasn't.

She frowned at him. "No, you're not. You're not the least bit sorry."

"Maybe a little," he insisted, then ruined it by adding, "But only because I didn't go for a kiss. Something tells me I'm going to regret that later tonight when I'm lying all alone in my bed."

"You would have regretted it more if you'd gone for it," she assured him, drawing herself up in an attempt to look suitably intimidating. "I know a few moves that could have put you on the floor."

He caught her gaze and held it, barely resisting the urge to laugh again. "I'll bet you do," he said quietly.

"Mr. Devaney…"

"Since we're old schoolmates, I think you can call me Patrick," he said.

"Maybe the informality is a bad idea," she suggested. "You tend to take liberties as it is."

He did laugh again then. "Darlin', when I really want to take liberties with you, you'll know it." His let his gaze travel over her slowly. "And you'll be ready for it."

"Is that some sort of a dare?"

"Do you want it to be?"

"No, of course not." She shook her head. "I really don't know what to make of you. I expected you to be more…"

"Difficult," Patrick supplied.

"Distant," she corrected.

"Ah, yes. Well, there's still a little life left in the hermit. You'd do well to remember that, before you come knocking on my door again."

"I won't be back," she said emphatically.

"You think soup and bread are sufficient thanks for me putting my life on the line to bail you out of a jam?" he asked.

"Absolutely," she said. "And your life was never on the line."

"That water was damn cold," he insisted.

"And you were in and out of it in ten seconds flat."

He gestured toward the outside. "You want to dive in and see how long ten seconds becomes when you hit those icy waves?"

She shuddered. "No, thanks. I'll take your word for it. You were very brave. I am very grateful. Let's leave it at that."

Probably a good idea, Patrick thought, given the way she tempted him. Fortunately, before he could ignore his good sense, he heard voices and yet more footsteps on the dock. Apparently, no one in the whole blasted town could read, or else, like Alice, they were all starting to assume that the No Trespassing sign didn't apply to them.

Alice apparently heard the noise at the same time. "You obviously have company coming. I should go," she said a little too eagerly.

Given the choice between the company he knew and the uninvited guests outside, he opted for the familiar. "Stay," he commanded. "I'll get rid of whoever it is."

But when he stepped onto the deck, he saw not one or even two people who could be easily dismissed, but three, all dark-haired replicas of the man he'd come to hate—Connor Devaney.

"Patrick Devaney? Son of Kathleen and Connor?" one of them asked, stepping forward.

Patrick nodded reluctantly, his heart pounding. It couldn't be that these three men who looked so familiar were really his brothers. Not after all these years. And yet, somehow, he knew they were, as surely as if they'd already said the words.

"We're your brothers," the one in front said.

And with those simple yet monumental words, his past and present merged.

4

A part of Patrick wanted to slam the door and pretend he'd never seen the men on the other side. He wanted to go on living the life he'd made for himself without family ties, without complications. These three men represented all sorts of uncomfortable complications.

Too late now, he thought, looking into eyes as blue as his own. He could already feel the connection pulling at him. It was an unbelievable sensation, knowing that three men he'd spent the past few years wondering about were now right here on his doorstep. He had yet to decide if that was good or bad, miracle or disaster. More than likely he wouldn't know for some time to come. The only way to tell would be to hear them out, see what sort of baggage they'd accumulated, thanks to being abandoned by their parents, and learn what their expectations were of him.

He scanned their faces with an eagerness that surprised him, looking for signs of resentment or blame. He saw only a certain wariness that was to be expected under the circumstances. These weren't old high school chums who'd come to call, but brothers—brothers he'd last seen when he was far too young for the concept to even register.

The one who'd spoken first seemed to sense his turmoil. "Did you know about us?" he asked, regarding Patrick worriedly. "Or did we just come busting in here and shock you into silence by telling you something you didn't know?"

"I knew about you," Patrick admitted reluctantly. When his words caused a flash of hurt to appear in one brother's eyes, Patrick quickly added, "But only for a few years now. Before that…" He shrugged. "I guess Daniel and I were just too young when we left to remember. I'm sorry. You have no idea how sorry."

"Don't be sorry. You were barely two when you left," his brother said. "How did you find out? Did our parents tell you?"

Patrick shook his head. "Daniel and I found some old photographs of us as babies. The three of you were in them. We asked our folks about the older boys in the pictures, and after a lot of denial, they finally admitted you were our brothers. We couldn't get them to say a lot more."

"Yeah, I imagine we're not their favorite topic," one of the others said with a bitterness that seemed to run as deep as Patrick's.

"Can it, Sean," the third one said, giving his brother's shoulder a squeeze. "Now's not the time. None of this is Patrick's fault."

"Given how we're related, it seems a little odd, but I guess introductions are in order," the first one said. "I'm Ryan, the oldest. I own an Irish pub in Boston."

Patrick would have guessed that, not just from the few strands of gray in his black hair or the lines in his face, but because he was the obvious leader. He turned his gaze to the brother standing next to him, the one with broader shoulders and the quick tongue.

"And you?"

"I'm Sean, next to oldest, a Boston firefighter and the one who doesn't know enough to keep his opinions to himself." He gave Patrick a rueful half smile that didn't quite reach his eyes.

"Hey, I can relate to that," Patrick responded. "Whatever's in my head tends to come out of my mouth. Daniel, well, he's not like that. He was always the peacemaker."

Sean's half smile turned into a full-fledged grin. "Sort of like our Michael here," he said, poking the remaining brother in the ribs with his elbow. "He's such a pacifist, it's hard to believe he's an ex-SEAL."

Michael rolled his eyes, then stepped forward with a decided limp and held out his hand. "I'm Michael," he said quietly. "I'm just a couple of years older than you and Daniel."

"Oh, my, this is so incredible." The soft murmur came from behind Patrick.

He turned and stared into eyes shining with unshed tears. For a moment he'd forgotten all about Alice, but she'd apparently followed him up onto the deck when he hadn't immediately returned. Now he seized on her presence like a lifeline.

Needing desperately to hold on to something familiar, if only barely so, he reached for her hand. Alice held on tight, communicating surprising understanding and support. It was almost as if this reunion meant as much to her as it did to him. Once again Patrick wondered about her past and the sense he'd had that they had experienced similar losses in their lives—a loss of people, perhaps a loss of innocence.

"Can we go somewhere and talk?" Ryan asked. He glanced pointedly at Alice. "Or is this a bad time?"

"Absolutely not," Alice said.

She spoke quickly, as if sensing that Patrick might try to think of some way to put off this encounter until he'd regained his equilibrium. "Jess's is close. Why not go there?"

Since the unanimous opinion seemed to be that this conversation was going to take place, Patrick finally nodded. Jess's would be better and far less intimate than trying to crowd four big men into the tight quarters below deck on his boat, and the chill in the night air made sitting on deck an uncomfortable alternative, although it might have the effect of shortening the encounter.

Still, Ryan waited, watching him sympathetically. "Is this okay with you?" he asked Patrick. "I know we've barged in here without warning, but we've waited a long time for this moment. We weren't absolutely certain we had the right man, but one look at you and there was little question that you're our brother. We'd really like you to fill us in on some things."

Patrick fought off doubts and reminded himself that he'd always preferred to confront things head-on. "Sure, why not?" he said, as if the prospect of a beer and a little get-acquainted chitchat were of no consequence. Admittedly he had a great deal of curiosity about these men who were his brothers. He might as well satisfy it, now that the opportunity had presented itself.

Besides, there was something reassuringly solid and normal about the three older Devaneys. He'd learned a lot about judging people since leaving home. He could tell at first glance that these were men of character. One of them had been a SEAL, for heaven's sake. If that didn't speak of courage and honor, what did? Maybe it was possible to outfox the Devaney bad blood, after all. If so, he wanted to know how.

As he led the procession toward Jess's, his steps dragged. Even though he'd satisfied himself that this was the thing to do, he couldn't deny feeling a certain amount of dread. What if things were even worse for his brothers than he'd imagined? What if they bore scars from being left behind? What if they blamed him, right along with their parents? Not that it would be a rational blame, since he and Daniel had been little more than babies, but in a volatile situation, logic and reason seldom mattered. Though he didn't even know them, he found that he desperately wanted them to accept him, and that terrified him. Discovering his parents' betrayal had taught him never to expect or need too much from anyone. Better to be a loner than to be hurt like that ever again.

Besides, his brothers had said they were here to fill in the blanks in their lives, not to answer all of his thousand and one questions.

With Patrick lost in thought, Alice kept up a barrage of inconsequential, nonstop chatter, mostly about Widow's Cove's history. It helped to defuse the tension as they made their way to Jess's.

As they neared the bar, they could hear the jukebox blasting. That, too, could be an inadvertent blessing, Patrick concluded. It was going to make real conversation difficult, if not impossible. And at this time of the evening on a typical Friday, Jess's was usually packed and noisy. Maybe they wouldn't even find a free table, Patrick thought, in one last hopeful bid to put this encounter off until tomorrow…or maybe forever. Maybe Daniel had it right, after all. Maybe it was better to keep his head buried in the sand. Maybe these strangers who claimed to be his brothers would go away. Sure, his curiosity wouldn't be satisfied, but what did that matter really? He'd made it through more than twenty years without having them in his life, and vice versa.

His halfhearted hope for a quick end to the evening was promptly dashed. He wasn't entirely sure how Alice managed it, but with a few whispered words to Molly, a table was magically cleared. Then Alice gave his hand one last reassuring squeeze. "I'll leave you with your brothers."

Fighting panic, Patrick gazed into her eyes. "Don't."

"You'll be fine," she assured him. "Obviously, I don't know the whole story, but I heard enough to know that this must be a life-altering moment for all of you. I don't belong here in the middle of it."

"I want you to stay," he said, needing some sort of familiar lifeline, someone from the world he'd made for himself to steady him as it rocked on its axis.

"It's okay," Ryan assured her. "If Patrick wants you here, it's fine with us."

Still, Alice shook her head and extracted her hand

from the death grip Patrick had on it. "Thanks, but I need to get home. I'm glad I got to meet you, though."

Ryan nodded. "Perhaps we'll meet again one day," he said, then headed over to join the others.

Still, Patrick held back. "I never thanked you for the soup," he protested with ridiculous urgency, just to keep her there and talking.

She grinned at that, obviously seeing straight through him. "And now you have."

She pushed him none too gently toward the table where his brothers were already seated. Patrick sighed and let her go, but his gaze followed her as she left the bar. Only then did he suck in a deep breath and go to join his brothers, pulling up a chair at the end of the booth rather than sliding into the vacant spot they'd left next to Michael.

"Pretty woman," Ryan observed. "Is she someone special?"

"I barely know her," Patrick said, forcing his attention to the three men seated opposite him like some sort of military tribunal. He should have slipped into the booth, he realized belatedly, made himself one of them, instead of an outsider. The symbolism was unmistakable. He wondered if they were aware of it.

Fascinated with the three men despite himself, he studied them. As Ryan had noted, there was no question about the family resemblance. All had the pitch-black hair and blue eyes of their Irish ancestors. He'd seen enough pictures of past generations—if not of this one—to know that Devaney men tended to be handsome rogues. Ryan's hair was a bit longer than the others and had those few errant strands of gray creeping in. He also had a tiny scar at the corner of his mouth.

Suddenly, completely out of the blue, a memory slammed into Patrick's head. There had been an argument, some sort of dispute between him and Daniel over a toy dump truck. Ryan had tried to mediate. Turning his temper on Ryan, Patrick had thrown the truck at him and split his lip. The image, obviously buried in his subconscious for years, was as clear now as if it had happened yesterday.

Tears swimming in his eyes, he swallowed hard and pointed at the scar. "I did that to you, didn't I? I threw a truck at you."

Surprise flickered in Ryan's eyes, then amusement. "I'll be damned. I'd forgotten that," he said, touching the scar as if he'd also forgotten its existence.

"You planning on getting even at this late date?" Patrick inquired warily.

Ryan rubbed his face. "Too late for that. I've been living with this face for a lot of years now. I'm used to it."

"Besides, Maggie thinks the scar's sexy," Sean chimed in with a grin.

"Maggie?" Patrick asked.

"His wife," Sean explained. "How he caught a wonderful woman like Maggie is beyond me, but I think that scar played a part in it."

Ryan laughed. "Could be. She does seem to be fond of kissing me, at any rate. I should probably thank you, Patrick, but I guess I'll let my wife do that when she meets you."

Patrick froze at the implication that they were here

for more than some very brief get-acquainted meet-ing. This invasion of his turf was disturbing enough. He wasn't ready by a long shot for wives and maybe even kids.

He regarded his brothers warily. "What are you talk-ing about?"

"I'm getting married," Michael explained. "That's why we picked this particular time to come looking for you."

"How long have you known where I was?"

Apparently, Ryan heard the tension in his voice. "Not that long. Honest. Besides, Michael was badly injured when Sean and I first found him. He wanted to be on his feet again before we came up here to see if we had the right man."

Patrick remembered the noticeable limp. "What hap-pened?"

"A sniper attack," Michael said succinctly. "It ended my career as a SEAL. It's taken me a while to come to grips with that. In the meantime, I've been a bear to be around."

"That's an understatement. He was being a total pain in the butt till his physical therapist badgered him into getting out of his wheelchair just so he could catch her," Sean teased. "Talk about motivation. Kelly was damn good at it."

"Very funny," Michael retorted. "The bottom line is Kelly and I are getting married, and we'd all like you to come back to Boston next week for the wedding. That way we'll all have a chance to get to know each other. Daniel, too."

Patrick instinctively shook his head. As much as he'd

thought about this moment, things were moving too fast for him. "I don't think so," he said, leaving aside the question of Daniel. The prospect of exchanging whatever tight-knit family ties they'd managed to forge for the ones he'd already broken held no appeal. Seeing them now was one thing. Exchanging an occasional Christmas card might be nice. But anything more was impossible.

Ryan regarded him with sympathy. "We're not a bad lot," he reassured Patrick. "And it's not as if we've been plotting and scheming together against you because you stayed with the folks and we didn't."

"I'm not worried about that," Patrick said. If only they knew how devastating it had been to learn that their parents weren't the models of decency that he'd always believed them to be.

"Really?" Sean asked skeptically. "I'm not sure the thought wouldn't have crossed my mind if I were in your position."

"That's because you're a cynic, Sean," Michael accused.

"Maybe he hates us for showing up here," Sean said, not backing down.

"I don't even know you," Patrick said. "As for hating you, why would I? You didn't do anything. If anything, you guys were the victims."

Ryan grinned. "What do you know? A Devaney with an open mind. Now that's something new."

"Oh, put a sock in it," Sean said good-naturedly.

Patrick listened to the bantering with amazement. "Can I ask you something?"

"Anything," Michael told him.

"After Mom and Dad took off with us, did you guys stick together? You seem so close, like the way Daniel and I used to be before…well, just before."

The three exchanged a significant look that spoke volumes. It was Ryan who responded. "No. We were separated and put into foster care."

Patrick got a sick feeling in the pit of his stomach. "With good families, at least?"

"My foster folks were the best," Michael said. "You'll meet them at the wedding. I've already filled them in about you. They can't wait to add another Devaney to the family. Hell, they've even opened their arms to these guys. Obviously, they're saints."

Ryan and Sean nodded. "That they are," Ryan said.

"Michael really lucked out in the foster family department," Sean said. "Mine were okay, but they were doing a job, you know what I mean?"

When Ryan remained silent, Patrick got the message. "You had a bad experience?"

"More like a dozen of them," Ryan said, though the words were expressed with surprisingly little evidence of bitterness. "But that got me to where I am now, so I have no reason to complain, I suppose. Not that I would have said that a few years ago. Meeting Maggie changed my outlook on a lot of things."

Patrick's anger at their parents deepened. "I'm sorry."

"Not your fault," Ryan said.

"Were you all in touch, at least?"

"Not until a few years ago for Ryan and Sean, and in my case, a few months ago," Michael told him. "Like I said, they tracked me down at a bad time in my life, right after my knee and thigh were shattered by that sniper and I was told I'd probably never walk again, much less go back to work as a SEAL."

"I'm amazed. You seem so well adjusted and so comfortable with each other," Patrick said. "I thought maybe…well, that you'd lucked out."

"Are you saying you didn't?" Ryan asked, his gaze sharpening. "What happened? Our folks didn't abuse you, did they?"

There was a protective note in his voice that stunned Patrick. "No," he said at once, not wanting them to get the wrong idea about his disenchantment with their parents. "Far from it. Daniel and I had it okay, actually. Mom and Dad did their best for us. Dad worked hard. I guess we were a typical family until Daniel and I found out about you guys. Then things kind of fell apart, at least for me. I couldn't believe what they'd done to you. They refused to offer one word of explanation or apology, so I took off and moved over here. I've seen Daniel once or twice in the past few years, but I haven't seen or spoken to Mom or Dad since I walked out. I don't think I'll ever be able to look them in the eyes again."

"You left because of us?" Sean said, sounding surprised.

Patrick nodded. "What they did, whatever reason they thought they had for doing it, it was wrong. It made me question everything I'd ever felt for them."

"That must have been hard," Michael said.

He was regarding Patrick with that sympathetic look that was beginning to get on his nerves. Why should his brothers feel sorry for him? They'd apparently gone through hell—or at least Ryan had—while Patrick had had a comparatively normal childhood. Evidently, though, they didn't want or expect his sympathy.

It was all too damn confusing. He suddenly wanted nothing more than to get back to his boat, to walk away from all of the conflicting emotions roiling around inside him. As for going to Boston for the wedding of a man he'd just met—or felt as if he had—forget it. It wasn't going to happen.

He stood up. "Look, I don't mean to be rude, but I honestly don't know why you came here. It can't be because you want another brother in your lives, especially one who got all the love and attention you should have gotten. And I sure as hell don't want to go to Boston and pretend that we're family."

"We *are* family," Ryan said quietly. "There's no escaping that. And we didn't come here to mess up the life you've made for yourself. We just wanted you to know that we're out there and if you ever need us, all you have to do is shout."

They were being so nice, so reasonable, it made him want to scream. He didn't deserve the way they were reaching out to him.

"Look, the way I see it, we're not family, not in any way that counts," Patrick said.

"We've got the same blood flowing through our veins," Michael told him. "Devaney blood."

Patrick frowned at that. "To tell you the truth, I've just about had my fill of being a Devaney."

"Because of what our folks did to *us?*" Ryan asked. "We're the ones who got abandoned, not you. We're the ones who have a right to be angry, not you."

"No, Daniel and I were just lied to our whole lives,"

Patrick said bitterly. "Maybe that's not the same as what you went through, but trust me, it makes you question just about everything—and it sure as hell doesn't make you anxious to try the whole family thing on for size again."

He was out of the bar before any of them could think of a response. Then again, maybe none of them even cared enough to stop him. This visit had been all about satisfying some innate curiosity, but they'd done that now.

All the way back to the dock, Patrick worked to convince himself that he didn't give a damn whether they left the same way they'd come, without a word to let him know. He sank into a chair on the deck of his boat despite the chill in the air and sucked in a deep breath. If he'd expected the salt air and solitude to calm him, he was disappointed. He tried to focus on Alice, figuring a beautiful, tempting woman ought to be able to occupy his mind, but that failed him, too.

No matter what he tried, he couldn't make himself stop thinking about meeting his brothers after all these years. He told himself that little instant of nostalgia back at Jess's was just that, a momentary glimpse of a past so long ago it didn't matter. He'd meant what he said—he'd had his fill of being a Devaney. The only one he missed these days was Daniel, but he'd made his peace with that, too.

Given the turmoil of his thoughts and his inability to put his brothers out of his head, he wasn't totally stunned by the sound of footsteps approaching once again.

"Who's there?" he called out with a resigned sigh.

"Your brothers," a voice—Ryan's—responded emphatically. "You're not getting rid of us so easily, and we have three women back in Boston who will kill us if we don't talk you into coming back for the wedding."

"Knowing Ryan's Maggie, she'll come here and pester you till you give in," Michael agreed. "And Deanna and Kelly are no slouches in the persuasion department, either. You may as well cave in now and save yourself the humiliation of letting them get the better of you."

"Why would they care? Why would it matter to any of you whether I'm there or not?" he asked, completely bewildered that he mattered to people who were essentially strangers. His own parents and twin hadn't pestered him to stick around when he'd left home. He was pretty sure his parents had been half-relieved to see him go after he'd put them on the defensive about the past. They lived less than thirty miles away and had never bothered to seek him out. After Patrick's initial lack of welcome, Daniel had called a few times, but even he had given up eventually.

But these three strangers weren't giving up. How ironic was that? They stepped into the dim beam of light coming up from below deck. Once again it was Ryan who responded.

"We want you there because you're family," he said simply.

"A helluva family," Patrick noted.

"Yeah, well, we're all getting used to it," Sean said.

"We've all learned just how important family is," Michael added quietly.

"And some of us had further to go in that regard than others," Ryan added. "Believe me, if you'd run across me a few years back, you'd never have caught me touting the virtues of marriage and kids. Now I have a wife I adore, a little girl who can wrap me around her finger and a baby on the way."

"Didn't the thought of all that terrify you?" Patrick asked curiously.

"You'd better believe it," Ryan admitted. "But once you meet Maggie, you'll see why I didn't stand a chance."

"I know you might feel a little awkward and out of place at first, but it won't last, believe me. Not with this crowd. Please, Patrick, won't you come?" Michael asked. "After that, if it's what you want, we'll leave you in peace, but at least you'll know where to find us if you ever change your mind and want us back in your life."

Patrick doubted it was possible they could leave him in peace. It had been a long time since he'd found any peace inside himself. And now he was more churned up than ever. He had a thousand and one questions he didn't want to have about these three brothers who'd popped into his life so unexpectedly.

He looked into three faces that were essentially mirror images of his own and nodded slowly. "What the hell? I've never been to Boston."

Michael grasped his hand and shook it, then abandoned the polite gesture and pulled him into a bear hug that pretty much knocked the breath out of him.

"I was as skeptical as you, when these two tracked me down in a hospital in San Diego," Michael told him, then grinned. "Turns out they're not so bad."

Patrick wasn't anywhere near ready to let go of his

skepticism. "I think I'll reserve judgment," he said stiffly.

"You've got every right," Ryan said solemnly. "Mind if we ask you one more question?"

"I imagine you want to know about Daniel and our folks," Patrick said.

Sean nodded. "You said you took off, so that must mean they don't live here in Widow's Cove. Where are they?"

"Living about thirty miles from here last time I checked," he said with undisguised bitterness.

"When was that?" Michael asked.

"Six years ago," he said without emotion.

"And they haven't come after you?" Sean asked, then shook his head. "I don't know why the hell that should surprise me. They never looked for us." He exchanged a look with the others. "As long as we're this close, do you want to go over there?"

Ryan's gaze turned to Patrick. "We could include Daniel at least in the wedding, or would that make things uncomfortable for you?"

"It's up to Michael. It's his wedding," Patrick said grudgingly. He didn't even attempt to hide his distaste at the idea.

Michael searched his face, then nodded slowly in apparent understanding of the unspoken message. "I think we can wait on contacting Daniel. At least we know where he is now."

Ryan seemed about to protest, then nodded. "Your call."

"I say we wait," Michael said.

Patrick couldn't hide his relief. "When the time

comes, I'll give you a phone number and an address. I doubt it's changed since the last time I was in touch with them."

Ryan studied him intently. "If you feel like telling us about your life, we don't have anyplace we need to be till our flight back in the morning," he said quietly.

Patrick suspected it wasn't so much his life they cared about, but the family that had excluded them. He wasn't up to it. It had been a day full of shocks, too many to end it by reliving one of the worst periods in his life.

He looked his oldest brother in the eye and promised, "Another time, okay?"

"That's fine, then," Ryan said agreeably. "We'll get on back to our motel. You going fishing in the morning, or can you join us for breakfast?"

Patrick longed to say he was going fishing. It would be the truth. That was usually how he spent his Saturdays. But something compelled him to make the time for these three men who'd searched for him. Whatever their reasons were, however little he wanted to care about them, they were his brothers. He knew what that sort of relationship could mean. He and Daniel had been close once, able to talk about anything, able to count on each other. He'd lost that, and he found the possibility that he could have that sort of tight-knit relationship again more alluring than he'd ever imagined possible.

"I'll be at Jess's at eight," he said. "If you're interested, Molly makes a pretty decent omelette."

"The omelette sounds good," Ryan said. "But the conversation sounds even better. We'll see you then, little brother."

Patrick watched the three of them walk off into the darkness with a sense of wonder. They looked as if they'd always been together, always been a team. And suddenly he felt more alone than he'd ever felt before.

5

With the tables filled with locals and tourists, Molly was moving at her usual brisk pace when Patrick wandered into Jess's. Her step faltered at the unusual sight of him at this hour on a Saturday morning, then she plastered a smile on her face.

"It must have been some night. You look like hell," she said cheerfully. "Go on over to the bar and I'll pour you a cup of strong coffee in a minute."

"I'll need a table," Patrick responded. "Four cups of coffee."

She nodded, clearly not half as startled by the request as he'd anticipated. "Over there, then." She gestured toward a more private booth in the back. "I'll be right there with the coffee."

His brothers still hadn't arrived by the time Molly brought the coffee, which meant she had no reason at all not to slip into the booth opposite him and study him with that frank, assessing look that meant she was about to start poking around in his life.

"Don't start with me, Molly," he said, hoping to forestall the inquisition.

"Is it a crime to want to know what's going on in the life of a man I consider to be a friend? Alice told me that those were your brothers who turned up here last night. I think I have a right to be curious," she said. Regarding him sympathetically, she asked, "Does Daniel know they've turned up?"

"I'm surprised you care what Daniel knows," he said.

"I don't," she insisted. "I'm merely curious."

"Okay, then, if it's only to satisfy your *curiosity,* he doesn't know," Patrick said tightly. "At least not from me. Who knows what someone in here last night might have felt the need to pass along to him."

She frowned at his testy tone. "Are you okay, Patrick? If you need to talk about this, you know I'll listen."

He shrugged off the question and the offer. "Why wouldn't I be okay?"

She frowned at him. "Is that all I'm going to get out of you on the subject?"

"Yep."

"Okay, fine," she said, giving up a little too readily. "Let's talk about you and Alice, instead."

Patrick glowered at her, but she knew him too well to be intimidated. It was one of his greatest frustrations that he'd lost the power to keep some people at a distance. Molly was the first to breach his reserve. Now Alice was gathering insights like little nuggets she could assemble to figure him out.

"I suppose you think that's off-limits, too," Molly said, when he remained stubbornly silent.

"It is," he said tightly. "Mainly because there *is* no me and Alice to discuss."

Molly rolled her eyes, clearly not buying it. "If you say so."

"I do," he said quite firmly. "And here come my brothers now, so make yourself scarce. Don't start poking and prodding at them."

"I imagine you won't object if I at least take your breakfast order?" she said tartly.

He grinned. "There you go, Molly. You could get the hang of being the polite hostess of this place yet."

"Don't count on it where you're concerned," she retorted, sliding out of the booth, then turning a beaming smile on his brothers. "Hi. I'm Molly. Your coffee's in the pot on the table, and I'll be back to take your order in a few minutes. As for him," she said, nodding toward Patrick, "try teaching him some manners."

"Too late for that, I imagine," Ryan said, grinning back at her. "And I doubt he'd take advice from us, anyway."

"You could at least try," she said.

"What did you do to rile the lovely waitress?" Sean inquired, studying Patrick.

"The lovely waitress is the owner of this place, and she takes after her grandfather Jess," Patrick said. "She thinks there's nothing that goes on in here or in all of Widow's Cove that's not her business."

"In other words, she was asking about us," Michael guessed.

Patrick nodded. "And when I refused to satisfy her curiosity on that count, she moved on to Alice."

"Which brings up a point," Michael said. "It never

occurred to me to ask last night, but would you like to bring her to the wedding?"

Patrick held up both hands. "Whoa! I barely know the woman. I don't think a wedding is the best idea for a first date."

"You've never even been out on a date with her?" Ryan asked, clearly shocked. "The two of you seemed pretty tight last night. You were awfully reluctant to let her leave."

"We met earlier in the day," Patrick explained, then told the story of Ricky Foster's untimely nosedive off his pier.

"Interesting," Sean said. "Our brother seems to be following our pattern of meeting his soul mate under unusual circumstances. Ryan's Maggie wandered into his pub after having a flat tire on Thanksgiving eve. I met Deanna after I put out the fire that destroyed her apartment. And Kelly came into Michael's life after he was shot."

"Alice is not my soul mate," Patrick protested, ignoring the fact that he had been more drawn to her than he had been to any other woman in a long time. That was chemistry, not some mystical connection. And whatever it was, he intended to ignore it, for sure.

"Denial," Michael noted, grinning. "Another part of the pattern."

"Yep, he's got it bad," Ryan teased.

Patrick gave the three of them a sour look. "Gee, if I'd known having big brothers was this much fun, I'd have gone hunting for you years ago."

Molly arrived just then, looking particularly pleased

to find them all laughing. "I'm delighted you all turned up when you did," she said.

Ryan looked up at her. "Oh?"

"Patrick was getting a little too hermity, if you know what I mean."

"Molly," Patrick warned, his voice low.

She gave him an innocent look. "Is something wrong?"

"You're treading on thin ice," he said.

"Is that so?" She stomped her foot on the old oak floor. "Seems solid enough to me." She turned to Ryan. "You seem like a man who knows his own mind. What can I get you?"

After she'd taken all their orders and gone, Ryan turned to Patrick. "Just how many women do you have in your life, little brother?"

"None," he said flatly.

All three brothers hooted at that.

"Look, did you come here this morning just to pester me about my love life? If so, I can leave now and still get in a few hours of fishing."

"I guess we're crossing the line," Sean said, though his eyes were twinkling with amusement.

"Definitely," Michael agreed.

"But this is such a fascinating topic, I hate to pass on it," Sean added.

"Maybe that's because we'd rather hear about the women in Patrick's life than talk about our folks," Ryan said wryly.

Sean and Michael instantly sobered, all teasing gone from their expressions.

"You've got that right," Sean said bitterly.

"Since I'm not crazy about talking about them, either, let's not," Patrick said. "We could talk about baseball. How do you guys think the Red Sox are going to do this year?"

Sean seemed eager to go along with the change of topic, but Ryan promptly cut him off.

"Locking the past in a closet doesn't work," Ryan countered. "Lord knows I tried for a lot of years. Now that I'm close to getting everything out in the open, I want to finish up so I can forget about it once and for all."

"There's just one problem with that," Patrick said. "I don't have the answers you want. Like I told you last night, the folks refused to answer any of the questions Daniel and I threw at them. As far as I know, they haven't opened up with him since I walked out. I think he'd have let me know if they had. If you want answers, you're going to have to look them up yourselves. I'll tell you where to find them, but that's it. Depending on what time your flight is, you could go today. It's only about a thirty-minute drive."

All three of his brothers fell silent at the suggestion. It was as if having finally neared the end of their long search, they weren't particularly anxious to start that final leg.

Ryan sighed heavily, his gaze on Michael. "Up to you. Do you want this over and done with before the wedding? Or will it ruin what should be the happiest time of your life?"

"I won't let our folks ruin anything for me," Michael said flatly. "But I still think we should wait. Finding them is going to affect all of us, and frankly I want all your attention focused on the wedding. If I walk into that church without the rings or miss the rehearsal dinner because you guys had your minds on what happened up here in Maine, Kelly will never let any of us forget it."

"You sure you don't want to make peace so the folks can be at the wedding?" Ryan persisted.

"*My* family will be at the wedding," Michael said emphatically. "The Havilceks and you guys are the only family I need to have there."

Ryan nodded. "Then we'll drop it for now," he told Patrick.

Patrick couldn't help the sigh of relief that shuddered through him.

"Since we've put the topic of the folks on the back burner for now," Sean said, a mischievous twinkle in his eyes again, "then I suggest we talk some more about Alice and Patrick. We owe it to our baby brother to see that he's on the path toward marital bliss like the rest of us. We can't have him up here living like a hermit, the way Molly says he is."

"Molly has a big mouth," Patrick complained, just as she arrived with the food.

"Watch it, buster," she said, "or you could wind up wearing these eggs."

"Just speaking the truth," he said unrepentantly.

"It's never wise to accuse your friendly neighborhood bartender of having a big mouth," Molly warned. "She might be tempted to spill all your secrets to certain interested parties."

"I don't have any secrets," Patrick retorted.

"I don't know. I think your brothers might be interested in knowing how lonely you've been since you left home. And while I never could figure out how you wound up with a brother as uptight and impossible as Daniel, I know you miss having him around."

He noticed his brothers watching him with a speculative look in their eyes and mentally cursed Molly for opening up that particular can of worms.

Patrick scowled at her. "There went your tip," he said, trying to inject a light note into his voice.

She shrugged. "Something tells me the rest of this crew will make up for it."

With that she strolled off to wait on other customers, who, Patrick surmised, probably managed to have their breakfasts served without the added ingredient of Molly's sass.

"Want to talk about it?" Ryan asked. "Is Molly right?"

"If you're asking if I miss Daniel, he's my twin—what the hell do you think?" he said heatedly. "Of course I miss him! But I'm not interested in mending that particular fence. He chose to stick by our parents." He looked his brothers in the eyes. "So you see, I know a little something about being shut out of the Devaney clan, too. And just because I was eighteen when I walked away doesn't mean it was a helluva lot easier on me than it was on you. I'd planned on college, but leaving home shot the hell out of that. I had to work. Fortunately, I love what I do. Being out on the water can be a hard life, but it's a good one."

Michael gave him a knowing look. "Amen to that. Not a day goes by that I don't miss being a SEAL. I almost took up a career as captain of a charter fishing boat, but the Navy convinced me that had a better use for my talents, even if it did stick me behind a desk. Still, I never miss a chance to get out on the water."

"You'll have to come up here sometime and go out with me," Patrick said, enjoying the sense of camaraderie he felt with his brother. Daniel had never loved the sea as much as Patrick did, and he certainly didn't understand Patrick's decision to become a fisherman rather than taking one dime of his college money from their parents.

Michael grinned at the invitation. "I'd like that. As for family, you have us now," he said. "We aren't your twin, but we are your brothers and we stick together."

Ryan nodded. "I went looking for these guys because I wanted to put the past to rest once and for all. I never expected to find men I felt connected to from the instant I laid eyes on them."

"Same with me," Sean said.

Michael nodded. "And me."

"And I feel the same about you," Ryan said to Patrick. "We've always been your brothers by blood, but from this moment on we'll be your family in every sense of the word, if you'll let us."

Patrick thought he'd long since passed the stage of being sentimental about family, but he found himself fighting against the unexpected sting of tears. He'd had no idea just how much he'd missed having family in his life until the prospect of having it again was dangled in front of him. Could he make himself reach out for it? Could he risk another hurt, another betrayal?

He honestly didn't know. And he had no idea at all how long it would take him to figure it out.

* * *

Alice usually spent Saturday mornings cleaning the little cottage she'd fixed up when she'd returned to Widow's Cove. She'd used the money she'd inherited from her parents to turn their home into her own. She'd once vowed never to set foot in it again and she hadn't, not until after they were gone. She had held on to all the anger right up until the second the policeman on the phone had told her about the accident. Then, in a heartbeat, she couldn't seem to recall why they had fought or why she had let it matter for so many years. Clinging to hurt had been cold comfort while she'd been all alone in Boston.

She sighed at the memory and tried to motivate herself to get busy with her chores. It didn't take all that long to run a vacuum through the four tiny rooms or to dust the few antiques she'd acquired since moving back. Still, it gave structure to her weekend, the two free days that always stretched out endlessly with way too many hours to think about the past.

She could hardly wait for warm weather to settle in for good so she could work in the garden she'd planned. She wanted spiky pink hollyhocks and bright daylilies to line the white picket fence of the seaside cottage. On the tiny patch of land in back she planned an herb garden. Her newly renovated home in Widow's Cove was going to be nothing at all like the dreary home in which she'd grown up. Her mother's taste had run to heavy drapes, plain white walls and sparse landscaping. Alice's walls were a cheery yellow, the woodwork white and white sheers billowed at her windows and let in lots of light and incredible shades of blue in the views of sky and sea.

Normally a thorough housecleaning, followed by an afternoon poring through gardening books, would have occupied her on a day like this, but today she was far too restless to sit still or even to clean. All she could think about was the amazing scene on Patrick's boat the night before, when his three brothers had shown up out of the blue.

As she'd followed him up to the deck and listened to their exchange, she'd been stunned, but Patrick's shock had been almost palpable. The fact that he'd turned to her and all but pleaded for her to stay had touched her more than she wanted to admit. It had been a long time since anyone other than her students had needed her for anything. There was something about a usually strong man turning vulnerable that could twist her inside out, too. She'd fallen just a little bit in love with Patrick Devaney at that moment.

As soon as she finished tidying up in the kitchen after her breakfast, she automatically reached into the closet for her cleaning supplies, only to put them right back. The curiosity was killing her. She had to know how last night had turned out. Patrick had been given the chance she'd always dreamed about, a chance at a reconciliation with his family. Had he taken advantage of it?

She wasn't quite brave enough to risk another visit to Patrick's boat, but there was someone who'd have the answers she was after. Because yesterday's balmy breezes were a thing of the past, and a cold front had turned the air wintry once more, she pulled on her sheepskin-lined jacket and headed for Jess's.

"I was wondering when you'd turn up," Molly called

out cheerfully when Alice stepped inside the dimly lit room. The window facing the street let in precious little light even on a sunny morning like this one.

"I'm not *that* predictable," Alice replied with a hint of indignation as she approached the bar.

"You are to someone who's known you since grade school," Molly said, then chided, "even if I don't see nearly enough of you these days."

Alice slid onto a stool and faced her friend. "I'm sorry."

"Don't apologize, just start coming around a bit more. You class up the place."

Alice laughed. "Hardly. If anything, having the kindergarten teacher around will kill your business."

"Since your visiting is such a rare thing, to what do I owe the honor…or need I ask? I imagine you came by to find out what went on with Patrick after you left last night," Molly said, giving her a sly once-over.

"Why would you think that?" Alice asked, as heat crept into her cheeks.

"Oh, please! When you were in here with the kids yesterday, you were watching the man as if he were covered in Belgian chocolate and you were in desperate need of a major fix of the stuff. You were no better last night."

"Don't be ridiculous!" Alice protested indignantly.

Molly grinned. "Then I suppose it is of absolutely no interest to you that he's sitting over in the corner, brooding over his fourth cup of coffee."

Alice barely resisted the sudden desire to bury her burning face in her hands. "He's here?"

"Has been for a couple of hours now. His brothers just left."

"Why didn't you say something sooner?" Snippets of their conversation came back to her. "Molly, what if he heard?"

"Honey, he's lost in his own thoughts. And I wasn't exactly shouting, you know. I do know a little bit about being discreet."

"Since when?" Alice asked, getting in her own barb. "Aren't you the girl who kept a record of the boys she'd kissed on the front of her English notebook in seventh grade?"

"I'm better now," Molly said primly. "All the juicy stuff about my love life is in the journal beside my bed." She studied Alice intently. "So, are you going to go over there or not?"

Alice glanced across the room and spotted Patrick in the corner. He was staring into his mug of coffee as if he'd never before seen anything so fascinating...or so sad.

Alice made a decision on impulse, something she'd done more in the past two days than she had in years. "Pour me two cups of coffee," she told Molly.

"Want me to slip a little Irish whiskey in his? It might loosen his tongue. I tried earlier, but I couldn't get a word out of him."

Alice was tempted, but she shook her head. If she could get a shy five-year-old to start chattering like a magpie, surely she could deal with one stoically silent male.

Coffee in hand, she crossed the room and slid into the booth opposite Patrick. He didn't even seem to notice her until she shoved one mug under his nose. Then he blinked and stared.

"Where'd you come from?" he asked, sounding cranky and not the least bit delighted to see her.

Relieved at the evidence that he'd heard none of Molly's teasing, she ignored the lack of welcome. "Are you asking in the cosmic sense?"

A half smile tugged at his lips. "It's too early in the morning for that."

"It's past ten."

Clearly startled, he stared at the clock over the bar. "How the hell did that happen?"

"The usual way. Time goes by, tick-tock, minute by minute."

"Very funny." He sat back and studied her, the tension in his shoulders visibly easing. "So, Alice Newberry, what are you doing hanging out in a bar at ten o'clock on a Saturday morning? Do the parents of your students know where you spend your free time?"

She bit back the first response that popped into her head. It would be way too revealing to admit that this was the first Saturday morning she'd ever ventured into Jess's. Patrick might have been lost in thought there for a minute, but he wasn't dense. He'd likely make the connection between her presence here today and his the night before. She didn't want him guessing that she was here to check on the outcome of his meeting with his brothers, after she'd made such a point of not intruding on it.

"Actually, I move from bar to bar so they can't keep up with me," she retorted. "This is my week for Jess's."

"How convenient for me," he said with what sounded like complete sincerity. "Have you eaten?"

"Hours ago," she admitted, almost regretting her early-morning habit of fixing a hearty breakfast to get her through a day that too often had no more than a few stolen minutes to grab a bite of lunch.

"Had enough coffee?"

"As a matter of fact, yes."

"Feel like going out on the boat for a couple of hours?"

"Sure," she said at once, telling herself it was only because he seemed eager for the company. "But for the record, I don't know anything about fishing."

"I know enough for both of us," he said, tossing some money on the table and grabbing his jacket. He shrugged into it, then held hers so she could slip it on.

He gazed into her eyes as he pulled her jacket snugly around her. "Besides, I just feel like getting out on the water. The salt air clears my head. The fish'll be there come Monday morning."

"If you want to clear your head, are you sure you want me along?" Alice asked.

"I wouldn't have asked you if I didn't want you there," he said. "Ask Molly," he added, raising his voice and nodding toward the woman who was blatantly eavesdropping. "I rarely do anything I don't want to do."

"That's true enough," Molly confirmed. "Have fun, you two. And you can both thank me later."

Patrick stared blankly at Alice. "Thank her for what?"

Alice knew but wished she didn't. "Believe me," she said fervently, "you don't want to know."

6

Patrick wasn't used to having anyone on board when he took the boat out, but Alice made a good companion. She didn't pester him with a lot of questions. In fact, she seemed perfectly content to sit on deck with a blanket wrapped around her and her face tilted up to the sun's rays. The wind was whipping her hair, but once again she seemed oblivious to the tangle.

"Your nose is getting sunburned," he said, tapping her gently on the tip of it before dropping down into the chair beside her.

She blinked in surprise, then yawned. "I think I dozed off."

"Must be my scintillating company," he said wryly.

She glanced around. "Not that I'm nervous or anything, but if you're sitting over here, who's piloting the boat?"

"I dropped anchor a few minutes ago," he explained.

"Where are we?"

"Not that far offshore, actually, just far enough away to keep from being bothered."

She grinned. "I gather you've concluded that the No Trespassing sign has lost its effectiveness."

He chuckled. "Given the parade coming down the dock yesterday, pretty much. From now on, if I want total peace and quiet, I'm moving out to sea."

"How come you invited me along, if you want total peace and quiet?"

"Maybe I knew you'd fall asleep the second you got a good dose of sea air," he teased, and pulled a tube of suntan lotion from his shirt pocket. He put a dab of the cream on his finger and spread it across her nose, then onto her cheeks. Her skin was so soft he lingered, reluctant to stop touching her. His gaze drifted to hers and lingered there, as well. The sudden and totally unexpected spark of desire in her eyes stunned him and sent a jolt of sexual tension racing straight through him.

Before he could think it through, he was following his instincts, leaning forward, his mouth covering hers. She uttered a faint gasp of surprise, then moved into the kiss with an eagerness that once again caught him off guard. The kiss turned greedy and hot in a flash that almost brought him to his knees. Who would have thought that the sweet little kindergarten teacher packed a wallop like that? He was shaky when he finally had the sense to pull back.

"Don't stop," she whispered, sending yet another jolt through him. She reached out and touched his cheek. "Please. It's been forever since anyone kissed me like that. It felt good. No, it felt great."

Her honesty rattled him. "Alice..." The protest formed in his head but died when she took the matter out of his hands by leaning forward and kissing him, holding on as if he had something to offer that she'd been missing for eons.

Who knew where it would have led had it not been for the blast of a ship's horn that shattered the silence. Alice was trembling, the color in her cheeks high, when he reluctantly pulled away for the second time.

"We aren't by any chance bobbing around out here right in the path of some cruise ship, are we?" she asked without any real evidence of fear.

"Nope. That was just a friendly greeting," he assured her.

"And a timely one," she said with obvious regret. "I don't know what I was thinking. I'm not in the habit of attacking men I barely know."

"I kissed you first," he reminded her, then added solemnly, "Besides, kissing isn't about thinking. It's about feeling." He tilted her chin up and met her gaze. There was no mistaking her need for reassurance, so he gave it to her. "I haven't felt like that in a long time, Alice."

She swallowed hard, her gaze drifting away, then back as she finally admitted, "Me, neither."

"Why is that?" he asked, wondering whether someone had broken her heart.

"Bad choices and the sudden realization that I needed to figure out why I was making them."

"Did you reach any conclusions?"

"A few."

"Care to share them?"

"And ruin your image of me? I don't think so."

"You don't know what my image of you is," he pointed out.

"You think I'm a little ditzy, a lot naive and very prim," she said.

Patrick chuckled. "That was my first impression. It's been changing quickly."

"I probably shouldn't ask about your current impression."

"Probably not," he agreed.

He looked into her eyes and instantly the laughter died on his lips. From the moment they'd met, Patrick had had the feeling that he was no longer in control, that something bigger had taken over. He'd blamed it on the circumstances of their meeting, on his brothers, on anything other than the attraction that was so obviously simmering now.

"So, what are we going to do about all of this, Alice Newberry?" he asked.

"Nothing, if we're smart."

Patrick grinned at that. "Then isn't it wonderful that no one's ever accused me of doing the smart thing? How about you?"

"I *always* do the smart thing."

Somehow he doubted that. He had the sense that she'd only recently made a resolution to do the right thing, but that she wasn't quite living up to it yet. He rubbed his thumb across her lips, saw the flash of excitement stir in her eyes once more. "Then I suppose one of us will have to change," he said.

Her mouth curved into a faint hint of a smile. "I suppose so."

He glanced sideways and gave her a lazy once-over. "You any good at change?"

"Not much."

"Neither am I." He reached for her hand and laced their fingers together. "How about this for now? There's nothing too dangerous about holding hands, is there?"

"Nothing at all," she agreed, leaning back in the chair and closing her eyes against the sun's glare, and quite possibly against his probing looks.

Patrick felt himself drifting off, oddly comforted by the feel of her soft, delicate hand in his much larger, rough one. What was it about a woman's touch that had the power to soothe when nothing else worked, he wondered.

The highly emotional meeting with his brothers faded from his mind. The complications ahead didn't seem to matter. All that mattered at this instant was the warmth of the sun on his face, the gentle rocking of the boat and the woman beside him. Life didn't get much better than this…unless, of course, a little hot, steamy sex was added in.

He fought a grin and resisted the desire to sneak a glance at Alice. Best not to go there. That one stolen kiss of his had unleashed unexpected passion in her. While he'd never been averse to uncomplicated, energetic sex, he had a feeling slipping into bed with Alice was going to be anything but uncomplicated. Besides, he'd hate to prove his brothers right about his level of involvement with Alice only a few brief hours after heatedly denying that he had any feelings for the woman.

Yes, indeed, he thought, his eyes clamped tightly shut, definitely best not to go there.

Alice could feel Patrick's gaze on her, but she absolutely, flatly refused to open her eyes. She was still simmering with embarrassment over her too-eager response to his kiss. What must he think of her? She'd all but crawled into his lap the instant he'd locked lips with her. She'd turned what might have been meant as an innocent, exploratory kiss into something wild and dangerous. She'd been so startled by her uncharacteristic reaction, it was a wonder she hadn't jumped overboard just to cool herself off.

Finally, when she felt his grip on her hand ease, she slipped her hand out of his and sighed. Risking a glance, she saw that he'd fallen asleep. His impressive chest was rising and falling with each steady breath he took. His long, dark eyelashes rested against his deeply tanned skin like smudges of coal. His lips—his magnificent, sweetly provocative lips—were curved into a half smile, as if he were dreaming something wonderful. She could have looked at him all day…and all night. The thought made her shiver with a sense of anticipation.

It would happen, too. She could feel it. The attraction wasn't one-sided. What she'd told Patrick was true. It had been so long since she'd felt anything like it.

When she'd first left home, she'd been so overwhelmed with work and difficult college classes that she'd had little time for romance. In her senior year, with the end of school in sight, she'd finally allowed herself the freedom to date and promptly fallen for the first man who'd asked her out.

Greg had turned out to be more interested in sharing her apartment than her life. She'd caught him at home, in their bed, with another classmate. An hour later everything he owned was on the lawn outside and he was sputtering protests and explanations even as she slammed the door in his face. It had taught her a lesson about getting involved too quickly.

Or at least she thought it had until she fell for the next man she went out with almost as rapidly. That hadn't ended quite as badly or as painfully, but it had been doomed from the outset. She would have seen that if she'd given the relationship a hard look at the beginning.

She'd spent the next couple of years taking a good long look at herself and her tendency to fall in love at the drop of a hat. It hadn't taken a genius to figure out that she was trying to find a replacement for the family she'd turned her back on. As the song said, she'd been looking for love in all the wrong places.

Until yesterday she'd thought she'd broken the pattern, but now here she was, all-too-fascinated with Patrick, and they hadn't so much as had a first date yet. Well, she wasn't going to make the same old mistake, no matter how tempting it might be. She was going to be smart this time, even if kissing him gave her a momentary sense of being connected and filled a huge void in her life.

Besides, there were flashing neon warning signs practically posted all around the man. He was a self-professed loner. He had major issues with his family. He was drifting through his life, quite literally at the moment, she thought wryly. He was the last man on earth she had any business falling for. She didn't even have to take one of those long, hard looks at the situation to figure that much out. Not that her hormones seemed to give two figs about any of that. Her body seemed to care only that he was a top-of-the-line kisser.

"Everything okay?" he asked, his voice husky with sleep.

"Sure," she said, a little too brightly. "Why?"

"You were frowning."

"Just wrestling with some old demons," she said, keeping her voice light.

"Who won?"

"I suppose that remains to be seen," she said honestly.

"Tell me about yourself," he encouraged, regarding her with unmistakable interest.

"There's not much to tell."

"You're from Widow's Cove, though, right?"

She nodded.

"Why don't I remember you from school? I thought I knew all the beautiful girls."

She grinned at the puzzlement in his voice. "I'm sure you did," she said. "I wasn't beautiful, and I was two years older, but I certainly knew who you were."

"Is that so?" he said with a hint of all-male arrogance.

She ticked off the obvious reason why the awareness had been so one-sided. "Star football player even as a sophomore. Advance placement in most of your classes. Girls falling at your feet. You were already a legend."

"And you let that scare you off?" he taunted.

"Absolutely. Besides, senior girls did not give sophomore boys a second look," she said airily, as if that had had anything at all to do with it. "We didn't want anyone thinking we were so desperate we had to rob the cradle."

"Oh, I think I could have held my own with you."

"No question about it," Alice said. "But senior

girls had a reputation to maintain, even the quiet ones like me."

"So, who did you date?"

"No one. I just had one goal back then, to get away. I wasn't about to let romance interfere. I headed for Boston the day after graduation."

His gaze narrowed. "And never came back?"

"Not until last summer."

"What happened last summer to finally get you back home?"

"My parents were killed in a car accident," she said, surprised that she could actually say the words without getting choked up.

His expression immediately sobered. "I'm sorry. That must have been rough."

"You have no idea. We'd never reconciled. I will regret that till the day I die." She gave him a sideways look. "Let that be a lesson to you. We never know how long we're going to have to mend fences with the people we love."

"Some fences can't be mended," Patrick said.

"They must be," she insisted.

"Alice, I can see where you're coming from, but trust me, in my case, you don't know what the hell you're talking about. If you understood the whole story—"

"Tell me," she urged.

He shook his head. "There's no point. The past is what it is."

"And your brothers, where do they fit in?"

"That remains to be seen."

"Will you be seeing them again?"

"I agreed to go to Boston in a few days for Michael's

wedding. After that, who knows?" he said with a shrug, as if it didn't matter to him one way or the other.

Alice ignored the shrug and went with what she thought she saw in his eyes, a need so raw that it probably scared him to death. She could relate to that only too well.

"Don't leave it to chance," she told him. "Do whatever it takes to keep them in your life."

His jaw tensed. "Again, not your call to make."

"I know that," she said impatiently. "But I also know what it's like to live with regrets, to know that it's too late to fix things. I wouldn't wish that on anyone. I don't want that for you."

"Why do you give a damn about any of this?" he asked. "You hardly know me."

"I know you better than you think," she said. "For a lot of years, I *was* you. I was angry and resentful and completely closed off from my parents. I made them miserable, and I lost something important that I can never get back. It's not too late for you to avoid the mistakes I made."

Patrick's expression softened ever so slightly. "I see where you're coming from, I really do, but I have to handle this my way, Alice. Maybe it's better if we steer clear of this particular topic from here on out."

She shook her head. "We can't, not if we're going to be friends. It'll be like the elephant in the room that we're trying to pretend isn't there. We can disagree over what to do about it, but we can't ignore it, Patrick."

"Friends, huh? That's how you see us, even after that steamy kiss?"

"Absolutely."

"That kiss didn't feel anything at all like a friendly peck," he noted.

Alice chuckled despite herself. "Which is why we're turning over a new leaf here and now. No more kisses."

Patrick groaned.

"I take it you disagree."

"I think that's pretty much as futile as trying to prevent a swamped boat from sinking by bailing with a teacup. It's not going to happen."

"I can control my urges, can't you?"

He reached for her hand and turned it over in his palm. She felt the warmth, the sandpapery, callused texture of a hand that worked hard. He rubbed his thumb across her wrist and sent heat spiraling through her to settle low in her belly. Her pulse jumped and he grinned.

"Still think you've got total control over those urges?" he asked.

"Maybe not total control," she admitted. "I'm working on it."

"Why fight the inevitable?"

"We are not inevitable," she insisted, even as she admitted to herself that she was lying through her teeth. Old patterns died hard. A part of her was falling fast, but she knew exactly how little judgment that part of her tended to exercise. She intended to fight it with every ounce of common sense she possessed. Real love didn't happen after two or three passing encounters. And she wasn't the kind of woman who could have a casual fling just because a man appealed to her.

She drew in a deep breath and steadied her racing pulse. Not this time. This time she was going to be smart and in control of her hormones and her emotions.

Besides, if Patrick was destined to ignore the wisdom she'd gained from her own mistakes, she didn't want to be around for the train wreck that followed. And that wreck really was inevitable. She could already see it coming.

It had been a perfectly pleasant, lazy afternoon, right up until the moment when Alice had gotten that bee in her bonnet about his family. Patrick regretted more than he could say that she knew anything at all about his history with his folks or his recent reunion with his older brothers. He had a hunch she could be a worse nag than Molly, and that was saying something.

Still, he wasn't totally inclined to send her packing the instant they returned to the dock. He enjoyed provoking her, seeing the quick rise of heat in her cheeks, the flash of desire in her eyes that she was trying so hard to ignore.

"Want to stay for dinner?" he asked. "I could run over to Jess's and bring back some of Molly's chowder, and there's half a loaf of your bread left."

She turned those golden eyes of hers on him with a sorrowful expression. "What would be the point?"

"Staving off starvation," he suggested wryly.

She frowned at that. "You know that's not what I meant. Sooner or later, we'll just butt heads again."

"I've got a hard head. I can take it," Patrick assured her.

She fought a grin. "Isn't that the problem, your hard head?"

"Only if you let it be," he responded. "We could play cards after dinner. Where's the harm in that?"

Her gaze narrowed speculatively. "Poker?"

"If that's what you want to play," he agreed, hiding his surprise at the choice. He'd figured on a few hands of gin rummy, maybe.

"Okay, you're on," she said. "But I'll warn you here and now that I'm very, very good."

Something in her voice alerted him that she was dead serious.

"Where'd you learn to play?" he asked, suddenly cautious.

"In Jess's back room."

Patrick stared at her. "Jess taught you to play poker?"

"When Molly and I were about ten."

"I see."

She grinned. "Still want to take me on?"

"More than ever," he said with heartfelt enthusiasm that wasn't entirely based on her self-proclaimed poker-playing ability.

"Then get the chowder," she said. "I need stamina."

"Is the chowder going to do it?"

"If Molly made an apple pie today, a slice of that would help, too." Her expression turned thoughtful. "And maybe some chocolate. Molly keeps a stash of Hershey bars behind the counter. Two ought to do it."

Patrick chuckled. Everyone in town knew about Molly's cache of chocolate. When she ran out, it was best to steer clear until she'd replenished her supply. Toughened seamen tended to slip extra candy bars into the box just to assure a pleasant Molly who wouldn't take offense at some slip of the tongue and dump a beer over their heads.

"Should I risk asking or just steal the candy?" Patrick inquired.

"Ask," she said. "And do it politely. It's too late to get any chocolate from the drugstore. It closes at five."

"Aye, aye," Patrick said. "Shall I grab a couple of beers, too?"

She shuddered. "With chocolate? Are you crazy?"

Patrick grinned. "Coffee, then. There's some below deck. You can make it while I'm gone."

"Well, hell," she muttered with a pretty little pout. "I was counting on that time to stack the cards."

He laughed, not entirely sure she wasn't totally serious. "Keep your hands off the cards. And just in case you lose control and don't, I'll be shuffling and dealing the first hand."

"I'll still win."

"We'll see."

"And I won't have to cheat to do it," she added.

"I'm thrilled at your level of self-confidence," he assured her. "The higher you climb, the harder you'll fall."

"You wish," she hollered after him, laughter threading through her voice.

Damn, but teachers had changed a lot since his school days. If he'd had a teacher like Alice, he'd have fallen in love on the first day of school and never recovered.

7

The salty air had sharpened Alice's appetite and dulled her brain. She almost fell asleep waiting for Patrick to get back from Jess's with their dinner. Only a strong cup of coffee revived her. Okay, that and the prospect of beating the pants off Patrick at cards.

She hadn't been lying about her skill with a poker hand. Jess had taught her and Molly not only how to gauge their own cards, but how to read their opponents' faces. Alice could spot someone trying to bluff a mile away, while concealing her own reactions with stoic control. She'd earned a good bit of her college tuition money playing cards with unsuspecting classmates in Boston.

Because of her pretty face and naive questions, she'd suckered more than one big-talking rich boy into coughing up a healthy chunk of his allowance from home. She'd socked away several thousand dollars before word had gotten around that playing cards with Alice Newberry was as risky as investing in junk bonds. Even then there had been takers, men with big egos who'd wanted to prove that they had the card sense all the other guys had lacked. Those weekly poker games had nicely supplemented the money she earned in tips at a local bar near Boston College.

She grinned at the memory. Patrick had no idea what he was in for.

When he finally got back to the boat, he was carrying two huge sacks. He set one on the galley counter, then upended the other one in her lap. Chocolate bars spilled all over, dozens of them.

Eyes wide, she gathered up as many of them as she could reach. "Oh, my, you didn't steal all of Molly's, did you?"

He seemed to sense her ambivalence about that. "You going to give them back if I did?" he taunted.

Just the faint scent of chocolate wafting through the wrappers tempted her. "Probably not," she confessed with total honesty. When it came to chocolate, she had few scruples.

"Then it's a good thing that I drove out to the fast-mart on the highway and bought out their stock. I'd hate to bring Molly's wrath down on our heads."

"You do know I can't possibly eat all this, don't you? Or are you hoping I'll take a stab at it and wind up in some sort of diabetic coma?"

"Why would I want to do that?"

"So you can beat me at cards."

"I don't need you unconscious to win," Patrick chided. "Those candy bars are just a token of my affection. Say thank you."

She met his gaze, saw the teasing glint in his eyes

and was captivated all over again. "Thank you," she said softly.

"Anytime."

The air in the tiny galley sizzled. At least it did right up until the second she caught on that charming her was his real means of attacking her concentration. If she was feeling all mushy and tender toward him, she might be distracted from playing cutthroat poker.

"It's not going to work, you know," she told him mildly, as she deliberately turned her back and ladled their soup into bowls.

"What's not going to work?"

"I'm not going to become so overwhelmed by my hormones that I can't concentrate on the cards," she said, setting the soup down in front of him.

His lips twitched slightly. "You think not?"

"I know not," she said emphatically.

"You're turning it into a challenge," he warned. "Men love challenges."

Uh-oh, she thought, recognizing the truth in that statement. Men were disgustingly predictable when it came to challenges, especially challenges uttered by a woman. She tried to regroup. "It wasn't a challenge, just a warning."

"Nice try, but I know a challenge when I hear one." He grinned as he cupped the back of her neck and held her mere inches away from his face. "And when I decide to take you up on it, you won't even see it coming."

Her stomach flipped over, even after he'd released her. She glanced a little frantically at her watch. "It's getting late."

"Oh, no, you don't, Miss Newberry." He moved

aside their untouched bowls of soup and slapped a deck of cards on the table. His gaze caught hers and held. "Ready?"

A part of Alice that had been too long dormant snapped to life. "Ready," she said, instantly revived, despite the lack of nourishment.

She leaned across the table and looked directly into his eyes. "Do your best, Devaney," she said defiantly. "It won't be good enough."

Instead of reaching for the cards, he skimmed his knuckles gently along her jaw. A half smile lifted the corners of his mouth. "We'll see."

Alice shuddered and fought the desire to lean into his touch. For the first time since she was ten years old and held her first poker hand, she had the distinct feeling that she was in way over her head in a card game.

She instinctively reached for her soup, ate several nourishing spoonfuls, then faced him with renewed determination as she looked over the cards she'd been dealt. It was the most pitiful assortment of five cards she'd ever seen, but she was used to overcoming the odds. She looked Patrick squarely in the eyes, chose two cards, when she should have dumped four, and laid them on the table.

"Two," she told him, her tone deliberately gloating.

His gaze narrowed. "Two, huh?" He dealt those and took three for himself.

Alice saw the faint twitch of his lips and knew that he'd gotten something, while her own hand was no better than it had been at the outset. Not even a pair, much less a high card to back it up. Still she tossed a few chips on the table to force Patrick to win the hand honestly.

He matched her bet. "Call."

Alice spread her woeful cards on the table, expecting to get a hearty laugh for her attempt at a bluff. As it turned out, Patrick had even less, a nine high card to her ten. She grinned and raked in the chips, noting that he didn't seem to be the least bit concerned.

"Nice bluff," he complimented her.

"You, too. You had me worried for about half a heartbeat."

She reached for the cards and shuffled. "Now I know what to look for."

"Oh?"

She grinned at him without explaining and dealt the cards. "Okay, Devaney. Time to get serious."

His gaze held hers. "Darlin', I've been serious since the minute we met."

Alice fumbled the cards and sent them flying. It was Patrick's turn to grin.

"Sorry," he apologized without a trace of sincerity in his voice. "Didn't mean to rattle you."

"You didn't," she assured him. How could he when she knew perfectly well that Patrick was never serious, not when it came to a woman? This time, though, she kept her eyes squarely on the cards.

A fat lot of good her total concentration did her, Alice thought when she'd lost three hands straight. Patrick was better than she'd expected. She was glad they were playing just for fun. Not that that had kept her competitive streak from kicking in. She still wanted to whip his butt.

"Don't get too confident, Devaney."

"I know," he said soberly. "It's just the luck of the draw."

Alice studied him. He'd sounded a little too uncharacteristically modest. "What are you up to?"

He gave her an innocent look. "Me? Nothing at all."

"You'd better not be."

"Or?" he said, barely containing a grin.

"Or you'll regret it," she said, and triumphantly spread her king-high straight on the table.

Patrick winced and folded his hand.

"Let that be a lesson to you," she gloated.

There was a devilish twinkle in his eyes when he met her gaze. "Oh, I imagine there's a great deal you could teach me, Miss Newberry."

There was no mistaking the fact that he was talking about a whole lot more than poker.

The evening was proving to be a lot livelier than Patrick had anticipated. Intrigued by Alice's competitive streak, he dealt, but when Alice would have picked up her cards, he placed his hand over hers. She gave him a startled look.

"Okay, enough fooling around," he declared.

"Fooling around?" she repeated, sounding breathless.

"Yeah, fooling around. It's time to get serious. What are we playing for?" he asked. "What do these chips represent? Pennies? Matchsticks?" His expression turned hopeful. "Clothes?"

Her look shot down that idea.

"Okay, you name it," he said.

"Points," she said. "Winner take all."

"And the prize?"

"When I win—"

"If," he corrected.

She frowned. "Okay, *if* I win, you have to contact your family."

Patrick froze. Not that he expected to lose, but there was no way in hell he'd agree to those terms. "Forget it."

"You said I got to choose. Are you backing down already? You're not scared I'll beat you, are you?"

She'd caught him there. He wasn't about to let her have the upper hand, not even for a second. "Okay, then, what if I win?"

"I suppose it's only fair that you choose that," she said.

"You go to Boston with me for my brother's wedding," he said impulsively.

He knew as soon as he saw her eyes light up that he'd made a huge miscalculation. Obviously, she now saw the bet as a win-win situation for her goal of reuniting him with his family. And of course if he showed up in Boston with Alice on his arm, his brothers were going to be wearing the same gloating expression she currently had on her face.

"Done," she said at once, before he could amend the bet.

"You're sneaky," he accused her.

"No, you just subconsciously want what I want," she told him.

Patrick frowned at the suggestion that he was in any way anxious to make peace with his folks or strengthen the bond between himself and his newly found brothers.

"I made my choice six years ago. I don't regret it," he told her flatly.

"Of course you do. Whatever happened shouldn't negate all the good years you had with your family."

"Those years were a lie, and I don't regret turning my back on my parents or even on Daniel, for that matter. Maybe you had regrets about leaving home, but I don't. Don't go projecting your past on me, Alice. Maybe your reasons for leaving home were less valid than mine."

Alice folded the hand of cards she held, set them facedown on the table and looked him in the eye. "I'll tell you my story if you'll tell me yours."

He saw the trap, but he was too curious to deny himself the chance to learn more about her. "Okay. You first. Why did you take off the minute you got out of high school?"

"Because I was determined not to be trapped here the way all of the women in my family had been for generations. They grew up, finished high school, got married to a local fisherman and stayed home with the kids. Many of them lost their husbands to the sea. It was a hard life, even for those who didn't lose their husbands, and I wanted more than that. I wanted my own identity, my own career to fall back on."

Patrick didn't see why that should have caused such a rift that she'd never seen her folks again. "What am I missing? That doesn't sound so awful."

She sighed heavily. "It shouldn't have been, not in this day and age, but my parents were very traditional. They saw my decision as a reflection on their choices. They said if what they'd given me wasn't good enough, then I should just get out and see how hard it was to make it on my own. So that's what I did. I left. I had just enough money to get to Boston and spend a few nights in a boarding house near Boston College. I had no money for classes and very little for food. I was lucky, though. I got a job after a few days, and it paid the bills with a little extra. Playing poker added to my savings, but even so it took me a year to save enough to start taking classes. I was twenty-two when I graduated and I've been teaching now for four years, three in Boston, one here."

"Good for you! You should be proud of yourself."

"I was. I *am*," she said with a touch of defiance.

He studied her intently, trying to figure out why she sounded as if she still felt she had something to prove. "In all that time your parents never contacted you?"

She shook her head, her expression unbearably sad. "Not once. I invited them to my graduation, but they didn't even reply. I heard after they died that my mother wanted to come, but my father refused and she wouldn't go against his wishes even then."

"I'm sorry."

There were unshed tears in her eyes when she looked at him. "It was all so silly. I was too stubborn and they had too much pride. If only any one of us had reached out, maybe we could have worked things out."

"Why didn't you?"

"I did reach out. I sent that invitation. I thought it was a gesture, but I don't know, maybe they saw it as a slap in the face, as me trying to show them how I'd done what I set out to do to spite them. And after that, I suppose their refusal to come to my graduation was one more blow. I felt as if I'd been rejected again. I'd been thinking about them a lot in the months before they died. I almost came home several times. I thought maybe if I just showed up it would be easier." She met his gaze. "Then it was too late. I'll blame myself forever for waiting too long."

"You couldn't have known that there wouldn't be years and years to mend fences."

"No, but it proved that things shouldn't be allowed to fester. We never know how long we have. The bitterness between us will be on my conscience forever."

Patrick looked away, thinking about the bitterness and anger and blame between him and his parents. As far as he could see, there was still no comparison between what they had done and what Alice's parents had done. The Newberrys had never abandoned three little boys. The Devaneys had, and they'd done it without once looking back. In his eyes that was unforgivable.

"You promised to tell me about your split with your family," Alice reminded him.

He had and he regretted it, but he wasn't going to renege on his promise. "It's an ugly story," he warned her.

"I still want to hear it."

He nodded. "Then I need a drink. You want anything?"

She shook her head as he poured a shot of Irish whiskey into a glass and drank it down. It burned his throat and made his eyes water, but a moment later he could feel the warmth stealing through him. It was a comforting sensation, which was one reason he rarely touched the stuff. It would be too easy to get lost in it.

"Okay," he began. "Here's the short version. Unbeknownst to me or Daniel, my parents had three sons before they had us. You met them the other night—Ryan, Sean and Michael. I guess on some level we knew about

them, because we were two when things fell apart. We
had to have been aware that we had big brothers, but
kids forget. They're adaptable at that age. At any rate,
our folks just picked up stakes and moved to Maine with
Daniel and me." He looked directly into her eyes, then
added so there could be no mistake about what he was
saying, "They left their other sons behind."

Alice stared at him, evidently not comprehending…
or not wanting to. "What do you mean they left them?
With friends? Another family?"

He shook his head. "They left them for Social Services to deal with. Ryan and Sean came home from
school, and the rest of us were gone. Michael was with
a babysitter."

"My God!" she whispered.

"It gets worse," Patrick told her, needing her to understand the full extent of his parents' treachery. "They
never once checked on them. Ryan, Sean and Michael
were separated. They were placed in foster care. Michael says his family was terrific and Sean's was okay,
but Ryan was understandably angry and hard to deal
with. He bounced from home to home. Because of the
way my parents left, there was no way any of them
could be put up for adoption, not with the laws on the
books then. Instead, they led makeshift lives with makeshift families."

"How awful for them," Alice said, obviously shaken.
"And you had no idea?"

"Not until I was eighteen. Daniel found some old
photos hidden in the attic. We asked our folks about
them. They admitted that they'd left their oldest three
sons behind in Boston when they moved here, that they

had no idea how they were. Maybe if they'd at least given permission for them to be adopted, I could forgive them, but to leave them in limbo like that…how could they?"

He met her gaze. "They refused to explain what they'd done. In fact, they acted as if we didn't even have the right to ask. Daniel stuck around. He's still hoping for an explanation, I guess. As for me, I will never forgive what they've done. There isn't an explanation they can give that would make what they did okay. I keep trying to put myself in my brothers' shoes on that day, coming back to an empty apartment, finding out that they'd been left behind. They must have been terrified. It makes me sick to my stomach just thinking about it."

"Your parents must have been desperate to do such a thing," Alice said, trying to explain away the inexplicable.

"Don't defend them to me!" Patrick said. "Put yourself in my brothers' shoes. Ryan was barely nine, the others even younger, and they were abandoned by their family, while Daniel and I were chosen to go with our parents. My God, what kind of selfish, cruel person does that to three little boys?"

"Only someone who's desperate," Alice insisted again. "Someone who can't see any other way out."

"They were adults. They had a responsibility to their children to find another way out," he said, his tone harsh. He sighed heavily. "For the longest time after Daniel and I found out, I dreamed about them. I kept seeing their faces, imagining them crying. I wanted to look for them, but I was scared."

"Scared of what?"

"That they'd hate me, or at the very least, resent me for being chosen to go with our parents." He regarded her with a sense of wonder. "The amazing thing is that they don't. They came here wanting answers, not revenge."

"Doesn't that tell you something?" Alice asked.

"That they're incredible men to have survived what our folks did to them," he said at once. "But I still don't feel right being around them. I feel as if I was given something they should have had, something they were entitled to—a secure home, parental love."

"It didn't seem to me as if they begrudge you that," Alice said.

"They don't," he admitted. "Like I said, they're better men than I am."

"No, they're not," she said fiercely.

Patrick grinned at her. "You don't know me well enough to be so quick to jump to my defense."

"Of course I do," she said. "Have you even been listening to yourself? You're not just upset with your parents because they lied to you and Daniel, you're filled with compassion and righteous indignation on behalf of brothers you didn't even remember. You're as connected to them as if you'd spent a lifetime together."

She gave him a sly look. "The only thing that might make you an even better man would be putting out the effort to make things right."

"Don't even go there," Patrick warned. "I'm not going to organize some big reconciliation between them and my folks. I don't ever want to see my parents again. The only reason I'm even going to Boston for this wedding is because it seems to mean a lot to Michael, Sean and Ryan. After that, if they want to track down Daniel and our parents, it's up to them. I want no part of it."

He expected her to deliver another lecture, but instead she merely said quietly, "Maybe you'll change your mind."

"I won't. If you're counting on that, you're going to be disappointed."

"We'll see."

"It's not going to happen, Alice."

"Whatever you say."

"Don't patronize me, dammit!"

She gave him a serene smile that almost sent him over the edge. He barely resisted the urge to pound the table to emphasize his point. Instead he picked up his cards and looked them over, relieved to see that he had a full house working. He tossed one card and waited for Alice to deal him another. After a long look, she finally did just that without further comment.

Patrick took that hand and then the next, but then Alice went on a winning streak that caught him by surprise. When she finally yawned and called it a night, she'd accumulated twenty points to his eighteen.

To her credit, she didn't gloat. Nor did she push overly hard for the reconciliation he'd declared wasn't going to happen.

"We'll talk about you paying up on our bet when you get back from Boston," she said mildly as she headed for the deck. Then she smiled up at him. "Of course, if you wanted to smooth things out with your brothers while you're there, then there won't even be anything to talk about except getting you back together with your folks."

Despite his annoyance, Patrick couldn't help admiring her tenacity. "We'll see," he said, snagging her hand and pulling her toward him. He brushed an errant curl away from her face and let his hand linger. "You're quite the little nag, aren't you?"

She grinned, obviously not taking offense. "You have no idea."

"Proud of it, too," he concluded.

"You bet, especially when the cause is such a good one."

"What if I were to threaten to kiss you each and every time you brought up the subject?" he inquired curiously.

She laughed at that. "Then you'd just be making it a whole lot more interesting."

He studied her with surprise. "Really?"

"Really," she said, keeping her expression serious, even though her eyes were twinkling merrily. "Good night, Patrick."

She pulled away and stepped onto the dock. "I can't wait to hear all about Boston."

"You could still come with me," he called after her.

"I don't think so. I think I'll just trust you to do the right thing."

He watched her until she reached her car and drove away, then sighed. He really, really hated having someone count on him to do the right thing. In this situation he wasn't even sure what the right thing was.

8

By Monday morning, Alice was already feeling restless and at loose ends. Spring break stretched out ahead of her like a prison sentence, rather than a relaxing vacation. Even though keeping up with a classroom full of five-year-olds was stressful, having time to herself with nothing to do but think about the past was worse. And now she had her conflicting emotions over Patrick to add into the mix. She would have given almost anything to have Ricky Foster around to give her a run for her money and keep her mind occupied.

Since she couldn't have that distraction, she opted for going to Jess's to see Molly. Molly was always good for some lively conversation, and she always knew the latest gossip in Widow's Cove.

Alice knew the second she walked through the door and saw her friend's face light up that she'd probably made a mistake.

"Over here," Molly ordered, gesturing toward a secluded booth. She brought the coffeepot and two cups with her. "Talk," she said as she poured the coffee.

Alice gave her a disgruntled look. "Any particular topic?"

"Don't even try to pretend you don't know what I'm asking about," Molly retorted. "You and Patrick. How's that going?"

Since Molly was unlikely to drop the subject, Alice concluded that the smart thing would be to turn Molly's fascination to her advantage. "What do you know about Patrick's brother Daniel?"

Molly made a face. "A pompous, self-righteous jerk," she said succinctly. She looked as if she wanted to say a lot more, but she didn't.

Alice's gaze narrowed. The description sounded more personal than objective. "Okay, spill it, Molly. What did he ever do to you?"

"Nothing," Molly said a little too quickly.

"Come on, Molly, tell the truth. You don't say things like that about someone unless they've done you wrong."

"Not me. Patrick," Molly insisted.

Alice studied her skeptically. "And that's it? You don't like him, because he what? Took Patrick at his word and left him alone?"

"Pretty much." She said it easily enough, but she wouldn't meet Alice's gaze.

"I'm not buying it," Alice said. "If that's all it was, you'd be moving heaven and earth to patch things up between them."

"The same way you are?" Molly asked testily.

"Exactly."

"Maybe I'm just not as inclined to meddle in something that's none of my business."

Alice gave her a wry look. "Since when?"

"Since it's Daniel Devaney we're talking about, if you must know. The man gets on my nerves, that's all."

"Oh, really?" Alice thought she was finally getting a lot closer to the truth. "It's only a tiny little leap from getting on your nerves to getting under your skin. Do you have a thing for Daniel?"

Molly looked as scandalized as if Alice had accused her of stealing from the poor. "Don't be absurd. The man would never give me a second look, and I don't waste my time pining for idiots."

Now there was a telling comment, Alice thought. She wondered if Molly realized she'd all but admitted to having feelings, even if they were feelings she was fighting.

"Is he as handsome as his brother?"

"They're identical twins," Molly retorted, then rested her chin on her hand and leveled a speculative look straight into Alice's eyes. "You tell me, does that make him handsome?"

Alice couldn't seem to prevent the blush that crept into her cheeks. If she expected total honesty from her friend, then she needed to repay it in kind. "It does in my book," she admitted.

Molly sat back with a satisfied look. "I thought so. How far has it gone?"

"It hasn't gone anywhere. We went out on his boat on Saturday, had dinner and played cards. Just a relaxing day. Nothing more."

"You were down in that cozy little place of his below deck till well after midnight and all you did was play cards? I am very disappointed in you," Molly chided.

Alice regarded Molly curiously. "How did you know I was there past midnight?"

"I wasn't down there peering in the portholes, if that's what you're thinking," Molly retorted. "Your car was still there when I closed up here. If you didn't want me to notice it, you should have parked someplace else or left earlier. The point is, you were with the man and wasting time on cards." Her expression brightened. "Was it strip poker at least?"

"No, it was not strip poker!" Alice said with feigned indignation. "As a matter of fact, the stakes were much higher."

"Oh, really? Maybe you didn't let me down after all. What were they?"

"If I won—which I did—he would make peace with his family."

Molly stared, obviously shocked. "Patrick agreed to that?"

Alice grinned. "He didn't expect to lose."

"You did tell him that Jess taught you to play poker didn't you?"

"I did, and apparently he wasn't overly impressed."

"Foolish man."

Alice shrugged. "His gullibility served my purposes very nicely."

"So now you're trying to figure out how to bring about this reconciliation?" Molly concluded. "Is that why you were asking about Daniel? You think he's the obvious link?"

"You disagree?"

"Let's just say I wouldn't turn to Daniel if my life were on the line, but that's just me."

Alice grinned. "Interesting. All that vehement protesting and your cheeks are bright pink."

"Don't make too much of that. The man infuriates me."

"My point exactly," Alice said. "I think I'll see what I can do about hooking up with Daniel Devaney while I'm on break from school."

"Patrick won't thank you for interfering in his life," Molly warned.

"Sometimes you just have to do what you think is best and to hell with the consequences for yourself," Alice said.

"You don't care if Patrick is furious with you?"

"I'd prefer it if he weren't," Alice admitted. "But I'm willing to take the risk."

"You're a braver woman that I am," Molly said, regarding her with admiration. "Just don't expect too much from Daniel. And don't go dragging him down here for this big reconciliation. I don't want him on the property."

She sounded dead serious. Alice studied her more closely. "How did he let you down, Molly?"

"I never said he let me down. I believe I said he was a pompous, self-righteous jerk."

"Because he let you down," Alice repeated confidently. "That just gives me one more thing to straighten out."

"I do not want to be your spring break project!" Molly shouted after her as she headed for the door. "I doubt that Patrick does, either."

"That's the problem with having a friend who has

good intentions and time on her hands," Alice called back. "We just go on about the business of doing our good deeds, anyway."

Patrick heard all about Alice's visit to Jess's the second he crossed the bar's threshold on Monday evening. Molly couldn't shut up about it.

"So what?" he asked, when he could finally get a word in. "It's not as if Daniel is going to come roaring over here to make peace just because Alice pesters him to do it. He knows better, at least where I'm concerned. What about you? You interested in making peace with my brother?"

"When hell freezes over," Molly said fiercely.

Patrick grinned. "You might want to tone down that response. It tends to give away the fact that down deep, you still have the hots for the man."

"I most certainly do not," Molly said. "And you, of all people, know exactly why that is."

Patrick sobered at once. "I do know, Molly, and you'll get no argument from me. He treated you badly, and you have every reason to hate him."

"To say nothing of the way he stood behind your folks rather than you," she said. "I can't forgive him for that, either."

"Leave me out of it. Daniel and I can wrestle with our issues. You don't have to take on my battle. And I won't hold it against you if you were ever to decide to give him another chance."

"I won't," Molly said flatly. "I'd say he's shown us both his true character, wouldn't you? Who needs it?"

Just then she glanced toward the door, and her expression turned sour. "Don't look now, but our meddling friend is back to report in on her day's adventures."

Patrick swiveled his stool around to see Alice marching toward them with a determined glint in her eyes. She looked as if she were returning from battle, though he couldn't quite read whether she'd been victorious.

"Have a busy day?" he inquired lightly.

"As a matter of fact, I did," she told him. "I went to see your brother."

"So I heard," he said, keeping his tone neutral.

Alice frowned at Molly. "You blabbed?"

"Of course, I told him," Molly said without regret. "He had a right to know."

"I suppose," Alice conceded.

Despite his irritation, Patrick was curious. "How'd it go?"

"He told me to mind my own damn business," she said indignantly. "And I am quoting him precisely."

Molly chuckled. "That's our Daniel. Never did mince words. Despite his tendency to want to keep the peace, the man has the diplomatic skills of Attila the Hun."

"Funny, he said pretty much the same thing about you," Alice retorted. "What the devil went on between you two, anyway? I have a feeling if I'd never mentioned your name, I might have gotten further."

"None of your business," Molly retorted.

Alice sighed. "I'm just trying to help."

Patrick understood that her heart was in the right place, but he'd tried to tell her not to waste her energy fighting his battles. Molly had apparently told her the same thing. "Leave it alone, Alice. Things are the way they're meant to be."

"Life is not meant to be lived like this. Families shouldn't be split up," she argued.

"Tell that to my folks," he said. "They're the ones responsible."

"Way back then, when they left Boston, yes," she agreed. "But you've only made it worse, and they've all let you get away with it."

"Which only means that we're all content with the status quo," he pointed out. "Leave it be." He tucked a finger under her chin and forced her to meet his gaze. "How about I buy you dinner?"

"I'm not hungry," she said, her expression glum.

"A drink, then?"

"Sure." She looked at Molly. "A diet soda, please."

Patrick grinned. "Big drinker, huh?"

"I know better than to drink anything else on an empty stomach."

"Then let me buy you dinner," he repeated. "The special's pork chops."

"Not interested," she insisted.

Patrick turned to Molly. "Make it one special, then. We'll be in that booth over there."

Molly frowned at him. "I don't get it, Patrick. Why aren't you more upset that Alice went meddling where she didn't belong?"

"Because he was secretly hoping I'd fix things," Alice said.

Patrick frowned at her. "No, because it's no big deal. I knew how it was going to turn out before Alice ever went traipsing after Daniel. So did you, Molly. You could have saved your breath trying to stop her. There was nothing to worry about."

"I wasn't worried. I was annoyed," Molly said. "I didn't like the idea earlier, and I'm no happier about it now." She scowled at Alice. "No more meddling on my behalf, okay? Promise me."

"Fine. I promise," Alice said.

She looked so dejected Patrick almost felt sorry for her. She'd obviously wanted to do something helpful, and she'd only been slapped down from all directions for her efforts.

"Come on," he said, steering her over to a booth. When she was settled across from him, he met her gaze. "Come on, Alice, cheer up. You tried. It didn't work out. I'm not unhappy about that. Molly is definitely not unhappy about it. You shouldn't be, either."

"Why is everyone being so stubborn?"

He grinned at the plaintive note in her voice. "I can't speak for Molly, but as for Daniel and me, we're Devancys. It comes with the genes."

"More's the pity," she muttered.

"Forget about it. Come to Boston with me this weekend. We'll have some fun, go to the wedding and you'll see that none of this matters in the greater scheme of things."

"I don't think so," she said as indignantly as if he'd suggested they go skinny-dipping in broad daylight. "I won our bet. I can't go to Boston."

He chuckled. "We can pretend I won. Or we can play one hand of poker right here and now, winner take all."

She shook her head. "I don't think so. I've already bumped up against two stubborn Devaneys. I'm not sure I could handle a whole crowd of them."

He laughed at that. "That makes two of us. Think

of it this way—you coming along would be a mission of mercy."

She finally grinned at that. "Nice try, Devaney, but you're not going to get me by playing on my sympathy. I will take those pork chops, though." She glanced at Molly, who was across the room taking in the scene with obvious fascination. "With mashed potatoes and gravy, please."

Patrick winked at Molly. "Give the lady whatever she wants."

"Naturally," Molly said. "Around here we aim to please our customers."

Alice gave her a sour look. "Then you can lay off all the I-told-you-so's that are on the tip of your tongue."

Molly grinned. "I'm not sure I can go that far."

"Try," Alice said. "Otherwise, I might be tempted to take one more stab at getting Daniel to listen to me."

"Then by all means, Molly, keep your mouth shut," Patrick said fervently. Given his own inability to resist Alice, he doubted his brother could withstand another persuasive onslaught, and the last thing he wanted was for Alice to manage to drag Daniel over here where he'd only stir up a lot of old issues for Patrick—and for Molly.

Patrick had second and then third thoughts on the drive down to Boston. Michael's wedding was just about the last place on earth he wanted to be, but he'd made his brothers a promise and he didn't intend to break it. If having him there made up for some of the old hurts inflicted by their folks, then it was the least he could do.

He drove straight to his oldest brother's pub, then

stood outside Ryan's Place trying to work up the courage to go in. At that moment he regretted, more than he could say, not trying harder to talk Alice into coming with him. Staring through the glass, he was grateful that the pub was packed. He doubted Ryan would have much time for him. He could say hello and head to his hotel, then try to regroup in time for tomorrow's wedding. With any luck there would be so much commotion at the wedding no one would even notice he was there.

When Patrick finally walked into the bar, Ryan spotted him at once and his face lit up.

"You're just in time," he called out. "I could use some help back here. You any good at pouring drinks?"

"I've filled in for Molly a time or two," Patrick admitted, relieved to have something to do. "Nice place you've got here. You always this busy?"

"It's a Friday night. We have music starting in an hour. If you think it's packed now, just wait."

"Aren't you supposed to be going to the rehearsal dinner in a little while?"

"Maggie and Caitlyn will stand in for me," Ryan said. "Besides, I wanted to spend some time with you. Since you turned down the invitation to the dinner, I figured this would be my best chance. Michael understands. He knows what it's like around here on the weekends. That's one reason he's having a morning wedding, so the reception will be over with in time for me to get back here tomorrow night." He grinned. "That and the fact that he's anxious to get Kelly on a plane to head for their honeymoon. They're going to some Caribbean island."

"Sounds romantic," Patrick said.

"Our brother has a romantic streak. I guess all the Devaneys do, once some woman manages to knock down the walls we've built around our hearts. What about you? Anyone ever gotten through your defenses?"

Patrick's heart thudded dully at the first volley from his big brother. Because Ryan was heading down a path Patrick didn't want to explore, he decided to turn the tables.

"Tell me about Maggie and your daughter," he said. "You have any pictures around here?"

Ryan regarded him with a knowing expression but didn't call him on the deliberate distraction. "Upstairs in our old apartment, where you'll be staying," Ryan said. "If you want to take your stuff on up and get settled, I can handle things here for a bit."

Grateful for the excuse to have a few minutes to himself, Patrick grabbed his suitcase and headed upstairs. He closed the door to the apartment behind him and drew in a deep breath. He felt as if he'd fallen into the middle of someone else's life. He was in a strange city, a strange apartment and trying to pretend that his own brother wasn't a complete stranger.

He set his one bag inside the door and flipped on the lights. The apartment was cozy and filled with the kind of touches only a woman could have put there. There were even fresh flowers in a vase on the coffee table and a welcoming note from Maggie propped against a family photo. He stared at the picture and found himself grinning.

Ryan looked as if he couldn't tear his gaze away from the two girls in his life. If he'd had to guess, he would say the photo had been taken in Ireland. The landscape was as green as could be, and they were standing on a rocky cliff overlooking the sea. A woman—obviously his beloved Maggie—had long red hair that had been caught by the breeze and a serene expression on her face. A pint-size miniature of her was wearing a bright-pink sweater, emerald-green pants and bright-yellow sneakers. She was obviously a child who had her own sense of fashion. And it was equally evident that the two adults doted on her. Patrick envied them the closeness that shone on their faces.

Turning his back on that momentary pang of envy, he quickly shut the door and went back downstairs.

Ryan looked up from the ale he was pouring and gave him a sharp look. "Everything okay?"

"Fine," Patrick said.

"You find everything you needed upstairs?"

"Yes," he said. He'd found everything he needed, along with something he hadn't even realized he wanted...evidence of what a thoroughly happy family was supposed to look like.

"You sure you don't mind if I put you to work?" Ryan asked.

"Not at all," Patrick said and meant it. It felt good to be needed. "Just tell me what to do."

Ryan pointed out where the various bottles of whiskey and wine were kept, showed him what beer and ales were on tap, then left him to it.

Patrick immediately fell into the rhythm of the pub, making chitchat with the waitresses, flirting just a little with the women who sat at the bar, then letting the familiar Irish songs wash over him in waves of nostalgia. Connor Devaney had played those same songs until the tapes wore out and had to be replaced by CDs. Not a day had gone by that he and Daniel hadn't felt ties to a land they'd never seen. And more than once, on a visit to Jess's, Connor had ended the evening with his own powerful voice singing "Danny Boy," as Patrick and Daniel sat on his knees. Now Connor never crossed the threshold of his old haunt, because Patrick had made it his own and all but declared it off-limits.

Funny how he'd pushed memories like that from his head during the past few years. He hadn't wanted to remember any of the good times, because he'd felt that they'd come at the expense of his brothers. Tonight, though, he could listen to that old familiar music without guilt. In a way, he owed Ryan for that, for giving him back a piece of himself.

Once the band finished for the night, the pub emptied out quickly. Ryan drew in a deep breath and gave Patrick a grin.

"Not bad, bro. I appreciate the help."

Patrick moved to a bar stool and sank onto it. "I thought fishing was hard work, but this was a thousand times worse."

"You said you'd worked at Jess's."

"Jess's is never packed like this. It's half the size, so even on a crowded night there's time to breathe."

"You want to head upstairs and get some sleep?" Ryan asked. "If you're exhausted at the wedding, I'll catch hell for it."

Patrick almost took him up on it. It would be better than sticking around for the questions that had been on the tip of his brother's tongue all evening. But that would be the cowardly way out, and Patrick had always prided himself on facing things.

"If you don't mind, I think I'd like a pint of that ale before I go up," he told Ryan.

"Coming right up," his brother said. He poured one for each of them, then rounded the bar and sat next to Patrick. "Now that you've had some time to think about it, how do you feel about Sean, Michael and me showing up last week?"

"To be honest, I can't quite get over it. I'm still feeling a little off-kilter, the same way I did when I first found out we'd run out on you." He looked Ryan in the eye. "And I can't believe you're not angrier."

"Believe me, I spent a lot of years being furious," Ryan said. "I caused a lot of trouble for a lot of foster families before I was finally old enough to go out on my own. And then I came damn close to landing in jail, but a good friend got me back on track. You'll meet Father Francis at the wedding tomorrow. The man's a saint to have put up with me. I owe him for all of this. He made me see what I could be."

"Obviously, he knew what he was talking about," Patrick said. "You've made a nice life for yourself here. The pub's really something."

"It's even better now that I've let Maggie into my life. Don't tell her I said this, but she's given this place the heart it lacked. It was a well-run pub before, but now it has her warmth, to say nothing of her clever way with a dollar. We've never done better." He grinned. "And we've another baby on the way, a boy this time."

"Congratulations!" Patrick said, feeling another surprising twinge of envy.

"You'll meet someone one of these days," Ryan told him, then gave him a sly look. "Or perhaps you already have."

"If you're talking about Alice, I told you I barely know her."

"Sometimes it doesn't take that long, when it's the right woman."

"She's a meddler," Patrick complained, feeling disloyal even as he said it. He knew better than anyone that Alice had a good heart, even if her attempts to help were misguided.

Ryan laughed. "Maybe so, but I imagine my Maggie could still give her lessons. Meddling's not a crime, if it's done for the right reasons. Not that I would have said that a few years back, with Father Francis and then Maggie thinking they knew what was best for me."

"You didn't appreciate what they were trying to do at the time?"

"Of course not, but I got over it eventually. If you're smart, you will, too. There's nothing like the love of a good woman to fill a man's heart and make his life worth living."

Patrick regarded him sadly. "Do you suppose our folks felt that way once?"

"They're still together, aren't they?" Ryan asked. "That says something. I'm not saying I understand or forgive what they did to Sean, Michael and me, or even to you and Daniel by keeping you in the dark, but they've stuck together. It takes a strong glue to do that, and the only one I know that powerful is love."

Patrick thought of the years when he'd thought the same. "I suppose."

"Weren't there happy times for all of you?" Ryan asked. "I'd hate to think that they caused such misery for the rest of us without finding some happiness with you and Daniel."

"How can there be any real happiness when it's based on a lie?" Patrick asked.

"Come on, Patrick," Ryan chided, "be honest. Were there good times? Was there laughter?"

Patrick wanted to deny it, but he couldn't. "Yes." He studied his brother curiously. "Don't you begrudge us that?"

Ryan took his time answering, clearly giving his reply some serous thought. "No, I don't think so. I think it would be unbearably sad if you had all been miserable, too."

"You have a generous heart," Patrick told him with sincerity. "More generous than mine. I doubt I'll ever forgive them for stealing so many years from all of us."

"We have the here and now," Ryan said. "In the end, that's all any of us have. The past is over, if not forgotten, and hating's a waste of time and energy. The future's out there, and the way it goes depends on what we do today. Maggie taught me that."

Patrick sipped his ale, then admitted, "Alice said something very much like it."

"A wise woman," Ryan said. "You should listen to her. I've been happier since I put aside my anger. I've been happier yet since I started paying attention to my wife. She sees things with a clarity that I can't. She's been a blessing, no doubt about it."

Was Alice the same sort of blessing? Patrick wondered. It was too soon to tell. But at that moment he couldn't wait to get back to Maine to find out.

9

Alice gave her tiny cottage a thorough spring house-cleaning, just to keep herself from thinking too much about what might be going on in Boston between Patrick and his brothers. She also needed to avoid her natural inclination to try to patch things up between him and Daniel and their parents. She'd promised to stay out of that and she intended to keep her word...unless, of course, she saw that they were making no progress on their own. Then she'd have a duty to step in, whether anyone appreciated her efforts or not.

For the most part, she managed to keep her thoughts of Patrick at bay as she washed windows till they glistened, scrubbed floors till they shone and dusted every single knickknack and surface throughout the four-room house. She lingered for several minutes over the photo of her parents taken during a family outing just a few months before her high school graduation. At that point they'd had no idea that she intended to leave Maine and go to college in Boston. She'd still been their cherished daughter.

"Oh, Mama," she whispered. "I never meant to hurt the two of you. I just needed you to respect my choice. If only you had...."

But they hadn't, and from the moment she'd announced her intentions, their world had been shattered. It wasn't as if she'd sprung it on them, either. She'd made no secret of applying to colleges, but they'd assumed she either wouldn't get in or would change her mind and stay right here in Widow's Cove, content to work as a clerk in some store until the right man came along.

Sighing at how naive they'd all been, she put the photo back on its shelf and went on with her cleaning.

With a warm breeze billowing the curtains and filling the house with fresh air, Alice finally collapsed into her favorite chintz-covered easy chair with a cup of tea and a slice of freshly baked apple pie. Before she took so much as a sip of tea, she closed her eyes and breathed deeply, feeling the tense muscles in her neck and shoulders finally ease. There was nothing like exhausting physical work to sweep the cobwebs from the mind, she thought as the faint sounds of a classical music station drifted from the radio.

Just when she felt herself beginning to unwind, the jarring sound of the phone startled her. She glanced at the clock and was surprised to see that the entire day had slipped away from her. It was after seven. Little wonder she was tired and hungry. She'd missed dinner completely in her frenzy to keep occupied.

The phone continued its insistent ringing as she conducted a frantic search for the portable receiver she'd left somewhere. She finally found it under a pile of throw pillows on the sofa. They'd done little to muffle the sound.

"Yes, hello," she said finally.

"What took so long? Were you asleep?"

"Patrick?" She felt her mouth curve into a smile at the unexpected sound of his voice.

"Yes."

"You're not back from Boston already, are you?"

"Nope. The reception ended a little while ago. I'm on my way back to Ryan's and decided to stop at a pay phone and give you a call."

Something inside her melted at that. "How was the wedding?"

"Okay, I suppose. They wrote their own vows. I guess Kelly played a big part in getting Michael back on his feet after he was shot. He talked about how much he owed her and how without her he wouldn't be standing at all, much less standing by her side. There wasn't a dry eye left in the church when they were finished."

"Even yours?"

"Yes, even mine," he said. "I'm not that cynical and jaded that a touching story can't get to me."

"Glad to hear it. So, tell me, what's your brother's bride like?"

"Beautiful, feisty— pretty much like the other two Devaney brides. Deanna has Sean wrapped around her finger. And Maggie, Ryan's wife, is really something. You'd like her. She's already nagging me about spending more time down here."

Alice felt her heart climb into her throat. What was there for Patrick in Maine, really? In Boston a whole new family awaited him. "What did you tell her? Would you consider moving down there?" she asked, trying to keep any hint of dismay out of her voice.

"Why would I do that?" he asked, sounding genuinely puzzled by the question.

"So you could spend more time with your brothers and their families," she explained.

"No way. Widow's Cove is my home. I love fishing. And lately, well, let's just say that I'm highly motivated to get back home."

"Why is that?" she asked, hardly daring to believe the implication that it had something to do with her.

"Well, you see, there's this schoolteacher," he began, lowering his voice to a seductive purr.

"Oh?"

"I can't seem to get her out of my head," he said. "She's thoroughly exasperating. She meddles. She cheats at poker."

"I do not cheat!"

"Oh, did you think I was talking about you?" he asked.

She could almost hear the smile in his voice. "Then this anonymous teacher has gotten to you, is that what you're saying?"

"I believe she has."

"Fascinating," she said, an unfamiliar warmth stealing through her at his admission.

"Yeah, it's definitely fascinating," he said. "I suppose we need to talk some more about that when I get back."

In Alice's opinion, talking was sometimes highly overrated, especially when you knew how cautious the other person was likely to be. Maybe she'd do some-

thing wildly impetuous to jump-start things, now that he'd given her a proper signal.

"What have you been up to today?" Patrick asked.

"Nothing much, just some spring cleaning."

"Meaning you probably turned the place upside down and inside out to scrub every square inch of it," he teased.

"Pretty much."

"Then I imagine you're tired. I should let you get some rest."

"And you should get back to your brother's," she said. "I'm glad you called, though. And I'm especially happy that things are going so well for you and your brothers. It must feel pretty amazing to have them back in your life."

"Better than I expected," he conceded.

"Have you talked about Daniel and your folks at all?"

"A bit with Ryan, but I imagine the subject will come up with the others before I manage to get out of town. I think everyone's waiting till after the wedding to get into anything else. I don't think they want anything to spoil this day for Michael and Kelly. Now that they've left on their honeymoon, I suspect the kid gloves will come off and we'll get down to the hard stuff."

"Have you thought about what you're going to do when the subject does come up?"

"I've already made my position plain. I'll tell them where to find Daniel and the folks, but I'm out when it comes to any grand reunion."

"Oh, Patrick," Alice whispered sadly.

"I've told you before that that's the way it has to be.

I won't change my mind," he said tightly. "Good night, Alice. I'll see you when I get back."

Filled with regret over having spoiled his good mood, she murmured a goodbye, then slowly hung up the phone. As she did, she realized that her palms were sweating and her pulse was racing. How long had it been since the simple sound of a man's voice had had the power to make her react like that? And why did it have to be Patrick Devaney, of all men, who'd reminded her of what it felt like to be a desirable woman? How could she possibly allow herself to fall for a man who was so clearly destined to make the very same mistakes she'd spend the rest of her life regretting?

Patrick's trip to Boston went better than he'd anticipated. Maybe if they lived closer, he could be friends with these men who were his brothers and with their wives. He was already crazy about his irrepressible niece, Caitlyn, and his too-wise-for-his-years nephew, Kevin.

But as he'd told Alice so emphatically, he wanted no part in their plan to get in touch with Daniel or their folks. He understood their need to make contact and find answers, but he already knew all he needed to know. He'd given his brothers an address and a phone number and left it at that. From here on out, they were on their own.

There had been no mistaking the disappointment in Alice's voice when he'd explained his stance to her. His brothers, however, had seemed to understand. They were going into this final stage of their search for answers with their guard up and their own share of anger.

"We'll let you know when we're coming up to Maine," Ryan had promised him.

"And we expect to spend time with you," Maggie had added firmly. "The trip won't be just about your folks and Daniel. We don't intend to lose touch now that we've found you. You have family, Patrick. We won't ever turn our backs on you."

Patrick had heard the total sincerity and love behind her words with a sense of amazement. Maggie and all of her huge family of O'Briens had welcomed him into their hearts. Michael's foster family, the Havilceks, had done the same. Though Patrick had lost the three most important people in his life when he'd left home, he suddenly found himself surrounded once again by family. It wasn't as suffocating as he'd feared it might be. Instead, it had healed a part of his heart that he'd been pretending wasn't broken.

Not that he entirely trusted this glow of rediscovery to last forever. Right now he was new to all of them, but in time they would settle into their own lives down in Boston and leave him to his. When that happened, he knew he would be lonelier than ever.

Still, he felt surprisingly good about the weekend he'd shared with his brothers. Their talks had reminded him of the many nights he and Daniel had stayed up as boys, talking over their day, discussing girls, planning strategy for the football field, where they excelled. He'd missed that kind of camaraderie.

It was late Sunday evening when he opened the gate on his dock and headed toward his boat. A faint whiff of perfume on the salt breeze had him smiling.

"Somebody's trespassing again," he said loudly enough to be heard. "Maybe I should call the police."

"Go right ahead," Alice said tartly. "But you'll miss the effect of finding me naked in your bed."

Patrick nearly choked. "Excuse me?" Surely she wasn't really naked…or in his bed, but the image was going to drive him wild for a long time to come. That she'd even suggested such a thing was enough to have his heart thundering and his pulse racing.

On the off chance that she was more daring than he'd realized, he all but ran to the boat. He found her standing on deck, wrapped in a blanket. He stared at her suspiciously. "Do you have anything on under there?"

"Maybe," she said with a coy smile. "Maybe not."

Patrick groaned. "What are you trying to do to me?"

"Isn't that obvious?"

"Drive me crazy? Seduce me?"

Her lips curved into a smile. "Both. I know how you have a tendency to overthink things, so I thought I'd be here to welcome you home. I couldn't resist. Do you mind?"

He studied her, from her wind-tousled hair to the pink in her cheeks, then searched her face. There was the faintest hint of uncertainty in her eyes. So Alice wasn't nearly as used to being brazen as she wanted him to believe. That charmed him all the more, even as it scared the daylights out of him. He'd intended to take things slowly, to be sensible.

"Quite a homecoming," he murmured, brushing a stray curl from her cheek. He felt her skin heat at the contact.

"Glad you appreciate it, because I'm actually freezing."

He skimmed a finger along the bare skin at the edge of the blanket. His touch raised goose bumps. "So I see. Your skin feels warm enough, though."

"Keep that up and you'll have me on fire," she said, a hitch in her voice.

Patrick dropped his suitcase with a thud and reached for the edge of the blanket, not entirely sure what he expected to find when he tugged. The soft navy chenille unwound slowly, then fell to the deck. To his shock and amazement, Alice was wearing only a lacy red bra and matching bikini panties. He was pretty sure his heart stopped.

"Sweet heaven, what did I do to deserve this?"

"You came back," she said simply. "I hope you don't mind my making myself at home to wait for you."

"Uh, no," he said in a choked voice as he tried to cling to one last shred of sanity. "Alice, I thought we were going to be smart about this."

Her smile spread as she reached for the buttons on his shirt. "We are. I bought an absolutely huge box of condoms."

"Woman, what are you trying to do to me?"

"Isn't that obvious?"

He picked the blanket up from the deck and draped it over her shoulders and pulled it closed in front. He couldn't think with all that bare skin tempting him.

"Why are you here, really?"

Her gaze faltered then, and she took a step back. "I guess I made a mistake. I thought…" She couldn't seem to get the words out.

"I know what you thought," he told her gently. "And I do want you. Believe me, I do. You've just caught me off guard. There are a million and one reasons why we shouldn't rush into anything."

"Name one," she challenged.

"This is a small town. You're a kindergarten teacher. There will be talk, and it won't do your career any good."

She tugged the blanket more tightly around her. "Thank you for your consideration," she said stiffly.

Patrick cupped her chin in his hand and forced her to meet his gaze. "I *am* thinking of you, you know."

Her gaze fell and then she sighed. "I know. I thought if I just showed up here like this, maybe you wouldn't think quite so hard."

He tipped her face up again and lost himself in those golden eyes now sparkling with unshed tears. "Don't you dare cry," he whispered, his voice husky.

"I'm not going to cry," she retorted.

"Good, because it would kill me to think that I'd hurt you, especially when I'm trying so damn hard to do the right thing."

"To hell with the right thing," she said fiercely.

Patrick barely contained a smile. "How about I make some coffee and we discuss that, darlin', because you are all about doing the right thing."

"Not always," she muttered, but she trailed him into the boat's cabin, grabbed up her clothes and went into the small head to change.

Patrick started the coffee and waited a very long time for her to emerge. "You ever going to come out?" he finally called out.

"No."

He laughed. "The coffee's ready. And I found an apple pie sitting on my counter. It looks delicious. I have some ice cream in the freezer I could put on top."

The door to the bathroom opened, and Alice emerged, her cheeks flushed and her eyes still just a little too bright.

"Sit," he said, putting a cup of coffee in front of her along with a slice of pie with ice cream.

He sat down across from her and took a long sip of coffee, watching her over the rim of the cup.

"I'm sorry," she said eventually.

"Don't you dare be sorry. You have nothing to apologize for," he said. "Any man would welcome what you tried to do tonight. I'm just trying to be sensible."

"Sometimes sensible sucks."

He laughed. "Tell me about it."

She regarded him with a wistful expression. "After you called last night, I couldn't get you out of my head. It's been a long time since any man made me feel the way you do. It's been an even longer time since I followed an impulse like the one that brought me over here to wait for you."

"I'm glad you followed this one," he insisted.

"Yeah, I could see that," she said wryly.

"I am," he repeated. "It shows we're on the same wavelength, even if the timing is a little off."

She studied him intently. "Okay, you're going to have to explain that one. What's wrong with the timing?"

"Can you honestly tell me that you're ready to get involved with a man who has as many issues with his family as I do?"

"I wasn't here to propose," she said with an edge of sarcasm.

"I'm aware of that, but a proposition is just as dangerous under the circumstances," he said. "I'm comfortable with the way things are with my family. For your own very valid reasons, you disagree. That's going to be a problem between us, especially if you think you're going to get me to change."

"But—"

"Let me finish," he said, cutting her off. "I know why you feel the way you do. I understand that you have regrets about not reconciling with your own family. I respect your feelings, but our situations are entirely different."

"They're not that different," Alice insisted. She leaned forward and added, "I'm not asking you to move back home. I just want you to open the lines of communication."

Patrick frowned at her. "And that's exactly what I mean about the timing being all wrong for us. I can't be with someone who doesn't respect my decision to cut all ties with my family. God knows, I wish that weren't sitting squarely between us, but it is. You'll be on my case nonstop and you know it. Next thing you know we'll be fighting all the time. What's the point?"

"You're just being stubborn," she accused. "About your family and about this."

"Maybe so."

She seemed startled that he didn't deny it. "Then you can change."

"I don't want to change."

"Patrick—"

He looked directly into her eyes. "Leave it alone, Alice, or we won't have anything to discuss at all."

She started to push back from the table and stand up, then sat back down and regarded him with a steady look. "Where did you see this thing between us going?"

"There's a part of me—a huge part of me—that wants exactly what you wanted when you came here tonight. I've spent a lot of hours this past week dreaming about taking you to bed." He sighed heavily. "Then my brain kicks in and I see how wrong that would be, because I can't give you what you really want from me."

Her gaze narrowed. "What do you think I want from you?"

He held her gaze. "A second chance to make things right with your parents."

She gasped at his words, and this time tears did spill down her cheeks. "You're wrong," she all but shouted at him. "That is so unfair."

"I don't think so. I think you believe if you can settle things between me and my folks, it will make up for the reconciliation you never got to have with your own. It won't, Alice. I can't fix what happened in your life. I can't make the regrets go away."

His heart ached as he watched her shoulders sag with defeat. Whether she admitted it or not, he knew he was right. Her expectations were totally unrealistic. Even if he agreed with her and made peace with his family, it would never be what she really needed. If she was going to find peace, she was going to have to dig deep inside and find a way to forgive herself.

He stood up then and held out his hand. "Come on. I'll drive you home."

"I have my car," she said, angrily brushing away the tears that were still falling.

"I know. I'll take you and walk back. You're in no condition to drive."

"I'm fine. I don't want you to drive me."

"Then I'll walk you home," he said, snatching the keys from the table and stuffing them into his pocket. "You're not getting behind the wheel of a car when you're this upset."

"As if I'd let a stubborn man like you upset me," she returned, but she stood up. "Fine. We'll walk." She scowled up at him. "But I don't want to hear a word out of you. I'm furious with you."

Patrick bit back a grin. "Yes, ma'am," he said dutifully.

"And don't even think about trying to kiss me goodnight."

"The thought won't even cross my mind," he assured her.

She sniffed, then blew her nose on the tissue he held out for her.

"Oh, don't look so damn smug," she said.

He tried to wipe all expression from his face. "How's that?"

"Better," she said, a hint of satisfaction in her voice.

They set off for her house, the silence between them thick with tension. Patrick remained true to his word. He kept his mouth firmly clamped shut. Alice kept sneaking little sideways glances in his direction, as if to reassure herself that he wasn't about to launch into some sort of chitchat.

The wind had kicked up, and the temperatures had

fallen. Alice was plainly shivering as they climbed the hill to her cottage, but he resisted the temptation to offer his jacket or to put his arm around her. She'd set the rules, and he intended to do his utmost to follow them, even if they were ridiculous.

When they reached her house, he noted the white picket fence with its tumble of climbing rose vines. In a few weeks, the roses would bloom in a profusion of color. He could hear the sound of the surf crashing against the cliff behind the house and the slap of a loose shutter somewhere on the house.

"I'll come by tomorrow and fix that shutter," he said.

"I can fix it myself," she said.

He grinned at her disgruntled tone. "Never said you couldn't. It was meant as a peace offering."

"You can't make peace with a couple of nails," she retorted.

"What will it take, then?"

She stared up at him, her face pale in the moon's glow. Her expression was bleak. "I honestly don't know," she said in a tone filled with regret.

"Alice, I was just trying to be honest earlier. I don't want to hurt you by letting you think that you can change me at some point down the road."

"As much as I hate it, I know that," she said.

Patrick shoved his hands in his pockets to keep from reaching for her. "What happens now?"

"I wish I knew."

"What do you want to happen?"

"I suppose you're going to continue to insist that there shouldn't be a difference between what I want right this second and what I want in the global scheme of things," she said wistfully.

"Probably, but try me," he said, fighting a grin.

"Right this second I want you to kiss me," she whispered, her gaze locked with his.

Patrick's heart slammed against his ribs. The woman was tormenting him. "And over the long haul?"

"A lot more kisses," she said, her expression hopeful.

"Alice," he chided.

"I want everyone to live happily ever after," she said.

"With my family," he guessed, finishing the thought.

She sighed. "Yes. So, sue me."

"No," he said. "But I think I will kiss you, if you don't mind. All this talk about kissing has made me just a little wild and crazy."

A smile tugged at her lips. "Oh, really?"

"Yes, really," he said. "As if you didn't know." Hands still shoved determinedly into his pockets so he wouldn't reach for her, he lowered his head and touched his lips to hers. His pulse bucked. "Oh, to hell with it," he murmured, dragging her to him and turning the kiss into something dark and dangerous and intoxicating.

He was aware of her soft gasp of surprise, of her body melting into his. The salt air left their skin damp and whipped her hair so that silky strands brushed over his skin like the tantalizing flick of a feather. He tangled his fingers in all those dark, silky threads of hair and savored the heat where his mouth held hers captive. Fire licked through his veins. The sweet taste of cinnamon and sugar and apple lingered on her tongue.

He wanted more. He wanted too much. And none of his thoroughly rational arguments seemed to matter.

"Come inside," she whispered. "Make love to me, Patrick. It doesn't have to be about tomorrow, or next week. It just has to be about tonight."

He was tempted. Oh, how he was tempted! His body was all but commanding him to take her up on her invitation, but of all the lessons he'd been taught over the years, at least one had stuck. A man didn't take advantage of a woman. And that's what he'd be doing, even if Alice claimed that she could be satisfied with tonight and nothing more.

Besides, buried deep inside was the first tiny kernel of a shocking discovery about himself. He—a man who'd seen the dark side of love and the devastating damage it could do—suddenly wanted to believe in forever.

"Go inside," he said, his hand gentle against her cheek.

Tears welled up in her eyes, along with a familiar flash of anger. "I won't ask again," she said.

"I know that," he said, filled with regret.

Maybe, if things ever changed—whether her expectations or his—he would be the one to ask. And if there was a God in heaven, Alice would forgive him for tonight and say yes.

10

Alice pretty much wanted to die of embarrassment. Twice she'd thrown herself at Patrick, and twice he'd rejected her. Oh, he'd said all sorts of noble things, but the bottom line was he'd been able to say no to everything she was offering. Which meant what? That he was a saint and she was a slut? Now there was a combination destined for happily ever after, she thought bitterly. She'd finally taken her heart out of cold storage and this was what she got for it.

Of course, maybe she'd again leaped too soon. Wasn't that a bitter lesson she should have learned long ago?

She stood under the shower for what seemed like an eternity, but she didn't feel one bit better when she emerged. Maybe that was because not even that much water could wash away all the salt from her self-deprecating tears. She was such an idiot.

She stepped into her bedroom, wrapped in a towel, just in time to hear the phone ring. She glared at it and almost didn't answer, but the ingrained habit of never ignoring phone calls prevented her from letting it ring more than three times.

"Hello." There was no mistaking the testiness in her voice.

"You sound cheery," Molly said. "Anything wrong?"

"Not a thing," Alice said, deliberately forcing a happier note into her voice if only to avoid all the questions likely to be on the tip of Molly's tongue. "Why are you calling so late?"

"Because your car's sitting in my parking lot, and Patrick's sitting at my bar staring into a beer with a moody expression," Molly said, her tone wry. "I figured there's a story there."

"Ask him."

"I did. He told me to mind my own business."

"Well, there you go. Sounds like good advice to me," Alice said.

"You're not going to tell me what's going on?" Molly asked.

"Nope."

"Then I'll have to draw my own conclusions," she said. "A lover's spat, that's what I think. Whose fault was it?"

"No spat. No fault." It wasn't entirely a lie. She and Patrick hadn't exactly fought over his stubborn refusal to have sex with her. He'd taken a stance and she'd had little choice but to accept his decision.

"Yeah, right," Molly said, her voice filled with skepticism. "And I'm Winnie the Pooh."

"Come to think of it, you do hear a remarkable resemblance to him," Alice said. "All round and with that cute little upturned nose of yours."

"Not funny," Molly retorted. "Okay, if you're not going to cough up any valuable information, I'll go back and try my luck with Patrick again. He usually caves after a few beers. He's on his second now."

"Leave the man alone," Alice advised, almost feeling sorry for him. Molly could be more relentless than a nor'easter when she put her mind to it.

"Because you don't want me to upset him, or because you're afraid he'll talk?"

"He won't talk," Alice said with confidence. What man would willingly admit he'd turned down sex when it was offered? Besides, if he was noble enough to say no, he was certainly too noble to kiss and tell.

"We'll see," Molly taunted. "And by the way, if I find out you did anything to hurt him, I'll be over there to tear your hair out."

Alice sighed. "He's very lucky to have you as a friend. You know that, don't you?"

"I like to think so," Molly said. "And it works both ways. Patrick's been a rock for me, too."

"When did you need someone to lean on, Molly?" Alice asked, overcome with curiosity. Molly had never seemed the type to need anyone to bolster her spirits or to drag her back from the edge of despair. Once more Alice had the feeling that it had something to do with Daniel Devaney.

"Everyone needs a friend," Molly replied lightly. "You should remember that."

"I know it all too well," Alice insisted.

"Okay, then. Stop by after school tomorrow. I'm making meat loaf and mashed potatoes for the special."

"I'll be there as long as they're not being served with a lot of personal questions thrown in for dessert."

"Can't promise that," Molly said. "Be here anyway."

"I may have things to do," Alice hedged. Scrubbing the toilet was an option. The bathroom could always use another thorough cleaning.

"Be here," Molly repeated, then hung up before Alice could argue.

Alice sighed. Once her friend got a notion in her head, there would be no peace until she had the answers she wanted. Alice figured she'd be up all night trying to come up with some that would satisfy Molly and not make herself look like a complete idiot in the process.

Patrick knew that Molly wasn't going to rest until she figured out what had gone on between him and Alice. She'd pestered him for an hour the night before until he'd finally left the bar just to get some peace and quiet. He also knew she was going to pull the same stunt with Alice. He doubted Alice would be up to fending off Molly, especially if Molly made it seem that she knew more than she did. She was tricky that way. She'd almost gotten to him by hanging up the phone and claiming that Alice had already told her side of the story. He'd realized differently at the last second and kept his own mouth clamped firmly shut. Alice might not be so quick to catch on.

He told himself that was why he was waiting outside the school when the bell rang at the end of the first day back from their late spring break. Kids streamed from the building, their shouts filling the air as they raced to meet waiting moms or to climb onto school buses. Ricky Foster spotted Patrick and came charging straight at him, hitting him with a tackle that would have felled a lot of people. Patrick merely absorbed the shock of contact and steadied the excited boy, thinking about the day when that energy and raw expertise could be put to the football team's advantage.

"Hey, Patrick, how you doing?" Ricky asked, as if they were longtime buddies.

Patrick grinned. "I'm doing okay, Ricky. How was your first day back at school?"

"Awesome. Miss Newberry bought us a hamster. We're going to take care of it."

Patrick couldn't hide his surprise. "School will be out in a few weeks. Who's going to take care of it this summer?"

Ricky shrugged. "She is, I guess. She said something about it reminding her of some rat or something. I didn't get it."

Unfortunately, Patrick did. Apparently the woman had bought the class a hamster to have a symbolic reminder of him right under her nose. That didn't bode well for the way the afternoon was likely to go.

"Does this hamster have a name?" he inquired uneasily.

"Miss Newberry let us choose. We're calling him Rocky. We figure he needs a tough name, 'cause he's kinda cute."

Patrick chuckled. "Rocky. That's a good one."

Ricky leaned close. "I thought I heard Miss Newberry call him something else, though, something not very nice."

"Did she indeed?"

Patrick looked up just in time to see Alice emerging from the building. The brisk wind plastered her dress to her curves and whipped the skirt above her knees.

He went hard just staring at her. That was a very bad sign. He'd hoped they could get off to a fresh start today without their hormones getting in the way.

Patrick felt a tug on his sleeve and looked down into Ricky's upturned face.

"I gotta go," Ricky announced. "Can I come see your boat sometime?"

"If your dad brings you," Patrick told him.

"All right!" Ricky enthused. "I'll tell him tonight."

He rushed off, tripping over his own feet twice on the way to the school bus. Patrick grinned. The kid was exactly like his dad. He couldn't help wondering what that would be like, having a pint-size version of yourself around.

"You shouldn't get so much enjoyment out of another person's pain," Alice said as she came closer.

"How can you not smile at a kid who's that full of energy and zest for life?" he countered. "Nothing keeps him down, not falling in the freezing ocean or falling on his face."

Her expression softened. "I know what you mean. Ricky's one of a kind."

He looked her in the eye. "So, Alice, do you bounce back, too?"

She regarded him warily. "That depends."

"On?"

"Whether I fall down or get shoved."

He sighed heavily. "I didn't shove you."

"That's what it felt like. Maybe you've never experienced rejection twice in one night. Trust me, it sucks."

"I had good reasons," he said, instantly on the defensive.

"So you think."

"Alice, be reasonable."

"Pardon me if I'm not feeling very reasonable at the moment."

"I gathered that." He met her gaze. "I heard about the substitute rat."

A smile tugged at the corners of her mouth. "Symbolic, don't you think?"

"You planning on cutting off any important parts to make a point?" he inquired.

"An interesting thought, but no. I'm not quite that bloodthirsty. Why are you here, by the way? Were you hoping to turn me down yet again?"

He scowled at her. "No."

"What, then? Are you thinking of enrolling in elementary school? I think you're a little too big for the chairs."

"Can it, Alice," he said, not even trying to contain his irritation at her attitude. "We need to talk about Molly. She has questions."

Alice sighed then. "Tell me about it. She called last night. When I wouldn't tell her anything, she said she was going to cross-examine you. Did you tell her anything?"

"No."

"Okay, then. There's no problem. We don't even have to try to keep our stories straight."

"If you think Molly's going to accept our evasions, you don't know her very well. She won't let up until one of us cracks."

"It won't be me," Alice assured him.

"Did she talk you into coming in this afternoon for meat loaf?" he asked.

Her gaze narrowed. "Yes. You, too?"

"Yes. I rest my case."

"I see your point," she conceded with obvious reluctance.

"Maybe we should stick together," he suggested.

She gave him a look that told him just what she thought of his idea.

"Why don't I go by Jess's and deal with Molly and you stay away?" she retorted.

"Because meat loaf and mashed potatoes are my favorites," he said, not about to be banished from the bar because he and Alice couldn't see eye to eye about sex.

"Get them to go," Alice advised. "Once you've left, I'll go in."

His annoyance with her attitude deepened. "Forget it. I prefer to eat right there where things are hot from the oven," he said. "Of course, you can always take your dinner home if you're scared to be around me."

She frowned at that. "I'm not scared of you, Devaney. I'm not scared of anything."

He actually believed that. "Then have dinner with me."

"Why? What's the point?"

He grinned at her testy tone. "Don't tell me you're one of those unenlightened women who believes that men and women can't be friends."

"Of course not. I just believe it's impossible for you and me to be friends."

"Why?"

"It just is, okay?"

"The sex thing, I suppose."

"Don't try and dismiss it. It's not as if it's a simple matter of you hating green beans and me loving them. Sex requires two people to be on the same wavelength."

"Then again, not having sex only requires one person to take a stance for all the right reasons," he said. "I never said I didn't want you in my life."

"On your terms."

"Yes, on my terms, because I'm trying to be sensible. You're not."

"How lovely that you think so highly of me. Since we obviously want different things from this relationship, it's better to cut our losses."

He leveled a look straight into her eyes. "So that's it? Sex is all you want from me?"

She frowned at him. The pulse at the base of her throat was beating rapidly. "I didn't say that."

"Didn't you? That's what I heard. If we can't sleep together, then you don't want anything from me. Correct me if I've got that wrong."

She looked as if she wanted to smack him, but she was far too ladylike to do it. "I'm just saying that the whole sex thing will get in the way of anything else."

"Speak for yourself. I learned to control myself a long time ago. I don't have to jump into bed with a woman just because she gets to me."

"Dammit, Patrick, this is getting us nowhere."

"No, I think it is. I think it's very telling that you don't think you're capable of keeping your raging hormones under control around me."

"Don't you dare twist this around and make it my problem," she said furiously.

"Then whose problem is it? I'm willing to be friends, to get to know you better. You're the one who won't settle for anything less than a passionate relationship, right here and right now."

"So, you're saying this is a matter of timing, that one day you might change your mind?"

Not if he had a brain in his head, but yeah, sooner or later, she was going to get to him. Better not to tell her that, though. "Maybe," he equivocated.

"Just what I love, a man who knows how to make a firm commitment." She glared at him. "Okay, then. You want a friend, I'll be your friend," she said through gritted teeth. "But I've got to tell you, right this second I don't like you very much."

He bit back a grin and reached for her hand. "Come on, friend. Let's have dinner."

She jerked her hand away. "Don't touch me."

He did laugh then. "*Too* friendly?"

"Too presumptuous," she shot back.

As they strolled toward Jess's he glanced sideways at her. "You know, if we walk into the bar barely speaking to each other, Molly's going to be all over us."

"Don't kid yourself. She's going to be all over us no matter what we do," Alice retorted. "At least this way, we're being honest about how we feel."

"Are we?"

She stopped and whirled on him. "What do you want from me? I'm doing the best I can to find some middle ground we can both live with. You think sex is too complicated with us, that's your right, but don't accuse me of being dishonest about my feelings."

He nodded slowly. "That's fair. You're right. There's

bound to be a certain amount of pretense while we're working this out."

"Do you even know how to be friends with a woman?"

"Sure. Molly and I have been friends for years."

"And the thought of jumping into the sack with her never once crossed your mind?"

"Never once," he said honestly. Molly had always had her eye on another Devaney. And even now, after things had gone terribly wrong between her and Daniel, she wouldn't look at another man, much less at Daniel's twin brother. Patrick had always respected that.

"Well, good for you. Maybe you are a saint, after all."

"Not a saint," he insisted. "I'm just trying to be an honorable man and not take advantage of the situation."

"Oh, whatever," she said. "From now on you're not going to have to worry about taking advantage of the 'situation,' as you put it. I wouldn't sleep with you if you were the last man on earth."

He met her gaze. "Is that so?"

She swallowed hard but didn't blink or look away. "Yes, that's so."

He nodded slowly. "Good. Then we have nothing to worry about."

Except for the fact that right that second he wanted nothing more than to sweep her into his arms and make love to her for about forty-eight hours, nonstop.

Pride was the only thing that made Alice walk into Jess's with Patrick by her side. It was also the only thing that had kept her from swinging her very hefty tote bag and smacking him upside the head when he got that smug expression on his face. It was going to be a long evening. She should have sacrificed the meat loaf and gone home to one of the frozen dinners she kept in the freezer for emergencies. Then again, that would have been admitting to Patrick that she couldn't spend a few hours in his company without getting all hot and bothered.

The minute they entered the bar, Molly gave the two of them a thorough once-over, then nodded in satisfaction. "Pick a booth. I'll bring you a couple of beers and the special in a sec," she said as she took a tray of icy mugs of ale to a table of fishermen seated in the middle of the room. She deftly managed to set the drinks on the table, all the while avoiding a few friendly, roving hands.

Molly rarely lost her cool, Alice thought with admiration. She could keep an entire room filled with rowdy men under control with just one withering glance. Alice wondered if she ought to take lessons from her. Maybe if she perfected her own withering glance, Patrick would stop tormenting her with all this nonsense about friendship. The odds of them sharing a purely platonic friendship were somewhere between slim and none. In her experience, once chemistry had been unleashed, it was all but impossible to pretend it didn't exist.

Still, since he'd insisted on the ground rules, she wasn't about to suggest that she couldn't follow them. She'd just have to train herself to pretend he was as attractive as sludge. Sooner or later, maybe she could make herself believe it.

Besides, Patrick was right about one thing: they hardly knew each other. She'd fallen for his heroics when he'd rescued Ricky, for the vulnerability she sensed in him and for the lost soul she imagined him to be. In truth, he seemed pretty darned determined not to be the least bit lost. In fact, he seemed pretty confident about himself and the decisions he'd made. Maybe if she got to know the real Patrick Devaney, she'd discover that without the imagined vulnerabilities, he didn't appeal to her in the slightest.

She clung to the icy mug of beer Molly had brought to the table and peered at Patrick thoughtfully. "Why did you decide to become a fisherman?" she asked.

His gaze narrowed at the question, as if he suspected it were some sort of trap. "I like being on the water," he said eventually. "It's a challenge."

Alice persisted. "Is it something you always wanted to do?"

He shook his head. "No. A long time ago I wanted to be a fireman, and then for a brief period I considered being an engineer on a train."

"How old were you when you changed your mind?"

"Seven."

A chuckle erupted before she could catch it. "What happened?"

"I caught my first big fish. I was standing on shore when it happened. My dad had to help me reel it in. It probably weighed no more than a pound, but I thought it was huge. My mom cooked it for dinner that night. It was the best fish I've ever had. After that, my dad started taking me out on his boat on Saturdays. He taught me everything he knew about commercial fishing." His expression turned sad. "I always thought we'd go into business together once I grew up."

Alice opened her mouth to tell him it wasn't too late, then clamped it shut again. She'd promised not to go there. Besides, he was opening up. She didn't want to do anything to jeopardize this momentary peace between them.

He sighed heavily. "But things change. I got my own boat and went into business for myself. I like the independence."

"Still, it must be exhausting."

"Some days, yes," he conceded. "But I'm my own boss."

"Ever give yourself a day off?"

"All the time."

"What do you do when you're off?"

He grinned at her. "I go fishing."

She stared at him in astonishment. "What?"

"I take a pole and go off to one of the lakes and stand on shore, just the way I did when I was a kid."

"You find that relaxing?"

"Absolutely. It's not the same at all. When I'm out at sea, I have to stay focused every second. Too many things can go wrong in a heartbeat. When I'm at the lake, I can close my eyes, feel the sun on my face, let my thoughts wander and wait for the fish to bite. If they do, great. If they don't, I've still spent the day outdoors in a great setting."

"It sounds tranquil," she said wistfully.

"It is. Play your cards right and I'll take you sometime."

Alice almost jumped on his reference to cards and that losing night of poker he'd had, then restrained herself. She saw that he was watching her expectantly, clearly anticipating that she'd remind him of their bet. All the more reason to avoid the subject.

"What kind of music do you like?" she asked instead.

He seemed startled by the change of topic, but went along with it. "Country-western, mostly. It gets at the heart of things."

"Movies?"

"Never go."

"Books?"

"Tom Clancy, John Grisham."

"Guy books," she scoffed.

"Hey, I *am* a guy. What do you want from me? Were you hoping I had a secret addiction to romance novels?"

She grinned at that. "You might learn something."

His lips curved into an irrepressible smile. "I might at that. You have any around the house I could borrow?"

"Buy your own."

"Maybe I will. Then, when I'm properly in touch with my feelings, we can have this conversation again." He gave her a long look. "Exactly what is this conversation we're having, anyway?"

"It's called friendly conversation," she said. "It's what you said you wanted."

He nodded slowly, as if trying to grasp the concept. "Okay, then, my turn. Why did you become a teacher?"

"I love kids, especially at the kindergarten age. They still have this incredible curiosity, and they can sop up knowledge like a sponge."

"They're also a little rambunctious," he pointed out.

"I love that, too. It keeps it challenging. I have to be on my toes to keep their attention."

"You want kids of your own?"

"Sure."

"How many?"

"Three, maybe four."

"Really? Then shouldn't you be getting started?"

She frowned. It was a sore point. She wasn't really old at twenty-six, but unless she wanted to have back-to-back babies, the clock was going to start ticking soon. "I'm not that old," she told him.

He grinned. "Older than me. I could have babies for, say, the next forty years or so."

"Typical of a man," she chided. "You think just because your parts work longer than ours, you'd make good daddy material."

"Okay, a valid point," he said, just as Molly appeared at the table, her expression thoroughly fascinated.

"Discussing having a family?" she inquired. "How interesting."

"Don't make too much out of it," Alice said. "We were talking in generalities." She barely resisted the urge to explain that it was all but impossible to have a child with a man who wouldn't agree to sleep with her. That was a can of worms best left tightly shut.

"Still, it's a start," Molly said cheerfully, settling into the booth next to Alice. "I've never heard Patrick mention a need to have children before."

"I said I could," he retorted. "Not that I intended to."

Alice stared at him. "You don't want children?"

"I didn't say that, either," he replied defensively.

"What then?"

"Just that I didn't have much of an example in the father department, as it turns out. I'm not sure I want to risk blowing things as badly as he did."

"That's absurd," Molly and Alice said together.

"You'd make a terrific father," Alice added. "Look at the way you were with Ricky the other day."

"And look at how the kids adore it when you coach Little League," Molly added. She turned to Alice. "You should see him. He's like the Pied Piper, with a dozen adoring kids trailing after him."

"I can imagine," Alice said, liking the image that crept into her head and wouldn't leave. "Are you coaching this summer?"

He shrugged. "Probably."

"I'll have to come to the games. I love baseball."

For the first time since she'd started poking around to discover his likes and dislikes, his eyes lit up. "You do?"

"I spent a lot of evenings at the Red Sox games when I lived in Boston. In a weird way, it made me feel close to my dad. He was a huge fan."

"Little League in Widow's Cove isn't quite the same as the Red Sox," Patrick pointed out.

"But where do you think I saw my first baseball games?" she said, suddenly filled with nostalgia. "My dad never went to Boston, but he did take me over to the ballfields here every Saturday afternoon. A lot of my friends were on teams. Then at night we'd listen to the Red Sox games on the radio."

"I did the same thing with my dad," he said, though his expression remained shuttered.

Alice instinctively reached out and covered his hand with her own. Funny thing how their relationships with their dads had brought them together yet again, this time over a shared interest in baseball. It was such a small thing, she thought, but maybe it was something they could build on.

11

Alice glanced out her classroom window just after lunchtime the next day and saw storm clouds building. It had been unseasonably hot and humid, and clearly they were about to pay for it. Normally there was nothing she liked better than a good, cleansing storm, but a sudden image of Patrick caught out at sea made her insides clench.

Come on, she told herself. He knows what he's doing. By his own admission, Patrick had been around boats all his life. Surely he knew enough to come into port with a storm on the horizon. Surely he knew to find a safe harbor.

But what if there hadn't been time? The thought hit her just as lightning streaked from the sky and thunder rumbled. Her already restless students reacted with alarm. Abandoning her lesson plan for the afternoon, Alice chose a favorite story about the Rainbow Fish and called the class to the front of the room.

Francesca crowded close to her side and even the usually independent Ricky pulled his chair closer than usual. She gave them all a reassuring smile, then tried not to ruin the effect by jumping at another bolt of lightning that seemed to hit far too close for comfort.

"Okay, now," she said, keeping her tone soothing. "Anybody remember what this story is about?"

"Sharing," Francesca said in her shy little voice, leaning against Alice.

"Exactly." Alice opened the book and began to read about the lonely fish with the glittering scales that set him apart from all the other fish.

Normally the story had the power to captivate her, but today just the mention of fish sent her thoughts ricocheting right back to Patrick. Still, the students' excited questions and rapt attention provided a distraction that lasted until the bell rang.

Alice noted the rain lashing at the windows in sheets and realized the kids were going to get soaked just getting to the buses and to their parents' cars. Since the day had started with bright sunshine, none of them had rain gear with them.

Grabbing her own umbrella from the coat closet, she herded her class into a line and led them to the front door, where several of the moms were already waiting. When those students were on their way, Alice put up her umbrella and took the rest one by one to their buses. The umbrella was virtually useless in the whipping wind, but it was the best she could do. She sighed when the last of her charges were finally safely aboard their buses or with their moms.

Her gaze instantly went toward the waterfront, but it was too far away for her to realistically hope to catch a glimpse of Patrick's boat. She was debating running across the park to get a better look when the principal appeared at her side.

"It's a nasty afternoon, isn't it?" Loretta said to Alice. "I understand several of the local fishermen were caught at sea."

Alice's heart began to pound. "Have you heard which ones?"

The principal gave her a knowing look. "I imagine it's Patrick Devaney you're most concerned about."

Alice didn't waste her breath trying to deny it. "Is he back?"

"No," Loretta admitted, "but I'm sure he's fine. Patrick's a smart man. Fishing and the sea are in his blood. He knows what to do to remain safe."

Alice nodded, but she wasn't nearly as certain as the principal seemed to be. Oh, she believed he was highly skilled, but she doubted that any man was a match for Mother Nature when she decided to stir the elements into a frenzy of wind and rain.

Loretta gave her a sympathetic look. "I've canceled the teachers' meeting, if you'd like to go down to the docks and check on him. Perhaps by the time you get there, someone will have more news."

Alice gave her a grateful look, went inside to grab her purse, then took off running, oblivious to the rain that soaked her dress and washed away the little makeup she wore. When she reached the dock with its useless No Trespassing sign, she skidded to a halt and stared out at the churning gray waters as far as she could see through the thick haze. If Patrick was heading for port, she couldn't spot him.

She shivered as the temperature dropped, then

wrapped her arms around herself in a useless attempt to keep warm. With the afternoon heat bumping straight into the cold air from the northwest, there would be fog soon. Getting back to port then would be an even trickier task, notwithstanding all the latest navigational equipment.

Getting colder by the minute, Alice found a blue tarp weighted down with an old anchor and dragged it free, then huddled beneath its scant protection.

That was how Molly found her hours later as darkness fell and more and more people gathered along the shore to watch for the handful of still-missing boats.

"I can't believe you're out here with no coat or hat," Molly scolded. "When someone told me they'd seen you, I was sure they'd been wrong. I thought you had more sense."

"Patrick's not back yet," Alice explained. "I couldn't leave."

Molly gave her a commiserating look. "You've got it bad, don't you?"

Alice sighed. "I suppose I do, for all the good it's going to do me." She shook her head. "I can't think about that now." She gazed at Molly worriedly. "Do you think Patrick's okay?"

"I think he's probably out there leading the rescue attempts for any of the other boats that are in trouble, that's what I think," Molly said with conviction.

"Really?" Alice asked, searching her friend's face.

"Absolutely."

There wasn't so much as a hint of doubt in Molly's voice, but Alice still wasn't entirely comforted. "I hope you're right," she whispered, trying to see through the gathering darkness for any sign of an approaching boat. He had to come back, if only so she could tell him that she would be his friend and ask nothing more, if that's the way it had to be. All that mattered was that Patrick be safe.

Patrick was cursing himself every which way as his boat rocked and rolled on the huge swells and lightning split the sky again and again. Normally he had a nose for bad weather and he could smell an oncoming storm in the air.

Today, though, his mind had been on Alice, on their dads and baseball and on the uneasy truce they'd reached the night before. He'd missed all the signs that the weather was about to change dramatically.

By the time he'd noticed the first dark clouds on the horizon, it had been too late. The storm was on top of him in minutes, with its fierce winds and pelting rain. The deck turned slippery and treacherous, and waves washed over the sides of the trawler.

"Blast it all to hell and back," he muttered as he tried to keep his hands steady on the wheel. He'd never gotten caught like this before. In fact, he was usually among the first to get back to shore and the first to head back out when a storm died down to look for others who hadn't been as lucky.

Today it was going to require every ounce of his concentration to keep from making a mistake that could mean certain death, either from the boat capsizing or him being washed overboard because of some misstep on the slippery deck. He thought of Alice and concluded he'd have to make damn sure nothing like that happened. He had fences to mend with the woman. He had to tell her that she was right and he was wrong. They needed to grab every second they could to be together, because life was filled with uncertainties.

Maybe their relationship would last, maybe it was doomed, but the only way to find out was to take a chance. He intended to say all that and to eat all the crow she wanted to dish up. Then he intended to make love to her for hours on end until he'd finally had his fill of touching and exploring and making her cry out with pleasure.

Hands clenched tightly to the wheel, he heard the sputtering static of his radio and a frantic Mayday call from another Widow's Cove boat. He peered around through the almost impenetrable wall of rain for some sign of a boat nearby.

"Where are you, *Lady Q.?*" he radioed back. "Give me your location."

He heard the hint of panic in Ray Stover's voice as he responded with the coordinants. Ray was a practiced seaman. If he was showing any hint of fear, then the danger had to be high.

"We're taking on water fast, Patrick. Are you any-where close?"

"Close enough," Patrick said, trying to hide his concern. "Not to worry. I'll get to you, Ray. Hang in there. Got your life vest on?"

"Of course."

"If anything happens to the boat, get the light on and keep signaling. I'll be there any minute now."

Totally focused on the emergency task, he set the boat's course and calculated that he could be there in ten minutes, maybe fifteen if the sea fought him, which it seemed inclined to do. Grabbing a spotlight he kept for emergencies, he sent its piercing beam in the direction where the sinking boat would likely appear.

"Ray, I've got a spotlight shining. Let me know when you see it."

"Roger that," Ray said, the tension in his voice less palpable. "Which direction?"

"I'm just east of you and approaching from the south."

"Got it."

The rain was finally easing and the lightning had moved farther out to sea, but the swells were still a challenge as Patrick cut through the water toward the distressed boat.

His radio crackled.

"I see the light," Ray shouted triumphantly. "You're about a hundred yards away now, and just in the nick of time, buddy. This crate of mine is about to go down."

Patrick still didn't breathe a sigh of relief, not until he was alongside the rapidly sinking *Lady Q.,* which was listing to port with water washing over its bow. As soon as he pulled alongside and held out a hand, Ray gingerly made the leap onto the deck of the *Katie G.* His lined face was stoic until the weathered and once-sturdy boat sank from view, then his expression filled with sorrow.

"Hey, man, you're okay. That's what counts," Patrick consoled him. "You can always get another boat."

Ray shook his head. "I'm done," he said, his voice heavy with resignation. "I've had three close calls in the past two years. I want to live to see my grandchildren grow up. Janey's been nagging at me to retire, but I figured I'd do one more season before calling it quits. This just pushes things along a little faster."

Patrick heard the regret in Ray's voice and knew he'd feel the same when the day finally came that the sea's challenges became too much for him, too. Before he could stop himself, his thoughts wandered to his father, who was almost the same age as Ray. Had he weathered today's storm? The commercial boats he captained were bigger and more seaworthy than the *Katie G.* or the *Lady Q.,* but in a raging storm, few of the boats were truly safe. A line of squalls was something a man learned to respect, if he intended to live a long and healthy life.

Because Patrick didn't want to care about his father's fate today, he busied himself with piloting the boat back toward Widow's Cove and keeping up a steady stream of distracting conversation to keep Ray's mind off of his own near miss.

As the lights of Widow's Cove pierced the darkness of the night sky, Patrick shone his spotlight toward shore to signal that he was coming in. He heard a shout go up.

"Wonder if we lost anyone out there today?" Ray asked. "Damn storm came up quicker than most."

"Yours was the only distress signal I caught," Patrick told him. "I imagine everyone else is making their way back now. If anyone's still missing, we'll know it soon enough."

When Patrick reached the dock, Ray helped him tie up the boat, then reached for Patrick's hand with a strong grip. "I owe you, son."

Patrick gave the old man an embrace. "If you start

getting restless being retired, you can go out with me anytime."

Ray grinned. "I might just take you up on that," he said, then cast a guilty glance toward the gray-haired woman standing on the dock with tears streaming down her face. "Assuming Janey ever lets me out of her sight again."

Patrick held back as Ray went to his wife and gently wiped the tears from her cheeks before putting his arm around her and leading her toward Jess's, where the town traditionally gathered in the aftermath of a storm that threatened the lives of the local fishermen.

After they'd gone, Patrick jumped onto the dock, only to walk straight into a shove that caught him off guard and almost landed him on his backside. Seemed like today was destined to be full of unexpected shocks. His gaze narrowed with speculation as he looked into Alice's flashing eyes.

"You scared the living daylights out of me," she said accusingly, her expression filled with a mix of anger and relief. "Don't you ever do that to me again, Patrick Devaney."

He stared at her in disbelief. "You were worried?"

"Look at me," she said, gesturing toward her soaked clothes and dripping hair. "I've been here for hours. I was terrified." Then the tears began rolling down her cheeks, a reaction every bit as heartfelt as Janey Stover's had been.

Shaken by the sight of Alice's tears, Patrick reached for her. "I'm here," he said, drawing her into his arms. "Ah, darlin', don't cry, I'm here now."

She poked him in the chest, though with slightly

less force than her earlier shove. "You scared me," she repeated.

He tucked a finger under her chin and looked deep into her eyes. "I can't promise it won't happen again. This is what I do."

She sighed, resting her cheek against his chest. "I know."

He decided to share some of his own discoveries made during the storm. "It did occur to me as I was sitting out there in the dark with the winds howling and the rain coming down that maybe I've been just a little hardheaded about the sex thing," he said casually.

Her gaze shot up to clash with his. "Meaning?"

Patrick felt himself drowning in those golden pools of light, still shimmering with tears. If he hadn't already been certain, one look into her eyes would have convinced him. "I don't want to waste any more time," he said, then added, "that is, if you're still interested."

She stood on tiptoe and kissed him, leaving no doubt at all in his mind about her response. That kiss could have melted steel, he thought, then wondered if maybe it wouldn't be worth weathering a storm every day to have a homecoming like this.

Alice apparently had no intention of giving Patrick one single second to change his mind, he concluded as she gave his chest a gentle nudge.

"Back on the boat," she ordered.

"I think I've had about all the bobbing around on the water I can take for one evening," he countered. "I had in mind a nice, warm bed on dry land."

"If you're considering mine, it's too far away."

"It's a few blocks," he pointed out.

"Too far," she repeated.

"There's always the room above Jess's," he suggested.

She gave him an incredulous look. "Are you crazy? We'd never hear the end of it," Alice said. "Okay, you win. My place, but let's make it snappy."

"I don't suppose I could grab a bite to eat first," he said.

She glowered at him. "If that isn't the most romantic thing I've ever heard. 'Darling, I'd really love to sleep with you after holding out forever, but I'd like my dinner first.'"

"You want me to have a little stamina, don't you?" he teased.

Alice rolled her eyes. "Okay, my place, I feed you and then no more stalling."

Patrick grinned. "No more stalling," he agreed.

As they walked up the hill to her cottage, he took off his jacket and wrapped it around her in an attempt to stop her shivering. As they neared, he spotted the warm light glowing in the front window.

"I thought you hadn't been home," he said. "There's a light on."

"It's on a timer," she explained. "I don't like coming home to a dark house."

Patrick sighed, unable to recall the last time he'd come home to a welcoming light in the window. Most nights his boat was dark as pitch when he got back from Jess's. Until he'd seen the light in Alice's window, he hadn't realized just how depressing the darkness could be.

Walking through the door of her cottage for the first

time, he got the oddest sensation in his chest. It felt as if he were coming home. She'd made the place cozy, even on a night like this. The fireplace was ready for the touch of a match. The walls were a soft shade of yellow, the furniture covered in blue-and-white prints and solids. There were fresh flowers in an old cobalt-blue jar on the coffee table next to a pile of books, and a bright-yellow chenille throw had been tossed over the back of the sofa. Patrick could instantly imagine Alice snuggled beneath the yellow fabric, the fire blazing and a book in her hands. He could just as easily imagine her wearing that soft throw and nothing else.

Best not to go there just yet, he admonished himself. To put a little distance between them, he said, "Why don't you go take a hot shower before you catch pneumonia? I'll see what I can rustle up in the kitchen."

She gave him one of those long, lingering looks that could vaporize water, then said, "Sure you don't want to come take that shower with me?"

Oh, yeah, he thought, feeling a little frantic. That was exactly what he wanted, but if he touched her now, if he so much as caught a glimpse of her naked, they'd be in her bed before either of them could say a word. He didn't want it to happen that way, not the first time they were together. He wanted to give her tenderness and romance and long, slow, tormenting caresses.

"I'll pass," he said mildly.

She gave him a grin that only a practiced vamp could have perfected. "Your loss."

"I'm sure it is," he murmured, turning away to go in search of the kitchen.

Compared to his own, Alice's kitchen was well

stocked with homemade soup, the makings for a variety
of sandwiches and even a leftover roasted chicken with
plenty of meat still on its bones. Patrick's mouth watered
as he pulled away a chunk of tender white meat and
munched on that while pondering all the other choices.

He put the beef vegetable soup on to heat, then made
two thick sandwiches of ham, cheese, lettuce and toma-
toes on homemade bread. After pouring two glasses of
milk, he set the feast on the kitchen table. He was about
to take his first bite, when the faint floral scent of Alice's perfume caught his attention. He glanced up, and
his mouth went dry.

She was standing in the kitchen doorway wearing a
perfectly respectable robe—that is, if fabric that draped
and clung to outline every curve could be described as
respectable. It was the same golden-bronze shade as
her eyes and it caught the light in much the same way,
shimmering provocatively. Suddenly the only thought
on his mind was slowly, ever so slowly, stripping that
robe off her and letting it slide to the floor.

"Alice, what are you trying to do to me?" he asked,
his breath hitching.

She tried to fight a smile, but it escaped, anyway. She
fingered the edge of the robe. "What? This old thing?"

"That old thing could drive a man wild."

She seemed genuinely surprised by the vehemence
in his voice. "Really?"

"Yes, and you damn well know it," he accused.

Her smile was full-blown now. "I could take it off."

Patrick forgot all about food, forgot everything,
including his own name, as his blood turned to fire.

"Okay," he murmured, when he could find breath enough to speak.

She blinked once. "Okay?"

He nodded and reached for the loosely tied belt on the robe. "That's what I said, okay. Take it off."

One tug on the belt untied it and had the front of the robe gaping open to reveal a body still glowing from her shower and slightly pink, though he couldn't be certain if the color was due to a thorough scrubbing or embarrassment.

"You take my breath away," he told her with total honesty.

"That's only fair," she said, sliding onto his lap. "You've been stealing mine since the day we met."

"What are we going to do about it?"

She grazed her knuckles along his cheek. "We could start with this," she said, lowering her mouth to cover his.

His pulse ricocheted wildly as he gave himself up to the kiss. She'd clearly intended it to be a light, teasing contact, but it turned greedy and all consuming in a flash. His heart slammed against his ribs, and he bunched a handful of that delicate, silky fabric into a wad to keep from putting his hands all over her.

How could he want her this much? he wondered with a hint of desperation. How had he allowed himself to need anyone this much? Did it even matter?

"Sweetheart, I think a kitchen chair is the wrong place for this," he said, scooping her up as he stood and heading for the door. "Where's the bedroom?"

Her head tucked on his shoulder, her breath fanning against his cheek, she directed him down the hall to her room. The colors in here were as soothing as those in the living room, Patrick noted vaguely as he settled her in the middle of a double bed on which the sheets had already been turned down. She regarded him with a lazy look.

"You're not climbing in here unless you lose some of those clothes, Devaney."

He grinned. "Which ones? Any preference about where I start?"

She studied him thoughtfully. "The shoes and socks first, I think, then the shirt. After that, I'll give it some more thought."

Patrick kicked off his shoes and stripped away his socks, then dragged his flannel shirt over his head without bothering to unbutton more than the top two buttons. "Next?"

"The belt, I think. Slowly, please."

He bit back a grin. "You sure you don't want a little background music for this striptease?"

"Nope. You're doing fine. Now, lose the T-shirt."

"Okay, then," he said, when he was standing before her, bare-chested and surprisingly self-conscious. "There's not a lot left. Do the jeans go or stay for now?"

"They go, of course."

Getting into the spirit of it and enjoying the mischievous pleasure shining in her eyes, he unsnapped the jeans then took his own sweet time unzipping them. He executed a little twirl before sliding them off and kicking them across the room.

Alice laughed. "Nice touch. I like the jockeys, by the way. Red is definitely your color."

"Probably matches my cheeks about now," he said, kneeling on the bed to press a kiss to her lips.

Alice cupped his face in her hands. "You aren't embarrassed, are you?"

"Darlin', what I am is hot and bothered."

Her smile spread. "Well, then, come on over here and let's see what we can do about that."

"I have a few ideas."

"Yes, I imagine you do."

He studied her expression, then chuckled. "But we're doing this your way, am I right?"

She reached for the waistband of his jockeys, her fingers grazing his belly. "Oh, yeah," she said, her eyes bright with anticipation.

"Then, go for it," he said, closing his eyes and lying back against the pillows. "I'm all yours."

He wasn't sure, but he thought he heard her murmur something that sounded a lot like "If only," but then her hands were playing their wicked games, and Patrick completely lost himself in her touch.

12

Alice had waited too long for Patrick to make love to her to want to rush through it. She intended to torment him until he was at least half as crazy with desire as she'd been for a couple of weeks now.

She sat back on her heels, her robe spilling open to display more bare flesh than she'd exposed to anyone except her doctor in a long time. Patrick was reclining against her pillows, clad in nothing except those bright-red jockey shorts, and she intended to savor the sight. The man was hard as a rock, every muscle well defined, not from working out in a gym but from his daily life. She reached out and ran her fingers over his abdomen and felt the muscles jerk at her touch. She could also see the effect on another well-defined portion of his anatomy, which his jockeys did nothing to disguise.

"Interesting," she murmured, as if she were conducting an experiment.

A low chuckle rumbled in his throat. "Having fun yet?"

"Absolutely," she said, moving on to the warm skin

of his broad chest. She tangled her fingers in the shadowing of dark hair that curled tightly against tanned skin. She could feel the heat radiating from him and uttered a little sigh of satisfaction. She hadn't realized how much she missed touching a man like this, how much she missed the closeness with another human being.

Even so, the closeness felt different somehow, more intense. More complete. She realized that because her feelings for Patrick ran deeper, she craved more than physical intimacy with him. She craved the emotional connection that had been building between them.

Not that the physical was all bad. No, indeed, she thought as she leaned forward and pressed a kiss to the base of his throat and felt his pulse leap. Then he clamped his hand on the back of her neck and held her still.

"Enough," he said just before closing his mouth over hers.

His tongue invaded in a heartbeat, stirring sensations low in her belly. Even as his kiss deepened and devastated, his hand was exploring, slip-sliding over silky fabric, rubbing it over nipples already taut and sensitive. She was aching and anxious by the time his clever fingers moved lower to dip into moist heat and send her jolting off the mattress.

The man was a wizard, his touch magic. She felt herself convulse from just one delicate flick across the tight bud of her arousal. Waves of pleasure washed over her.

Patrick waited, letting her ride them out, before starting all over again. The buildup was even faster this time, and far more intense. Her already aroused body responded to each caress, to each kiss, with restless movements that quickly turned more frenzied and demanding.

"Not just yet," he said, holding back, his gaze locked with hers.

"I need you now," she insisted, thinking she might die of anticipation if he insisted on waiting another moment. She lifted her hips, seeking the joining he was denying her. "Patrick, please. Inside me."

He smoothed a hand over her brow as if soothing an anxious child. "When the time is right."

Alice bit back a gasp as he swirled his tongue around one nipple, then another, before tugging hard and sending sensation slamming through her. Her hips lifted off the bed, once more seeking relief, seeking him…but still he remained beyond reach.

Those clever fingers tormented and teased and inflamed until she thought she'd scream from the sheer wonder of it. Every muscle in her body strained for release, every inch of her skin was hot and aching for a touch that he now passed out with stingy deliberation. Her nerves were raw, her body achy and needy, when at last he thrust into her and took her breath away.

She felt her body stretch, then mold to his, felt the friction as he moved inside her and then the quick rise of sensation, the overwhelming tide of pleasure as heat and desire exploded. Rather than shattering them into a million fragments, the explosion melded them into one single unit, like the fusion of metals into something so strong, so powerful it could withstand the test of time.

Alice clung to Patrick's shoulders and rode out the waves of sensation until, at last, peace followed. And with peace came the certainty that this love she felt for Patrick Devaney would last a lifetime.

If only he would let it.

Morning came too darn soon. Patrick would have stayed right here, Alice warm and flushed in his arms, if there hadn't been the outside world and all its demands to consider. He might be master of his own fate, but she wasn't. She had a classroom full of five-year-olds who were counting on her. He glanced at the clock, noted it was only six and concluded they had at least a little time before Alice would need to start on her workday.

He brushed a finger lightly across her lush lips, then felt the soft whisper of a sigh as she snuggled against him. "Hey, darlin', if you wake up now like a good girl, there's time to be bad before the day gets underway."

"Bad?" she murmured. Then her eyes snapped open, alight with interest. "How bad?"

He grinned at her instantaneous eagerness. That was just one of things he'd come to love about her during the long night. Alice held nothing back. There was no pretense of reticence, no game playing. When it came to making love, they were completely, shatteringly attuned.

He leaned close to whisper in her ear, the taunt designed to make her cheeks flame and her hands rove. She slid on top of him in a heartbeat, taking him into her and riding him, her head thrown back, her expression triumphant, as another climax tore through them both.

She collapsed on top of him, her breath coming in gasps. "There's a very good chance I won't be able to move for the rest of my life," she murmured eventually.

Patrick grinned. There was far more satisfaction than dismay in her tone. "I think you'd better," he advised lightly. "I'm not sure you want to try explaining away an absence from school today."

She groaned and rolled over. "You could call in for me."

"And say what?" he teased. "That you spent the night making mad, passionate love with me and can't even crawl out of bed?"

"It would be the truth," she said, her eyes still closed, a smile on her lips.

"And it would be all over town by suppertime. It just might give some parents second thoughts about entrusting their precious kindergarten students to you."

She opened her eyes and frowned. "Yeah, I see your point," she conceded with obvious reluctance. "What about you? Are you going to work today? Or are you going to laze around in my bed all day? Come to think of it, I rather like the idea of daydreaming about that all day long. I'd be highly motivated to get home after school."

"Unfortunately, I, too, have to work," he said. "I need to go over the boat to see if there was any damage from the storm. Then I'll probably take it out for a few hours."

Alarm flashed in her eyes for just an instant. "Are you sure? Have you checked the weather?"

"Not yet." He smoothed away the furrow in her brow. "Alice, yesterday was a fluke. I was distracted. I missed all the signs that a storm was approaching. Usually I'm one of the first ones in."

"What happened yesterday?"

"You were on my mind," he admitted.

The furrows instantly formed again. "It was my fault you almost got yourself killed?"

"No. It was mine. I know better than to allow myself to get distracted. It won't happen again." He gave her a nudge. "Now scoot. I'm not sure I can drag myself out of this bed as long as you're in here tempting me."

"I tempt you?" she asked.

"Don't fish for compliments," he scolded. "You know you drive me crazy. There are a million and one reasons why you and me being together is a bad idea, and you managed to make me forget every one of them."

She grinned then. "Good, because you drive me crazy, too."

He watched her finally slide from the bed, then head for the bathroom, unable to tear his gaze away from her amazing body. No question about it, she'd bewitched him.

Unfortunately, there was also no question that their relationship remained every bit as complicated as it had been before they'd slept together. There were some things that making love—or even falling in love—simply couldn't change.

Alice felt as if everything in her life was changing and, finally, for the better. She'd spent her whole life dreaming about a man like Patrick Devaney—solid and dependable and amazingly tender, a man in whom to place her trust, whom she could love with her whole heart, with whom she could build a family. Maybe, at long last, she would be able to fill the hole in her heart that had been left when her own family had died.

"You're certainly glowing this morning," Loretta

Dowd said when she came across Alice in the school office. "Obviously, you found Patrick last night. He made it home safely?"

Alice prayed she wasn't blushing furiously, though her cheeks felt hot under the woman's knowing gaze. "He's fine," she said. "He rescued Ray Stover. Ray's boat capsized."

"Janey will be glad enough of that, I imagine," the principal said. "She's been wanting Ray to retire for some time now." Loretta studied Alice with a knowing look that seemed to zero straight in on her heart. "What about you? Any second thoughts about giving your heart to a fisherman?"

A twinge or two, Alice was forced to admit to herself. Aloud she said, "None at all."

"Really? I find that surprising. I always thought that was one of the reasons you left Widow's Cove, because you didn't want to fall into the trap that so many of your ancestors had fallen into. I thought you viewed the sea as your enemy."

Alice shuddered at the reminder. "If I've learned nothing else in the past few years, it's that the heart makes its own choices."

The principal patted her hand. "Indeed it does. I only regret that you came to that wisdom after your parents were gone."

Alice sighed. "I know. I wish I could have told them and begged their forgiveness for making judgments about their choices."

"They bore their own share of the guilt," Loretta reminded her. "They were too hard on you. You were young. You had a right to your choices, as well."

"I know, but I regret that we didn't have a second chance to discuss it more rationally. Maybe I could have made them see how happy I was with the choice I'd made."

"Living with regrets is a waste of time." Loretta gave Alice a sly look. "Have you had any luck making Patrick see that?"

"None at all," Alice admitted.

"I thought not. He's a hard case. It wouldn't surprise me if he took his anger to the grave."

Alice regarded her with surprise. "You don't think there's any hope for a reconciliation with his family?"

"As long as there's breath, there's hope. Keep trying, Alice. I see Patrick's parents from time to time. There was always something a little lost and sad about them, but it's been worse since Patrick left. I don't know the whole story, but it would be a shame if it kept them apart for too long. Mending fences is never easy once pride gets in the way, but without forgiveness, where would any of us be?"

"I know," Alice said. "I agree."

"Then do something about it. He'll listen to you. Once a man's heart opens to love, it's more accepting of a lot of things."

"I don't know that Patrick loves me."

The principal gave her another of those too-knowing looks. "If not, then what was last night about, my dear?"

Alice blushed furiously. "How…?"

A surprising twinkle lit the principal's eyes. "You're wearing your blouse inside out. It's not like you, so I suspect you dressed in a rush this morning."

She grinned at Alice, then strode into her office and firmly shut the door.

Alice stared down at the exposed seams of her blouse and felt as if she might die of embarrassment on the spot. She rushed off to the ladies' room to remedy the telltale mistake before anyone else noticed and the story made its way around town.

She was still completely off-kilter when the day ended and she made her way to Jess's, hoping for at least a glimpse of Patrick before she went home.

At three o'clock the bar was quiet and Molly was sitting in a booth in a darkened corner, her expression brooding. Alice slid in opposite her and studied her worriedly.

"Bad day?" she asked when Molly volunteered nothing, not even a halfhearted greeting.

"Bad enough."

"Want to talk about it?"

"No." She sounded very sure of it, too.

"Sometimes talking helps," Alice pressed.

"And sometimes it's just a waste of breath."

"Now there's a cynical view."

"I have a right," Molly retorted, her tone and her expression unyielding.

"Of course you do, but it's unlike you. People around here know they can count on you for sound advice and a cheery greeting. You'll scare them off if you keep the sour look on your face through happy hour."

Molly feigned a mocking smile. "Will that do?"

"It might fool some, but not most. Talk, Molly."

"I've nothing to say, and if you're going to keep pestering me, I'll be forced to head into the kitchen and start dinner preparations."

"Does that involve sharp knives?"

"Of course."

"Then maybe you should put it off."

Molly gave her a wry look. "Very funny."

"I didn't mean it to be."

Molly started to push herself up, then sank back against the cushions of the booth. The effort was so halfhearted, so counter to everything Alice knew about Molly's usual energy level, that Alice's alarm grew.

"Dammit, Molly, are you sick?"

Molly's gaze turned sad. "Not the way you mean."

"Sick at heart, then?"

She nodded eventually, then cut off all questions by adding firmly, "But I don't want to talk about it."

"It has something to do with Daniel Devaney, though, doesn't it?"

"I said I didn't want to talk about it," Molly repeated, though her voice lacked her usual feistiness.

"Oh, Molly, what did he do to you?" Alice whispered, reaching for her friend's hand.

"Nothing Patrick won't do to you, if you're not careful," Molly said.

The sting of the words was so unexpected that Alice felt as if she'd been slapped. Before she could even think of an adequate response, Molly leaned forward.

"I'm very fond of Patrick," Molly said, her tone filled with urgency. "He's a wonderful man, and he's been a good friend to me, but that's all he's capable of, Alice. That's all either of them are capable of, thanks to those god-awful parents of theirs. Neither of them will ever trust anyone enough to let them into their lives."

Alice refused to believe that was true, at least of Patrick. In fact, she was still convinced that if he could only forgive his parents and make peace with them, his heart would be open to anything. He'd allowed her into his life, hadn't he? That had to mean something.

"You're wrong," she told Molly.

"Am I? What makes you so certain of that? Is it because Patrick slept with you? Because, if you're counting on that to make a difference, I'm here to tell you that it's only the first step on the path to heartbreak."

"You're wrong," Alice said again, unwilling to admit how deeply Molly's words had shaken her. "And it's cruel of you to project whatever happened to you with Daniel onto my relationship with Patrick."

"I'm only trying to warn you because I care about you," Molly said. "And I care about him, as well. Leaving you will hurt him as much as it hurts you, but he'll do it just the same."

"I can't accept that. Keep your warnings to yourself, Molly. I know Patrick. I know what we have together." If she hadn't before last night, she did now, and she didn't intend to let Molly's dire predictions sway her.

Molly merely gave her a sad smile. "I feel sorry for you."

"Why would you feel sorry for me?"

"Because I once felt the same about Daniel. I thought I knew who he was and what we shared. It turned out I knew nothing about him at all."

Alice regretted that she wasn't Ricky Foster's age, that she couldn't clamp her hands over her ears and make nonsense noises to block out Molly's hurtful words.

"Molly, I'm sorry for whatever Daniel did to you. I really am," she replied instead. "But it's got nothing to do with me and Patrick."

"It has everything to do with him," Molly insisted. "They're twins, for goodness' sakes. Identical twins."

"That doesn't mean they see the world exactly alike," Alice said, still fighting for what she'd found with Patrick the night before. She refused to believe it had been nothing more than an illusion, nothing more than incredible sex with no meaning behind it.

"Do you think because Patrick broke free of his parents after he and Daniel found out about their brothers that he's somehow more well adjusted than Daniel?" Molly asked.

"No." The opposite, in fact, though Alice wasn't ready to admit that, not when Molly was in this odd mood.

"Well, I'm glad you can see that much, at least," Molly said with evident relief.

"One day he'll make peace with them," Alice said.

Molly stared at her. "For a minute, there, I thought there was some hope for you, but now I see that you're delusional, after all."

"He will," Alice insisted.

"And then what? The Devaneys will all live happily ever after?"

"Yes."

"No," Molly said flatly. "You've been spending too much time with five-year-olds. This isn't a fairy tale, Alice. It's real life, and some betrayals are too huge.

You're not going to have some picture-perfect family to make up for the one you lost."

Once again the sting of the words had the power to take her breath away. For Molly to be so harsh, so unbelievably cruel, her own pain had to be overwhelming. Alice wished she could look Daniel Devaney in the eyes and tell him what a heartless fool he was for whatever he'd done to Molly. She doubted she could fix this, though. Molly was probably right about one thing—some betrayals *were* too huge.

"I'm so sorry he hurt you so badly," she told Molly. "One of these days you'll meet someone else and forget all about Daniel."

Molly gave her a sad, tired smile. "If only it were that easy," she said.

Before Alice could respond, Molly visibly pulled herself together and stood up.

"I'm sorry you caught the brunt of my foul mood," she told Alice. "I'm usually better at keeping it under wraps."

"Why not today?"

"An anniversary of sorts," Molly said.

"You can tell me, you know. And I can even manage to hold my tongue, if you're not anxious for my advice."

Molly laughed at that. "Now it would almost be worth testing you on that, but I have things to do in the kitchen. If you want to make yourself useful, there's an inventory checklist for the liquor that I meant to get done this afternoon."

Alice nodded. "I imagine I can count a few bottles and write the totals down without messing up. Jess always left that to me, because you were too easily distracted."

Molly chuckled. "He did at that. I'd forgotten. Your parents would have had a fit had they known that my grandfather was letting you near the whiskey and teaching you to play poker."

"Which was exactly why I loved coming here so much," Alice told her. "I think I already had a well-developed rebellious streak, even in grade school."

"You did, indeed," Molly concurred. "That's why it's such a wonder that they're letting you teach at that very school. Now, get busy, before Patrick wanders in and distracts you all over again."

Alice watched her friend go into the kitchen, then sighed. She would give anything to ease Molly's pain, but how could she, when Molly wouldn't even reveal what the problem was beyond an obviously bitter breakup?

Of course, Patrick probably knew the details, she realized as she found the inventory sheet and began counting the stock behind the bar. And she knew all sorts of clever ways for making him talk. She'd have to put a few of them to good use later tonight.

13

Patrick found Alice hunkered down and bent over in a fascinatingly provocative position when he walked into Jess's. Fortunately the bar was empty, or he'd no doubt have had to bust the chops of a few male patrons eager to get an eyeful of her delectable backside. Since they were alone, he walked up behind her, snagged her around the waist and pulled her against him.

She gasped in surprise, then twisted to face him. "Trying to take advantage of me?" She seemed more intrigued than upset by the possibility.

He grinned. "Looked to me as if you were waiting for me to come along."

She feigned a scowl. "Hardly. I was doing inventory to help Molly out."

"Remind me to have you come by the boat and take inventory for me sometime," he said.

She gave him a look that had his pulse jumping. "I'm almost finished here," she told him, a deliberate taunt in her voice. "Just what do you have to be inventoried?"

"Oh, I think you'd find it more interesting than this," he assured her.

"Ask me again after dinner," she suggested, wriggling free in a way designed to torment him some more. "The special's herb-roasted chicken. I've been smelling it for the past hour, and I'm not leaving here till I've had some."

"Then let me get our order in while you finish up here. Where is Molly, by the way?"

"Hiding in the kitchen," Alice said, her expression suddenly sobering. "She's having a bad day, Patrick. Worse than usual. Any idea why?"

Patrick glanced at the calendar on the wall behind the bar, then muttered a curse and shoved into the kitchen without another word to Alice. He trusted her to stay where she was and give him a few minutes alone to offer whatever comfort he could to Molly. He should have remembered the day without a reminder from Alice. He always made it a point to stick close by when this particular anniversary came around.

When he burst into the kitchen, Molly glanced up from the pot of mashed potatoes she was whipping. Her face was streaked with tears. She swiped at them ineffectively, her movements jerky and impatient.

"Unusual way to salt the potatoes, don't you think?" he said gently.

"I'm not going to discuss my tears with you," Molly said, sniffing. "They'll pass. They always do."

"Oh, Molly," Patrick said, drawing her into his arms and letting her renewed flow of tears dampen his shirt as she finally relaxed in his arms. "Sometimes I could string my brother up from the tallest tree in town and flog him." He felt her mouth curve into a smile against his shoulder. "You like that idea, do you? Just say the word and I'll do it. You always were a bloodthirsty little thing."

"Only where Daniel's concerned," she said, her voice catching. She pulled back and met his gaze. "It's been three years. I don't know why it still catches me off guard like this."

"It's been longer than that since I discovered the truth about my folks and left home. The pain of their betrayal still surprises me sometimes. It's as fresh as if it happened yesterday," he said. "There's no timetable on something like this. Your heart will heal when it's ready."

"And yours?"

He avoided her gaze. "Mine's cold as stone."

"If that's true, then you shouldn't be with Alice," she chided, her expression worried.

Patrick sighed. "You're probably right, but I can't walk away from her, Molly. And I don't want to discuss my relationship with her with you, not till I've got it figured out for myself."

"We're quite the happy little trio tonight, all of us with our secrets and forbidden topics," Molly said with a rare touch of bitterness. "They could make a TV soap opera about Widow's Cove, with our lives as the central plotline."

"Why not suggest it and make us all rich?" Patrick said. "There should be some benefit to going through the kind of anguish you and I and Alice have been through."

"You'd have to do it," she said. "I can't write worth a damn."

"Neither can I," Patrick lamented. "Oh, well, it was just an idea."

Molly sighed. "I could sure use a drink."

"You're entitled," he said.

"Which is why I won't have one," she said. "It would be too easy to use liquor to numb the pain. And in the end, what does that accomplish?"

Patrick was hit with a sudden flash of insight. "Which is why Alice is out there poking through your liquor stock, isn't it?"

She nodded. "I started doing the inventory, but the temptation was too great. When Alice offered to help out, I grabbed at the chance to turn the chore over to her."

"Good for you. Seeing you upset worries her. She needs to be doing something to help."

"I know, but I can't explain it to her," Molly said. "You'd better get back out there before she starts to wonder what we're up to in here. Alice has never been one to ignore her curiosity for long. She's been pestering me about Daniel all afternoon, but I refuse to discuss him."

Patrick studied Molly's face. Her tears had dried, but there was still unbearable sadness in her eyes, and his brother had put it there. He felt partly responsible for that. He should have done a better job of protecting her, but no one had been able to get through to Molly once she'd fallen under Daniel's spell.

"You sure you're going to be okay?" he asked.

"I'm not sure of much," she said, "but I am sure of

that. You and me, we're survivors, Patrick, you in spite of being a Devaney, me because of one."

"Don't ever forget that, Molly, not even for a second."

She gave him a forced smile. "Get on out of here—the potatoes are going cold. I'll have to reheat them in the microwave, and you know how that goes against my grain. I'll bring your dinners out in a minute. I imagine you both want the special."

"The special and a smile on your face."

"I can promise one but not the other. I'll do my best, though."

He gave her a long, lingering look, then finally nodded, satisfied with what he saw. "Five minutes more of hiding out and not a second longer," he warned. "You don't want me back in here."

"You're right about that," she said. "You get in the way."

He left her with some regret and went in search of Alice, who'd poured them each a beer and found a booth where the light was dim.

"That took a while," she said, searching his face. "Is Molly okay?"

"She's fine."

Alice looked skeptical. "She's not fine, Patrick."

"She will be," he insisted.

"Can't you tell me what happened? She's my friend, too. I want to help."

"She'll tell you what she wants you to know. It's enough that she understands you care," he said, then reached for her hand and pressed a kiss against her knuckles. "Let's talk about this inventory we're going to do at my place tonight."

"You know, if you keep secrets from me, there's a good chance we won't *be* at your place," she told him tartly. "Not tonight. Not ever."

He pulled away from her and sat back, feeling his defenses slip into place the way they always did when a woman tried to back him into a corner, however innocently. It didn't seem to matter that the argument was over Molly's secrets and not his own.

"Your choice," he said.

Hurt flashed in her eyes. "Would it be that easy for you to stop this, Patrick?" she asked. "Could you let me turn my back and walk away?"

He deliberately shrugged. "Like I said, it's your choice."

She kept her gaze steady on him, then sighed. "In that case, I think I'd better do just that and go home," she said, slipping out of the booth. "Tell Molly I'm sorry about dinner. Not that either of you will apparently give a damn whether I'm here or not. It's nice that you have each other's shoulders to cry on."

The implication that they had deliberately shut her out of something important cut through him. Patrick wanted to reach out and stop her. One heartfelt word of apology was all it would have taken, one touch. But he couldn't make himself do it. Instead, he watched her leave and told himself the ache in his heart had nothing at all to do with her going. He almost believed it, too. After all, over the years he'd gotten damn good at lying to himself.

Alice glanced up from the notes she was making for end-of-the-year report cards and saw Patrick coming across the school yard, a bouquet of lilacs in hand. It had been four days, four endless days, since she'd last laid eyes on him. Her heart did an automatic flip even though she'd vowed at least a hundred times to steel herself against the effect he had on her. She'd almost convinced herself that Molly was right, there was nothing to be gained by clinging to a false hope that Patrick would change.

Walking out of Jess's, waiting as she crossed the room for Patrick to give even the tiniest sign that he didn't want her to go, had almost killed her. She'd seen it as evidence that Patrick might enjoy sleeping with her, might even have feelings for her on some level, but he wasn't letting her into his heart, not really, not if he could let her go so easily. It saddened her that Molly knew him better than she did. And she was just the teensiest bit jealous that the two of them had a history she knew nothing about.

Outside the window, he had disappeared from view, which could only mean he was in the building. She listened for the sound of his footsteps in the silent hallway, trying to brace herself against the impact he always had on her. She needed to be cool and distant and unapproachable. Unfortunately, she didn't have the vaguest idea how she was going to pull off such a lie.

Suddenly he was there, without a whisper of sound to announce him, only the faint scent of lilacs to capture her attention. He filled the doorway, looking oddly uncertain as he waited for her to give some indication of whether he was welcome. She said nothing. She couldn't gather the words or her thoughts. None of the heated words she'd mentally flung at him over the past few days were coming to her now. She was too darned glad to see him.

"Want me to leave?" he asked eventually.

"What I want and what I should want are two different things," she told him candidly, then threw his own words back at him. "I guess that makes it your choice."

"Then I'll stay," he said, stepping into the room. "That's what you should have done at Jess's, Alice. You should have stayed."

"Why, when it was plain you didn't care which I did?" She frowned at him. "Don't try making what happened my fault, Patrick."

"I cared," he said. "I'm just lousy at saying it. I'm even worse at looking ahead more than a minute or two."

She sighed then, noting that he'd opted to ignore the fact that their fight had to do with Molly's secrets. Since he was focusing on his own mistakes, she would, too.

"Do you think that will ever change?" she asked.

"I doubt it."

"I see. So where does that leave us?"

"Can you try to hear what I'm not saying as well as what comes out of my mouth? Can you take here and now?" he asked plaintively. "Can you not worry about the future?"

How could she, when she wanted a future with this man so desperately? But he wasn't offering one, not yet anyway. Once again he was giving her the choice of taking him as he was…or not. She had a feeling what she said and did in the next few minutes would make or break any chance they had.

She blinked away the tears that threatened and faced him. "Are those lilacs for me?"

He nodded.

"I suppose I should put them in some water." She got to her feet, found an old vase in a cupboard, filled it with water, then took the flowers, burying her face in them before setting them on a corner of her desk.

"Is there an answer in there I'm missing?" he asked eventually, regarding her warily.

She turned slowly, lifted her gaze to meet his. "The classroom is a little inappropriate for my answer. How about your place?"

Relief spread across his face, and she took heart at the sight of it.

"How fast can you gather up those papers?" he asked.

"I may as well leave them here," she said, grabbing only her purse. "Something tells me I won't be getting to them any time over the weekend."

He grinned. "Not if I have my way."

It wasn't just about the fabulous sex, Patrick told himself a thousand times over the weekend, as he and Alice shut themselves away on his boat. He wasn't using her. He would never do that to her.

But he couldn't bring himself to define what it *was* about. He'd never let a woman get this close, never felt so needy and out of sorts when she was away. The four days before he'd swallowed his pride and gone after Alice had been the most miserable he'd spent since the early days after he'd left home.

"You know," she said, staring at him across his tiny

kitchen table. "I really should go home and get a change of clothes."

"Why, when I'd only make you take them off?" he teased.

She grinned. "Maybe that's why. I'm thinking something with lots and lots of tiny buttons, so you can fumble and be adorable as you try to undo them."

"You think I have the patience for that? I'm more likely to rip them apart."

"That could be interesting, too. I'll make it something *old* with tiny buttons."

"Forget it. I like the way you look in my shirt. I had no idea that an old T-shirt could look that sexy on someone."

"If it's that enticing, why am I still dressed in it?"

"Sometimes anticipation is every bit as important as the sex," he said, realizing it was true. He liked the slow buildup of heat. He liked knowing where it would lead, knowing how her body would respond. He liked the teasing, the exchange of smoldering looks and lingering caresses.

But even as he thought of his own amazing level of contentment, Alice's grin faltered.

"Patrick, are you sure you're not getting tired of having me underfoot?"

He stared at her in shock. "Do I act as if I'm bored?"

"No, but it's not as if you're used to sharing these quarters with another person."

He studied her with a narrowed gaze. "What are you really saying, Alice? Is being shut up here on the boat with me getting on your nerves?"

"Don't be ridiculous."

Relief washed over him. He hadn't realized how desperately he'd begun to want this to work. If she'd said she wanted to go home, he wasn't sure how he would have reacted.

"Okay, then," he said.

"But I will need to get back to my place tonight," she told him.

Immediately he tensed. "Why?"

"I have school tomorrow. There's no way I can put that off, and I can't very well wear the same thing I had on on Friday."

As reasonable as the explanation was, it made his stomach tighten. He was the one who wanted things to be temporary, but hearing her making plans to take off upset him in ways he couldn't explain.

"Patrick?"

"What?"

"You do know I can't just stay here forever, right? It's not as if we've sailed away to some idyllic island. We both have responsibilities."

There was that word again—*forever.* He seized on it and nothing else. Over the past couple of days, the word and its implications had lost some of their power to terrify him. "Of course I know that."

"You could come to my place," she suggested casually. "It would make it easier during the week. That is, if you wanted to."

"I don't know," he said, the cautious words coming out before he could consider them. It was an automatic, knee-jerk response. His turf was one thing, hers was something else. He thought of that cozy little cottage, and it made his palms sweat. Being there had made him want things that he'd learned couldn't be trusted—a home, a family.

"Think about it," she said. "And school will be out soon. I could stay here then, if you'd prefer it. I could even go out fishing with you."

A part of him liked the idea of sharing his life with her that way. Another part was terrified. All this talk about tomorrow and the day after tomorrow and beyond was treading on turf he normally avoided like the plague. He didn't do plans. He didn't look into the future. Forever might not be as frightening as it had once been, but it was still off-limits. He wasn't ready to toss all of his rules and common sense out the window, just because the mere thought of them no longer panicked him.

"Let me know when you're ready to go and I'll take you home," he said tightly, ignoring all of her bright and cheerful plans for the summer.

There was no mistaking the quick rise of hurt in Alice's eyes. That, of course, was the problem. He was going to hurt her eventually. There was no question about it. He'd been deluding himself when he'd tried to pretend that they could take things one day at a time. Alice was a forever woman. She had every right to expect permanence and commitment, but he didn't believe in either one.

"Whenever you want me to go, just say the word," she said stiffly.

"I don't *want* you to go," he retorted, more exasperated with himself than with her. He was the one who wasn't making any sense. "I just think it's for the best."

"Because you're scared," she guessed.

"Because I'm smart," he corrected.

"And if I disagree about what's smart?"

"You're entitled to your opinion."

She stood up in that oversize T-shirt of his that skimmed her thighs and managed to emphasize her curves. He expected her to flounce from the room, but instead she rounded the table to sit in his lap. She draped an arm loosely around his neck and skimmed a finger along his stubbled cheek.

"It is my opinion," she said, "that we're doing entirely too much talking all of a sudden. It always gets us into trouble. You get that worried frown on your forehead." She pressed a kiss to the place in question. "And lines right here," she added, kissing the downturned corners of his mouth.

"We can't go through life making love whenever we butt heads," he said, trying to maintain his grip on reason even as she tried to torment him with sneaky little kisses.

"Can you think of a better way to remind ourselves of what's really important?" She looked him in the eye. "I love you, Patrick. All the rest of it—" she waved her hand dismissively "—we'll work it out."

"Alice," he began, but the protest died on his lips when she covered his mouth with hers.

He sighed and gave himself up to the desire instantly slamming through him. Maybe she did know what was important, after all. He could wrestle with his doubts when she wasn't around to torment him.

* * *

"This thing between you and Alice, is it serious?" Molly asked Patrick several days after Alice had gone back to her place.

He frowned at the question. "What thing?" he asked, being deliberately obtuse. This was not a conversation he intended to pursue, not with Molly. He thought he'd made that clear to her.

Molly scowled at him. "Oh, please. Half the town knows the two of you never left your boat all weekend. Only an idiot would assume she was helping you work on the engine or clean the galley for that long."

Patrick bit back a curse. He'd forgotten what small towns were like when people got hold of a juicy piece of gossip. He didn't give a damn for himself, but it couldn't be good for Alice to have people talking about the two of them. Maybe if he'd put an engagement ring on her finger, it would dispel the talk, but that was out of the question.

"Sweetheart, you know nothing I do is ever serious," he told Molly, adopting his devil-may-care tone of old.

Her gaze narrowed. "Does Alice understand that?"

"Of course," he said at once.

"Does she *really?*" Molly persisted. "Because if you hurt her, Patrick Devaney, I swear I'll come out on that pitiful dock of yours and set fire to it *and* your boat."

She would do it, too. He didn't have any doubts about that. Molly had a mile-wide protective streak when it came to her friends, and a built-in aversion to the way Devaney men treated women. He'd always been glad to count himself among the friends, despite his last name.

Obviously, though, she considered Alice to be the friend most in need of protection now…from him.

"Look, I'll talk to her, okay? I'll make sure we're both on the same page," he said. He recalled how the last time he'd tried to have that conversation with Alice it hadn't gone so well. She'd seemed to hear only what she wanted to hear, dismissing everything else.

"When?" Molly pressed.

"Tonight," he promised.

"What's wrong with now?"

"She's at school."

Molly clearly wasn't satisfied with his response. Hands on hips, she asked, "Why put it off, Patrick? The kids are only there a half day today. The teachers are all alone in their classrooms grading papers and stuff in the afternoon. Knowing Alice, she had all that done days ago and is sitting there bored to tears and staring at the walls."

"Molly, you can't actually expect me to have a conversation like this with her in her classroom. It's totally inappropriate," he said. Besides, if he kept showing up in Alice's classroom, that was going to set off its own round of speculation. He'd run into Loretta Dowd on his last visit, and she'd given him an approving grin that had completely rattled him.

"It's not an ideal situation, no, but if you put it off, you'll just think of some other excuse. I know you, Patrick. You'd rather run than stick around and settle things. Isn't that what you did with your folks?"

"Leave my folks out of this," he retorted heatedly. "I'll talk to Alice. I'll spell things out for her one more time, but I'll decide when and where. This is none of your business."

"I'm making it my business. I like her, Patrick. And she's in way over her head with you. She's in love with you."

He wanted to deny that, but the echo of Alice saying those very words had rung in his head all week long. The words had meant more to him than he wanted to admit, but he wasn't about to let Molly know that.

"So what if she is?" he asked, his tone cavalier.

Molly scowled at him. "Do you honestly need me to answer that?"

Patrick sighed. "No. I'll talk to her."

There was just one problem…once he talked to Alice, really talked to her, things might never be the same. And for the first time in his life he didn't want to lose the feelings he'd discovered in her arms, feelings he'd never imagined himself capable of.

14

Even if she hadn't been taken aback earlier in the day when Patrick had sent a written summons to her classroom, Alice would have known something was wrong the minute she stepped aboard the *Katie G.*

Patrick was waiting for her on the deck, a brooding expression on his face and a beer in his hand. He didn't look especially happy to see her. The fact that he'd been avoiding her most of the week only added to her alarm.

She hesitated when he said nothing, then finally sat down next to him and put her feet up on the railing. The afternoon sun was warm on her face, but the breeze held a promising hint of rain. There would be a storm before nightfall, no question about it. And she had a feeling there would be one on board between her and Patrick even sooner.

She finally dared a glance in his direction. "Is everything okay, Patrick? Have you heard something from your brothers in Boston? Or from Daniel or your folks?"

"No, it's nothing like that."

"What then?"

"We need to talk."

Something inside her froze at the tone in his voice. Those words never meant anything good. "About?"

"Us."

She'd been anticipating this for days now. In some ways she was surprised it had been so long in coming. As much as she'd wanted to pretend that Molly's warning was misplaced, she hadn't been able to forget it. Patrick intended to dump her before things got complicated, or, rather, any *more* complicated. She'd told him she loved him and that had been the kiss of death. It would be with a lot of men, but especially with a man who had the kind of trust issues Patrick had. And he was too damned noble to let her go on loving him when he was convinced he could never love her back.

Her pride immediately kicked in. She had no intention of being the one dumped. She looked him straight in the eye. "Okay. Are you going to start or shall I?"

He stared at her in surprise, as if it had never occurred to him that she might have an opinion on that subject. "You, by all means," he said politely.

"You're going to say that what's been going on between us has gotten out of hand, that I might be misinterpreting what it means, and that you never intended for it to get serious." She met his gaze. "How am I doing so far?"

He scowled at her. "Am I that predictablc?"

"You are when it comes to relationships. When they get too difficult, you run. I suspect you never even allow most relationships to get to that point."

"Dammit, you're the second person today to say something like that to me. I'm getting sick of it."

"You heard it first from Molly, I imagine," she said, trying not to be angry at a friend who only thought she was looking out for Alice's best interests by pushing Patrick to be honest with her. "I also suspect she's the one who told you that you needed to spell things out for me for my sake."

"She thinks I'll hurt you," he said defensively.

"What do you think?"

He met her gaze, his expression miserable. "That she's probably right, eventually I will hurt you, Alice. It's what I do."

"You could stop the pattern. All you have to do is quit running," she countered.

"Simple as that?" he said, his expression wry.

"Why not? I've never hurt you or given you any reason to distrust me. That was your parents. And from what you've said, you never really gave them a chance to explain why they did what they did to your older brothers or why they kept it from you and Daniel. You had one conversation that caught them completely off guard, then turned your back on them—and on your brother, who's as much a victim in this situation as you are—and ran."

Alice met his turbulent gaze. "Believe me, Patrick, I know all about running. I did the same thing. I shut my parents out of my life because of one hurtful argument. I made one more halfhearted attempt to reconcile by sending them that invitation to my graduation, and then I wrote them off. Before I realized how ridiculous that was, what a waste, it was too late. I'll regret that for the rest of my life."

"I'm sorry," he said.

"So am I." She regarded him with a penetrating look. "Let me ask you something. Has being alone made you happy? Or has it only made you feel safe?" She held up her hand when he seemed about to speak. "Don't answer me now. I want you to think long and hard about that when I'm gone. I knew the risks when I got involved with you. I don't know about you, but I've felt more alive lately than I have in years. In my opinion, that's a helluva lot better than safe and alone. You can protect your heart, Patrick. Or you can live. I protected myself once and it cost me everything. Never again. I'm going to live my life as if there's no tomorrow."

She stood up, leaned down and pressed a quick kiss to the grim line of his mouth, then walked away before the tears that were threatening could fall.

Patrick stared after Alice and cursed himself for letting her walk away yet again. She'd caught him completely off guard when she'd taken the decision to call it quits out of his hands. She did that a lot—in fact, she had a way of taking him by surprise that should have made him nuts. Instead it filled him with anticipation. It also made him ashamed that he wasn't nearly as brave as she was. Not only was she brave enough to go, but she'd been brave enough to take a risk on staying if only he'd met her halfway.

But no more. She'd left no doubt in his mind that she was finished. She'd seen the handwriting on the wall, handwriting he'd scrawled there in big, bold, unmistakable letters, and had wisely decided to cut her losses.

He should be dancing for joy at being free of a commitment he'd been incapable of making in the first place. Instead all he felt was the sense that he'd lost something precious, something he'd never be able to replace.

He would have gone to Jess's and gotten blind, stinking drunk, but he wasn't sure he wanted to listen to any more of Molly's comments on his love life. He sure as hell didn't want to argue with her over whether or not what had happened was for the best. Of course it was. But he didn't have to like it.

He should take his boat out to sea and let the demands of fishing tax his muscles and clear his head, but the prospect held no appeal.

Ironically, he had a sudden urge to call Daniel. His twin had always been able to put things into perspective for him when it came to women. Not that Daniel had much wisdom in that area of his own life—the mess he'd made of things with Molly was testament to that. But when it came to Patrick, Daniel had always seen things more clearly.

Patrick almost reached for the phone, then caught himself. He could make that call only if he was willing to take everything that went along with it. He would have to reconcile with his brother, and that would be only one step away from letting his folks back into his life. He almost did it anyway, but the weight of all that old baggage kept his hand off the phone.

For the first time since he'd moved away, Patrick felt unbearably lonely. He'd been alone before and never minded it. Today, though, it made his heart ache. With Alice he'd had a taste of something incredible. He could call it companionship or sex and demean it, but he was honest enough not to do that. What he'd shared with her had been love in its purest, most incredible form, and he'd let it slip through his fingers.

"Hey, Patrick. You look as if you've lost your best friend," Ray Stover said, calling out to him from the end of the dock.

Grateful for the interruption, Patrick waved the older man on board. "What brings you by, Ray?"

"I wanted to thank you again for coming to my rescue." He handed over a package wrapped in bright-yellow paper and tied with string. "A little something from Janey. Judging from the shape of it, it's probably one of the sweaters she knits when I'm not around. The truth is, they're usually too big and she tends to drop a lot of stitches, so I won't be offended if you hang it on the back of the door and forget about it."

Patrick laughed as he untied the bow around the package and opened it to find a dark-green sweater that was every bit as large and unevenly made as Ray had predicted. "Nice color," he said, seizing on the one thing Janey had gotten exactly right.

Ray grinned. "That's very diplomatic, Patrick. I'll tell her you love the color and she'll be pleased as punch."

"Is that the only reason you came by, to deliver Janey's thank-you gift?"

Ray looked sheepish. "To tell you the truth, I'm going stir-crazy around the house. Janey's already lost her enthusiasm for having me underfoot—she says I disrupt her routine. I thought I might take you up on that invitation to go out fishing—that is, if you're heading out this afternoon."

"I was just debating whether to try to get in a couple

of hours before nightfall," Patrick said. "I'd be glad of the company."

Ray leaped to his feet with an agility that belied his years and began untying the boat from its moorings. Patrick moved more slowly, amused by the man's enthusiasm.

"Something tells me you're going to be looking around to buy a new boat one of these days," he told Ray.

"Not as long as you'll let me help you out from time to time. I'm retired for good. That's the way it has to be," Ray said, not sounding as unhappy about it as he had when the decision had first been taken out of his hands.

"Is that because it's what your wife wants?"

"No, it's because it's what's right for the two of us. That's what marriage is about, son, making compromises for the good of both of you."

"Don't you both wind up losing that way?"

"Only if that's the way you choose to see it," Ray told him.

"Is there another way?" Patrick asked, genuinely curious.

"You can see it as both of you giving up a little bit for the good of what you have together. Then you both come out winners—though, to be honest, as soon as you start thinking in terms of winners and losers you're in trouble." He gave Patrick a speculative look. "Is that what was on your mind when I got here a bit ago? You and that pretty young teacher at odds over something?"

"In a way."

"Is what she wants unreasonable?"

Patrick wasn't sure how to answer. She wanted him to love her enough to forget about the past. She wanted him to trust in their love. The requests weren't unreasonable. Maybe just a little unrealistic, given where he was coming from.

"No," he told Ray eventually.

"Do you want to lose her? Is clinging to your position more important than keeping her in your life?"

"No," he said more quickly.

Ray grinned. "Well, then, I think you have your answer."

Patrick sighed. He had an answer, all right. He just had no idea at all about how to put it into practice. How could he compromise a little bit when it came to letting go of the past? There was no way to open the door just a crack to his parents and Daniel. It had to be all or nothing.

The same with acting on his feelings for Alice. If he went back to her, he had to be prepared to love her with all his heart. He had to allow himself to be vulnerable to her. He couldn't protectively close himself off to his feelings without shortchanging both of them.

But one thing was certain, he didn't want to go on like this. He'd had a taste of what a full life could be, and anything else was unacceptable.

Alice was attacking the weeds in her garden when she heard the doorbell ring. She stayed right where she was. There was no one she wanted to see. There hadn't been anyone she wanted to see for days now. She grabbed another handful of weeds and tugged viciously, then flung them over her shoulder.

"What was that for?" Molly demanded irritably.

Alice sighed and turned around, only to see her friend wiping traces of dirt and weeds from her face and the front of her blouse.

"Sorry," Alice said without any real sincerity in her tone. She was almost as furious with Molly these days as she was with Patrick. She knew that Molly was behind that little talk Patrick had insisted they needed to have. Even though Alice had gotten in the first word, the handwriting had been on the wall from the instant she stepped aboard his boat. Molly might have meddled out of affection for both of them, but she'd set off a chain reaction that had been as painful as anything that might have come down the road.

"Yeah, I can tell how sorry you are," Molly replied.

"What do you expect from me?"

"Why don't we start with an explanation of where you've been lately?"

"At school, working here in the garden, around town."

"Just not at Jess's," Molly concluded.

"Pretty much."

"Avoiding me or avoiding Patrick?"

"Both."

"Why?"

"As if you don't know," Alice accused.

"I don't," Molly said. "Patrick's been making himself scarce, too."

"Then go chase him down and try all your questions on him. Maybe he'll be more receptive to them than I am."

Molly answered by sitting down on a chaise longue

and stretching out. She looked as if she had no intention of leaving anytime soon. Removing her sunglasses,
she turned her face up to the sun. "Nice day, isn't it?"

Alice rocked back on her heels and sighed. "You're
not going to go away, are you?"

"Not until I get the answers I came for."

"Okay, here it is in a nutshell. Patrick called me over
to break up with me. I broke up with him first. You were
right. It wasn't going to work. You got us both to face
that fact. Happy?"

"No, I am not happy," Molly said, her own expression glum. "How could I be, when you're so obviously
miserable?"

"I'm not miserable," Alice retorted heatedly. "I'm
furious."

"With Patrick?"

"And with you. You were so sure we couldn't make
it work. I know you were bugging him to be straight
with me because you care about me, but all you did was
to back him into making a decision before any decision
needed to be made."

Molly looked her in the eye. "How long were you
willing to wait?"

"As long as it took," Alice insisted.

"Really? Then you don't care about having children?
You were willing to put your whole life on hold while
he wrestles with all those demons on his back?"

"Yes."

"Even if after all that waiting around and wasting
your life, you could still lose him?"

"Even then," Alice said.

"You're crazy," Molly said flatly. "You'd wind up hating him and blaming me for not stepping in sooner."

"It was my decision, Molly, not yours. You took it out of my hands."

"I merely wanted you both to face the truth before it was too late."

"What truth? I'm in love with him. Is that the truth you meant?" she retorted vehemently. "That's not going to go away just because it might be more sensible if I weren't."

Molly stared at her in shock. "If you're in love with him, really in love with him, then why the hell did you break up with him?"

"Because it was what he wanted."

"So basically you just let him off the hook?"

"It was easier on both of us to get it over with."

"Why make it easy for him, Alice? Why not make him squirm and say the words?"

Alice frowned at the hint that she'd somehow taken the easy way out. She especially resented it coming from Molly, who'd set all this in motion. "What purpose would that have served?"

"If it had been hard for him to let go, he might have had to question whether it was what he really wanted. Now he thinks it's what *you* wanted. You've given him one more reason to believe that love isn't strong enough to weather anything."

"That's not fair," Alice said, though she couldn't help wondering if that wasn't exactly what she'd done.

"One of you needed to fight for what you had. It was never likely to be Patrick—that left you. I thought you understood that, Alice."

"Maybe you should have explained the rules before you started meddling."

"I didn't think I needed to. You were so certain of how you felt, of how Patrick felt. I expected you to fight like a banshee to keep him."

Alice studied Molly speculatively. "Did you fight for Daniel, Molly?"

"No," Molly admitted. "I don't know that it would have changed anything, but I'll still regret it till the day I die."

Alice forgot for a moment how angry she was about Molly's role in her breakup with Patrick. She reached for her hand. "I'm so sorry. Why don't you do something about it now?"

"It's too late for some things."

"It's never too late," Alice said fiercely.

Molly gave her a sly look. "Then why not go to Patrick and tell him you made a mistake, that you want to fight for a relationship with him?"

Alice frowned at her. "Nice try, but I don't think so."

"Why not? Too much pride?"

Molly's words lingered in Alice's head long after Molly had left to go back to work. Was it just stubborn pride that kept Alice from going to Patrick? Or was it that she'd really finally seen the light and accepted that they couldn't make a go of things?

Images of the way they were together tumbled through her head, like snapshots falling to the floor in a jumble. She wanted to freeze each one, linger over it, but they slipped away in rapid succession, leaving only an overall impression of a joy she'd never expected to find.

Wasn't that worth fighting for? Of course it was, even if it was an uphill battle. She'd painted a rosy picture for herself of the way it could be, of marrying Patrick and making his family her own. But to make that happen, Patrick had to do something he felt was wrong. He had to be willing to let go of the past. If he couldn't, who was she to demand it? No one had been able to make her see the light when it came to her own parents. Why should she expect so much more of him?

Maybe his stubbornness was a mistake he would come to regret…or maybe it wasn't. But it was his decision, not hers.

She sighed and stuck her trowel back into the well-worked soil, then brushed the dirt off her hands. Love was a little bit like gardening. It required patience, and sometimes things got messy. But the end results were worth any amount of effort.

Pleased with her analogy, she headed inside to shower and change into something that would send an unmistakable message to Patrick that they weren't over. Not by a long shot.

15

For days after Alice had gone, Patrick wrestled with his conscience and his heart. He knew she would never accept a halfway attempt on his part. He had to be ready to face the past before he could stake any claim at all on a future with her.

Because he couldn't bring himself to call Daniel, he picked up the phone and called Ryan, turning to his oldest brother for advice as if it were something he'd been doing his whole life.

"I know what Alice wants from me, but I don't know if I can give it to her," he told Ryan.

"Has it occurred to you that all she really wants is for you to be truly happy?" Ryan asked. "It took me a while to understand that that was what Maggie was after with me. She could see how burying the past had only given it a power over me that it didn't deserve. I wasn't happy. I was just denying my real feelings."

Like Ryan, Patrick wanted to deny that his folks or even Daniel had any power at all over his life, but he knew that wasn't true. Without doing a thing, they were standing squarely between him and the future he wanted with Alice.

"Funny thing about finding the right woman, isn't it?" Ryan said thoughtfully, when Patrick remained silent. "It was Maggie who made me face the fact that I needed to find my family before I could ever move on. She was right. I still have one more step to take, and there's no way of knowing if it will turn out okay, but once I've taken it, I'll be free of all that weight I've been carrying around inside me. It takes a lot of energy to go on hating people, especially after all these years."

Patrick thought of how consumed he'd been with bitterness and resentment. It had colored the choices he'd made, the lifestyle he'd chosen, even the people he saw and those he avoided because their connections to his folks were too painful. Ryan and Alice were both right. It was no way to live. There was only one way to be rid of it, and it wasn't by burying his head in the sand.

He slowly drew in a deep breath and said, "I could set up a meeting. It wouldn't be the last step for any of us, but it might be a good place to start."

"You set it up, anytime, anyplace," Ryan said at once. "The rest of us will be there. We've been waiting until you were ready. We agreed that it needed to be that way. The Devaney brothers stick together."

Hearing Ryan include him with his older brothers filled Patrick's heart with surprising joy, but because he wasn't entirely certain he was ready to face his folks, at least not without Alice by his side, he said, "I'll start with Daniel. Will that be okay?"

"Start wherever you're comfortable," Ryan said. "We've all had to make up the rules as we went along, to take things at our own pace and compromise when compromise was called for. I wrestled with all sorts of emotions before I finally made that first call to Sean. It's not as if there's a guidebook we can follow for this kind of thing. There aren't a lot of families who've been through what we've been through."

"Thank God for that," Patrick said with heartfelt sincerity. He pitied anyone who'd been in their shoes. "I'll call you once I've spoken to Daniel."

"Make it soon, little brother. Not for our sake, but for your own—it sounds as if Alice is too special to risk losing."

Patrick smiled. "Yeah, she is. She really is."

Even though Patrick was anxious to put his plan into motion, years of keeping his distance from his family were too ingrained to be overcome in a heartbeat. With almost any other dreaded chore, he would have tackled it at once to put it behind him, but with this, he spent days trying to work up the courage to pick up the phone. He was consoled by Ryan's admission that he'd had a similar struggle before he'd contacted Sean.

Patrick was still tormented by indecision when he heard footsteps on the dock and looked up to see Alice coming toward him with a purposeful stride. She was wearing something designed to make his heart race and his palms sweat. His breath caught in his chest. He was forced to admit that even if she'd been covered from head to toe, he wasn't ready to see her, not yet. He'd wanted to have something to offer her before they talked.

"So, this is where you've been hiding out," she said, as if she'd found him tucked in a cave somewhere.

"It's hardly hiding if I'm on my own boat in broad daylight," he retorted. "You must not have been looking too hard. What's up?"

"I actually had a request for your presence at the kindergarten graduation ceremony next week. Ricky Foster would be honored if you'd attend."

Patrick bit back a grin. "Is that so? They hold graduation ceremonies for kindergarten? Why is that?"

"We've found it motivates them and gives them a greater sense of purpose when they start first grade and things get more serious," she explained.

"I see. Was there some reason Ricky couldn't come over here and ask me himself?"

"I agreed to do it. He seems to think I might have more influence where you're concerned."

"Really? Where would he get an idea like that?"

She blushed just enough to put some color into her pale cheeks. "Around town."

Patrick flinched at the idea that they were still the subject of gossip, especially as now people were probably speculating about why they were no longer seeing each other. "I'm sorry."

"Don't be. I think it's rather sweet that he's joined in the matchmaking. He might be better at it than Molly."

Patrick grinned. "Yeah, her skills in that department could definitely use some work."

"So, will you come to graduation?" she persisted.

"Sure. Where and when?"

"The school auditorium on Monday. Ten o'clock."

"I'll be there," he promised.

Alice looked as if she weren't quite sure what to do next. She finally met his gaze. "Any chance you can have dinner tonight?"

As desperately as he wanted to say yes, knowing how irresistible she was in that slinky sundress, he shook his head. "I don't think so."

"I guess that would be too much like a date," she said, "and we're not doing that anymore."

Because she looked so miserable, he wanted to tell her everything about how he was trying to put his life back together just for her, but he didn't want to get her hopes up in case he failed.

"It's not that. I just have some things I need to do."

"Sure," she said, her skepticism plain. "No problem, I'll see you at school on Monday."

"Maybe we can talk after the ceremony," he suggested. "You going to be around?"

She nodded. "There's always a lot left to do after the kids finally leave."

"I'll see you then."

"Fine."

She looked so dejected as she began to walk away that he called out to her. "Alice?"

She turned to look at him.

"It's a date, okay?"

A faint smile touched her lips. "It's a date."

"And you could wear that dress again, if you wanted to. It takes my breath away."

The smile that spread across her face was his reward for being honest for once and saying what was in his heart.

As soon as she'd gone, Patrick knew what he had to

do. He went inside the boat, picked up his phone and dialed the once-familiar number of his brother's office in Portland.

Daniel answered, as always, on the very first ring, but he sounded distracted.

"Daniel, it's Patrick."

Silence greeted him, then a long sigh. "Hey, bro, what's up?"

Just like that, the years of separation faded away. "We have some catching up to do," Patrick told him. "Can we get together?"

"Anytime," Daniel said at once.

"Over the weekend, maybe Sunday around one?"

"That works for me. Where?"

"Here, on my boat." He needed this first meeting to be on his turf, not Daniel's.

"Want to tell me what this is about?"

"I'll explain when I see you. There are some people I want you to meet. I think you'll really like them."

"If they're friends of yours, I'm sure I will," Daniel said. "Or are we talking about a woman, Patrick? Are you getting married? I've heard some rumors about you and a teacher at the elementary school."

"Maybe one of these days," he admitted. "But this isn't about that, not the way you mean, anyway. Just be here on Sunday, okay?"

"I'll be there," Daniel promised. "I'm glad you called. I've been waiting a long time."

"I know," Patrick said with a sigh. "Too long."

"Something's going on with Patrick," Molly told Alice on Saturday. "Any idea what it is?"

"Beats me. I had the same sense that something was up when I saw him yesterday. What tipped you off?"

"He's just hauled enough coleslaw and potato salad down to his boat to feed an army, along with hamburger patties and an entire keg of beer."

"Sounds as if he's having a party," Alice said slowly, then gasped. "What if he's getting together with his brothers?" She met Molly's gaze. "*All* of them."

"Even Daniel?" Molly asked, an unmistakable hitch in her voice.

"That would be my guess. Do you know of anyone else Patrick would invite for a party?"

"To be honest, no," Molly said. "At least, not without telling me about it. Daniel's the only person he wouldn't want me to know was around. If he's being secretive, then Daniel has to be involved. I think maybe I'll close the bar tomorrow and go hiking somewhere."

Alice studied her friend's miserable expression. "Wouldn't you rather stay here and see who turns up?"

Molly shook her head. "I'll leave the spying to you."

"I'm not going to spy," Alice denied heatedly.

Molly grinned then. "More than one stroll past that dock and it's considered spying. Get a good look the first time."

Alice grinned back at her. "Believe me, I intend to."

Patrick was as nervous as if this were the first time he'd ever thrown a party. Of course, it was the first time he'd ever held one for his brothers. He checked the food at least a hundred times, counted napkins and plates, rearranged the bowls of potato salad and cole-slaw, then fussed over the grill, which was one of the old-fashioned ones with charcoal. It was already burning red-hot, perfect for cooking the burgers that waited in the refrigerator below deck. It was crazy to be this worked up over the food, when it was likely to be the last thing on anyone's mind. But it was easier to think about potato salad than the past.

There was nothing else to do but wait. He paced the deck, and when that seemed too confined, moved to the dock and paced up and down that. He finally spotted the rental car as it pulled into the parking lot and his older brothers emerged. They were halfway down the dock when Daniel's familiar SUV turned into the lot. Patrick wasn't the least bit surprised that his twin was still driving the same car he'd had for years. Daniel had always claimed a car was nothing more than transportation. He'd never cared about style or speed.

"Here's Daniel now," Patrick said quietly to Ryan, Sean and Michael.

They all turned to watch their brother as he walked to the dock, then caught sight of them and hesitated, a dawning sense of recognition on his face.

"Too late to turn back now," Patrick said, going to meet his twin just in case Daniel had any crazy ideas about fleeing.

Daniel searched his brother's face, then drew him into a fierce hug. When the embrace ended, he met Patrick's gaze. "Tell me I'm not dreaming. Are those...?" His voice caught.

"They're our brothers," Patrick told him.

"When? How? Why the hell didn't you say something?"

Patrick grinned at the litany of questions. "I'll let

them explain, unless you're planning to stand here at the end of the dock all afternoon trying to figure it out on your own."

A grin spread across his twin's face. "You sound like your old self."

Patrick thought about that, then released a sigh. "You know, I'm beginning to feel like my old self, only better."

"Complete?" Daniel asked.

Patrick nodded. "That's it."

"I know. That's the way I felt the second I heard your voice on the phone. Next time you get some fool idea in your head about losing touch, I'm not going to let you get away with it."

Patrick leveled a gaze at him and thought of Alice. "There won't be a next time," he assured Daniel.

"Hey, you two going to stand down there all day?" Ryan called out. "Sean here is starved."

"Sean's always starved," Michael noted, poking his brother in the ribs.

Patrick led Daniel to the boat, made the introductions, then stood back while his older brothers peppered Daniel with questions until his head was no doubt spinning. Being here with all of them felt right, as if this day had been way too long coming. The only thing that could possibly have improved on it would have been having Alice here by his side.

Just as that wish crossed his mind, he thought he heard a whisper of sound on shore. He turned, but caught only a fleeting glimpse of movement. He couldn't prove it, of course, but it had been Alice. He knew it. He should have known he'd piqued her curiosity. He knew he'd stirred Molly's when he'd bought the food for today. Obviously, they'd put two and two together, and Alice, at least, hadn't been able to resist coming by to confirm their suspicions. He suspected Molly was a hundred miles away. That was the distance she preferred to keep between herself and Daniel.

Suddenly Ryan was by his side. "Brooding over Alice?" he asked.

Patrick shook his head. "I'm going to make things right with her."

"When?"

"Tomorrow."

"Good for you. Maggie's anxious to come up to meet her. I convinced her to stay home today, but by next week there'll be no holding her back."

"Tell her if she waits a few weeks, she could come for a wedding," Patrick said. "I don't intend to let Alice drag her heels."

Ryan grinned. "Think she might try?"

"She will if she's smart," Patrick said. "But I can be pretty persuasive when I set my mind to it."

Ryan's expression sobered. "That might be a good time to get together with the folks. Weddings always bring out the best in families."

Patrick promptly shook his head. "I'm not taking any chances with mine."

"You sure you want to get married without at least inviting them?"

"I'm sure," he said with conviction. "That doesn't mean you all can't get together with them while you're here. I'm sure Daniel will set it up." In fact, if he knew anything at all about his twin, Daniel would be eager to do it. It was probably taking every ounce of restraint he possessed not to call them right now.

"We'll play it by ear," Ryan said. "We've waited this long for an explanation of why they abandoned us. A few weeks or even months longer won't make any difference. It's a big decision, and we all need to be agreed that the timing's right."

Patrick gave his brother a grateful smile. "Thanks for understanding."

"Trust me, we all understand what a mixed bag of emotions are getting stirred up here. And none of us are all that anxious to hear why we were left behind. It's enough for now that we've seen Daniel again."

Patrick's gaze drifted to where his twin was laughing with Sean and Michael and felt his heart fill to bursting. "Yeah," he told Ryan. "That's enough for now."

Alice was staring out her classroom window at the turbulent June sky. It was going to storm any minute now. She ought to pack up her papers and head for home before the clouds opened up, but the prospect of going back to that empty house held no appeal. At least here at school there were other teachers in the building.

She'd been expecting Patrick to turn up ever since the end of the graduation ceremony, but there'd been no sign of him. Apparently, it was a promise he didn't intend to keep. She shouldn't be disappointed, but she was, especially after the scene she'd witnessed on his boat the day before. It had reduced her to tears and stirred hope in her heart once more.

A tap on the door startled her. When she turned, she was even more stunned to see Patrick in the doorway.

"You busy?" he asked.

Unable to find her tongue, she simply shook her head. He looked fabulous. Overnight it seemed as if his tan had deepened, so that his eyes seemed even bluer. He looked more carefree, too, as if a weight had been lifted from his shoulders. It took every ounce of restraint she possessed not to race across the room and throw herself into his arms.

He came in, glanced around at the small chairs meant for five-year-olds and settled for perching on the corner of her desk. That put him close enough that she could feel the heat radiating from him and smell his familiar masculine scent. She wanted desperately to reach out and rest her hand on the hard muscle of his thigh. Instead she sat perfectly still and waited impatiently to hear what was on his mind.

"You look beautiful," he said quietly.

"Thank you."

"I meant to be here right after graduation, but Ricky caught up with me and asked if I'd come to his party over at Jess's. I broke away as soon as I could."

"I see."

He held her gaze. "I've missed you."

"I saw you on Friday," she reminded him.

"But it's been longer than that since we were together, since we were on the same wavelength."

"True."

"I've been using the time to do some thinking."

"That's always good," she said, since he seemed to be waiting for a response.

"I saw my brothers yesterday. Daniel was there, too."

Alice blinked back tears. "I know. I saw."

He grinned. "I thought I saw you. I should have guessed you'd figure out something was up and poke around until you found out what it was."

She shrugged. "I care. Sue me." She studied him intently. "How did it go?"

"Awkwardly at first, but then it was like it was when they came here to meet me, almost as if we'd never been apart. I guess the bond between brothers is more powerful than I ever realized."

"And the bond between parent and child?"

"I'm still thinking about that one."

"With an open mind?"

He grinned. "At least as open a mind as any hard-headed man can have."

"Was there some other reason you wanted to see me today?" she asked.

He swallowed, then glanced toward the blackboard. "Do teachers still make kids write on the blackboard when they've misbehaved?"

"Sometimes," she said. "It's a little hard with kindergarten kids. They can't print or spell that well."

He grinned and stood up. "I can't say much for my handwriting, but my spelling's pretty good." He walked over, picked up a piece of chalk and began to write.

Alice held her breath as the words began to form.

Patrick Devaney loves Alice Newberry.

He turned to face her, a hopeful expression in his eyes. "How many times do you want me to write it?"

Her own eyes swimming with tears, she stood up. "Just say it."

Eyes locked with hers, he took a step toward her. "I love you, Alice Newberry," he said softly.

Alice tilted her head at the sound of the sweet words she'd wondered if she would ever hear. "Say it again."

"I love you," he repeated dutifully. "How many more times?"

"A million will do," she said.

"That could take forever," he pointed out.

She grinned at him. "I have the time. How about you?"

"Only if you'll marry me. And in case the fact that I love you is not enough incentive, I have it on good authority that I can get my brothers to come to the wedding."

"All of them?" she asked cautiously.

He nodded. "All of them."

"And your parents?"

"I'm not sure I'm ready to invite them to the wedding, but I promise that I'm working on forgiving them," he said, his expression neutral. "There's a lot of water under the bridge. Is the promise that I'll try good enough for now?"

Alice threw her arms around him. "Trying is the most I'll ever ask of you." She met his gaze. "That and that you'll never stop loving me."

He brushed a stray curl away from her cheek, then gave her one of those devastating Devaney smiles. "Darlin', that one's easy."

Epilogue

Alice had drawn on every bit of persuasive skill she possessed to try to convince Molly to be the maid of honor at her wedding. She'd even gotten Patrick into the act, hoping he could charm Molly into reconsidering the firm "No" she'd uttered each time Alice had asked.

"I wish you all the luck and happiness in the world. You know I do," Molly told Alice when she made one last plea. "But I can't do it, not if Daniel's going to be there, and especially not if he's going to be Patrick's best man."

"But how can I possibly get married without you as my maid of honor?" Alice asked. She could see the stubborn light shining in Molly's eyes and knew she was defeated.

"You pick someone else and walk down that aisle with your head held high and your eyes focused on your handsome groom, that's how," Molly said. "I'll be thinking of you every second."

"You won't even come to the wedding?" Alice asked.

"I can't," Molly said. "I wish I could, but it's not possible. If that's being selfish, I'm sorry."

"You're not being selfish," Alice insisted, giving her a fierce hug. "And I'm the one who should be sorry. I shouldn't have tried to put you in that position, knowing it would make you miserable."

Molly gave her a halfhearted smile. "It was nice to be asked," she said, then added wistfully, "I love weddings."

"You'll have your own, one of these days, and you'll be the most beautiful bride Widow's Cove has ever seen," Alice assured her.

"A pretty thought, but you don't have to butter me up. I'll still do all the cooking for the rehearsal dinner."

Alice regarded her with surprise. "You agreed to have it here?"

"As if Patrick would give me a choice in the matter," Molly said. "But I've brought in help for the night. I'll be far away."

"Licking your wounds," Alice said.

"So what if I am? Believe me, I'm entitled."

"I just wish the wounds had healed by now. If they run that deep, they could infect the rest of your life. If you'd only talk about what happened between you and Daniel, maybe you could move on."

Molly frowned at her. "I have moved on. I just don't care to set eyes on that weasel ever again."

Alice grinned at the heat in her voice. "Yes, you've moved on all right. I can hear it in your tone."

"I have," Molly insisted.

"Then you could catch a glimpse of Daniel and not have it turn you inside out?"

"Of course."

Alice regarded her with a speculative look. "I'll keep that in mind."

"Don't go getting any wild ideas," Molly said, alarm in her eyes. "Concentrate on your wedding and leave my life to me."

"Oh, I have plenty of time for both," Alice assured her.

"Not if you expect to live to see your wedding day," Molly said, her expression grim.

It was the heartfelt sincerity behind her words that told Alice everything she needed to know. Molly wasn't over Daniel. Not by a long shot. Maybe their relationship couldn't be fixed, but Alice had never let long odds stop her from trying. Besides, she was deep in the throes of her own bridal joy. She couldn't be totally content until everyone around her was just as happy. Unfortunately, in this instance, she might have to wait till after her own wedding to pull it off.

Patrick's nerves had been pretty much shot by the time Alice finally walked down the aisle and stood next to him. He hadn't believed they were going to pull it off until he actually heard her say, "I do," and the priest pronounced them man and wife. Then he let out a whoop of joy that could be heard in the next county.

Alice grinned at him. "I hope I always make you this happy," she said, her tone dry.

"No question about that," he said as he took her hand and marched her out of the church. Outside on the steps, he pulled her into his arms and gave her the kind of kiss he'd feared would send the priest into heart failure.

When he finally released her, he tucked a finger

under her chin and looked into her eyes. "I love you, Alice Devaney."

She rested her hand against his cheek. Her fingers were trembling. "I love you, Patrick Devaney. And all your brothers."

He gave her a searching look. "Even Daniel?"

"Why wouldn't I love Daniel?"

"Because he hurt Molly. Even I have a hard time with that one."

"We're going to fix it," she said with confidence.

"Maybe we should concentrate on us," he said, regarding her worriedly. "Molly and Daniel are adults. They can fix their own problems, assuming they even want to."

"But I want everyone to be as happy as we are."

"Not possible," he told her, pulling her close for another kiss. "No one on earth could ever be as happy as we are."

"Speak for yourself," Ryan said, coming up to slap him on the back and give Alice a kiss. "Maggie and I are doing okay."

"So are Deanna and I," Sean said, joining them.

"And Kelly and I aren't doing so bad in the joy department, either," Michael chimed in.

They all turned to look at Daniel, who simply stared. "What?"

"There's something missing from your life, little brother," Ryan said.

Patrick gave him a sympathetic look. "You might as well go with the flow, Daniel. Besides, they'll be back in Boston soon. That's too far away for any meddling."

"But I'm here," Alice said, regarding her new brother-in-law speculatively.

Daniel frowned at her. "Meddle at your own peril. I'm a hard case."

"So was I," Patrick pointed out, tightening his arm around Alice's waist. "Look at me now."

"See," Alice said. "Look at all these fine examples your brothers have set for you."

Patrick saw the fire in Daniel's eyes and knew Alice was about to push him too far. He wanted nothing to spoil this day, so he cut off her words with another kiss.

"I think we should be getting to the reception," he said. "I want to dance with my bride."

Alice looked up at him, a question in her eyes, but then she sighed with understanding. "I guess I only get to fix one thing in this family at a time."

He grinned at her. "You've done more than your share with me. Let Daniel take care of himself."

"I suppose," she agreed with obvious reluctance.

"I'll make it worth your while," he teased.

Immediately her eyes lit up. "How?"

"I'll show you tonight."

"Why not now? I'm told there's a room at the Widow's Cove Hotel with our name on it."

"And a room downstairs filled with guests waiting to toast to our happiness," he said, fighting temptation.

"Just think how much happier we'll be if we take a little detour," she said.

"You have a very wicked mind," he told her.

"Does that bother you?"

"Not as long as I'm the only one in those wild fantasies of yours."

"The only one," she assured him. "Always and forever."

Forever, Patrick thought, and waited for the first
twinge of panic. It never came. Instead, all he felt was
contentment and anticipation. Their life was going to
be one hell of a ride.

* * * * *

*Read on for a sneak peek at the next new book
in the* Sweet Magnolias *series,*
SWAN POINT,
coming soon.

1

Adelia watched with her heart in her throat as the moving van pulled away from the crumbling curb in Swan Point, one of Serenity, South Carolina's, oldest and, at one time, finest neighborhoods with moss-draped oaks in perfectly maintained yards. With backyards sloping to a small, man-made lake, which was home to several swans, the houses had been large and stately by early standards.

Now, though, most of the homes, like this one, were showing signs of age. She found something alluring and fitting about the prospect of filling this historic old house with laughter and giving it a new lease on life. It would be as if the house and her family were moving into the future together.

Letting go of the old life, however, was proving more difficult than she'd anticipated. Drawing in a deep breath, she turned to deal with the accusing looks of her four children, who weren't nearly as convinced as she was that they were about to have an exciting fresh start.

Her youngest, Tomas, named for his grandfather Hernandez on her ex-husband's side of the family, turned to her with tears streaming down his cheeks. "Mommy, I don't like it here. I want to go home. This house is old. It smells funny. And there's no pool."

She knelt down in front of the eight-year-old and gathered him close, gathered all of them close, even her oldest, Selena.

It was Selena who understood better than any of them why this move had been necessary. While they all knew that Adelia and their father had divorced, Selena had seen Ernesto more than once with one of his mistresses. In a move that defied logic or compassion, he'd even had the audacity to introduce the most recent woman to Selena while he and Adelia were still making a pretense at least of trying to keep their marriage intact. His action had devastated Selena and it had been the final straw for Adelia. She'd seen at last that tolerating such disrespect was the wrong example to set for her three girls and even for her son.

"I know you'd rather be in our old house," she said, comforting them with a hitch in her voice. "But it's just not possible. This is home now. I really think you're going to love it once we get settled in."

* * * * *

Limited time offer!

$1.⁵⁰ OFF

#1 *New York Times* bestselling author

sherryl woods

brings readers back to
Serenity, South Carolina

*Available July 29, 2014,
wherever books are sold!*

www.Harlequin.com

$14.95 U.S./$17.95 CAN.

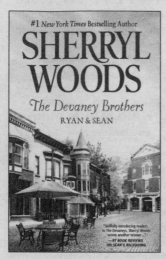